always mine

Wade Legacy Series
Book Two

n. w. brown

table of contents

dedication

For the women who've learned to live with the weight of what they never said out loud.
For the women who've buried truths to protect their peace.
For the ones who are hard on themselves, and keep moving forward anyway.
For the ones who built something beautiful on the ashes of what once broke them.
May this story remind you:
Your softness is not a weakness.
You deserve a love that chooses you, over and over.
Even in the rebuilding.
Especially *in the rebuilding.*
May this story feel like a soft place to land.
~ N.W. Brown

content trigger notice

This book is a second-chance romance with an HEA, but the journey there includes content that may be difficult for some readers, including;

- Medical emergency during pregnancy and childbirth
- Anxiety and panic attacks
- Grief related to the loss of a parent and parental abandonment
- Open door intimacy

Readers sensitive to any of these may want to proceed with care.

this book has a soundtrack

The music in this book isn't just background. It's heartbeat, memory, and mood.

Every song was chosen with intention, sometimes saying what a character cannot.

Chapters with soundtracks are marked at the start. If you'd like to listen as you read, scan the code below

to access the songs in order, or visit *chapterandsoul.com/playlists*.

prologue

simone

one year ago

I HAVE A FOUR-YEAR-OLD SON. HIS NAME IS ZHAIRE NOVA WADE, AND he has his father's eyes, dimples, and joyous laugh. His father is the love of my life, and has no idea that his son exists.

Today was supposed to change that.

I hadn't worn heels in months and my feet reminded me of that with every step through the Spectrum Center. Taryn was walking fast ahead of me to our seats, hellbent on making sure I confessed to the man whose DNA created half of my son. She was my best friend, soon to be my sister-in-law, and the only person on earth who knew the full scope of the mess I'd made of my life.

"Damn, Taryn. Can we pretend we're not on a mission?" I muttered, pulling my coat tighter. "At least *look* casual."

She glanced over her shoulder at me. "This is me being casual. You're the one out here dressed in all black, wearing sunglasses inside, like somebody's guilty conscience."

Our seats weren't courtside, thank God. Taryn had gotten us a box suite. Far enough for cover, close enough for a good view.

"There he is," Taryn announced as she sipped her drink.

My eyes snapped to where she was pointing, and there he was. Raschad Nova Carter. Number seventeen, warming up before the game, laughing with teammates. Orange and blue Knicks uniform, a little more mature in the face than the last time I'd seen him nearly five years ago. More tattoos, more muscle, more swag in his step. More... *every-thing*. My heart started to race even faster as I swallowed hard and forced myself to sit down. The noise inside the arena barely registered to me. All I could hear was my own pulse.

"Forgot he was that fine?" Taryn smirked as she continued saying something about genetics. I could see her mouth moving, but she had begun to sound far away.

"Simone, I'm gagged! He looks exactly like Zhaire. Or I guess

Zhaire looks exactly like him. Your DNA didn't even put up a fight, girl. That man's genes said 'copy, paste and to hell with you'." She laughed at her own joke, nudging my arm, waiting for me to laugh with her.

I couldn't laugh back, because the first thing that went was my hearing. It faded slowly, like someone turning a dial. The roar of the arena, the squeak of sneakers on hardwood, the bass from the speakers pumping Kendrick Lamar, all of it pulling away from me like a tide going out. Replaced by a sound that wasn't a sound. More like a pressure. The inside of my skull becoming the loudest room I'd ever been in.

The second thing to go was my vision. Twenty thousand people, a full NBA court, a jumbotron the size of a building, all of it collapsed inward, the edges going black like a photograph burning from the outside in. The only thing left in focus was the court. The only thing on the court was him.

The man who'd fathered my son and didn't know it stood at the free throw line, bouncing the ball three quick times, the exact way I'd watched him do it on screen for years, following his career from the international league in Spain to the NBA, to this moment.

He sank the free throw and the crowd erupted, as my hands started shaking. Then the third thing to attack me was my breathing. It sped up, then went shallow, like my lungs had morphed into fists grabbing at air, but unable to catch any. My chest constricted like someone had placed both hands flat against it and dropped their full weight.

Panic attack.

I knew what this was. I'd known what it was since I was twelve years old, standing in the living room with my brothers Zion and Tre, while our oldest brother, Julian, read a Dear John letter our father left for us, four months after we'd buried our mother. She'd been seven months pregnant when she hemorrhaged alone in our kitchen on a Tuesday afternoon. And now, our father, who had loved her in the consuming, total way that leaves nothing left over for anything else, was gone.

Julian gathered us in the living room reading the letter with an expression I'd never seen. *I failed you… I cannot move on without her… I'd only hold you back… Take care of each other.* I remember Julian's voice shaking on that last part. I remember Tre cursing, and Zion punching a wall.

And I remember the moment my chest locked for the first time. My vision tunneled, my hands went numb, and my legs gave out. My brothers thought I was dying, hysterical because they'd already lost our mother, then our father, and now their little sister was on the floor. My body learned something that day it would never unlearn. People leave, and when they do, you might not survive it.

So, that was my first panic attack, but not my last. Over the years they came and went. Triggered by things that seem small from the outside but felt like the end of the world from the inside. Coming home to a quiet house when I expected someone to have been there. Julian working late and not answering his phone. Anything that smelled like absence. Anything that looked like a door about to close on me.

I saw a therapist for a few years. Dr. Mobley, a Black woman with locs and a voice like warm tea. She gave me a diagnosis that had too many syllables, prescribed anxiety meds, and taught me coping mechanisms and grounding techniques. And it helped. By the time I left for college, the attacks were less frequent, and more manageable. I stopped seeing her because I felt like I'd outgrown them, the way you outgrow a childhood fear of the dark. Not because the dark stops being dark, but because you learn to sleep in it.

But you don't necessarily outgrow anxiety and panic attacks. You get longer stretches between them. Until something happens that smells like loss and feels like leaving, and your body responds the way it would to a car crash. Flooding your system, shutting down everything that isn't essential, and bracing for impact. Your child mind taking over, while your grown woman mind can only watch.

Something like seeing the man you'd fallen in love with sink a free throw in a Charlotte arena, while the son he didn't know about was home in Lennox Falls, asleep wearing his father's exact face.

Raschad had become everything he said he would. Right on schedule. The plan he'd outlined tangled in sheets in Los Angeles, while I lay beside him, daydreaming about the future we might have together. And now, there I was sitting in a suite forty feet above, with a secret eating me alive.

"Simone?" Taryn's voice broke through the hum. "Simone! Oh shit. Okay. Look at me. Look at me."

I couldn't look at her. I was locked on him. He was jogging back on defense, smiling, and his smile was Zhaire's smile. A wide, easy grin that took over his whole face, and my lungs felt like they had collapsed.

"Okay. Come on. We're going to the bathroom."

Taryn's hand closed around my wrist and pulled. She'd done this before. Talked me off this ledge in bathrooms and parking lots and the front seat of her car at two in the morning. I let her pull me. My legs moved, but I couldn't feel them as she wove us past people quickly, her hand locked in mine and I followed her blind and numb, trusting her legs because mine had forgotten how to work properly.

She found the women's bathroom a few feet down from the suite, checked the stalls, and locked the door behind us. She didn't say anything, just took slow breaths for me to mimic, holding the silence and waiting for my nervous system to stop screaming. My breathing eventually slowed. My exhales got longer and my inhales deepened. The gray at the edges of my vision receded. The hum in my head faded and the bathroom came into focus. Tile walls, fluorescent lights, the muffled roar of the arena bleeding through the door. I pressed my palms flat against my thighs, grounding myself in the solidity of my own legs.

"I'm okay," I said. My voice thin and scraped out. "I'm okay."

"I know you are." Taryn's voice was calm and steady. "Take your time."

Then the tears came leaking like my body had held everything in during my panic and now was releasing the overflow. Silent tears tracked down my face while I stared at the mirror and tried to summon the confident, self-assured Simone who'd walked into this arena with resolve and a plan.

"I can't do this," I declared.

"Yes you can, Simone. You're already here. You already did the hardest part. You showed up."

"I *can't*. Taryn. The second he sees me he's gonna want to know where I've been. Why I left. And I don't have an answer that makes sense. I'm going to have to stand there and explain myself, and—"

"That's kind of the point." She looked at me in the mirror. "The game's not over. There's still time. And after, we'll go to the tunnel. The pass will get us through. You don't even have to say everything tonight, Simi. Just open the door, speak to him. Say hello at least. That'll be the start. I'll be right next to you."

I looked at myself. Mascara streaked. Eyes swollen. What exactly was my plan? Walk up to a man I hadn't spoken to in five years and say: *Hi! Remember me? We fell in love in California and I got pregnant and disappeared on you. And by the way, your son has your smile, and your middle name is on his birth certificate, but the line for "father" is blank because I couldn't bring myself to tell you.*

"Okay," I heard myself say. "After the game. The tunnel."

Forty minutes later the final horn blared. The game ended and I didn't know the score or who won. Taryn and I walked through the concourse, or maybe she dragged me through it. The hallway smelled like Gatorade and floor polish and sweat. I could hear voices ahead, reporters, staff, and the squeak of sneakers on concrete as we rounded a corner.

And there he was again. Twenty feet away, laughing with a teammate, tall and glistening with sweat, a towel draped around his neck. His voice carried, that deep baritone voice with a youthful undertone, the one I still heard in my dreams sometimes.

My feet stuck to the ground, and I couldn't move, as I stood there staring at the side of his face. Then he started to turn, scanning the tunnel. My hand shot out and I grabbed Taryn so hard she flinched.

"No. No. No. Let's go. Please. Come on."

"Ouch! Simone!"

"Not like this. Not here. This was a bad idea." I put my head down and turned away, already walking. Then, not walking, *running*. Heels clicking against the concrete like gunshots, as my coattail flew behind me, and tears blurred the exit signs into smears of red.

I heard Taryn behind me a moment after. She told me later that their eyes met for two seconds. Maybe three. That his brow furrowed, and he tilted his head at her as my back was to him, running away like I'd stolen something. Which... I kind of had. His fatherhood. His expression shifted from casual to curious to confused and he took a half-step forward before she turned and beat it behind me.

OUR HOTEL ROOM WAS DARK EXCEPT FOR THE CITY GLOW THROUGH THE window. I threw myself onto the bed, face in the pillow, while Taryn came in quietly, unzipped her boots, and decided that $18.99 a piece for two mini bottles of liquor wasn't criminal. She handed me one as she plopped down next to me.

"You wanna talk about it?"

I shook my head.

"So you want me to pretend I didn't just watch you sprint out of the stadium like you owed its light bill?"

A weak laugh escaped me, turned into a sniffle. "I froze."

"I know. I was there."

"He looked so happy and content. And he's built this amazing life, and here I am about to blow it up because I made this choice alone."

Her voice was quiet but precise. "You made the choice *without* him. And now you're making it again. Deciding *for* him, every time you stay quiet."

She was right. She'd been right for five years. I knew I was wrong, but knowing and doing are different languages.

"I just need more time to figure it out," I said.

She sighed in frustration. "This can't go on, Simone. You're waiting until you think there will be some magic moment where it won't hurt him as much. Where the damage won't be so heavy. But the longer you keep holding out, the greater the damage will be. He's in Charlotte *right* now. Three hours from Lennox Falls. The world is getting smaller. One day you're not going to have the luxury of telling him on your terms."

"I know. You're right. I know."

She studied me for a moment. "You want me to just tell him for you? Get the initial shock out the way? 'Cause you know I will. Or let me tell Zion at least. He'd know how to handle this."

"No, it has to come from me, Taryn. Do *not* tell Zion. You know the first thing he will do is tell Julian and Tre, and then the three of them will be on a plane to the next city Raschad is playing in, pulling up. No. No. That can't happen."

She took a deep breath, "I get it Simone, but I need you to know, it was easier to carry this with you before. Now I'm about to be married to your brother. *Married.* And I'm starting to feel like I'm lying to him, babe. He's gonna be pissed at me when this comes out. At some point you're gonna have to just rip the fucking bandaid."

I nodded, guilt settling in over the position I'd put her in that I had never really stopped to consider. "I'm sorry to put you in this situation, T. I don't want you in trouble with Zion because of me."

She bumped her shoulder against mine. "Trouble? Girl, I'm not afraid of Zion. I got that man wrapped around my pinky."

I raised an eyebrow and managed a smile, "You sure it's not the other way around?"

"Yeah, you right, who am I kidding." She cackled. "But, I'm just saying, we don't keep things from each other, Simone. Except for this. And I'm starting to feel guilty about it."

"I hear you. I'm gonna fix this. I will."

"Okay," she replied skeptically. "And I love you, but don't think years from now I won't be telling the story of how you sprinted away from your six-foot-six NBA playin' baby-daddy like he was the boogeyman."

"Shut up."

"You were *booking* it, Simi. I'm talking full-on track meet. Usain Bolt in a pair of Kendall Miles heels. It was impressive. Zhaire's got athleticism on both sides apparently."

"Goodnight, Taryn." I shoved her playfully. And for a moment the weight lifted enough for me to relax.

Later, I lay awake staring at the ceiling. I'd been twenty feet from him. Twenty feet from the beginning of something terrifying and necessary and long, long overdue. And I'd run. Like I'd always been running. Like a coward.

I kept thinking about what Taryn said about the world getting smaller. She was right. I just wasn't aware then of just how small it had already gotten, and how much smaller it was about to get.

part one

FATE

when we collide

simone

present day

Bathtime had been a negotiation, and the final round of *ONE MORE story, Mommy, please* had nearly broken me, because Zhaire had discovered that if he widened his eyes just right and said "please" in a sweet whisper, I'd fold like a lawn chair. He was five, and he already knew how to negotiate leveraging his strengths.

Finally, my house was quiet, giggles faded and my five-year-old finally powered down for the night. I sat on the edge of his bed and stared at him. He was curled up under his dinosaur comforter, half his stuffed animal collection surrounding him like security detail. His twists fanned across his pillow, the ones I'd spent part of the day detangling and retwisting while he squirmed and told me I was "doing too much." Another too-grown phrase I was gonna have to get on Uncle Tre for teaching him.

"Night, sweet potato," I whispered.

His eyelids fluttered, not asleep yet. "Are you still going out?"

"Just for a little while," I answered, smoothing the blanket over his chest. "The studio is having a mixer tonight. I'll be with Uncle Julian and Uncle Tre."

"What about Uncle Z and Auntie Taryn?"

"They won't be there tonight. Still enjoying their newlywed time."

"Yuck." He said like he knew exactly what that meant. Thanks also to Tre, who had explained the concept of a honeymoon by telling him *"it's when grown-ups go somewhere fancy to kiss and act real weird."*

He burrowed deeper into the comforter, already drifting. I stood there a moment longer. Watching the way his lashes fanned across his cheeks. Absurdly long, and unfairly the kind of lashes women pay money for. He didn't get those from me. Those were from his father, along with the single dimple on his right cheek. People told me all the time how much he looked like me. I always nodded and smiled when they said it. Let them believe it.

I kissed his forehead. "I love you, sweet p."

I pulled the door almost closed and left the hallway light on, the way he liked it. Then I thanked my babysitter Xeena on the way out.

THE MONARCH WAS ONE OF MY COUSIN KHAZ'S CLUBS. HE'D BUILT IT from an abandoned warehouse into the kind of place that made people feel important the moment they walked in. WadeHouse held events there all the time. Familiar, family-run territory. I wasn't there to party. I was there to represent the family brand: show my face, drink my one glass of champagne, then get back home by ten. Julian and Zion typically did the real talking, and Tre did the real charming.

I'd chosen a simple black dress, nothing dramatic, just well-cut and form-fitting. My hair was silk pressed past my shoulders, in a middle part bust down, which had become my signature style over the past couple years.

I'd settled into a booth with Tre, and my other cousin Khairos. Tre was in the middle of a story about a sound engineer who'd accidentally deleted an entire session and blamed it on "spiritual interference." He was mimicking the guy's voice as Khairos fell out laughing.

I laughed along, while sipping my drink and scrolling on my phone, pretending to check something important when really I was rewatching a video Zhaire's pre-K teacher had sent of him doing a "presentation" on dinosaurs, when suddenly Julian appeared at the edge of the booth.

"Simone, I want you to meet someone real quick."

I looked up from my phone, casually and professionally, like I'd done a thousand times. The introductions, the handshakes, the *nice to meet you, we should connect* dance that these events ran on. I was already arranging my face into the polite, interested smile I used for business, when Julian stepped to the side and the man behind him came into view.

My brain didn't process it immediately. There was a lag, a full three, maybe four seconds where I was looking at him without understanding what I was looking at. The way you hear a sound you recognize but can't place what it is.

And then it hit me, realization exploding throughout my body like fireworks. Or, more like a nuclear blast. *Raschad?*

I told myself I had to be hallucinating. But then I blinked, and he was still standing there. It *was* him. Raschad Nova Carter. The father of my child. The man I had spent every day of the past nearly six years agonizing over reaching out to, and avoiding it at all costs. I could hear my heart beating in surround sound in my head.

Up close, he was even taller than I remembered. Or maybe I was smaller, sitting down, looking up at him, feeling like the booth was swallowing me whole. He'd filled out, broader through the shoulders, more settled in his frame, the lean athleticism I remembered replaced by something denser and more solid. His beard was trimmed low along a jawline that I knew well because I'd traced it with my fingers in a bedroom in California, and now traced it every day on my son, when I greased him down before school.

His eyes hadn't changed at all. Dark, warm, and impossibly focused. The exact same eyes I had just kissed goodnight an hour ago. He smiled slightly with the lazy smirk with a lone dimple that Zhaire flashed when he was caught doing something he shouldn't be.

I think my heart actually stopped for a split second. If I'd been hooked up to an EKG, there most definitely would have been a flatline alarm. My entire cardiovascular system looked at this man, said *"nope, absolutely not"*, and clocked out for a moment.

He stepped closer, and six years of distance collapsed in an instant. Six years of streaming services, and Instagram lurking, and Google alerts, and late-night stat checks, and jerseys in a closet box, and unsent messages, all folding in on itself.

Raschad stood in front of me, and my body didn't know how to act. Heat rose in my stomach, tightness clawed at my throat, and a tremor shook in my hands that I hid by pressing them flat against my thighs under the table.

"Raschad's in town for some production collaboration talks," Julian said, but his voice sounded like it was coming from very far away… underwater… in another country. "A few of his tracks have been gaining traction, and we've been in talks about possible collabs with WadeHouse. He'll be around the studio for a week or so, and we've got that kickoff meeting with him on Monday. Thought y'all should connect."

Julian was completely unaware of the fire he'd just tossed me into. My brain began running a parallel process recalling every half-heard reference to an "R. Carter deal" in status meetings I'd skimmed through. Every line-item agenda I'd barely read. Julian mentioning something about a new production imprint. Zion saying something about demo sessions. Names and numbers I'd tuned out the way I always tuned out early-stage deal chatter, because that was their lane and I only got involved when something was final and needed an ops or marketing strategy.

R. Carter. Raschad Carter. My own brothers had been building a business relationship with my son's father for months, and I'd been too busy not paying attention to clock it. But why the hell would I have made the connection? He's an NBA player for God's sake. Now he's a music producer too? What the actual fuck?

Though, that shouldn't have surprised me. He'd always said it: Basketball first, music after. That was the plan he'd laid out, clear as anything. I'd believed him because he meant everything he said. I just hadn't expected "after" to be *now*. He had at least another good five years of NBA small forward in him.

Julian was giving me a confused look. Raschad was staring at me. *Everyone* at our table was staring at me, because this was the part where I was supposed to say something. Shake his hand. Be professional. Be normal.

My brain had short-circuited completely. Every intelligent thought and bit of social training I'd developed vacated the premises. I was standing in the smoking ruins of my own composure with nothing to offer but the emergency default that lived in my muscle memory.

I stood up. "Ni…Nice to meet you," I heard myself say. It came out with a stutter. The same bland, industry-standard greeting I'd given at a hundred events. *Nice to meet you.* The most generic phrase in the English language. A phrase so automatic I could say it in my sleep, and apparently also while having a complete psychological breakdown.

But what else was I supposed to say? In front of my brothers, my cousins, and a room full of industry people? *Oh, we've already met! You know how y'all finally stopped asking me who your nephew's father is, even though it still bothers you that I never told you? Surprise! Oh, and Raschad, remember how we fell in love, and then I ghosted you, and never told you why? Double surprise!*

I don't think so.

So I defaulted to the script and smiled my worst, most unconvincing smile. Too wide, too stiff, all teeth and no soul. I was having an out-of-body experience, floating two feet above myself watching it all happen.

Raschad held out his hand, and I took it. The moment his fingers closed around mine, something detonated. My body *reacted* physically, immediately, and without mercy. A current ripped through me, every nerve ending I had firing off at once. My breath caught in a tiny gasp, and my pulse, which was already sprinting, broke into a full gallop.

His grip was firm and his thumb grazed the back of my hand with the lightest brush, and I felt it in my knees.

"Pleasure," he replied.

His voice was a little rougher and deeper than I remembered, and his hand lingered a moment too long for a business introduction. Then he let go, and I could breathe again. Barely.

I studied his face looking for clues, for something I could use. Was there a flicker? A pause? Anything? I scanned every micro-expression. The set of his mouth, the movement of his eyes, the rhythm of his breathing, the bob of his Adam's apple, searching for even the smallest sign of recognition. Some flinch of *oh shit, it's you.* Some crack in that swagged-up exterior that said *I remember everything.*

But there was nothing. Just an easy smile and the effortless composure you'd expect from a man who'd spent years being introduced to strangers at events.

He doesn't remember me. The thought hit me like cold water. And the first thing I felt, shamefully and pathetically, was relief. Pure, dizzying relief that flooded my body like a drug.

Then the second wave came.

Wait. He doesn't remember me? What in the actual fuck!

I know he's in the NBA. I know what that world looks like. The endless rotation of women and the probable hookups in every city. He'd probably met hundreds of women since me. And I was what? A chapter so brief it didn't even warrant a bookmark?

But we'd talked every day, multiple times a day for months. We fell asleep on FaceTime. I flew to LA to see him. He held me through a moment in San Diego while I told him about the worst days of my life. We lay in his bed talking about our goals and dreams after he'd made love to me so thoroughly I couldn't feel my legs.

All that was forgettable?

The thought made me want to throw up. But then I caught myself. Because what kind of delusional, audacious, irrational nerve did I have to be upset? I disappeared on him. Vanished without a word. Ignored his calls and messages. I had his child and hadn't told him. And now I'm mad he might not remember me? The audacity. The absolute, uncut audacity of my own emotions.

Fine. Cool. If he didn't remember me, that was actually the best possible outcome at that moment. I could play stranger, get through this night, and figure out the rest tomorrow. I could do this. I just had to stop trembling first.

"Oh snap!" Khairos said, standing to dap Raschad up. "Carter, whaddup! Good to see you again, bruh."

"Khairos! What's up, man," Raschad took his eyes off me, *finally*, and greeted Khairos with the warmth of familiarity. "It's been a minute. How you been?"

I sank back into my seat, floating like a ghost attending her own haunting. From what I could piece together through my fog, Khairos had met Raschad through Tre. Apparently he'd gone to New York with

Tre a couple times, courtside games, afterparties with the team, and studio sessions. The kind of hangouts that turn strangers into homeboys. My family had been circling this man for months; award shows, Knicks games, studios, business talks; and I'd been clueless. The universe wasn't being subtle. It was being hostile as hell.

Julian tapped the table at me. "You okay, Simone?"

I blinked. "Huh?"

"Are you okay?"

"Yeah. Fine." I lied, sipping from a drink I couldn't even taste anymore. They were all talking. Raschad, Tre, Julian, Khairos, and Khaz, who'd come back to join the table. Talking sports and music and whatnot. Normal conversations that normal men have, while I was in my own silent episode of *Black Mirror: Baby Daddy Edition.*

I couldn't follow much of the conversation. My brain was running a split screen, one half pretending to be present, smiling at the right moments; the other half cataloguing every detail of the man across from me. The new tattoo on the side of his neck. The cadence of his voice when he talked about his music, the same passion I remembered from late-night calls when he'd play me melodies he made on his laptop and watch my face for a reaction.

Every now and then, I'd catch him glancing at me. And every time our eyes met, I looked away quickly, hoping I didn't look as crazy as I felt. This went on for maybe twenty minutes. Twenty excruciating minutes of smiling and pretending and dying inside.

"Nah, I'm not suiting up this season," Raschad said, and my ears locked onto his words like a homing device. "Coming off an injury. Some trade stuff might be in the works, but looks like I might be here for a while getting this collab going in the meantime. We'll see what happens."

I choked. A full-body, eyes-watering, coughing fit that made every head toward me. Raschad was on his feet and next to me before anyone else moved. "You alright?"

I nodded, eyes streaming, waving him off, while still coughing. He reached for napkins and put his hand on my back between my shoulder blades, and when his palm touched me through the fabric of my dress, the jolt hit again. A full-body shiver that I disguised as more coughing.

"I'm good. I'm good," I wheezed, standing up fast, putting distance between us. "Really. I'm good."

"You sure?" He was scanning my face, brow furrowed, eyes up close searching mine. And for one terrible second, I thought I might pass out.

Tre was standing too and frowned. "You sure you're okay, Simone?"

"Yes, yes. I'm fine." I grabbed my clutch and pulled my composure together with all my might. "But I've got some stuff in the morning and this is turning into a guys' night anyway. I'm pretty beat. I'll talk to y'all later."

"I'll walk you to your—" Julian started.

"No, no, stay. I'm good. I parked right out front."

I made quick, efficient rounds. Giving Julian a kiss on the cheek, a quick hug for Tre. A dap for Khairos. A nod for Khaz. And then Raschad. I couldn't skip him without it being obvious. So I turned to him and extended my hand. Stupid. Why did I volunteer to touch him again?

"Um… bye." I looked up at him.

He closed his hand around mine, and looked at me with intensity. "Good night, Simone. Get home safe," he replied with a slight smile.

I cleared my throat, pulled my hand away, turned and walked toward the exit. *Don't run. Don't run. Don't run.*

I ran.

Booked into the cool night air, with my heart hammering so hard I could feel it in my fingertips. I made it to my car, got inside and locked the doors like someone was chasing me, sitting there for I don't know how long. Shaking.

What the hell was that? What the hell was that? What the HELL was that? I clutched my chest, trying to breathe normally. My phone. I needed my phone. I fired off a text to Taryn:

> Is Zion with you?

> 911

Seconds later, my phone rang. "You okay?" Taryn asked.

"He's here" My voice came out barely a whisper.

"Who?"

"*Raschaaaad!* I just saw him at the damn mixer! Julian just introduced us like it was nothing! No idea, T! I-I couldn't breathe. I practically ran out of there. Oh my God, I'm gonna throw up. I'm having a full-on panic attack right now. Or a heart attack. Or both. I don't know what to do."

"Where are you?"

"Outside. In the parking lot. Sitting in my car like an idiot."

"Okay. Go home. I'll be there in twenty."

"Taryn…"

"Go *home*, Simone. I'm coming."

I drove home on autopilot. Paid and relieved Xeena when I got there, checked on Zhaire who was still asleep, then sat on my couch. In the dark. In a trance.

Taryn let herself in and came barreling through my door like it was a police raid.

"Girl!" she said when she spotted me half comatose, sitting on my couch, staring at a blank TV screen, "You look worse than you sounded on the phone."

I let out a whimper, jumped up from the couch and started pacing.

"Okay. Just calm down so you can think. You're sweating, your lashes are hanging. Sit down and talk to me."

"I can't — I can't breathe, T. I can't..." I stopped pacing and grabbed the back of the couch. My legs felt like they'd been filled with sand.

Taryn rubbed my arm. "Hey. Hey. You're okay. You kept it together well enough at Monarch, you can keep it together now. Deep breaths, Simi."

"I can't..."

"You *can*." She breathed in and out and I matched her.

I exhaled and it came out in a sob.

"It's gonna be okay, Simone. We knew this time was coming," she said softly. "Everything is gonna be okay."

I wasn't okay, and I knew it was going to get much worse than okay very soon. She guided me back down onto the couch, went to the kitchen and came back with a glass of water.

"Okay," Taryn said, settling beside me. "Tell me everything."

I explained every moment of the night down to the fact that my entire family had been orbiting this man without me knowing, and that he planned to be in Lennox Falls working with them for who knows how long.

Taryn sat very still through all of it, and when I finished, she exhaled slowly. "So your brothers have been building a relationship with your baby-daddy for *months* and you had no idea? How is that possible?"

"I never pay attention to early-stage stuff! It's always just names and line items to me. I didn't connect it until Julian said his actual name to my actual face."

"There's no way he doesn't remember you Simone. *No* possible way."

"That's what's killing me. He played it so smooth then. But what if he was playing me, playing it cool, while I was playing him cool, but spiraling inside, completely *uncool* the entire time?"

"Jesus be a fence," Taryn shook her head, raising both palms to the ceiling. Then she looked at me with concern on her face "Do you think he knows? About Zhaire? Planned this?"

"Knows as in you think he came here to find me? Oh my God! Like bounty hunters?!"

"Girl, no, that's for criminals."

"I *am* a criminal, Taryn! I stole his child!"

"You did not steal — okay, you know what, we're not doing the legal analysis right now." She grabbed my hands. "Slow down, you're gonna spiral."

"I *am* spiraling! Do you know what it's like to look at a man and see your son and know you've been lying about his existence for *five years*?"

Taryn shifted her eyes to the side, then back again, "Um… can't say that I do. No."

My voice cracked and the ugly tears came flooding. "What if he takes Zhaire from me? What if he sues me? What if I ruin everything? When everyone finds out what I did and they all hate me! What if my brothers never talk to me again? What if Raschad takes me to court and a judge deems me an unfit mother because of what I've done?"

"Stop. Just stop. Sit back and breathe." She handed me a tissue. "Now. Let's separate the real fears from the panic fears."

"They're all real."

"No. Some of them are your brain on a five-alarm fire, making up scenarios." She ticked them off on her fingers. "Is Raschad going to take your child? No. Is he going to destroy your family business out of spite? No. Is Julian going to disown you? That man raised you. He'd walk through fire for you. No. Will Zion and Tre stop speaking to you? That would never happen."

"What *is* real is this: Raschad is here. In your city. Working with your brothers. And you have a secret that is *going* to come out, Simone. There is no way around it now. Whether you tell him, or whether he sees his face in Zhaire across a room and does the math himself."

The image hit me like a fist. Raschad walking into WadeHouse and Zhaire running through the halls the way he often did.

"Oh God," I whispered.

"Yeah," Taryn let the silence sit. Then she softened. "Look. I know you're scared. I know this is the thing you've been running from since the day you got that positive test. But there's nowhere to hide now, Simi. Not anymore. Raschad is *here*."

I stared at the water in my hands. "What if he hates me?"

"Then he hates you," she said simply. "And that would be his right. But you'd still have your brothers. You'd still have me. And you'd still have Zhaire. That little boy knows your love. He knows your heart."

I nodded, but barely.

"You have to tell him now, Simone. Not just for him. For *you*. You've been carrying this burden and guilt like a second skin for years. And for that baby, who *deserves* the full truth of where and from who he comes from."

I wiped my eyes and took a shaky breath. "How? How do I even start that conversation?"

Taryn was quiet for a moment, thinking. "You ask him to lunch. Somewhere private. You feel out his energy. And when the moment is right, you just say it. Face to face. Like a grown woman."

"And if he flips out on me and it all goes left?"

"Then I'll handle the getaway car and new identities."

I chuckled, wiped away more tears and blew my nose.

"You can do this," she said. "You've survived harder things than this, Simone." She squeezed my hand. "You can do one hard conversation."

After Taryn left, I sat in the dark all night. This was a sign if there ever was one. A second chance to fix what I broke. And then I started crying again because I didn't deserve a second chance, and I had no idea what to do next or how to fix this gaping crater I'd dug myself into.

raschad

I KNEW IT WAS HER BEFORE I FULLY SAW HER. JULIAN AND I WERE walking through the club toward a booth in the back, as he talked about their studio expansion. I was listening, nodding, doing the things you do when someone important is talking about important things. But my attention snagged the way a current shifts in the ocean, letting you know something is coming, even if you can't see what it is yet.

Then I saw Simone. Sitting at the end of a booth, scrolling her phone. My heart raced then cracked, a tiny quiet, internal fracture. The kind of crack where something you thought had healed splits open again making you realize it was never healed at all. Just covered up.

Julian was still talking and I willed my face to do all the right, professional things. But inside, every system I had was adjusting to the reality that the woman who'd broken my heart, who I'd spent six years trying to forget, was casually sitting three feet away.

She looked up, our eyes met, and I watched it happen in real time. The recognition, and the flash of pure, undiluted panic that crossed her face before she buried it. Her smile went stiff and too wide, the kind that's not a smile at all, but a shield.

"Ni-nice to meet you," she stuttered.

And that stutter told me enough. She knew me. But instead she looked me dead in the eyes and introduced herself like I was a stranger. I didn't know why, or what she needed from me in that moment, but I knew enough to follow her lead. That was her call to make, not mine. I was in unfamiliar territory, and I wasn't going to put her on the spot in front of her brothers because I was caught off guard. So, if she wanted to play that game? I could play that.

You forgot me? Cool. I forgot you too, then.

I played it cool through the introductions. Dapped up Khairos. Sat down when Julian offered a chair and listened as Tre lead the conversation into music and business, the reason I was actually there in the first place.

But the whole time, through every handshake, every joke, every exchange, I was tracking her. She was sitting there silent, not contributing or engaging. Just holding her drink with both hands, smiling at intervals that didn't always match the conversation, like she was on a two-second delay. Her body was there but her attention was somewhere else.

Every few minutes, I'd casually look her way. And every time, she was already looking at me. Then she'd snap her eyes away so fast I swear I could hear it. Every time I looked away, I'd feel her eyes come back on me like gravity. She couldn't help it any more than I could.

We did this for a while. This silent, stupid, electric dance of her looking at me looking at her looking away. Then, when I mentioned I'd be out for the rest of the season because of my injury, and would be in town for a while, she actually *choked*. A full, dramatic, eyes-watering choke that stopped the table.

I was on my feet before I thought about it, with my hand on her back. She flinched *into* me, her back arched under my palm, then she pulled back, putting distance between us. But in that second of contact, I felt it. The exact same charge from the first time she'd pressed against me on a beach in San Diego. Six years and it was still there, still alive, still humming.

She left immediately after that with some excuse that nobody questioned because they didn't know what I knew. She hugged Tre. Kissed Julian's cheek. Gave nods to her cousins. And then she extended her hand to me for a second handshake, I took it and held her eyes, then she pulled away, turned, and broke into an actual run, disappearing into the night.

I waited, giving it a ten-count, taking a slow sip of my drink, then turned to Julian. "She always dip out early?" Going for my best just-making-conversation voice, leaning back.

"She just had to get home," Julian answered. "Being a mom, she doesn't like being out too late."

A mom? That hit my gut like a speed bump. But I absorbed it, keeping my face neutral, pretending to glance around the lounge. "Oh, okay. Her man probably needed a break from diaper duty, huh?" I said it light, like a joke. But I was digging and I knew it.

Tre's eyes cut to me. The man had stealth radar. "Why you asking?" he said, a grin spreading across his face.

"I'm not asking. Just making conversation."

"Nah, that was a question." Tre looked at Khairos. "That was definitely a question, right?"

Khairos was smiling and cosigning. "That was absolutely a question."

"It wasn't a—"

"You asked if my sister has a man," Tre leaned forward, pointing his drink at me. "You asked about her man. Specifically."

"I can't make small talk? Just being polite."

"I know when a man's investigating."

Khairos was dying with laughter.

I rubbed the back of my neck. "Aight. Y'all got it."

"She's a single mom," Tre answered, still smiling but with a protective edge to it. Just enough to let me know his jokes had a fence around them. "And let me find out you're feelin' my sister, bruh. I don't wanna have to fuck you up," he laughed.

"Noted." I held up my hands.

"He's feeling her. Was staring at her since he sat down." Khairos said to Tre.

"Oh, he's *definitely* feeling her," Tre confirmed.

"I'm sitting right here."

"We know," they said at the same time.

Julian shook his head, "Leave the man alone."

"Jules, your boy just ran a full background check on our sister with one sentence," Tre argued. "I'm supposed to ignore that?"

I laughed. Because Tre was funny and also completely right. I was obvious. The kind of obvious that would've gotten me clowned in any locker room in the league.

"My bad," I said. "She seems cool. That's all." I tried to play it off.

Tre studied me then his face softened just a fraction. "She *is* cool. Best person I know. Which is why if you come at her, come correct. Or we're gonna have a very different kind of conversation. Got me?"

"I got you." The irony almost made me laugh out loud at the wrong moment. Tre threatening me if I come at his sister wrong, and I'm sitting there knowing I've already held her. Already had a whole season of her. Whole months of her voice in my ear at 2am, whole mornings. I'm a man who kissed her goodbye at an airport thinking it was the beginning of something. Who spent the better part of six years trying to figure out what I'd done to make her vanish. And this man is over here like: *don't even think about it.*

I almost said it. Felt the words right there. Watched, for a half second, the version of this night where I told the truth and let everything rearrange around it. Sitting there, drinking with Julian, watching Tre clink his glass against mine like I was just a new business associate with a little crush, I felt the weight of my history with Simone. Not guilt, but something adjacent to it. The discomfort of knowing things about someone that the people who love them clearly don't know.

I stayed another hour or so. Talked music, business, the expansion plans. Letting the evening settle. But underneath it, my mind kept drifting back to her. *Single mom.* That detail kept circling back. She'd moved on. Six years is a long time. People don't wait around, I knew that. But single mom hit me in a specific way.

I'd told myself I'd closed the chapter on Simone. A few good months in my early twenties that ended abruptly and didn't mean as much as I'd thought. That's the easy to carry story I'd been running for years.

Tonight blew that apart. Because the second I saw her face, every defense I'd built imploded. Like they'd been held together with tape waiting for one good shake. Seeing her didn't feel like running into an ex. It felt like finding something I'd lost and pretended I didn't need.

She was still stunning. Same rich brown skin, perfect face… that mouth. Thicker now in a way that suited her. But something else had shifted that I couldn't pinpoint. The Simone I remembered had this restless energy. Never fully still, always like she was about to say something that would catch you off guard, could talk your ear off effortlessly about everything and nothing at the same time. The woman at that table tonight was much quieter. Holding herself careful, like she'd learned to take up less space. That wasn't from getting older.

I didn't know why she'd disappeared. Didn't know what had happened between our last late night conversation and the silence that followed. She'd never given me a reason.

Maybe I'd finally get that answer. Not because I was going to demand it or corner her. But because I was going to be *here*, in her town, working with her brothers, in her world.

I finished my drink and realized my most urgent question was no longer *what did I do wrong?* It was *what happened to you?* And I was going to be around long enough to find out.

2 /

breathe, peach

THIS CHAPTER HAS A SOUNDTRACK

Redbone by Childish Gambino | *Location* by Khalid | *Come Thru & Chill* by Miguel | *Pink + White* by Frank Ocean

simone

six years ago

THE RESORT SAT ON A CLIFF IN SAN DIEGO, OVERLOOKING THE PACIFIC like something out of a magazine. Bougainvillea dripped from every railing, infinity pools melted into the ocean, the air smelled like hibiscus and sea salt, and the cabanas lining the pool deck had gauzy white curtains that turned everyone behind them into a silhouette.

I was reclined on a lounger with oversized sunglasses on and a mango margarita sweating in my hand. My bikini cut exactly right, a royal blue two-piece Taryn had talked me into that made my body look criminal and my confidence on ten.

Julian and Zion were there to speak at the West Coast Music Futures Conference. Tre had backed out last minute, so his tickets were suddenly free. And I was a Wade, part-owner of WadeHouse Music, and more importantly, a woman in need of a break. So I made myself essential and brought Taryn along. She rolled her eyes at the conference part but perked up the second I said *beach resort.* By the time we checked in, she was already plotting outfits and mapping which champagne brunch would hit hardest.

She was beside me with her legs crossed, and her curls catching the ocean breeze, perfectly unbothered in a fire orange two-piece that had caused a three-man near-collision on the pool deck. She never had to try.

"Julian texted." I checked my phone, squinting against the glare. "Meeting ran long. They're gonna miss lunch. Said go on without them."

Taryn sipped her drink without opening her eyes. "Thank God. They've been killing the vibe since we landed. Julian told us not to go anywhere after dark. A curfew, Simone? We're grown women. At a luxury resort. He called it a suggestion, but we both know what it was."

"True," I agreed, "Zion looked like he wanted to file an HR complaint about your bikini."

"Please. That man's been mad at my hips since forever." She pushed her sunglasses down her nose and gave me a quizzical glance. "You sure he's not adopted?"

"Don't do my brother like that." I laughed.

"I'm just saying."

"I don't know why y'all try to act like you can't stand each other." I grinned.

She leaned back and waved the topic away. "Let's enjoy this sunshine before your brothers come back and ask us to join some dry-ass networking session."

I exhaled, letting my shoulders drop. The sun pressed against my skin like warm hands, and I took it all in. No meetings. No family gatherings to coordinate. Just sun and salt and the weightlessness of being somewhere nobody needed me.

Then, I noticed a man sitting a few loungers down and across from us. He was impossible to miss. Six-five at least. He'd taken off his shirt and slung it over the back of his chair, showing off a chest and stomach that made me briefly forget what I was thinking about. He had deep brown skin, an athletic build that suggested his body was a tool he used seriously, and tattoos climbed from his forearm up past his elbow.

His fade was fresh, cut close with a crisp lineup that said he didn't miss appointments. A close-cropped shadow of a beard traced his jawline. He had an ease about him. He sat at the end of his lounger, legs apart, strong back straight, phone loose in his hand, like the whole ocean behind him was his personal backdrop.

"You see him, right?" Taryn didn't even turn her head to indicate who.

"I don't know what you're talking about."

"Mmhm." She turned fully. "He's been eyeing you since he got here. I gave him ten minutes to grow a pair. We're at minute seventeen."

"He's probably just people watching."

"Simone. The man has been looking at you like you're the only other person that exists out here. Don't play dumb."

I tried not to smile.

"He is fine," she conceded. "Not my type though. A little too *I read motivational quotes for breakfast*, but I'll allow it."

"You're ridiculous."

"I'm observant. And by my observation, he likes you, and you like him. So if he doesn't come over here in the next five minutes, I'm walking over there and getting his number for you."

"Please don't."

"You're always talking about how you need to live a little more, but then you get all precious when life actually starts flirting."

That's when he stood up, and started walking towards us. I pressed my sunglasses higher on my face and tried to steady my racing heartbeat. Taryn smiled wide like she'd won a bet.

He stopped two feet from our loungers and looked right at me. "I've been sitting over there for twenty minutes," he said. His voice was low and deep in a baritone that matched the rest of him. "Trying to come up with something clever to say." He paused. "Couldn't."

Taryn crossed her arms. "That's it? That's your line?"

He raised an eyebrow at her, not offended, more amused. "You must be the security detail."

"She prefers gatekeeper," I replied.

"*Gatekeeper.*" He gave Taryn a nod that was equal parts respect and challenge, then he turned back to me. "I'm Nova. Raschad's my first name. Nova's the middle. Family calls me Nova."

He extended his hand and I took it. His palm large enough to make mine disappear, and when his fingers closed around mine something moved through me that I had no business feeling in broad daylight. We held the shake before letting go.

"Simone," I said.

"Simone," he repeated it slowly. "Fits."

"Fits what?"

"You. Classy, but has a little bite to it."

I looked away and pursed my lips in my mouth before he could see me smile.

"Can I?" he gestured toward the empty end of my lounger. I shifted my legs and he sat. His arm rested near me and the proximity did something inconvenient to my nervous system. We talked for a bit. An easy conversation that shouldn't have flowed the way it did between two strangers. He asked where I was from, and I asked what brought him to San Diego.

"Basketball training. I'm heading overseas in a few months. Recently graduated UCLA, and just got a contract in Spain."

"Spain? That's far."

"Yeah. Two, maybe three years. Then it'll be the NBA." He said it with a quiet certainty that wasn't arrogance. "Spain's just a stop. Not the final destination."

"Okay. Man with a plan."

"Have to be." Something flickered across his face. "Family's counting on it."

He was funny too, in an understated way. And he kept looking at me with a steady, open attention that made me feel like whatever I had to say mattered to him. At some point Taryn had gone quietly back to her Kindle, and I almost forgot she was there.

Later, one of his boys materialized behind him, with the confidence of a man who'd never been told no to his face. "What's good? I'm Damon." He looked at Taryn. "And you are?"

Taryn didn't look up from her Kindle. "Not the group activity type. Just 'cause your boy and my girl are vibing doesn't make this a two-for-one special."

Damon blinked. "Damn."

Raschad laughed and whispered to me. "Yeah. She's a little dangerous."

"She's a full-time job with no lunch breaks," I said.

When Damon continued to hover, Taryn shot me a look over her sunglasses that said *I will not be responsible for what happens next.* She started gathering her things, and stood up.

"We're gonna go find food," she announced, giving me a look loaded with subtext.

Raschad stood, holding his hand out to help me up. Then he pulled out his phone. "There's a beach bonfire tonight. Resort lounge, down by the water. Music, drinks, all that." He handed me his phone, with the screen open to a new contact. "Stop by? I'll look for you."

I typed in my number and handed it back. He looked at it, then at me, with a quiet expression. "Simone." He said my name again and smiled. Then he walked off with Damon, who was still shaking his head at Taryn's rejection.

The second they were out of earshot, Taryn turned to me. "Okay, important question. Did you wax before this trip?"

"Taryn! I just met him."

"Exactly. Prime vacation conditions."

"I'm not sleeping with someone I just met."

She pushed her sunglasses down and looked at me over the frames. "One day I'ma get you to admit you're not as innocent as you try to be."

"Not today."

"Mmhm." She pushed her sunglasses back up. "We'll see what that man's trimmed facial hair has to say about that tonight."

The beach party had already settled into itself by the time we walked down from the hotel that night. Tiki torches lined the path down to the sand, their flames bending in the cool ocean breeze. Fire pits glowed as people gathered around them in low chairs and on blankets. The ocean was a dark, endless thing, catching moonlight in pieces and giving it back in shimmer. The DJ had the vibe calibrated exactly right. A mellow playlist that said *you're not leaving anytime soon.*

I remember the song playing when we stepped onto the sand, even now, with a clarity that shouldn't be possible for a detail that small. *Redbone* by Childish Gambino. That bass line that starts in your spine and climbs up, reorganizing your center around the groove. Taryn made a low "mmm" of approval and linked her arm through mine.

"Now this is a vibe," she said.

It was. I scanned the crowd, trying not to be obvious.

"Three o'clock," Taryn said, like she'd been tracking Raschad for me with radar.

He was leaning against the bar, one elbow propped, a pineapple drink in hand, laughing at something with his friends. He'd changed into a UCLA hoodie, sleeves pushed up to show the tattoos on his forearms, and he looked even better at night. Then he looked up and saw me. His head tilted with a small, private acknowledgment. *There you are.* My stomach flipped.

Taryn spotted a group of women we'd met earlier and squeezed my arm. "Go handle your business. I'll be over there."

She disappeared into the crowd and I was standing alone in my white maxi dress when he materialized beside me.

"You made it," he said, like he thought I wouldn't.

"I considered other offers."

"Oh yeah? What did I beat out?"

"Room service and a bad movie."

"And here you are." He tilted his pineapple drink toward me, offering it. I raised an eyebrow.

"I don't drink anything I didn't see poured."

He nodded without a flicker of offense. Then flagged down a bartender. "Can she get one of what I'm having?"

That small thing? The way he didn't get defensive, just understood and handled it? I took a note. My drink arrived and we migrated toward one of the fire pits further from the speakers, where the music softened into something you felt more than heard. Two low beach chairs angled toward the water, and we settled in.

Khalid's *Location* played in the background as we talked. He told me about UCLA, about the years of work that led to his Spain contract.

The coaches who doubted him, and the ones who didn't. He talked about basketball as something he was born to do, and his hard work as honoring it as a gift he was given.

But then he talked about music. He made beats and instrumentals as a hobby. His eyes changed when he talked about it, softer and more interior.

"Basketball will pay the bills. Set me up for life," he said. "Music is something that..." He searched for the word, mouth working around something he couldn't quite land on. "It's the thing that makes sense when nothing else does."

Coming from the family I came from, I understood that more than he knew. "So you're telling me you're a baller and a musician." I sipped my drink. "That's a lot of talent for one person. Seems unfair."

He laughed. "Says the woman running marketing for a music label at twenty-three."

"Associate Director," I corrected. "I only started full-time two years ago when I finished school. I don't technically run it."

"Still impressive. I see you're the type who downplays herself." He looked at me. "We're gonna have to work on that. You gotta pop your collar, talk your shit every now and then."

"*We?*"

He didn't respond. Just smiled. I told him about the label my parents built. And then, without meaning to, in the space between one sentence and the next where truth sometimes flows out of you like water finding its level, I told him how my mother died and my father left when I was a child. It just came out like the night had loosened something in me.

He didn't rush to fill the silence with sympathy. Didn't say *I'm so sorry* with that automatic sincerity people offer when they don't know what else to say. He just sat with it.

"That's a lot to carry," he finally said.

I looked at him. "Sometimes."

"You carry it well."

"Not all the time."

"My dad left when I was eight," he said. Not as a trade. Just offering it up the way people show you their wound when you've shown them yours. "It's just been me, my mother, and my four older sisters. I was always the default man of the house."

We talked about what it meant when life taught you adult lessons too fast. About both of us being the youngest and only sibling of our gender. What it was like for him growing up in a house with five women.

"I bet you can do no wrong in their eyes," I said. "The only boy *and* the baby? I know your behind is spoiled."

"Who's talking? You've got three older brothers." He studied me. "You're probably both spoiled *and* the bossy one."

"What's your sign?" I asked. "I'm a Virgo."

"Leo. August third." He gave me a look.

"Leo." *Of course.* "What time were you born?"

"Like six in the morning I think. My mom loves to remind me I woke her up at dawn."

I pulled out my phone and opened my astrology app. "Leo sun, Scorpio moon, Sagittarius rising."

"What's that mean?"

"You're intense," I said. "You love hard and you feel everything more deeply than you let on."

He stared at me, "You really believe in all that?"

"It's interesting. It's not a crystal ball, but some traits in people I find accurate."

"Ok, then what do those 'traits' say about us?" he asked.

The word *us* hung in the air. Two letters that had no business carrying that much weight after a couple hours and one drink.

"Depends," I said.

"On what?"

"On things that can't be predicted."

The party shifted around us. What had started as a mellow beach gathering had grown, tipping from chill to crowded. The music had moved on to Miguel's *Come Through and Chill,* an insistent groove that enters your body through the soles of your feet and works its way up.

"You wanna dance?" I asked, surprising myself. The night and the music and the pineapple drink had built a version of me that was braver than the one who'd packed her suitcase in Lennox Falls.

He stood, reached for my hand, and I took it. We moved to the other side of the fire pits where the crowd had made a makeshift dance floor on the sand. Raschad could move. I'd half expected him to be stiff the way tall men sometimes are, but he was smooth in the way athletes can be, who used their bodies as instruments, understanding rhythm as physics. His hand found my waist, fingers resting along the curve of my hip. We danced through two songs, until the crowd pressed in and an elbow caught my shoulder. I stumbled forward into him, hands flat against his chest.

"Wanna walk?" he asked.

"Yeah."

We drifted from the party, shoes already off, feet in the sand, heading down the shore as the waves came in, fizzing around our ankles before pulling back. The further we got from the bonfire, the colder the breeze was off the ocean. I crossed my arms and shivered, and without a word, he shrugged off his hoodie and held it out.

"I'm fine," I said.

He kept holding it out, until I took it and put it on. It swallowed me, and smelled like him, and I told myself to remember to give it back before the night was over.

I didn't.

At some point, absentmindedly, we ended up holding hands. Then I stopped walking. He stopped too and faced me, reached out and gently brushed the side of my face. We looked at each other.

"Can I kiss you?" he asked.

I didn't answer. Just stood on my toes and leaned in. That was all the permission he needed. Our kiss wasn't rushed or greedy or performative. His lips were full, and tasted like rum and pineapple. The contact sent a current through my body that started at my mouth and ended in my hands, which found the back of his neck. My other hand fisted the front of his shirt.

His hand slid to the small of my back. His other hand cradled my jaw, thumb tracing the edge of it tenderly. When we pulled back, just enough to breathe, he pressed his forehead to mine. His exhale was slow and a little unsteady.

"Nah," he said quietly, his voice frayed at the edges. "You kiss me like that and I'm supposed to leave here and never see you again? Like you didn't just ruin me on the beach in the dark."

My laugh was breathless. "I ruined you?"

"Completely."

He kissed me again as the waves hit our ankles and neither of us moved. When we finally came up for air he stared at me, and the moonlight made his eyes look like jewels.

"I know what you're thinking," he said.

"Oh? Are you psychic?"

He smiled. "No. But I know what a moment feels like."

"What does this moment feel like?"

"Like if I asked you to stay the night with me, we'd both be conflicted in the morning."

My lips curved. "That bad?"

"No. That good."

He dropped his hand and stepped back. "I like you," he said. "And I don't want you thinking everything I said tonight was just to get you in my bed."

I nodded slowly. "I like you too."

He offered his arm like a gentleman born in the wrong century. "Come on. I'll walk you back."

I took his arm and we walked the path back to the resort.

"How long you here for?" he asked as we reached the lobby.

"A day and a half."

"Good. Spend tomorrow with me. I heard there's a spot up the coast with the best empanadas in California."

"My brothers have a panel in the morning," I said. "But I'm free after."

"I'll meet you there then."

He walked me to the elevators and before I could step inside, he kissed me one more time, quick on the lips. "Text me in the morning," he said. "If you're still thinking about me."

He smiled as the elevator doors closed between us and I watched him through the glass until the lobby disappeared below.

I SLIPPED INTO MY ROOM STILL FLOATING, STILL FEELING THE SHAPE OF his mouth on mine. Taryn whipped up from her bed before I'd even closed the door, with her bonnet slightly crooked, phone in hand, and eyes wide with the energy of a woman who had been tracking my situation all night.

"*Biiitch,*" she sat straight up. "Did y'all fuck on the beach?"

"What? No!"

She pointed an accusing finger. "I checked your location *multiple* times. You barely moved. Y'all were out there for *hours.*"

"We talked. We walked. We kissed. He asked me out tomorrow."

She let out a squeal pitched at a level that only best friends and dolphins could properly interpret. "Tomorrow you're gonna get some. I can feel it in my spirit."

"We're just getting empanadas."

"Nobody drives up the coast for empanadas, Simone. That man is trying to date you, even though he knows you're leaving. He likes you for real."

I sat on the edge of my bed, smiling. Taryn studied me and her expression softened into the version of her that lived beneath the jokes. The friend who remembered I hadn't smiled like that in a long time. Maybe ever.

"Look," her voice was gentle. "I get it. You're careful. But not like my style of careful. I can walk into something knowing exactly what it is, get what I need, and walk back out, without a second thought. You can't do that. Which is why you don't let yourself go there at all until you're sure. And tonight?" She tilted her head. "You looked sure. Which is why I'm excited, because it's been a looong-ass minute, and that man clearly did something to your brain chemistry."

I laughed. "You are so dumb."

"But not wrong." She flopped back dramatically and her bonnet slid off. "All I'm saying is if you do decide to ride that man's wave into the sunset tomorrow, don't let some imaginary hoe-meter hold you back. You're grown. Your body. Your pleasure. Own it."

Sometimes Taryn caught me off guard. The way she could be crude and wise in the same breath, the way she wrapped real concern in ridiculous packaging.

"Okay, Queen of Sexual Enlightenment."

"Damn right. Now get some good sleep. You've got food and other possibilities on the menu tomorrow."

I plopped on the bed replaying the night in fragments, when my phone buzzed.

RASCHAD NOVA

> Thank you for tonight. See you tomorrow.
> Goodnight.

I pressed the phone to my chest and smiled at the ceiling like a fool, still wrapped in his hoodie.

The conference hall was past capacity with three hundred people packed into the room. I slipped in just in time for Julian and Zion's panel, and sat at the back, close enough to the exit to make a quiet escape before the rest of the day's speakers. Taryn had warned she'd be "dead until noon" and not to disturb her unless the resort was on fire. So it was just me. My mind was absolutely somewhere else, because Raschad had texted me at eight that morning.

RASCHAD NOVA

> Still thinking about you. In case you were
> wondering.

I'd stared at it for a full minute. Typing and deleting four different responses before settling on

> I wasn't wondering. I already knew. 😏

> See you later.

Bold for me, which made him send back a single smirk emoji.

I sat there half listening to my brothers' panel, half thinking about Raschad, when he suddenly slid into the seat beside me. His knee was a careful inch from mine and his cologne mixed with the conference air.

"Your brothers are impressive," he whispered, leaning in close.

"Yeah," I whispered back. "They are."

Julian was at the center of the panel, commanding the stage the way he'd been commanding rooms since he was nineteen and suddenly responsible for a business, a legacy, and three younger siblings. He spoke about WadeHouse's evolution with matter-of-fact precision and quiet authority. Beside him, Zion was his counterweight. Looser, warmer, with a natural charisma that made people lean forward. They were talking about independent labels, building something from nothing, and legacy.

I was proud of them. Fiercely, achingly proud in the way only siblings who've survived something together can be. The moderator was wrapping up, preparing for audience questions, when the screen behind them lit up.

"Before we close," she said, "as we speak about legacy, we'd like to take a moment to honor the foundations of WadeHouse Music the visionaries who started it all."

My stomach dropped to the floor as photos appeared on the massive screen. My father first. Isaiah "Zay" Wade, standing at a mixing board with headphones around his neck, wearing the smile I used to think could fix anything. The smile of a man who believed in what he was creating and had no idea he'd one day walk away from all of it. He looked alive and full of a future he'd never finish.

Then my mother. Denise "Niecy" Wade. Mama. On a stage beside my father, radiant under the lights, her head tilted back mid-laugh while my father looked at her like she was the only person in the room. He used to do that at every show she came to; pull her onstage, sing her praises, sometimes sing directly to her like the audience wasn't there. Once in a while she'd sing back to him, her voice filling the space the same way it filled our house.

The two of them were the first beautiful thing I ever knew.

"Zay and Niecy Wade," the moderator continued, narrating my parents' lives like they were historical figures and not the two people who made me and left me, breaking my world apart. "Pioneers who helped shape the sound of a generation."

Another photo. Then another. The last one at an awards show, my mother in sequins, my father's arm around her shoulders and his hand resting low on her stomach. You could barely tell. But I knew exactly when that photo was taken. They looked like people in love who had time.

Mama was gone a few months later that year.

Onstage, Julian blinked once, slowly, and his jaw tightened by a fraction so small nobody would notice. But I noticed. I'd been reading that controlled tick since I was twelve. Zion's shoulders went rigid. He swallowed hard and shifted slightly in his seat. They knew how to mask it. They always did.

But me? My body had never learned to mask anything. Something went wrong with my hearing. The sound warped, the applause hitting me like physical contact, every clap feeling like a hand pressing against my heart. My vision narrowed at the edges and the room collapsed into a tunnel with my parents' faces at the end of it, on a screen for strangers to admire, while I began to come apart in the back row.

I stood up, knocking into chairs, and somehow got my legs to move. Not gracefully, just *away*, toward the exit. Toward air. Toward anywhere that wasn't a room full of applause for two people I still needed more than anything and would never stop missing.

I made it to the hallway and my knees buckled. I pressed my back against a wall, hand on my chest, trying to physically push the panic back down. My breath came in short, broken gasps, shallow and useless.

The worst part about panic attacks is the awareness. You know you're not dying. The rational part of your brain is screaming that this is neurological, your body misfiring in response to a threat that isn't real. But your body doesn't listen during an attack. It runs its own program.

Then I felt a hand. Warm and firm, closing around my elbow. I didn't see him approach.

"Hey." Raschad crouched in front of me, balanced on the balls of his feet, eyes locked on mine, looking completely unbothered by the fact that I was dissolving in a conference center hallway. "Can you look at me?"

I was getting dizzy, my breath still sticking.

"You're having a panic attack," Raschad said, matter-of-factly. "Come on. Let's get you some air."

He guided me to a bench against the wall right outside the entrance, sat beside me, and began rubbing circles between my shoulder blades.

"Breathe, Peach," he said softly, taking slow exaggerated breaths, guiding mine with his. "In… out. That's it. In… out."

Peach?

I heard it but couldn't process it. I cried without making a sound as my lungs continued not to cooperate. Then he reached into his jacket pocket and I felt the gentle weight of headphones being placed over my ears. He fumbled with his phone and soft, dreamy music filled my head.

Pink + White by Frank Ocean.

The melody drifted in like weather. Just sound, layered and warm and gentle, filling the space where my anxiety had been fighting for territory. The rhythm gave me something to follow. My breathing synced to it, matching the pace. In… out. In… out.

I found myself leaning into him, with my head against his shoulder. My breath found its rhythm and my pulse finally began to slow down. He put his arm around me and we sat like that for a long stretch of quiet. The muffled applause from inside the ballroom felt like it belonged to another world.

"You okay?" he finally asked.

"Yeah. I… yeah."

"Good."

"Raschad?"

"Hmm?"

"Did you call me Peach?"

He broke into a small smile. "I did."

"Why?"

His eyes moved over my face. "Peaches are my favorite fruit," he said. "They're soft. Sweet. Full of flavor. But you have to be gentle with them. They bruise easy if you're careless."

I lifted my head from his shoulder and looked at him, so caught off guard I couldn't find a single word. We sat in the quiet a while longer.

"That was my mom," I finally said. "And my dad… in those pictures."

"I figured," he said softly. "You look exactly like her. Same face. Same beauty."

A sad, grateful smile found my lips. "Thank you."

"You handled that really well," I said. "My panic attack. You knew what to do."

Something flickered in his expression. "My mom deals with anxiety," he said carefully. "She's been through a lot. Health stuff. So I've seen it with her."

"Is she okay?"

He hesitated. "She's fighting cancer. Got diagnosed about a year ago."

"Oh no, I'm sorry."

"She's strong. She's gonna beat it." He said like a reminder to himself. "That's part of why Spain matters. Most of the money's going home. The cost of living is much lower there, so I won't need it. Better doctor for her. Best treatments. Let her stop working and truly focus on getting better."

"That's a lot of pressure." I squeezed his hand.

"Not pressure," he said simply. "Just… my responsibility as a man."

We looked at each other.

"You know," I said, shifting the energy, "this is the most emotionally intense second date in the history of second dates."

He laughed. "We haven't even gotten to the empanadas yet."

"Right. You promised me empanadas."

"I did. And I'm a man of my word." He stood and offered his hand. "Come on, Peach. Let's go find some food and talk about something that doesn't make you cry."

I took his hand and he pulled me up.

<hr />

We ate empanadas at a roadside spot up the coast and talked the whole way back. By late afternoon we were sitting on a bench near the hotel, watching the water.

"Can I be honest with you?" he asked.

"You've been doing okay so far."

He smirked, then his expression settled into something more serious. "I don't want this to be the last time I see you, Simone."

My heart thudded, but I didn't know how to respond.

He glanced at me. "Too much?"

I shook my head and we sat with that as the sun began to set. "You wanna come up?" The words spilled out of my mouth before I'd fully decided to say them, but sitting there with the sky painted in front of us, I knew I wasn't ready for it to end either.

He looked at me with a small smile. "I do want to."

Then I caught myself. "I mean, I'm sharing a room with Taryn though, so…" He paused. "I've got my own room… if you're comfortable."

"Yes. Yeah," I nodded. "Let's go."

He stood and offered his hand. "Okay, then let's go."

In the elevator he stood behind me. Close enough to feel the warmth radiating off his chest and his breath grazing the back of my neck. I watched his eyes find mine in the mirrored doors. We didn't say anything the entire ride up.

His room was on the twelfth floor. When the door clicked shut behind us he set the key on the desk, turned to face me, and just… waited.

"You sure?" he asked.

I opened my mouth to say yes, and something in my face must have moved, because his brows drew together and he touched my arm gently.

"We don't have to do anything you don't want to. I mean that. We can order room service. Talk. Debate about music. I'll even let you win."

That made me laugh. "Why are you so good at saying the right thing?"

He shrugged, half-smiling. "Five women raised me. I learned early what not to do."

Lucky me, I thought. And then I stepped toward him and placed my hand flat against his chest feeling his heart going just as fast as mine. That was the thing that finally settled me. He was nervous too. He just wore it differently.

"I'm good," I said. "I just…" I looked up at him. "This feels different."

"I feel the same way, Peach."

He leaned down, and when his mouth found mine I wasn't second-guessing a single thing. He walked me backward, never breaking our kiss, with his hands moving up my sides. His shirt came off somewhere in the middle of it, I don't remember which of us did it, and then my hands were on his bare chest and I remembered why I'd been stealing glances at him across the pool yesterday. The tattoos I'd only half-seen were detailed and close now, and his body was hard under my palms in a way that made thinking in full sentences nearly impossible.

The backs of my legs found the bed and we stopped kissing. He pulled back enough to look at me. I reached up and pulled him down to kiss me again, and he groaned low against my mouth, as his fingers gathered the fabric at the sides of my sundress, slowly pulling it up until it bunched around my waist. Then he lifted me up and I wrapped my legs around him, as he turned us around and sat on the bed. Me straddling his lap, and his hands gliding up and down my thighs, then settling to cup my behind.

His mouth found my neck and he licked circles with his tongue at the curve, making me arch into him with jolts of pleasure.

He smiled against my skin. "Sensitive there?"

"Mhmm." I couldn't form more than that.

His hands slid higher, grazing the underwire of my bra, and my whole body lit up, a quiet gasp slipping past my lips as he unclasped it, then trailed his lips over my breasts.

That's when my brain chose that moment to start overthinking.

You don't do this, Simone.

I didn't. I had never in my life been the woman in a hotel room with someone she'd known for less than forty-eight hours. I had a whole internal framework a man was supposed to clear before I'd even consider this.

And yet there I was. Braless in just my panties, straddling a man in a hotel room in California.

But it didn't feel reckless. Didn't feel like a one-night stand. It felt like the beginning of something, which made no sense because I was leaving the next day, and the math did not work no matter how many times I ran it.

I felt different with him. A version of myself I didn't usually have access to. Lighter. Less managed. Like I'd set down something I'd been carrying so long I'd forgotten it had weight. Safe in a way I couldn't justify after such a short time. I felt it anyway, bone-deep and certain.

But what if I was the only one feeling this? What if to him this was just another weekend? A girl at a beach resort, a good story? What if he woke up tomorrow completely fine while I got on a plane home with my whole heart rearranged?

He reached down for his pants at the floor and grabbed his wallet, pulling out a condom. I watched him and something in my face must have moved because he looked at me and stopped.

"You okay?"

"I'm fine," I said too fast.

He set the condom on the bed and shifted. "You went somewhere. In your head. What is it?"

I almost said *nowhere*. The word was right there, but instead what came out was: "I've never done this before."

He went very still. "Are you —" He stopped, then started again, carefully. "Simone. Are you a virgin?"

I blinked. "What? No…. No. That's not…I mean, I don't *do* this. I don't sleep with people I'm not in a relationship with. I don't do one-night stands. I don't —" I gestured at the room, at him, at myself sitting there having apparently lost my entire personality. "This isn't something I've… done before."

He looked at me for a moment, then his expression shifted, understanding sliding into place. "I hear you," he said, wrapping his arms around my waist.

I exhaled. "But with you it doesn't feel like that. And I don't know what to do with that because logically…" My voice dropped. "I leave tomorrow. And I'm sitting here running the math and it does not work, and I don't know why I feel this comfortable with you, but I do, and that's making me nervous because I don't know what this is to you and—"

"Simone," he cut me off, and rubbed my back.

I stopped talking, as he took my face in both hands, and waited until my eyes found his.

"It's not a one-night stand," he said simply. Like he'd already decided. "That's not what this is to me."

"How do you know that?"

"I know what a one-night stand feels like, and this isn't it."

"We live on opposite coasts."

"I know."

"You're leaving the country in a few months."

"I know that too."

"So how?"

"Because when I want something," he said quietly, "I figure out how. And I already know I'm going to want to figure this out."

He kissed me. Then he pulled back and exhaled, hard, his forehead dropping to mine. He let out something between a laugh and a curse under his breath.

"Listen. I want you. Bad. I have been wanting you since you walked onto that pool deck yesterday." He kissed me again. "But not when you got that look on your face. I'd rather wait han rush you, and have you second-guessing it on the plane home tomorrow."

I stared at him. "You're twenty-three years old, Raschad," I said.

"Yeah."

"You should not be this emotionally intelligent at twenty-three."

He gave me a tired, lopsided smile. "I'm not, really. I'm just trying. My body's not on the same page as my mouth right now, in case that wasn't obvious."

I laughed, the last of the tension left my shoulders. He kissed me, smiling into it.

He laughed too, "Plus, like I told you, five women raised me."

He pulled me back against him and we kissed some more, one hand at the small of my back and the other in my hair. It would have been easy to keep going. Both of us were warm and breathing hard and back where we'd been a minute ago, except now there was a decision behind it. He kept finding the discipline. I felt him lose it for a second and pull me tighter against him, then exhale and ease me back, his mouth on my temple while he caught his breath.

"Okay," he said more to himself than to me. "Okay."

He reached to where my dress had bunched at my hips and gently tugged it back down for me. Picked up my bra from where it had landed on the floor and set it on the nightstand. His shirt stayed off. My dress went back on but barely.

He pulled me down to lie against him, my head on his chest, his heart still going too fast under my ear. Eventually we settled.

"Okay?" he asked.

"Very," I said, and meant it completely.

He pulled me in closer, my back against his chest, arm across my waist, chin at my shoulder. And then we talked. The way you talk when there's nothing left to perform. Scattered and easy, drifting from one topic to the next.

Every now and then his lips would find my shoulder, or my neck, and the conversation would pause. His hand would slide along my hip, my stomach, up and down my back. He'd kiss me until I forgot what I'd been saying. Then we'd settle back in, and he'd ask me a question, and we'd pick up like we'd never stopped.

He told me about his sisters. About his mom and how she'd held the family together after his dad left, and how he'd promised himself he'd take care of her one day. "Once I'm established. Stacked money up, I'm gonna buy her a house. Retire her. That's the goal."

"Big plans," I murmured against his chest.

"Mm. Got 'em mapped."

He turned my face toward him and kissed me some more. Then went back to whatever he'd been telling me before.

I told him about my first day taking on a real role at WadeHouse, how terrified I was of being taken seriously in a room that had watched me grow up. He told me about his first college game, feeling like maybe he wasn't cut out for it. We talked about what we wanted out of life. The emptiness of missing someone who was still alive. His father. My father.

Somewhere along the way his sentences started getting slower, trailing into nowhere. His hand on my waist went still. His voice dropped, then went quiet. I listened to him breathe, amazed at how much we'd talked about, how easy it was, how much I liked him.

I am in serious trouble, was my last lucid thought before I fell asleep too.

I was still wrapped in the hotel duvet when morning came. The sheets were tangled around our legs, my leg draped over his, his arm tucked under me. I stretched slowly and turned to find him already awake, eyes on me like I was the sunrise.

"Morning," he smiled.

"Morning," I whispered, back suddenly shy.

"You slept hard."

"We talked each other's ears off. I was drained," I said, a slow smile finding my lips.

He chuckled and we lay there a few minutes in silence. I studied his face. *Did this man actually get finer overnight?*

"You hungry?" he asked.

"I could eat a whole damn buffet."

He sat up. "Say less. I'll be right back."

I watched him throw on a t-shirt and slides and leave. I sank deeper into the pillows, trying to convince myself to stay grounded in the moment, not in what it meant, or what it couldn't be.

He came back with arms full of plates like he'd robbed the breakfast bar. "Complimentary breakfast buffet. I may have overdone it."

"So you're a breakfast hoarder. Noted."

"Didn't know if you were a grape or strawberry jelly kind of girl."

I blinked. "You brought me options?"

He shrugged like it was nothing. "Didn't want to get it wrong."

That shouldn't have hit the way it did. He climbed back onto the bed and we sat there, plates between us, like a cozy morning-after-no-sex picnic. We ate slowly. Trading bites. Stealing glances. Our knees kept knocking and neither of us moved. Every now and then he'd pass me a slice of melon or tear off a piece of croissant and hold it out for me to eat.

"You always this charming?" I asked, licking honey butter from my thumb.

He looked at me over the rim of his cup. "This is low-level charm."

We finished most of the food and stayed there, talking.

"You better call me when you get home," he said at some point, his tone shifting more serious.

"Oh please," I tried to joke. "You're the one who's not going to call. I give it a week before some groupie has your full attention."

He laughed, then looked at me. "Not interested in that. I'm going to call you, Simone. I really like you. A lot."

"Okayyy." I arched a brow, playing at lightness. "But we live on opposite coasts. We may never actually see each other again."

"We can see each other if we want to," he said, looking at me like he meant every single word.

I didn't say anything. Just nodded, then I glanced at the clock, and reality slid in like a slow tide.

"I leave this afternoon," I said quietly.

"We don't have to name it," he leaned back and looked at me. "But we don't have to pretend it's nothing either."

He pulled me into a hug and we stayed like that a little while longer, my heart was already filing all of it away. Every brush of his hand. Every smile. Every little thing he said.

Leaving his room was harder than it should have been after two days. I stood at the door, and he leaned against the frame, arms crossed.

"Call me when you land," he said.

"You'll be asleep. Time difference."

"Call me anyway."

I nodded. Then I went to my room to pack. I still had his UCLA hoodie. I meant to give it back to him. Thought about texting him to drop it off to him. I folded it and packed it instead.

r. carter

raschad

I DIDN'T PLAN ON ENDING UP IN LENNOX FALLS. AND OF ALL THE LABELS to start a new chapter of my life with, I didn't plan on it being with WadeHouse. But if I'm being honest, none of this was a complete accident either.

Simone Denise Wade. She told me what her family did when I met her six years ago. We were on a beach in San Diego, talking for hours, and I'd asked what she did back home. *"Family business,"* she'd told me. *"My brothers and I run a label in North Carolina. WadeHouse."* She said it casually, like it was a small thing, so I looked it up that night. It wasn't small.

I filed it away the way you file everything about someone you're falling for. Not because I was planning something, but because my brain decided on its own that every detail I'd learned about her was important and worth remembering.

One minute I was laying in a blanket fort in Los Angeles with Ari Lennox on the speakers, and Simone naked in my arms, telling me I was free to go to Spain with no labels and no commitment. Me telling her she was giving me freedom I didn't want or need. That she was building a door so she could survive me walking through it, but that I wasn't going to even open that door. And I meant that. But then, she decided to walk through it herself instead.

One day she was there, her voice and face on my screen at midnight, and then she was gone. Like smoke. Leaving a hole in the space in my chest I had carved out for her. I tried to give her space, but then two days passed, then another, then another. I texted:

> Hey, everything okay?

I got no response. A few days later I tried again:

> Missing you. Hit me when you can.

Still nothing.

> Did I do something wrong? If I did, tell me. I'll
> fix it.

By week three, I was scrolling back through our thread, replaying conversations, looking for clues. Maybe there was something I missed.

> Saw something today that reminded me of you.
> Call me, please. Hope you're okay.

She gave me nothing back but read receipts mocking me. Eventually, I got the hint and stopped reaching out.

The last voice note she'd sent me was still in my phone. I don't know why I kept it. I'd eventually cleaned out everything else from our thread, the photos, the long voice messages, all of it, but that one note that I kept going back to. It was ordinary. She'd sent it early morning her time, knowing I was still asleep. Her voice was soft and slightly hushed, as she talked about something she'd seen on a walk. Then she got quiet and took a deep breath.

"I miss you."

Then she gave a little exhale and the message ended. That was it.

I had listened to it so many times the words stopped being words. I was just hearing the sound of her. In the months that followed, while I was in Spain and basketball was the only thing keeping me from wallowing in the full weight of her silence, I carried that sound around in my bones.

My sister Jordan noticed I was in a funk on one of my video calls home. "What's wrong with you?" she asked. "You're moping like you got dumped."

"I didn't get dumped," I replied. "I got ghosted. Like vapor. Like I imagined the whole thing."

"By who?"

"Simone."

I texted her the photo I'd taken of Simone on the last day of her visiting me in LA. Her smiling in a Venice Beach backdrop, radiant and stunning in the sun.

Jordan whistled. "She's beautiful."

"Yeah. I know."

"Did she meet somebody else?"

"Maybe." I looked down.

She studied my face, "Aww, Nova. Want me to reach out, see if she responds?"

I looked at my last messages to her. "Nah, I'm good. Over it."

But I checked my phone more than I wanted to admit. Wondered if her texts got lost. Wondered if I said something wrong. If maybe she had a man back home. Hell, maybe she was playing me the whole time. Or maybe I just caught her mid-flight. Wrong time, wrong place. But I didn't even get the respect of a simple "hey, I'm not feeling this". No reason. Just silence.

Eventually, I got the message. No response *is* a response. So I stopped trying, silenced our thread, and buried her number, telling myself I'd imagined what we had, that it wasn't that deep. That it was nothing. That's what I told myself. Over and over.

I dated, of course. Women were always available. Some of them were smart and beautiful and kind, and I'd take them out and bring them home, but none of it meant anything. None of them were her. I know how that sounds. I know it's absurd to be holding every woman up against someone who didn't even care enough about me to give an explanation or a goodbye. But, that's the truth.

I spent a year and a half in Spain in the Liga ACB, proving myself, and perfecting my game so well it finally got me noticed by NBA scouts. I poured myself into basketball the way you pour yourself into anything when you're trying not to think about something else. It worked, mostly. I made the league, got my contract. Sent money home for my mother's treatments which allowed her to stop working and focus on her health. Helped my sisters out and did everything I'd promised myself I'd do since I was a child watching my mother work fourteen-hour days to keep the lights on.

There would be nights in Madrid when I couldn't sleep and I'd open my phone without thinking, pressing play on that last voice note from Simone. I don't know how many times I'd listened to it. One of those times, I picked up my laptop, dubbed over her breath, the deep inhale and small exhale. Then the fragment, *"I miss you"* that she'd said before the exhale. Three seconds of audio from a voice note that over time I ended up building something around. Layering it under the bass, and slowing it down until it stopped being her voice and became texture. The quality of someone who was there and then wasn't. Something you felt underneath everything else rather than heard fully.

I built a beat around the sound of Simone's voice telling me she missed me.

Then I wrote words that I had no one to say them to. Just trying to put something down that wouldn't stop circling:

Were you real, or did I dream you
Did you feel it too

I sat with those lines for a long time. Then eventually wrote the rest.
I called the track *Ghost.*

GHOST
Written and produced by R. Carter

VERSE
Left your perfume on my pillowcase
Your laughter in an empty space
Keep reaching for a frequency
Plays only in my memory
Were you vivid, or a fever dream
More than it was meant to be
Now I'm standing in the in-between

CHORUS
Ghost ([exhale]) (miss you)
Hovering where you used to be
Ghost ([exhale]) (miss you)
Breath in my periphery
Ghost ([exhale]) (miss you)
Gone but never left
Stuck in the aftermath of your breath
Ghost ([exhale]) (miss you)

VERSE
Your voice in my ear
Six am like you're here
Run every moment back
Looking for the thing I lacked
I know how to move on
Still you live in every song
Every beat
Every note

CHORUS
Ghost ([exhale]) (miss you)
Hovering where you used to be
Ghost ([exhale]) (miss you)

Breath in my periphery
Ghost ([exhale]) (miss you)
Gone but never left
Stuck in the aftermath of your breath
Ghost ([exhale]) (miss you)

MY PLAN WAS ALWAYS TWO CAREERS. MOST PEOPLE ONLY SAW ME AS Raschad Nova Carter, small forward, New York Knicks, All-Star, six-foot-six, kid from Jersey. That's the version of me that exists on Sports-Center and social media. But the other version of me checks his keyboard in on every flight, and every bus trip, to every city I travel to for games. Plays it at two in the morning, building beats in hotel rooms, layering tracks on a laptop while teammates played cards in the next room. I put music out under R. Carter, because I wanted no distractions, and to know if my music could stand on its own. No face, no athlete story, just my sound.

Music was the thing I did when the noise and politics of basketball got loud and I needed to remember that I exist outside of holding a ball. My plan was to play a few more years, keep stacking my money, then pivot to music full-time, with maybe sports commentating on the side. A second act that wasn't a consolation prize but something I'd been building all along, beat by beat.

R. Carter was supposed to be a slow build. I started sending tracks to indie artists, and a couple of those tracks caught fire. One picked up by an artist whose album went platinum, and *Ghost* landed a BET Award nomination. I didn't tell the artist I eventually brought the song to who it was about. Just played them the track, and the scratch vocals I'd had done for reference, and watched them sit with it, leading to *Ghost* getting a nomination I hadn't expected. The song had built slowly word-of-mouth at first, then radio play. People called it haunting and intimate. Critics wrote about the production technique, and the texture under-neath it. Suddenly people were asking *who is R. Carter* and my phone was ringing with people who didn't know at first they were calling a New York Knick.

I met the Wade brothers about a year ago at BET Awards weekend. WadeHouse had nominations that weekend, a couple of their artists, and a production credit for Tre. I didn't know any of that going in. I was at the afterparty when Tre found me and started talking about my nomi-nated track. Said it had a quality he couldn't stop going back to. Zion came over. Then Julian. I knew exactly who they were. Couldn't ignore the irony: The song that had gotten me into that room, was a song I had built out of their sister's voice. But I also told myself that didn't matter. The chapter of my life that involved Simone was over. But standing in a corner of a loud room with her brothers, talking music until the party cleared out around us, I understood that closed and over were two different things.

I didn't mention her to them. What could I have said to men I'd just met? So I pushed that reality away the same way I'd done everything about her, carefully, into the back of my mind.

We exchanged numbers that night, and over the next several months, a friendship built the way good things do. Naturally, without forcing it. Tre and I traded beats. Zion and I talked trends and artists. Julian asked smart questions about how I was thinking about the transition out of basketball and strategy and planning with intention.

Tre was the one I connected with most, we had a similar instinct and thought process when it came to production, and what made a track hit. Over that year, the Wade brothers came through New York pretty regularly for business. When we were in town at the same time, we'd link up. I got them courtside seats a couple of times and invited them to hang with the team after. They'd invite me to whatever studio session they had going. I'd play them what I was working on. We'd mess around with beats together, no pressure, just vibing. Once or twice, their cousin Khairos came through too. Good dude, same energy. It wasn't strategic, it just naturally clicked. What started as industry respect turned into something that felt like real friendship.

And through that time, not once did I mention Simone. They never brought her up either. In no scenario could I ever see myself telling them: *"Funny story, I slept with your sister years ago, thought I loved her, but then she disappeared on me, so to process that I made a song, and that song is why we're vibing today."* Nah. That's not a conversation you have with a woman's brothers. That chapter was closed. So what did it matter? Life kept moving and I moved with it.

Then my injury happened. A season-ending torn meniscus, requiring surgery, and months of rehab. That gave me more time alone with my thoughts than I'd had in years. I'd be back on the court next season, but my hunger for basketball, the thing that had driven me since I was a child, began to get quieter, and what got louder was the music. The thing I actually loved versus the thing I was just good at.

When the universe hands you unexpected time, you don't waste it. So while my body healed I kept building. And that's when Julian and I began talking business more seriously.

"You've got an impressive career," he told me, matter-of-factly. "But you face the reality of a body that might not let you play as long as you planned."

Julian, I was learning, didn't mince words, or tiptoe feelings. He was as direct as they come. "Most guys in your position are panicking. Hoping somebody throws them a lifeline. But you've been building. Laying a foundation. Putting in even more work, before you have to. Before your hand is forced. That's discipline most people never develop."

He paused, studying me. "I saw an interview where you talked about how you retired your mother. Got her a house. How you look out for your sisters. Five of them?"

"Four," I corrected. I didn't ask how he found that out. Julian struck me as the type to do his homework before any meeting. Probably knew my credit score and my high school GPA too.

"That kind of responsibility changes how you move. Makes you think further ahead than most people your age. I can appreciate that. Recognize that."

He let it sit for a moment. "You're embarking on a new chapter, Raschad. WadeHouse can help you write it. And if you're open to it, I'm happy to share what I've learned along the way. Might be useful."

I nodded, taking in everything he said. With Tre, it was music, beats, and unwinding. He was a friend. But sitting across from Julian, I understood this was something different. This was strategy and mentorship. The long game.

"I am open," I said.

Julian nodded once. "Good."

WadeHouse was expanding, building its production arms, bringing in new talent and collaborators. I had other offers. Safer offers, that didn't come with the complication and gravitational pull of a woman I'd never fully gotten over.

But I chose WadeHouse, because they were building something the big studios couldn't see yet. Because my instincts told me it was the right fit. Because Julian had a sharp business mind, and a thought process that reminded me of my own. I knew I could learn a lot from him. And Zion had connections and instincts that ran deeper than his laid back demeanor suggested. And because Tre had an ear you can't teach and can't fake.

And, yes, because Simone was there.

I could admit that to myself, even if I couldn't say it out loud. She wasn't *the* reason. But she was a factor. A quiet hum underneath my logic. That the unanswered question I'd been carrying for six years had a potential answer walking the halls of that building.

I didn't expect what happened at the mixer. The physical reality of seeing her again hit me hard. And the look on her face when she saw me? That was enough to let me know that whatever made her disappear, it wasn't indifference. You don't react that way at the sight of someone who didn't matter.

I had a lot of questions and a kickoff meeting on my calendar that would land me across the table from Simone. Maybe she'd be ready to tell me what happened to her… to us, all those years ago.

rain check

raschad

THE WADEHOUSE OFFICES WERE NOT WHAT I EXPECTED. HIGH CEILINGS, natural light, plants everywhere, and covering almost every wall, were black and white photographs. Artists in the booth, label events, people mid-laugh in hallways. Years of it, displayed the way a family covers the walls of a home. A family tree made of music.

Julian ran introductions at the head of the conference table. I catalogued faces and names until he got to the far end of the table. Simone was sitting the way you sit when you've calculated the maximum possible distance between yourself and another person. Laptop open. Pen moving. Looking at me briefly from the corner of her eye, never directly.

Her title on the agenda read Vice President of Operations and Brand Strategy. When I met her she was Associate Director of Marketing. Something like pride expanded in my chest. Which made no sense. She wasn't anything to me except still unanswered questions in a meeting that was running long.

I looked back at Julian and tried to stay there. He laid out their vision, R. Carter under the WadeHouse umbrella, full creative autonomy, their infrastructure. I caught maybe eighty percent of it. The other twenty percent kept drifting to the end of the table, where her pen was moving steadily across her notepad and she hadn't looked up once.

Zion mentioned almost in passing that SZA's camp had been circling a track Tre and I cut last month. "Nothing confirmed. But her people played it and word came back she's feeling it."

I glanced toward the end of the table. Her pen slowed for just a second, then kept moving.

Tre looked at Julian. "See? I told you." Then leaned back. "And we haven't even gotten started. We bout to fuck it up out here." he reached across and dapped me up.

"That's the plan." I smiled.

Julian nodded then turned to Simone. "Simone, operationally, you'll be the point on getting Raschad set up. Studio access, office space, scheduling systems, partner relationships. Everything he needs to function inside this building."

She nodded without looking up from her notebook. "I'll have an onboarding doc to you by end of week. Studio availability, key card access, the session booking system. We'll need to coordinate with legal on the workspace agreement before I can assign permanent space, but we can get interim access set up immediately."

"With the traction his recent placements have had," Zion was saying, "especially *Ghost...*"

Simone's pen stopped, first time since I sat down. "You produced *Ghost?*" she asked me, almost involuntarily.

"Yeah," I said trying to meet her eyes.

She looked at me directly for the first time in the whole meeting. Recognition moved in her expression. "It's a beautiful song," she said carefully. "Didn't know it was yours."

The awkwardness that followed was brief enough that no one in the room would have noticed it. Julian moved on. Zion nodded at something on the screen. Tre glanced between us with quiet radar, probably still thinking I had a thing for his sister and was trying to get with her.

I kept my face exactly where it needed to be. But underneath, my stomach flipped, because I knew what wound I had built that track from. And now she was sitting twelve feet away telling me she'd heard it.

The meeting ended with handshakes, and Zion clapping me on the shoulder with "welcome aboard." Tre was already talking about meeting him in his studio that afternoon. Julian nodding with quiet approval. And Simone closing her things with careful movements, not looking at me.

Everyone was filing out and the doorway cleared as she walked toward it. It was just us left in a conference room with the remains of a meeting scattered across the table.

"Simone."

She stopped and turned to face me, and her expression was a mixture of what I can only describe as fear and something else unreadable. I stood up, keeping my voice low.

"How long we gonna keep playing pretend, Simone?"

She went still. I watched her try to find words and come up empty. Her hands were shaking slightly and she was looking at me like I'd said something she understood but hadn't expected to be asked.

"Raschad, I —"

"I played along the other night, because it seemed like you needed me to." I gestured outside to the hall where her brothers had gone. "I get it. Your brothers were there. It was public. I respect that. But we can't keep pretending. Not when I'm going to be in this building working for a little while."

I took a step toward her. "It's good to see you, Simone."

Emotion flooded in her eyes. "It's good to see you too, Raschad. You… you look great," she replied with an exhale.

"And you look incredible."

She laughed. "You don't have to…"

"I'm not just being polite. It's the truth."

She looked at the floor, then back up at me. And whatever war was happening behind her eyes, I watched her set it aside. "This isn't the place to talk," she said.

"I know."

She caught herself and swallowed the rest of the sentence. "It's not that this is a problem, it's just… my brothers don't know we already know each other yet, and — "

"I figured that out at the mixer. I'm not going to say anything. That's your call."

Her shoulders dropped, just slightly. "Raschad, I'm—" she started to speak but her voice was barely a whisper.

"Raschad," Julian's voice cut through the moment like a knife and he poked his head back into the room. "We're late for that call."

My eyes didn't leave hers. "On my way," I said to Julian, then I smiled at her. "Talk again soon, Pe—," I caught myself. "Simone."

"Soon." She held her laptop against her chest, then rushed out of the conference room.

I stood there, in the empty room with the unmistakable certainty that I was not over this woman. That I had never been over this woman. And she was right in front of me after all this time, because I'd finally found my way to this small town, that I'd chosen, maybe on purpose, maybe not.

Probably on purpose.

Okay, I admit, definitely on purpose.

simone

I PRACTICALLY SPEED-WALKED OUT OF THAT CONFERENCE ROOM AND down the hall with my laptop clutched to my chest, heels clicking in time with my heartbeat. I needed to get to my office before anyone caught

WHAT WAS HAPPENING ON MY FACE. I MADE IT, CLOSED THE DOOR, AND sank into my desk chair.

How long we gonna keep playing pretend, Simone?

I pressed my palms flat on my desk and breathed. Lord. Judgement day had arrived. After years of avoidance and distance, I was going to have to do this. Blow up my life, and his, by telling this man that the reason I disappeared on him was currently ten miles away in a karate uniform… wearing his exact face.

I sat there for a long time without moving. At some point I picked up my phone and searched for Raschad's song. *Ghost.*

The song bled through my earbuds. I had heard it so many times before. In the car. At home doing laundry. I had called it haunting without knowing what I was naming. Now I sat in my office with everything I knew, and I listened like it was my first time hearing it.

> *Left your perfume on my pillowcase*
> *Your laughter in an empty space*

I gasped and my eyes began to sting.

> *Keep reaching for a frequency*
> *Plays only in my memory*
> *Were you vivid, or a fever dream*

I pressed my hand over my mouth.

> *More than it was meant to be*
> *Now I'm standing in the in-between*

Guilt-ridden tears began to fall. This song I'd called haunting, that I had felt move through me like something I recognized… was actually about me.

He had written this song about me. About how I had… *hurt* him.

> *Run every moment back*
> *Searching for the thing I lacked*

He thought he'd done something wrong. And he'd done nothing. He'd done nothing and I let him believe otherwise because I was too afraid to pick up the phone. And he had taken that silence, all of it, my unanswered calls, my read receipts and years of nothing, and he had made something out of it. Something that found me anyway, the way he'd found me before, slipping past every wall I built and settling somewhere I couldn't reach to remove.

> *Still you live in every song*
> *Every beat*
> *Every note*

I sat in my office and cried in a way I hadn't let myself cry in years. Not the contained, functional kind I'd perfected. The ugly, snot-nosed, guilt-ridden, regret-filled and long overdue kind.

Finally, I wiped my face, blew my nose, reapplied my lip gloss, and texted Taryn.

> Need to talk. Come by tonight. Bring alcohol.

Her response was immediate.

> TARYN

WADEHOUSE RAN ON TWO SCHEDULES. BY FIVE-THIRTY THE CORPORATE side had emptied out in waves, the quiet that only happened when the business stopped and the building handed itself over to the other thing it was. The studio side was just waking up.

Julian had picked up Zhaire for me. Karate, then dinner, probably a movie he'd let him stay up too late for, because Julian had never once enforced a bedtime when it was just the two of them.

I'd asked him to keep him once I knew I'd be spending part of the day in the same building as Raschad trying to breathe normally, not knowing how the day would play out. And Taryn was coming over later, probably with wine, ready for the full debrief she'd been texting me all day for.

I saved the file I was working on, closed my laptop, and grabbed my bag, to head out the door.

"Simone."

His voice found me before I turned the corner. Raschad was leaning against the wall outside Studio A, phone in hand, looking like he'd been there a while. He had this easy, unhurried posture that made it impossible to know if he was being intentional or just existing in a space and letting the world come to him.

"Hey," I said, trying to be casual.

"You heading out?"

"Um... yes."

He nodded and pushed off the wall. "I'll walk you."

He fell into step beside me and we walked in silence for a bit, surprisingly comfortable in a way that shouldn't have existed between two people who hadn't spoken in years.

"So," I said, trying to think of small talk besides *'wanna meet your son'*. "How's your mom? Is she... how's her health?"

He stopped walking, a half-step pause, like I'd caught him off guard. "You remember that?"

"Of course. You talked about her every night." I thought about the way he talked about his mom, with pride, worry, and the weight of being the only son. I could've drawn a portrait of that woman from his words alone.

The last time he'd told me, his mother was stage two. He had just got his first check in Spain, and was excited to be able to send it home because her treatments were bleeding her dry, and his sisters were stretched thin.

That was one of the reasons I'd told myself was noble. The reason that felt like protection instead of cowardice. *He has to go to Spain. He has to make this money. His mother needs him focused, not derailed by a pregnancy from a woman he's still getting to know.* I'd wrapped my fear in his mother's illness like a gift I was giving him. Like keeping his son from him was an act of generosity.

It wasn't. I knew that now. Had known it for years. But standing in this hallway asking about the health of a woman I'd never met, my guilt was specifically painful.

"She's in remission. Cancer-free," he said, and his whole face softened. "Almost three years now. Clean scans every checkup. She's good. She's really good."

"I'm so glad," I said.

We pushed through the side door into the parking lot. The evening was warm, and my car was maybe twenty feet away. Twenty feet of borrowed time.

"What about you?" I asked. "How are you? Really."

He laughed. "You asking the polite version or the real version?"

"Real."

"Fair." He rubbed the back of his neck. "I'm... figuring it out. The injury set me back, but I should get cleared soon, so physically I'm good." He paused. "But being here, making music, working with your brothers, it's the first time in a while I've felt like myself. Not the basketball version of myself. Just me. The kid from Jersey who used to make beats in his bedroom."

"You were always more than basketball."

We reached my car. I didn't unlock it. He didn't step back. We just stood there in the parking lot light with the night pressing in and neither of us doing the smart thing.

"Can I ask you something?" he said quietly.

My pulse spiked. "Yes."

"Back then," he was looking at me with honest curiosity. "What happened? I went to Spain. I called. I texted. And then nothing. You just. Vanished."

The truth rose in my throat like bile. Hot, urgent, and demanding to be said. *I found out I was pregnant. I was terrified. I thought I was going to die the way my mother did. I ran and by the time I stopped running it had been too long and the lie was bigger than I could control.*

But my words caught, the way they always caught. Snagged on the hook of the fear that lived in my body. He must have seen it on my face. The shift, the tension, whatever it looked like from the outside when I was drowning on the inside. Because he softened.

"Hey." His voice dropped gently. "We don't have to do this right now."

"No, I need to —"

"Simone," he stepped closer. "This probably isn't the best place for this conversation. I've waited years. I can wait a little longer. I'm not going anywhere."

I'm not going anywhere.

The words crushed me, because that was the promise, wasn't it? The one I'd never let him make. The one I'd run from before he could offer it, because my trauma convinced me that sometimes the people I needed to *"not go anywhere"* the most, would, in fact, go. My mother hadn't gone anywhere on purpose, but was gone nonetheless. My father had promised the same in different ways for the first twelve years of my life, before he packed a bag and walked away.

And here Raschad was standing in a parking lot looking at me with sincerity, and he was saying *I can wait, I'll be here* and he meant it. I could see it. His patience wasn't a performance. That was him.

"I owe you an explanation," My voice was shaking. "And I'm going to give you one. I promise. But you're right, it can't be here in the parking lot."

He studied me, reading my face. "Okay. Whenever you're ready."

"Soon."

"Okay."

The silence that followed wasn't awkward. It was full. He was looking at me. I was looking at him. And the distance between us, collapsed. I don't know who moved first. Maybe both of us. Maybe neither. Maybe it was just the evening and the light and the years and the ache and the simple, devastating fact that we had never stopped.

His hand came up to my chin, and when I didn't step back, he leaned down, gently placing his lips on mine, and kissed me. Sweet and simple. The kind of kiss that isn't about passion, but that says *I remember you. I remember us.*

My hand rested on his chest, feeling his heartbeat under my palm. When we pulled apart, the air between us had rearranged itself.

"Rain check on that explanation?" he said, half-smiling.

"Yeah." I could barely speak. "Rain check."

"I'm here for a week," he said. "Head back to Jersey next Tuesday, then be back again maybe a few weeks after that."

I nodded. "Ok, then this weekend before you go? I will let you know the time and place… soon."

"Okay." He smiled. "Soon." Then he stepped back, giving me space to open my door, and as I slid into the driver's seat, he leaned down, one hand on the roof of my car.

"For the record," he said, "I don't believe in coincidences. I think there's a reason I ended up here. In this town. In this building. And I don't think it's just about the music."

I looked up at him. This man who had no idea that the reason fate put us in the same place again was a five-year-old.

"Drive safe, Simone."

"Yeah." I swallowed hard. "You too."

He tapped the roof of my car, stepped back, and watched me pull off.

I GOT HOME AND LOCKED THE DOOR BEHIND ME, LEANED AGAINST IT, AND let out a noise I could only describe as a "whew-chile-this-man-is-too-much" exhale.

I dropped my bag by the door, and stood in my kitchen for a moment just listening to the quiet. He kissed me. I kissed him back. And I still hadn't said a word.

I should've told him. *Right* then, parking lot be damned. He asked me what happened directly, and I said nothing. What kind of sociopath doesn't say something in that moment? Me. Apparently.

And now I'm over here, heart tap dancing to the rhythm of his damn smile, when I should be planning how to break the most life-altering news of his existence. I kissed the father of my child. The father who doesn't know he's the father. And I liked it. My lips still feel tingly. My soul? Fighting for its life.

"I kissed him," I whisper to a throw pillow like it was my homegirl. I collapse on my couch, arms stretched out, staring at the air like it could give me answers. Because why does he have to look like that? Why does he have to smell like that? Why did God give him dimples, depth, and discipline? For what?

I was unwell. Because now I wasn't just lying by omission. I was lying to his face while catching feelings all over again. With this secret getting heavier, pulsing like a bomb on a timer.

Taryn blinked at me, with her mouth slightly open, as I recapped the meeting, the song, and parking lot kiss. Her eyes widened, her mouth dropped open like she'd just watched a plot twist on a reality show. "Girl. GIRL."

"I know," I groaned, dragging a throw pillow into my lap.

She stood up, hands flying around. "This is some soap opera-level shit. I mean, whew!"

All I could do was nod, while wiping away fresh tears.

"Look, Simone. I'm not gon' hold you. This is messy. But it's not unfixable."

I sank further into the couch. "Feels unfixable."

"You know what fixes a lie? Telling the truth. You ever seen those shows where they have to pull a bullet out before it causes more damage? That's this. Every day you leave it in, the worse it gets."

"Yeah, but if I pull it out wrong, I could bleed out."

Taryn gave me a look. "That's dramatic as hell, but also, yeah... I get it. But keeping it in means it's still killing you too, just slower."

My eyes began to water. "He's gonna hate me."

"Simone. You had his son. You're raising him with love and care. You didn't do it perfectly, but you're doing it. He might be mad. Yeah, he's *gonna* be mad. But that's his child. And he loved you once. It might not be as bad as you think. And I gotta be real with you; this isn't about him forgiving *you*. It's about that little boy knowing where he comes from."

She reached over and touched my hand. "You are not the first woman to make a mistake, Simi. But you could be a woman who turns that mistake into a masterpiece if you stop being so scared."

I blinked fast to keep more tears from falling.

"You gotta let go of the version of you that made this decision and step into the version of you who's ready to own it. You owe that to yourself and Zhaire. *And* Raschad."

"I'm gonna tell him. I just don't know how yet."

She grinned. "Girl, lucky for you, I'm good at planning dramatic reveals. Let's rehearse what you're gonna say."

"Right now?"

"Absolutely. I'm thinking… since the chemistry is *clearly* still there, you may as well sample the goods one last time before you drop the real bomb on him."

"Taryn, I swear. Don't try to make me laugh, this is serious."

"I am being serious," she gave a devious grin. "You ride that man like your life depends on it, and then right when he's about to cross over to glory, you lean in real soft, kiss his ear and whisper: *'you got a son.'*"

I choked on my wine, couldn't help from laughing.

"I'm tellin' you, if you make him see stars first, he might just say, *'Word? That's what's up.'* You'll confuse his nervous system. His body won't even know how to be mad."

"You want me to sleep with him and then tell him he has a child? You are not right in the head. I'm worried for my brother at this point."

"Please, you need to be worried about *me*. Zion's been wearing my ass out. You know I literally had to ice it the other day?"

"Taryn, no! TMI! TMI!"

Her face got serious. "I'm glad I can still get you to smile in the middle of your Greek tragedy. And I don't mean to pile it on, Simi, but I gotta remind you that I *am* married to your brother, and until you face this, I'm the wife helping you hide this. I'd like to be the one who helped you fix it instead. I'm just saying. I have real skin in this game now. *Literally*. Okay?"

I sat with that for a moment. She was right. This had to end.

"Real advice? You need to ease into it," she continued. "Like an emotional warmup. Don't just blurt it out. Set the scene and make it intentional."

I nodded slowly.

"Do it somewhere private. Maybe invite him over this weekend. Cook for him. Catch up for a bit. Explain where your head was at back then, but not as an excuse. Then tell him."

"That's actually good. You're good at this."

"I know. I can be useful beyond comic relief, thank you very much."

"Thank you, T. For listening. And not judging me."

Taryn reached for the wine bottle between us and poured me

another glass. "Please. I *been* judging you." She smirked. "I just love you anyway."

We both laughed, but she grabbed my hand and held it. "You can do this, Simone. You *need* to do this. And no matter how it goes down, I've got you. Okay?"

I nodded. I could do this. I *would* do this. This weekend. A little food. A lot of honesty. And maybe the start of redemption.

Or the beginning of everything falling apart.

night session

raschad

WADEHOUSE AFTER HOURS WAS A DIFFERENT BUILDING. WHEN THE front desk cleared and the lights shifted, the place exhaled into a building for people who loved sound more than they loved sleep.

Tonight it was me, Tre and his sound engineer, locked in on a track Tre had been building. A dirty South bounce underneath jazz samples, layered in a way that shouldn't have worked, but did. I'd come back after walking Simone to her car, needing something to distract me from my own thoughts.

"Run that back," I said. "The bridge feels boxed in. What if you drop it a half step?"

Tre adjusted and hit play. The track opened up, with the bass line stretching, and the horn sample finding space it didn't have before. We all nodded. That was the pocket.

"See?" Tre pointed at me without looking up. "Fresh ears. I been saying it was off all day and couldn't pinpoint it."

We worked through two more passes when Tre's phone buzzed on the console. He glanced at it and went still for half a second. "Zion says SZA's A&R hit him back on that track."

I stopped what I was doing.

"Her team's feeling it." He looked up. "She's doing a show in the area in a few days. Zion's seeing if the schedules can align for a listening session while she's close. If she vibes with it, this could turn into something."

"Nice. What needs to be done before that?" I asked.

"Still need to clean the mix on the second verse."

"Bet. I'll handle the production pass tonight if you want to focus on the arrangement."

Tre looked at me. "You sure?"

"Man, it's SZA. I'm not sleeping anyway."

He nodded and turned back to the board. We were deep into the arrangement when the studio door opened and Julian walked in. Behind him was a kid in a karate uniform with a backpack on one shoulder and two action figures in his hand.

"Just checking in before we head out," Julian said, dapping each of us. "Had this one at karate, then had to swing by to grab something from my office. He remembered he left Bumblebee up here the other day." He looked down at the boy. "Say hi."

The kid was already on his way to Tre, running through an elaborate handshake of multiple steps, clearly practiced. Tre executed it without looking up fully from the board.

"This is Zhaire, Simone's son." Julian said, nodding toward me. "Zhaire, this is Mr. Raschad. He plays in the NBA, and he makes beats like Uncle Tre."

Zhaire assessed me with the appraisal of a kid deciding whether you were worth his time. Then he extended his fist.

I bumped it. "What's good, little man."

"Hi!" he said. "You play basketball?"

"I do."

"Do you know how to dunk?"

"Of course."

He immediately pivoted toward the console. "How does this button—"

Tre's hand came down over the controls. "Nice try, buddy."

Zhaire pulled his hand back. "I was just gonna ask how it works."

"You know how it works. You also know you're not supposed to touch it."

Zhaire turned to me. "He said I can't. But you didn't say I can't."

I kept my face straight, working hard not to laugh. "Your uncle said no."

He sighed, accepted his fate then dropped onto the floor cross-legged with his Transformers in his lap.

Tre started noodling on the keys, and Zhaire's whole body responded. Head first, then shoulders, then a full-body bounce. "This one's Optimus Prime," he said, holding up the bigger figure at me. "And this one's Bumblebee." He held up the other. "He's my favorite because he can't talk so he uses the radio to say words."

"That's cold," I replied.

He looked up. "You like Transformers?"

"I had a Starscream when I was a kid. He turned into a jet."

His eyes went wide. "A JET?"

"Yep."

He spun around. "Uncle Julian! Starscream! That's the one I want! Can we go to the store to get it?"

Julian's eyes cut to me. "Thank you, Raschad."

"My fault."

Zhaire was already back in motion, his full-body bounce going again, doing some move that was half robot, half something else. Entirely committed.

"Little man's got rhythm," I said.

"He was practically born bobbing his head," Tre said.

I slid over to my keyboard and started messing around with a drum pattern I'd been working on, tapping it out on the pads. Zhaire abandoned his toys on the floor and came beside me, staring at my hands with intense focus.

"How come it sounds like a drum?" he asked. "There's no drum."

"These pads," I said, tapping one. "Each one makes a different sound. This one's the kick." I hit it. "That one's called the snare." I hit another. "You play them together and it sounds like a whole kit."

"I like drums," he said.

"Yeah?"

"Mhm. My teacher has a real drum at school. She lets me play it sometimes."

"I used to play real drums too."

He looked up at me. "Why do you use this?"

"Because I can bring this on a plane," I said. "And my neighbors appreciate it."

Tre laughed. "Don't let Simone hear him talking about drums. She'll have him signed up for lessons by Monday and then we'll be the ones having to take him."

Julian looked up from his phone. "He's already at capacity. Karate, soccer, swim lessons. The boy has a fuller schedule than I do."

"She just has to hear 'Mommy, can I?' and it's a wrap," Tre shook his head.

Zhaire looked like he was thinking about this seriously. "Can I try?"

"Zhaire, no." Julian started. "Time to go."

"Not tonight," I said. "But next time you come through, I'll show you how to build a drum beat from scratch. Deal?"

His whole face lit up. "Deal!"

Zhaire started his rounds, the elaborate handshake with Tre again, murmuring something that made Tre laugh. Then he came back to me as I went to the fridge to grab a water.

He held out his fist, and I bumped it. Then he grabbed my hand and pulled himself into a quick hug around my legs, letting go before I could react.

"Bye Mr. Raschad." Already turning toward Julian. "Don't forget about the drums!"

"I won't forget."

Julian took his hand and steered him toward the door. "Say goodnight."

"Night!"

The door closed and Tre reached over and turned a dial.

"Good kid," I said.

"The best." He said simply. "Simone's doing an amazing job with him."

We worked through a few more bars. Then, I asked as casually as I could: "His father around?"

Tre shrugged, "Nah. Just Simone on her own since day one. Her and us."

I nodded and let it sit. No man. She'd been doing this alone. I didn't know what I'd expected the answer to be, but something settled in me when I heard it. Not relief exactly. Just information I didn't know I'd been waiting for.

"Alright," I said. "Let's get back to it."

Tre looked up from the board. "Before we do. Tomorrow night. It's my birthday. Monarch Lounge. Family, friends, good music, open bar." He nodded at me. "Didn't know you'd be in town, or I would have invited you sooner. Come through."

"I'm there."

"Good." He turned back to the board. "Simone'll be there."

"I'd assume so. She's your sister."

"Just letting you know." He adjusted a dial without looking up. "Dress nice."

6 /

the monarch

THIS CHAPTER HAS A SOUNDTRACK

Man of the Year by Schoolboy Q | *A Milli* by Lil' Wayne | *Get Low* by Ying Yang Twins | *Touch It* by dvsn | *Up Late* by Ari Lennox

simone

THE MONARCH ON ANY GIVEN NIGHT WAS ALWAYS A VIBE. BUT FOR TRE'S thirty-third birthday it was something else. The club was at capacity, the entire Wade clan of course, anyone who was anyone in Lennox Falls, a few notable faces in from out of town, and a plethora of women who looked like they belonged on a video set. Apparently he'd given specific instructions on the guest list ratio; three women for every man on the list. I shook my head laughing as I surveyed the scene. I would expect nothing less from Tre.

I'd chosen my outfit carefully, a blue form-fitting dress, strappy heels, hair in soft waves, makeup subtle with a matte maroon lip. Taryn was already inside holding court in the VIP section with my cousins Zenobia and Marlowe, all three of them looking absolutely gorgeous.

"There she is!" Zenobia pulled me into a hug. "Girl, that DRESS."

"Just trying to keep up with y'all." I smiled.

Our "Wade" section was already claimed in full. Julian was sitting back talking to my other cousin Khaz, doing his watchful oldest-brother-and-cousin thing. Zion was hugged up on the other side of Taryn because the two of them were forever joined at the hip these days. Tre was working the room, moving from group to group, greeting people as they arrived. He spotted me across the section and cut through the crowd.

"Happy birthday, baby brother."

"Baby? Simi, I'm older than you."

"Baby of my brothers. That makes you baby bro."

"That's not how that works," he laughed and kissed my forehead, then leaned back to look at me. "You look good, sis." Then he gave me a look, "Man ain't here yet. But I invited him, said he's coming."

"Who?"

"You know who, Simi," he grinned.

"Go enjoy your birthday." I ignored him, then was saved as he was pulled somewhere else.

I got a drink and settled into our section, when one of Tre's friends, Nasir, caught my eye and walked over.

"Simone," his eyes moved over me once. "You look amazing."

"Hi, Nasir. Thank you."

"Been a minute since I've seen you around."

"Yeah, I've been working mostly."

"I hear that." He leaned against the wall beside me. "We should fix that sometime. Link up."

Before I could answer I felt the energy in the room shift, a ripple traveling from the entrance inward. Taryn materialized at my side, clutching my arm.

"Don't look yet," she said under her breath. "Okay, look."

Raschad had just walked in. The club was already taking him in as women near the entrance clocked him immediately, and another cluster by the bar leaned in, whispering and pointing. He'd only been in the building thirty seconds.

"Maybe we can catch up later?" Nasir asked. I gave him a noncommittal smile, and he read it correctly, stepping away without making it awkward.

Raschad stopped near the bar with Khairos, his tall frame cutting through the crowd. When he turned and caught sight of me, a slow smile spread across his face showing off that dimple, and my heart did an annoying flutter I couldn't control. Then the guilt hit right behind it.

"You alright?" Taryn asked.

"Fine," I lied.

She squeezed my arm and dropped her voice. "Just relax and enjoy the night. What you've got to tell him… this is *not* the night and it's *not* the place. Just breathe and have fun."

"You're right."

She surveyed the room. "Damn, it's a groupie's wet dream tonight. Wade bachelors, the usual who's who, and now an NBA player? These bitches think they won the lottery." She spotted Zion across the section, as a woman tried to strike up a conversation with him despite his ring. "Let me go post up before I have to make a scene."

"Please do, because I don't wanna have to jump into any fights on GP." I laughed.

She squeezed my arm again then was gone. I turned back toward the room. Raschad's eyes swept the crowd until they found mine again. He said something to Khairos and started walking over, stepping around a woman who'd positioned herself directly in his path without breaking stride.

"Was hoping I'd see you here," he said.

"Well, it is my brother's birthday."

"I know," he flashed that dimple again. "Still hoping. You look beautiful."

"Thank you." I tried not to blush.

Raschad folded into the section with my family comfortably. He and Tre fell into a conversation immediately. Julian and Khaz asking him something about his injury timeline. Khairos showed him something on his phone, Raschad's head tilting to look, with a grin breaking across his face.

I was talking to Zenobia and Marlowe. Mostly present, until his laugh carried. Then I thought, *he's laughing right now but he doesn't know yet what I'm about to hand him.*

Then Tre appeared in front of me, grabbing my arm, as he called over his shoulder, "Raschad, bruh, come here…"

And just like that we were standing next to each other again.

"Tell him," Tre said.

My stomach dropped. I looked at Tre. Then at Raschad. Then back at Tre. *Tell him? Right here? In the middle of his birthday party? How does Tre even — does he know? Did Taryn —*

"Tell him… what?" I asked carefully.

"About our battles." Tre grinned. "Tell him who holds the record."

The relief hit so fast I nearly laughed out loud. *Oh, that's what he meant.*

"Tre. No."

"Simone is the undefeated champion of Wade family rap battles," Tre announced to Raschad. "Never lost. I say that even though I was her primary opponent and I object to the official record on several counts."

Either he was several drinks deep already, or if I didn't know any better, he was genuinely trying to set me up with my own baby daddy. Probably both.

"There are no valid objections, Tre." I said.

"I'll let that slide. She is my sister and it's my birthday. But I want her to know I see her greatness… even when she cheats."

"I have never cheated. I'm just better than you."

Tre looked at Raschad. "You wouldn't believe it by looking at her. But Simi's got flow."

"I definitely believe it," he replied to Tre but he was looking at me like he was remembering something.

I looked away before he could see that I was remembering too. Then *Man of the Year* by SchoolBoy Q dropped.

"Op! That's my cue." Tre left us there, making his way to the elevated platform at the top of the VIP section, like a man ascending a throne. Four women flanked him on either side, before he reached the top. Someone produced a chair. Someone else was fanning him. The crowd parted and cheered.

Then the cake came out, with sparklers blazing, and the whole section erupted as Tre led his own birthday song like a conductor, arms spread wide, accepting the room's devotion.

Raschad watched the whole thing standing next to me, chuckling. "He planned that, huh?"

"Every year," I said. "Different song, same energy."

"The chair was a nice touch."

We laughed together, and I looked over and found Taryn across the section. She held my gaze for a second. Then looked pointedly at Raschad and back at me.

I know, I told her with my eyes.

Watch yourself, her expression said back.

When the birthday moment settled, Tre happy and fully in his feelings pointed directly at me as I watched him stop at the DJ booth, lean in, say something. The DJ nodded. Then he was walking back toward us with a mischievous look on his face.

"Simi," he stopped in front of us. "Show him."

"Tre. No."

The opening bars of Lil' Wayne's *A Milli* started threading through the speakers.

"It's my birthday," he said. "Can't tell me no."

I looked at Raschad, who was looking at me, trying and failing to keep a straight face. Something inside me said *screw it* and I turned directly to Raschad and gave him every bar. Right in his face. Delivering Lil Wayne with the precision of a woman who'd been made to memorize those verses at eleven years old by her brother.

His eyebrows went up slowly, then he broke out in a wide smile, as Tre stood next to me, hyping me up.

"TALK THAT SHIT, SIMI!"

By the second verse a small circle formed the way circles form around a moment. I got through a few more bars before I began to feel self-conscious, catching myself. I held up a hand. "Okay. That's enough."

The circle dissolved laughing. Raschad was still looking at me and smiling, as Tre pointed at him triumphantly. "Told you."

Get Low hit and the room shifted instantly. The bass dropped and Tre spread his arms like he'd ordained it, and women around him took it as their cue. Then the call came. "*To the window*" — Every hand in the club section swung left pointing. "*To the wall*" — Every hand swung right. Tre's face was pure joy as a woman next to him dropped it to the floor on cue to "*get low*". Two more women followed suit around him.

Then *Wipe Me Down* dropped and it was over. Heels came off without hesitation. Someone cleared space and my cousins hit the floor on the first bar. Tre planted himself in the center and went off. The stomp, the twist, the whole sequence. Zenobia matched him. Marlowe dropped lower just to be competitive about it. A circle formed fast and loud. Then Zenobia grabbed my arm. "Simi. Come on."

"I will not —"

Marlowe had my other arm, the circle opened and I was in it before I could finish my sentence. My body finding the rhythm before my brain could argue. At some point the circle shifted and I found myself facing Raschad. He hadn't moved. Arms loose, chin slightly down, something at the edge of his mouth that wasn't committing to being a smile. He bobbed his head, watching me dance.

"Uh huh," he said, staring at me as I wiped down in front of him.

I laughed and did it again.

"And I thought Jersey had the vibe," he said.

"Lennox Falls has something to say." I joked.

"I see that."

The way he looked at me like I was worth taking in slowly? I wanted to swim in it. I wanted to stay beside him all night and let him keep looking at me like that, lean into him, and let the whole night feel like we were building back to something. I wanted to let him keep looking at me like I was a second chance. But had to remind myself that tonight was not mine to spend the way I wanted to spend it.

"I'm going to find Taryn," I said.

He nodded. I found Taryn. Made a lap. Talked to Zenobia longer than necessary. Watched Tre's birthday descend further into its natural chaos from a comfortable distance, and I kept Raschad in my peripheral, conscious of him, but not looking directly at him. He'd folded back into the night easily, back to being a person at a party who was not the center of my attention.

Eventually the crowd thinned, with people saying goodbye for twenty minutes before anyone actually left. The DJ read the room and shifted to something slower. *Touch It* by dvsn came through. The speakers the remaining guests exhaled into it.

I wasn't looking for Raschad, but I knew when he was close. Suddenly, he appeared beside me.

"Dance with me."

I looked at him. I thought about the parking lot, and our kiss and the truth I was carrying, and what it was going to cost both of us the moment I said it out loud tomorrow. And about how this was the last time I would be able to pretend this chemistry between us had a chance to turn into anything other than heartbreak and resentment.

I didn't want to say no, so I didn't.

His hand settled at my waist, pressing me against him, and we moved together devastatingly easy. No finding the rhythm, or adjustment. Just… fitting. Like time hadn't passed. Like our bodies remembered the feeling of being that close and slipped back into it with muscle memory.

Butterflies was too small a word for what was happening inside me. It was more like my whole internal architecture had shifted, everything rearranging around the way he held me. I let myself pretend that six years hadn't happened the way they did. That his hand at my back was just his hand at my back, uncomplicated. That tomorrow wasn't coming with everything it was bringing. That the ease of being held by him, was something I would get to keep.

I knew it wasn't true. I knew that the moment the truth left my mouth whatever lived in this man's eyes when he looked at me would be replaced by something I deserved and may not survive. This dance was the last of something. The counting down to a detonation I'd set for myself.

So I stayed hugged up close, and let the music move through me. I let myself have it.

Suddenly, *Up Late* by Ari Lennox came through the speakers. I recognized the opening sound before my brain caught up. A warmth of muscle memory that had nothing to do with the room. Raschad looked down at me the same moment I looked up at him. He already knew.

"This song," he said quietly, almost to himself.

"Yeah," I said.

"I'd kiss you right now…but I don't wanna have to fight your brothers tonight."

"They're harmless."

"Julian keeps watching us."

"Julian watches everything."

As if on cue Tre's drunken voice cut through from two feet away. "Bruh. You really rubbin' all up on my sister like her brothers aren't right here?"

Raschad went still, then stepped back from me slightly, unsure if Tre was seriously joking or seriously pissed. Tre looked at him for a long moment.

"You lucky we like you, Carter," then he laughed.

Julian, from somewhere behind Tre said nothing, just looked at Raschad with a measured expression, then raised his glass once. Which was somehow more alarming than anything. Zion just shook his head and smiled. Raschad and I looked at each other, a laugh still in his eyes but underneath it a look of desire that had no business being that visible in front of my family.

"SIMONE!"

Taryn's voice was piercing. "Come here."

Raschad leaned down slightly. "Find me before you leave."

"Okay," I said, then went over to where Taryn was standing with her arms crossed.

"What?" I asked.

She didn't look at me right away, just scanned around us, making sure no one was close enough to hear. "I said relax and have fun," she muttered. "I did *not* say dry hump your baby daddy who doesn't know he's your baby daddy in front of half your family."

"I wasn't —"

"Girl, you were two songs away from conception part two."

"You're being dramatic."

"And you're digging a deeper hole for yourself Simone!"

She made her voice softer, then added: "Zion said he was glad to see you like this. Said you'd closed yourself off since you became a mom, and he was starting to think you'd decided that was just your life." She kept her eyes forward. "He said Raschad was good people, and that it was nice to see you relax with someone."

I swallowed my gasp, as Taryn turned back to look at me. "Every day this goes on is another day your brothers are out here loving this man and not knowing why they already have every reason to."

"And then look at you… you're glowing. I haven't seen you look like this in…" She stopped. "I don't actually remember the last time. This is dangerous, Simone."

"I know. I know." I exhaled. "It's been six years, Taryn." I looked at her and let her see it. The thing I hadn't said out loud to anyone. "I forgot what this feels like. I *know* it's selfish. I *know*. I'm standing here melting because he put his hand on my waist. I know how that looks."

"It doesn't look like anything," Taryn said quietly. "Except a woman who's been starving herself and then the love of her life just shows up like a meal placed in front of her."

I closed my eyes, that landed square in my chest.

"I get it, Simi. And he might feel the same way. *But...* he doesn't have all the facts. I just don't want this to hurt worse for you when it finally comes out."

"Tomorrow." I took a breath. "I'm going to tell him."

"Ok. Good." She put her arm around me and we walked out together as the rest of the party started to file out too.

We hit the sidewalk, the cool air hitting after hours of heat and bodies. I found Tre, hugged him hard, told him I loved him and let him spin me once. Said goodnight to Julian, who squeezed me and kissed my cheek, and made my rounds to the rest of my family.

Raschad was next to me when I turned. "Heading home?" he asked.

"Yep." I looked at him. "Um… are you free tomorrow? To talk?"

"Yes," he replied with no hesitation. "Come to me? My extended stay has a kitchen. I can make us something, or order some food."

"Six o'clock?" I asked

"Six works."

"Ok, see you then. Goodnight, Raschad."

"Night, Simone."

Zion was waiting for Taryn and me by their car, as I took her hand and we walked away from Raschad.

"He really does like you," she said into my shoulder. "It's absolutely obvious."

"Until tomorrow," I said sadly.

She exhaled and squeezed my arm. This woman who had been holding my secret since before Zhaire was born, and had sat with me through middle-of-the-night panics and years of quiet guilt. Then she stopped in the middle of the lot and pulled me into a hug that said everything words hadn't.

"Tomorrow," she pulled back and looked at me. "And then we deal with whatever comes next."

7 /

capacity: two

THIS CHAPTER HAS A SOUNDTRACK

Shea Butter Baby by Ari Lennox | *GOAT* by Ari Lennox | *40 Shades of Choke* by Ari Lennox

simone

six years ago

I'D TOLD MY BROTHERS I WAS VISITING A FRIEND. IT WASN'T ENTIRELY A lie. I was vague on purpose, letting their assumptions do the work, then I hopped on a plane to Los Angeles to spend five days with the man I'd been talking to every single day, for the past three months. A man I'd met once in person, on a beach in San Diego, who had somehow become the first voice I reached for in the morning and the last face I wanted to see at night.

If my brothers knew I was going to stay with a man they knew nothing about, Julian would have tried to put me on a no-fly list, Zion would have popped a blood vessel, and Tre would have booked himself on the same flight. So I said *a friend from school,* knowing they'd assume it was a female, and packed my best outfits and new lingerie at the bottom of my suitcase.

Our daily calls and texts had become routine. Not because we scheduled them, just because neither of us wanted to go a day without hearing the other's voice.

"Come to LA," he said one night while we were on FaceTime. He was fresh from practice, towel around his neck, and I was lying in bed with a face mask on, looking absolutely ridiculous, yet he looked at me like I was wearing couture. "Before I leave for Spain, so I can see you."

So I went. This was going to be my first time seeing LA, so of course I'd made a list. Color-coded, and organized by neighborhood, with star emojis next to the non-negotiables. Raschad had laughed at it, but then added his own stops. "Your list plus my list," he'd said.

The flight to LA felt like the longest four hours of my life. I spent the entire flight worrying if I was making a mistake.

What if it was awkward?
What if we had nothing to say in person?
What if I'd built something in my head that didn't actually exist?
When I landed, my phone buzzed immediately.

RASCHAD NOVA:

Here. I'll meet you at baggage claim.

My hands were shaking as I walked through the terminal, and then I saw him, leaning against a pillar, holding flowers, and wearing a huge smile. Our eyes met, and I practically ran to him.

He lifted me up in a bear hug, then set me back down and pulled me into him. I pressed my face into his chest, breathing him in, and every hesitation I'd carried on the plane evaporated. I knew then, it wasn't a mistake.

"Hi," I whispered into his shirt.

"Hi," he kissed the top of my head. "I missed you, Peach."

"Missed you more."

"Not possible."

HIS APARTMENT WAS A TWO-BEDROOM IN CULVER CITY. A CLEAN, SIMPLE bachelor pad with a couch that had seen better days and a kitchen that looked like it got moderate use. In a loft area, he had a home studio setup with monitors, keyboards, a mic, and headphones hung on a hook.

"This is where the magic happens," he said, watching me take it in.

"I thought the magic happened in the bedroom?"

He laughed surprised, and almost delighted. "Damn, Peach. You came out swinging."

His roommate Darius was there briefly, gave me a once-over, nodded approvingly, and said, "So you're the one who's got my man writing love songs at three in the morning. Nice to meet you. I'm out. Y'all have the place." He grabbed his keys and was gone before I could say hello.

Whatever restraint we'd both been exercising since San Diego evaporated several times over those first two days. We made up for lost time… several times, and it was exactly what I'd been trying not to think about for three months.

The first couple of days, what was *his* became *ours.* His place, his city, his favorite spots, his Honda Accord with the UCLA bumper sticker, all of it opened up and made room for me. He showed me where he trained, and introduced me as *"my girl"* to people at the gym. By day three we'd found a rhythm in every sense of the word.

I knew he was leaving for Spain in a month. I knew that every hour we spent together was one fewer hour before a goodbye we hadn't figured out how to talk about yet. I knew all of that. And I fell harder anyway.

Roscoe's was on my list and he took me there on day three. It was worth going just to say I'd been. The chicken was crispy and seasoned and I ate like I'd been raised without manners.

"You have syrup on your chin," Raschad smiled at me.

"I'm in a flow state. Don't interrupt my process."

He laughed and reached across the table with his napkin, wiping my chin himself. Then the bill came and he grabbed it.

"You've paid for everything since I've been here," I said trying to take the bill from him.

"And I'll pay tomorrow, too."

"You don't have to. I brought money."

"I know I don't have to," he looked at me, his voice was firm. "You flew out here. The least I can do is take care of you."

I wanted to push back. He was twenty-three years old and weeks away from his first professional paycheck. Everything he'd spent on this weekend was money I knew he'd carved from a budget that didn't have a lot of margin. But there was pride and intention in his face. It wasn't about impressing me with what he had. It was about showing me what he was willing to give. So I let him pay.

"Thank you," I said.

"You're welcome," he said, pocketing his wallet, "When I start getting those league checks, I'm gonna spoil you rotten. Just so you know." He paused. "First check that hits—" He caught himself.

"First check that hits *what?*"

"Nothing. We'll see."

Venice Beach in late February was not what I expected. Not the shoulder-to-shoulder chaos I'd seen in movies, but spacious, and breathable. The sky was a blue that looked edited, and the air was cool enough for a hoodie. Nothing like February in Lennox Falls, where the wind came off the mountains brisk enough to make your eyes water. Here the palm trees swayed lazily like they'd never heard of winter.

We walked the boardwalk and found a bench facing the water. A seagull argued with something down the beach, and somewhere behind us a man was playing saxophone. We talked about our families. He told me stories about his sisters that made me laugh until my ribs hurt. I talked about my brothers, and how different their personalities were. I went deeper and told him how we'd managed after my parents, and about how my nightmares about my mother were less frequent as time went on. But how the grief could hit me out of nowhere, fresh as the day it happened.

Raschad went quiet. "You know my mother is sick," he said eventually. "I worry about losing her everyday. Cancer is no joke. She's fighting though, and she's headstrong, so I know that's working in her favor."

I took his hand and squeezed it.

"The bills are a lot though, and she's still working two jobs. She's tired, and I know that can't be helping her healing."

He looked at me. "I've had a plan since I was thirteen. Scholarship, go pro, retire my mom. Maybe get her a new house. Make sure my sisters are good. And music, that's building too. I know the body doesn't last forever."

"That's why Spain matters. Two years, three max. Enough film to make the NBA case, enough checks to help my family. Every decision I make right now is about making sure the women in my life can rest." his thumb moved back and forth across my knuckles and he looked at me.

I didn't say anything to that. Just sat there, holding his hand and watching the water. "This is so beautiful," I said softly, feeling the breeze and watching the waves.

"Yeah, it is." he said, but he was looking at me.

I turned toward him and his forehead came to rest against mine.

"I don't want to go to Spain," he said.

"What?"

"I mean, I'm going. I have to go," he exhaled. "But right now, being here with you... I don't want to go."

"I know."

He pulled back enough to look at me. "I'm gonna miss you, Peach. Bad."

"I'm gonna miss you too, Nova. One month," I said quietly. "And then you're gone."

"I know we're going to be on different continents. I know it's complicated," he laced his fingers through mine. "But we've already done months on the phone and it didn't slow us down. We'll figure it out."

<hr>

ARI LENNOX HAD FOUND ME SOMETIME IN COLLEGE AND NEVER LEFT. I'D played her album *PHO* on repeat until my roommate asked me to please listen with headphones. She was the kind of artist who made you feel like she'd written songs specifically about your life, which was probably everyone's experience of her, but felt personal anyway.

Raschad knew this about me. I'd told him somewhere in month one of late-night calls, talking about music the way we talked about everything without running out of things to say. He'd filed it apparently. The day I got to LA he told me he'd gotten us tickets for her show at the El Rey, an intimate venue of a few hundred people in a room small enough to feel her voice like she was right next to you.

"You did *not!*"

"I did, Peach."

"Raschad!" I squealed jumping up into his arms and peppering kisses all over his face. Then I started singing *GOAT* to him. *"Yoooou're the greateeeest…"*

"Don't make it weird, Peach," he smiled, pecked me on the lips, then set me down and smacked my ass. "It's the night before you have to fly back. I figure that would be the perfect ending to your visit."

"You figured right."

Day four started slow the way we'd let all of them start. Breakfast at the counter, a walk around the neighborhood that stretched longer than intended because neither of us was in a hurry to be anywhere. Then the couch. His laptop open to practice film, my feet tucked under his thigh, a book in my hands I read the same paragraph of four times.

The kind of morning that tricks you into thinking this is just your life. Tomorrow I was flying home and I was trying not to think about that.

Later that afternoon, his phone buzzed on the coffee table. He checked it. His face changed — not dramatically, just a dimming, like someone had turned the brightness down one notch.

"What?" I sat up. *"What happened?"*

He handed me the phone.

TONIGHT'S ARI LENNOX PERFORMANCE AT THE EL REY THEATRE HAS BEEN POSTPONED DUE TO A VENUE MAINTENANCE ISSUE. WE APOLOGIZE FOR THE INCON- VENIENCE.

"I'm sorry," he said, watching the disappointment on my face.

"It's fine. It's not your fault."

"I know, but, still…"

"Raschad. It's fine." I said it brighter than I felt.

He heard everything I wasn't saying. I could tell by the way he went quiet, not accepting it, just deciding what to do with it.

"Okay." He stood up and grabbed his keys off the counter. "I gotta run out for a bit."

"Now?"

"Be dressed by six, Peach." He smiled at me. "Whatever you were gonna wear to the concert. Put that on."

"For what?"

"Trust me?"

"Yeah. I trust you."

"Six o'clock." He paused in the doorway. Looked back at me on his couch, his hoodie, his blanket. "Look pretty."

"I always look pretty," I teased.

"You definitely do," he said quietly.

I took my time getting ready in Raschad's room. Showered, oiled my body down, spritzed my perfume in strategic places. Laid my edges down, added wavy curls to my flat ironed hair. The skirt I'd packed for exactly this kind of moment, rust silk, midi length, that moved right. A light beat, mascara, lip gloss and highlighter on my collarbone.

5:45 PM, I heard the front door open, bags being set down, cabinets opening and closing, the shuffle of rearranging. Then music, faint at first, climbing, a bass line I felt before I heard it.

Raschad called from down the hall: "Stay back there for a few more minutes."

"What are you doing?"

"Ten minutes, Simone."

I sat on the edge of his bed and waited. Finally he called out to me. "Okay, come on out, Peach."

The overhead lights were off, instead a string of warm dim lights hung from the ceiling beams, draped in loose uneven arcs, and with candlelight tracing the room. Thick pillar candles on a table. Votives along the windowsill. A few on the floor near the walls, their flames swaying and throwing shadows that moved like breathing.

The couch was pushed back out of the way and the coffee table was gone. In its place was a large nest on the floor, covered in oversized cushions, layered and stacked, surrounded by blankets and more pillows, a low table in the center set with two plates and two glasses. I could smell garlic and smoke and something sweet.

Ari Lennox was playing, her melody moving through the room. Raschad stood in the center of all of it in a white tee and gray sweats. Barefoot with a smile, studying me, like he wanted to catch all of my reaction.

"Nova…" My voice split open on his name.

He stepped closer. "Show got canceled. But that don't mean we can't make our own show." He spread his arms, gesturing at the room. "Welcome to the Dreamville living room experience. Capacity: two."

My eyes were burning. "How did you do all this?"

"Grand Central Market for the food, best birria in the city. Drug store for the string lights and candles and a few extra pillows. Borrowed some extra candles from Darius. Well, I think they are his girlfriend's."

"He's going to kill you."

"He's in San Francisco. I might have borrowed a throw pillow or two from his room though, so he actually might kill me."

I pressed my hand to my mouth, not sure if I wanted to laugh, cry or some messy combination of both.

"Too much?" he asked, uncertainty flickering across his face.

"It's perfect." My voice was barely there. "It's so perfect I want to be mad at you for setting a standard no one else will ever reach."

He exhaled, then he held out his hand. "No one else will have to reach it, Peach. It's always gonna be me."

I looked at him standing in the middle of all of it and felt the truth of his words swell in my chest. Something that had been building since San Diego and hadn't stopped. *I love him.*

Not out loud. Not yet. But I knew.

"Okay," I said softly, and I took his hand.

Then *Shea Butter Baby* began to play through the speakers. I couldn't help but sing along, giving it my whole voice the way I only did when nobody was paying attention.

J. Cole's verse came in and something said *"go"*, so I went, rapping every syllable, the internal rhymes caught, the rhythm sitting right in the pocket. When I finished the last bar I looked up and caught his expression.

"What?"

"You can rap."

"Obviously."

"That's not obviously." He leaned forward. "How are you —"

"My brother Tre." I settled back against the cushions, legs folded under me. "He used to make me learn every verse on every song he liked. Female, male, feature, bridge, spoken word interlude… if it played anywhere I had to know it. Said the best rapper in the room should know everything." I shrugged. "We used to battle. Julian and Zion would judge."

"Who won?"

I gave him a look. "I don't lose rap battles," I bragged. "That's just not something that happens."

He looked at me for exactly one second and grinned. "Prove it."

"Excuse me?"

"Right now. Let's go."

I studied him with a smile. "You make music, Raschad. That means you have an ear. It does not mean —"

"I can hold my own."

"Raschad."

"Unless you're scared?"

"Don't do that."

"It's okay if you —"

"Give me a word," I said.

He looked around the apartment. "Blanket."

"Blanket."

He started a beat. Mouth percussion, *tsk tsk boom, tsk tsk boom,* snapping on the two and four. I watched him with my arms crossed, shook my head, squared my shoulders, and went in:

> *"Aight, aight, aight…*
> *You built this fort from scratch cause that's how you do*
> *Lights up, blanket down,*
> *The vision came through*
> *You play games for a living,*
> *Yeah you like to compete*
> *Challenged me to battle*
> *Then you gave me a beat*
> *Think you can win?*
> *That's what you said to my face*
> *But this my game, Nova,*
> *Better stay in your place*
> *I'll take it easy on you*
> *'Cause the vibe is right*
> *And the blanket hits different*
> *On this LA night."*

He broke the beat laughing before I finished. "Stay in your place? You're telling me stay in my place in MY apartment, Peach?"

"Your word." I pointed at him. Then I said it quietly, testing it. "Spain."

Something shifted on his face, then he fake-cracked his knuckles and went in:

"A month before I cross the ocean
NBA dreams and European motion
Not gon' act like I ain't notice the date
Every time it come up something flips in my chest, wait —
But this is a battle
So I'll keep it light
I'm going to Spain,
You staying right— in North Cackalack
Where the sweet tea cold
Not gon' lie, I'm getting bold
Talking every day
Tryna stay close
Voice notes and FaceTime
Peach got me doin' the most
So I'll go to Spain
Do what I gotta do
Every city I'm in
I'll be checking for you
Think I found you just to let the wifi drop?
Nah, Peach, that's not how this go —
I mean — that's not how this STOP"

He lost the rhyme and I covered my mouth, giggling. "You said GO when you meant STOP."

"I recovered."

"You did not recover."

He fixed the cushion wall behind him. "Okay, One more round. Your word." He thought for a second. "Real."

I swallowed, nodded once and started:

"Flew here with a bag and a bunch of excuses
Told myself this was nothing,
These feelings are useless
Said San Diego was just a good weekend
No, these walls won't be weakened
Then you made a beat and a blanket fort
Lost the rhyme and got back on course
Got me thinking, wow, this man is it
I been knowing since the beach but ain't wanna admit
What's happened between us is as real as it gets
But I'm scared of real, Nova, so I called it a trip
Said it's just a week, have to get a grip

> *But then you built this whole world out of candles and*
>   *string*
> *And I ran out of reasons to pretend it ain't a thing."*

I stopped, both of us went quiet, the only sound was Ari singing. I could feel his eyes on me before I looked up, and his expression wasn't smug, or triumphant. It was just… open.

"Okay," I said, too quickly. "Your turn." I held out the imaginary mic before he could say anything about what I'd just put in the room. "Final word is mine to give."

He took the mic slowly, still looking at me. "Peach…"

"Your turn, Nova."

"Okay," he said. "Give me a word."

I looked at him, looked away, then looked back. "Heart," I said.

"Heart." He went in slow:

> *"If you ask me what I want*
> *I'ma give it to you straight*
> *Not the distance, not the timing,*
> *not the Spain debate*
> *It's the way being with you feels like home*
> *It's the way you rap J. Cole bars straight off the dome*
> *It's the way you looked at me that first night at the beach*
> *Something in me said 'yo, she's what you need to reach'*
> *I don't say this light, don't say this for sport*
> *But my heart been talking and the message is short:*
> *You can have it."*

He paused and looked straight into my eyes, "You can have it," he said again, still looking directly at me.

I was very still. "I'm done rapping," I said softly.

Neither of us moved for a moment, just sitting with what had been said, the rap battle and the real thing underneath it occupying the same space, both of us pretending we hadn't just told the truth.

He broke first, reaching over and lifting the lid on the birria container.

"Eat with me," he said simply, like we hadn't just said what we'd said to each other.

I smiled, relieved, grateful for the redirect. "Yeah, I'm starving."

We ate on the floor, cross-legged on the nest. The birria was rich and warm, the churros still hot from the bag. He'd thought about every detail and the care in it made the food taste like more than food.

"Tomorrow I go home," I said.

He set his plate down. "I know."

"And in four weeks, you go to Spain."

"I know that too."

"So what happens?"

He poured me more to drink, taking his time. "We keep doing what we've been doing. Talk every day. Once I get settled you come visit."

"To Spain?"

"To Spain." He caught my eye and held it. "It's not forever. Two years, maybe three, then the distance part is over."

"Three years is a long time."

"We'll make it work, Simone."

Ari's voice drifted between us and he reached across and took my hands. His fingers closed around mine.

"I don't want to go home tomorrow," I said quietly.

"Then don't."

"I have to."

"I know." He lifted my hand and kissed the back of it.

The food was gone. The candles burned lower and we'd migrated deeper into the cushions, lying on our sides, facing each other, close enough that our breath mixed.

"We don't need to call this anything," I said.

"What do you mean?" His voice was careful.

"You're about to move to another country. You're going to be living a completely different life. I don't want you worrying about me or feeling guilty or tied to something six thousand miles away." I pressed my lips together. "You're free. No label. No guilt."

He was quiet for a moment, "You're being scared, Simone."

"Maybe I am." I admitted. "But I'm also being practical. You're twenty-three. Your whole life is about to change in ways you can't predict and I don't want to be the thing that holds you back."

I told myself this was the right call. Keeping it open was mature, not labeling it was wise, and giving him room to be young and free in a new country was the generous adult thing to do.

He sat up and pulled me up with him so we were facing each other, cross-legged in the blankets, knees touching. The string lights made his eyes look liquid.

"Peach, I hear you. But I don't need the freedom you're offering me. I'm not looking for it." He squeezed my hands. "I'm not going to walk through the door just because you left it open."

"So what do you want?" I asked.

"To talk to you every day. FaceTime every night. Send you pictures of Spain and hear you make fun of my terrible Spanish and count down the days until I see you again." He paused. "I don't need a label to do any of that. If you need this to be undefined, fine. But I want you to know, whatever we call this, whatever we don't — I'm not out here looking. The freedom you just offered? I don't want it."

"You say that now."

"I'll say it in Spain. I'll say it at three in the morning on FaceTime when we're both exhausted and the time difference is killing us." His thumb moved across the back of my hands. "You don't have to believe me yet. Just don't shut the door because you're afraid I'll walk through it."

"Okay," I said. "Undefined. But real."

"Real," he confirmed.

There was a version of me that existed with Raschad. And in that apartment, in that nest of cushions, in the warmth of being close to him.

I have never been her before. She is soft, and safe and unguarded. She sits in his lap without asking. She lets him hold her face when he's talking to her. She presses her head to his chest just to feel his heartbeat and doesn't have a reason for it except that she wants to be that close. She makes small involuntary sounds when she's comfortable, the kind you make when something feels safe, and she doesn't catch and correct them. She isn't self conscious or worrying about being too silly or too awkward. She had never once in her life just been held without thinking about what the holding meant, or how long it would last, or what it would cost her when it ended. She wasn't running calculations. She wasn't managing the outcome. She was just there.

Tomorrow I was flying home. Soon he'd be leaving for another continent. This was the last night of the last day and something about knowing that, the counting down, made the managing stop.

I looked at him in the candlelight this man who had built me a concert out of string lights and cushions, who had breathed with me in San Diego hallway, who had just refused the door I'd opened for him… and I stopped thinking.

raschad

---

40 Shades of Choke came through the speaker. A low groove arriving like a challenge, changing the temperature of the room. Simone tilted her head slightly and smiled at me with a playful sparkle in her eyes. She got on her hands and knees and moved toward me slowly, then hiked up her skirt, and climbed onto my lap, settling over me.

"Peach," I whispered, as my hands grazed up her thighs, finding their way up her skirt.

"Hmmm?" She ran one hand down my chest and stomach and placed the other on my face, pulling me in for a kiss.

My hands were all over her as she straddled me, and whatever I was about to say next was forgotten. Gripping her waist, palming her thighs, roaming up her lace-covered ass, squeezing hard enough to make her gasp. My mouth dropped to her neck, licking and sucking until she shivered and ground against me.

"Raschad…" she whispered, pulling my head tighter to her neck.

I pulled back just enough to look at her, hands still gripping her hips, as she pulled her shirt up over her head. I slid my hands up her back, my fingers finding the clasp of her bra, unhooking and freeing her. My mouth watered and my lips were back on her before I could stop myself. Licking, sucking, nibbling her breasts, pulling soft gasps out of her while she held me there, fingers laced behind my head, grinding against the erection trying to fight its way through my pants.

"I love how sensitive you are here." I continued worshiping her breasts.

"Mmmm," her moan answered, as her hips rolled harder. My hand roamed down her stomach, parting her thighs wider until I reached her center. The second I brushed her there, I smirked, eyes locked on hers as I tugged her panties to the side, slipping my fingers inside the lace.

She moaned and kissed me hard, tongue sweeping mine, while I stroked her with my hand, teasing her clit until she whimpered against my mouth. Her hands roamed everywhere, my chest, my shoulders, gripping me like she couldn't get enough.

I tugged my shirt off and lifted my hips to shift my pants down and free myself, and then, in one slow glide, she found me, and with a slow, steady push, she slid down, taking me one inch at a time.

Her moan broke loudly, and her head fell back. My mouth found her throat again, cursing into her skin as she sank fully onto me.

"*Peeeach*," I groaned, gripping her hips, fighting for control.

Her thighs squeezed around my waist as she rode me, hips grinding in a rhythm that was pure poetry. I sat up straighter, hands caressing her body as I watched her lose herself as she took me.

I dropped my head, eyes glued to where our bodies met. The way she swallowed me whole then pulled back, only to sink back down again? The sight alone made me groan, deep and guttural. I gripped her hips, thumbs pressing into her soft skin.

"Simone!" I rasped, head falling back as she picked up the pace, her moans vibrating in my ear. She was moving faster, riding me like she owned me, and I was this close to falling apart.

"Slow down, baby," I hissed, voice strained. "Let me take my time with you."

She leaned in, lips brushing mine, breath hot. "I'm gonna miss you, Nova," she moaned, and I felt it in my knees.

I took control, gripping her waist tighter, lifting her up and down on my length, guiding her movements as our bodies slapped together, the sound echoing off the walls, as her cries grew louder.

"You gonna miss this? Huh, Peach?" I growled, each thrust rougher than the last. "Show me how bad you gonna miss it, baby."

She rocked on me faster, biting her lip, as she rode me with more purpose. My hands gripped her waist, trying to set the rhythm, but she wasn't having it. "This much," she teased, grinding down harder. Her voice was breathless, taunting, as her nails scraped down my chest.

I kissed her again, groaning into her mouth, her body clenching around me so tight I was about to lose it. "You feel—*fuck*—" My head tipped back, eyes shutting for a second. "So good, Peach. So good..."

My fingers dug into her ass, squeezing as I bucked my hips up into her. "Shit..." I cursed as she tightened more around me. My grip locked down, but she just moved faster, hair in her face as she tilted to kiss my mouth, swallowing every ragged sound I gave her.

I bit back another curse, and slid a hand up to find her breast again, taking it into my mouth. Her moans turned desperate, and I knew she was close.

"Raschad!" Her cry cracked, broken, right against my ear.

I gritted my teeth, drove up into her harder, lifting her half up with each grind. My body burned, every muscle straining. "Go 'head and come for me, Peach."

She shattered against me, head thrown back, a scream ripping out of her throat. Her body clenched hard, pulsing and pulling me over with her.

I roared, holding her down as I spilled deep, her name breaking out of me again and again as we both came undone, our bodies locked, sweat glistening, breath tangled. She collapsed against me, head on my shoulder, shaking.

I wrapped my arms around her tight, still buried inside, kissing along her temple, her cheek, her mouth, every part of her, trembling with her. We stayed locked together, both of us gasping for air, hearts slowing.

I should have stopped to get a condom. Done the responsible thing. I knew that. But neither of us stopped. We didn't talk about not using a condom. When I moved inside her, all I could do was *feel*. We didn't ask, didn't reach, didn't pause. Our bodies made the choice before our minds could form the thought, and mouths could form the words. Maybe it was the intimacy. The way we held each other. Trusted each other. The way it felt like whatever it was between us, was already ours, already belonged to us. It was that dangerous, messy space between desire and decision.

Simone fell asleep before the playlist looped, lying against me, head and hand on my chest. I covered her hand with mine. I couldn't sleep.

I made my first plan when I was thirteen years old. My father had been gone long enough that I'd stopped caring. My mother was working two jobs and selling dinners on weekends to provide for my sisters and me. I was thirteen and I sat at the kitchen table with a composition notebook and I wrote down everything I was going to do.

Take care of Mama. Get a scholarship. Go pro. Make enough money that nobody in my family ever worried again.

There I was, twenty-three and on track for every single item on that list. Spain was happening. The NBA would follow. I knew it with the same certainty I have always known the things I've decided. I never leave room for doubt. I decide what happens. Then I make it happen.

I learned early that if you understood everything faster than everyone else you could stay ahead of it. Ahead of loss. Ahead of instability. You mapped it out and you executed and you didn't leave room for things to surprise you, because surprise meant unprepared, and unprepared was something I couldn't afford.

And then I met Simone.

Suddenly there I was laying in a blanket nest, with her asleep on my chest and I was completely, genuinely, for the first time in my life… unplanned.

I didn't plan to like talking to her more than sleeping.

I didn't plan to pick up every call regardless of where I was or what I was doing.

I didn't plan to start thinking about what she would think about things.

I had dated beautiful women before. Great women and I never once thought about them when they weren't in the room.

I watched her sleep. She had no idea what she did to me. She thinks she's in my space. She doesn't know she is my space. She doesn't know that every room I've been in since San Diego has been missing a frequency and she is the frequency.

I have a plan. Years of it, mapped out with intention, every variable accounted for. She was not in the plan. But in that moment, the only thing I could think about was how I might have to tear the whole thing up.

And I wasn't even a little bit mad about it.

I HELD HER HAND THE ENTIRE DRIVE TO LAX. NEITHER OF US SPOKE much. What was there to say? Five days. The best five days of my life and now they were ending. Not permanently, we'd both been saying that, *not permanently*. But the space between us was about to get a lot wider than Los Angeles to Lennox Falls.

I walked her as far as security would let me and held both her hands.

"Two years," I said.

"Two years," she repeated.

"I'll visit. You'll visit. We'll make it work."

"I know."

I kissed her, full of everything I wasn't saying out loud. Every version of a future I was already building in my head. Phone calls and plane tickets and faith that a connection this strong wouldn't just stop because of an ocean.

"Call me when you land, Peach."

"Okay."

We kissed again, and she walked toward security. Then she turned back. I stayed where I was, leaning against a railing, and waved. She waved back, turned again and kept walking. Then she stopped and looked back a second time. I was still there, smiling. Then a third time, I smiled again, and waved once more.

And then she was gone and I stood there for a long moment staring at the space where she'd been.

pregnant. pregnant. pregnant.

simone

six years ago

I KNEW IT BEFORE I EVEN TOOK THE TEST. SOMETHING CELLULAR SHIFTED and my body knew. The nausea started a few weeks after I got home from LA. A roll in my stomach I tried to blame on stress, and the particular wreckage of leaving someone you'd fallen in love with at a gate, holding yourself together through security. But underneath all of it, I already knew.

I bought three tests, because one truth wasn't going to be enough to convince me. I got the nerve to take them at one in the morning, and lined them up on my counter in a neat row.

Three little windows, with three identical verdicts:

Pregnant.

Pregnant.

Pregnant.

I sat on toilet and stared. My pills. I'd forgotten them in Lennox Falls, left them on my bathroom counter when I packed, and told myself I'd only be in LA for a few days, and I'd just finished my period, so it wouldn't matter. And we used condoms. Mostly. Except the time we got lost in each other and neither one of us stopped ourselves. *Foolish.* Now I was pregnant, and he was leaving for Spain in two days.

I picked up my phone, then set it down. If I told him tonight, he might not go. Or he would go and his head would be everywhere else but where it needed to be. Focused on achieving his goals. Or he would not get on that plane. He'd eat whatever penalty was in the fine print, and come back. Because he'd told me the kind of man he was and I'd believed him.

If I ever have children, I'm going to be there. He meant every word of it, and that was a problem. He didn't need to be here, he needed to be there.

I put the tests in the trash and went to bed.

RASCHAD BOARDED HIS FLIGHT TWO DAYS LATER. HE CALLED ME FROM A layover in London, then again when he landed in Madrid. He called from the hotel they'd put him in before the apartment was ready, his voice thin with exhaustion and buzzing with barely contained anxiety. We talked for forty minutes at midnight his time and I lay on my bed with my hand flat on my stomach and told him *you've got this*, and said nothing else.

I would tell him once he was settled, I told myself. Once the season started and he'd found his footing.

We continued to talk every day. Morning messages and late-night calls and voice notes when the time difference made our schedules impossible. He'd hold his phone up to his laptop speaker so I could hear new beats he was working on. Every call, I'd think *today. I'll tell him today.* And then the call would end and I'd put the phone down and exhale.

I'd had panic attacks before. I knew what they felt like, but the shape of these new ones I was having, I didn't know. They'd come in the middle of calls, during the silence between sentences when I had the words lined up, and my mouth open, and my body would simply shut it down. Heart slamming, breath going wrong. The paralysis of having watched a pregnancy kill my mother, translating into my inability to simply say the word out loud, without my body reacting like an imminent threat was near.

My first trimester came and went. And I hadn't told a soul. Not Taryn, not my brothers, and still, not Raschad.

Around week fourteen the calls got harder. My belly wasn't visible yet but the pregnancy was real in ways that made the pretending increasingly impossible. He noticed, and I could hear him trying to figure out what was wrong and not wanting to push, and I was out of language for all of it. There's only so many times you can use the excuse *I just had a long day*.

I HADN'T DREAMED ABOUT MY MOTHER IN A COUPLE OF YEARS. BUT AT fifteen weeks pregnant, at two in the morning, she came back. In the dream I was twelve again, standing in a kitchen doorway. The light is wrong, too yellow and there is a woman on the floor. She is on her hands

AND KNEES, WITH ONE ARM REACHING TOWARD THE WALL, THE FLOOR beneath her was dark and wet. It was Mama.

I couldn't move, or make a sound. I was stuck, frozen in the doorway while Julian pushed past me, while Tre started crying, while Zion called 911 with shaking hands.

She turned towards me, and when she looked up it wasn't her face. It was mine. My face with one hand pressed to my stomach, looking back at me from the floor with an expression of terror.

I woke up gasping, with my hand on my belly and my heart slamming against my ribs. I lay there for a long time without moving, catching my breath and waiting for my pulse to slow down. And one thing kept circling in my mind over and over.

My mother was pregnant when she died.

My mother died because she was pregnant.

No warning. Gone in an afternoon because her body made a decision she never agreed to. And the man who loved her most in the world couldn't stay. Couldn't look at the children she'd left behind without seeing everything he'd lost.

I knew what Raschad would do if I called him right now. If he heard my voice at 2:47 in the morning, shaking, hand pressed to a belly I hadn't told him about. He would hear my fear before I'd finished a sentence. He would stay on the phone until my breathing steadied. And he would book a flight the moment we hung up. Not because of the baby. *For me.* Because that was who he was, the man who had breathed with me in a hallway in San Diego without being asked, who had been steady and clear in the middle of my panic like he'd been built for exactly that. He would come home and hold me in his arms and tell me to breathe with him, tell me, *I've got you.* And I would let him, and I would feel safe, and that was the problem.

Because what came after safe? What happened when my fear got too big even for him to steady? What happened when the thing I was terrified of actually happened? When my body made the same decision my mother's body had made, when the floor went dark and wet, and he was left standing in a doorway looking at a child he didn't know how to love because loving that child meant remembering what he'd lost? His dream, his girl. Or worse, what if he lost his mother because he wasn't able to execute his plan?

Because of me.

I didn't call him that night. Not because of one nightmare, or one fear. Because of every reason I had stacked on top of every other reason until I couldn't see the bottom of it. I was protecting his career. I was protecting his mother. I was protecting the plan he'd made at thirteen when the world required him to be older than he was.

And underneath all of it, the thing I couldn't say out loud even to myself yet:

I was protecting myself. From calling him at 2:47 in the morning and letting him hear how scared I was. From letting him show up and then watching him eventually realize that I wasn't worth what it would cost him.

I showed up at Taryn's house the morning after I dreamt about my mother. I sat on her couch in silence until she put down her phone, looked at me and said:

"Okay. You either killed someone or you're pregnant."

My lip quivered, I nodded rapidly and that was it, everything I'd been holding alone for weeks broke. I was shaking, crying, full-body sobbing.

"I don't know what to do," I cried. "I can't tell him."

Her voice sharpened. "Why not? Simone! Is he married?! Abusive? A liar? Just tell me now, 'cause you know —"

"No," I interrupted. "None of that. He's good. Kind. Thoughtful. Responsible." My voice broke again.

She paused. "So what's the problem?"

"He just got there, Taryn. He *just* got there. He's been working toward this his whole life and he's finally there, and his mom's medical stuff, and his sisters, he talked about them all the time, he sends money home to them." I pressed my hands against my face. "He needs this to work. I can't be the thing that ruins it."

Taryn was quiet for a moment. "That's a beautiful reason," she said flatly. "But it's also not the real reason, Simi."

I looked up. "What?"

"You can say it to me….you're afraid. You're scared, Simone. And we both know why."

I looked at her and let the rest out. "What if he comes home and tries and eventually leaves? What if I —" I stopped. "My mother was healthy. She was fine and then she wasn't, and what if that happens to me? What if I tell him and something goes wrong and he gave up Spain for a pregnancy that —" I couldn't finish it. "What if he comes home and I'm not here? What if our baby grows up the way I grew up?"

"Hey." She wrapped her arms around me. "Those are very different fears," she said carefully. "And you stacked them all on top of each other so fast you probably didn't even notice. The first one is about protecting him. The second is about protecting yourself from him leaving. And the third one…" She stared at me. "The third one has been sitting in your body since you were a child."

"They're all real. Every one of them," she continued. "But I'm listening to you use each one to justify the next. And underneath all of it, you're leaving before he can leave you. Trust me I get it. No one gets it more than I do. But you are having his *baby*, Simone. And you're making his choice for him, so you don't have to watch him make the wrong one." She took my hand. "That's not protecting him, babe. That's *robbing* him. That's robbing y'all's baby. That's robbing *you*."

"I know," I whispered. "I just need more time. I need to know everything is okay before I —"

"Simone."

"I'll tell him. I'm going to tell him. I just need to get to a place where I can say the words without…" I pressed my hand to my chest.

She watched me for a long moment, then she exhaled.

"Okay," she said. "One thing at a time. We get you a doctor. A good one. Healthy baby, healthy Simone, that's the most important thing on the list right now." She squeezed my hand. "But I want it on record that I loudly disagree."

In the weeks after I ran the numbers. Not financial ones. Emotional ones. If I told him, and he stayed in Spain, he'd try to be there from across the ocean. And eventually, the distance would win anyway.

If he came home he wood eventually resent me, maybe even resent out chid, and leave the way men leave, the way people always left when the weight got too heavy, my child would inherit the same wound I've spent years trying to survive.

Underneath all of it, deeper than any of the logic, was that I was terrified of dying. What if something went wrong, and this baby was left with a father who barely knew him? A man across an ocean who might grieve and then move on, because men can do that, men can leave, men can choose their pain over their children.

I STOPPED ANSWERING ON A THURSDAY. I COULDN'T HEAR HIS VOICE AND hold this at the same time. Couldn't do the math of telling him and then imagine all the versions of what came after.

He texted.

RASCHAD NOVA

Hey, been trying to reach you. Call me when you can.

RASCHAD NOVA

You ok?

RASCHAD NOVA

Did I do something, Simone?

RASCHAD NOVA

I'm trying to give you space, but I'm confused. Let me know you're okay.

RASCHAD NOVA

I don't know what I did, Simone. I wish you'd give me a chance to fix it. Whatever it is.

You didn't do anything, I wanted to say. The baby was kicking now. Hard, insistent kicks that felt like accusations.

RASCHAD NOVA

Thought of you today. I hope you're doing okay.

I pressed my hand to my stomach, feeling him roll, and typed:

I'm pregnant.

I stared at the words until the letters blurred.
Backspace. Backspace. Backspace.

RASCHAD NOVA

Message received. I won't bother you anymore.

That one hollowed me out. The final message from a man who'd given everything he had and gotten silence back. I typed with trembling fingers:

You're going to be a father. A boy. I want to name him Zhaire...

My thumb hovered over send. The baby moved, hard, right beneath my ribs, like he was reaching for the phone himself. A sob cracked through my chest.
Backspace. Backspace. Backspace.
Before I knew it, the decision I'd meant to make temporarily had calcified into something permanent without me ever actively choosing that.

. . .

I TOLD MY BROTHERS WHEN I WAS TWENTY WEEKS ALONG. I'D HIDDEN IT as long as I could, so finally I sat across from all three of them in Julian's living room, trying to get the words out.

"Simone," Julian said gently. "Whatever it is, just say it."

"I'm preg—" I couldn't get the word out, so I stood up and lifted my oversized shirt up exposing my round twenty-week belly.

I watched their faces shift, silence and shock first, then something else that lived underneath. Fear. They were all remembering the same thing at the same time and I could feel it move through the room like a dark cloud.

"I'm okay," I said quickly. "The baby's okay."

"How do you know?" Julian's voice was shaken in a way I'd never heard. "How do you *know*?"

"I've been seeing a doctor. Everything is fine —"

"How?" Tre asked, standing. "When?"

"Who's the father?" Zion asked quietly.

My heart spiked. "That's not important right now."

"The hell it isn't." Julian was on his feet now too. "Who is he? *Where* is he? Why isn't he here with you?"

"Julian, please."

"Is he taking care of you? Is he going to —"

"I don't want to discuss that right now."

"Simone! You need to tell us who he is. I'm not playing..." Tre demanded.

"Is he denying it's his?" Zion asked angrily, "Who the fu— I will find his ass and beat the— "

"I can't, I can't right now. I..." and then I couldn't breathe. I heard someone say *shit* and then Julian was in front of me, hands on my face, and Tre was somewhere behind him, and my body had simply shut down the conversation the way it always shut down things it couldn't face.

"Okay, Okay." Julian's voice dropped a register, trying to anchor me. "Give her space. Zion... water."

He breathed with me and the room reassembled itself.

"Better?" he asked when I had calmed down.

I nodded.

"Okay." He sat back and I could see it in all three of their faces, the questions still there, stacked and unanswered. But underneath the questions was the thing that had been living in all of us since when we were kids. They had seen what a pregnancy could do to the body of someone they loved. And now their baby sister was carrying a child.

Ultimately, their fear won, and they backed off, deciding to follow my lead and not push me on who the father was.

"Okay," Zion said. "We're not going to discuss the father right now. But, every child deserves a dad, Simone. At some point, you need to let us help you deal with whoever he is."

The irony of that statement, coming from a man whose own father had vanished, hit me so hard I almost told them everything. Almost said *his name is Raschad, he's in Spain, he plays basketball, he loves his mother, he calls me Peach, and I'm destroying him because I'm too afraid to let him love me through this.*

But I didn't. And they dropped it. Because my brothers loved me more than they needed answers. Choosing my peace over their own curiosity. They were afraid, and keeping me calm was more important than interrogating me about a man they'd never met.

They showed up instead. Julian decided the doctor I was seeing wasn't good enough, switched me to one he'd researched and took me to every appointment. Zion put together the crib and rocking chair and bassinet. Tre painted the baby's room yellow as a compromise to blue, telling me *"Wade intuition. We make kings first."*

They loved me, and they were terrified, and those two things pointed in the same direction. Don't stress her out. Don't push. And while I'm sure they always wondered, none of them asked me about the father again.

ZHAIRE NOVA WADE WAS BORN ON NOVEMBER TWENTY-SECOND. SEVEN pounds, four ounces with a full head of curly hair, and his father's face.

When they placed him on my chest I fell apart, with relief. From the overwhelming, impossible relief of having survived the thing what had taken my mother from me. I held him and I shook and I cried.

"Hi, baby," I whispered. "I'm your mama."

He blinked up at me like he already knew my voice. Julian was beside me with his arms crossed and his eyes wet, losing the battle he was trying to win against his own feelings. When I looked up at him he shook his head slowly.

"He looks just like you, Simi."

He did. But he also looked like the man who should have been in that room. Who should have cut the cord and held his son and told me he was proud of me and how I'd done good.

I thought hard about what to name him. I wrote it on the birth certificate in careful neat letters:

Zhaire Nova Wade.

When Julian asked about the middle name I told him it meant light. A new chapter. A star reborn. That was true. But the truth underneath the truth. The kind you only admit to yourself at 3 AM with a newborn sleeping on your chest, his face a map of the man he came from, was simpler. I named him after his father. The imprint of him. The spark and the love that had made this child possible.

Raschad Nova Carter had given me the greatest gift of my life. And he didn't know it yet.

THREE WEEKS AFTER ZHAIRE WAS BORN, I FOUND A STREAMING SERVICE that carried EuroLeague basketball. Fifteen dollars a month. I watched his games with the volume low and the lights off and Zhaire asleep in his bassinet beside the couch, and I'd cry through the whole thing. The first game I watched he scored twelve points. The announcers kept saying his name wrong. I wanted to call in and correct them. Instead, I took screenshots when the camera zoomed in close and saved it to a folder on my laptop I labeled *Z's Dad.*

I learned his teammates' names. Watched his minutes go up. Watched him become their best player. And every time the camera found his face, that smile, those eyes, pride and grief moved through me so close together they were indistinguishable.

When Zhaire was seven months old, after many failed attempts at making that phone call, I wrote Raschad a letter, telling him everything. His son's name, his birthday, his weight at birth. I wrote *I'm sorry. I love you. You have a son.* I addressed it to his agent's office in California, walked to the mailbox, and stood there in the cold for a long time.

I walked back inside with the letter still in my hand.

The months continued to pass the way months do when you stop counting them. Next thing I knew, Zhaire was eighteen months old, and the NBA draft announcement came:

"With the 16th pick in the NBA Draft, the New York Knicks select Raschad Nova Carter from Real Madrid"

I saved the clip to my folder and watched it over and over. Two to three years, he'd told me. And he'd done it. On screen he put on the hat and shook the commissioner's hand and hugged his mother and the camera caught his face and I shouted *"he did it!"* out loud to an empty room.

The interviewer asked how his mother was doing and he said *she's was doing well* and his voice cracked. I watched him compose himself in real time, and I thought: *see? I made the right choice. His mother is alive. He achieved everything. I did the right thing.*

I told myself that enough times to almost believe it. I was lying to myself. I knew it even as I thought it. By then I'd had two years of practice.

9 /

linea nigra

THIS CHAPTER HAS A SOUNDTRACK

La La La La by Ari Lennox

raschad

present day

I'D PUT THE MUSIC ON BEFORE SHE KNOCKED. ARI LENNOX. HER BEST songs on a playlist, set on repeat, low enough to sit underneath the room rather than fill it. I'd put it on without pretending I hadn't made that decision. I knew what I was doing.

When she knocked I took a breath and opened the door. She had on jeans and a graphic tee and her hair was pulled back in a low ponytail. Just her, the way she looked when she wasn't thinking about being looked at, which was the version that got me every time.

"Hey," she said.

"Hey."

She stepped inside and I watched her register the music before anything else. A slight pause, with her eyes moving toward the speaker on the counter, then quickly back. Neither of us said anything about it.

I'd ordered food and had set it on the counter. She looked around the space while I fixed our plates, taking it in quietly.

"Not bad for an extended stay," she said.

"Honestly I've barely been in here. Studio most days, out with your brothers the rest of it."

"I heard." She almost smiled.

We sat on the couch with the food between us on the coffee table, and we fell into an easy conversation. She asked about the music I'd been working on and I told her, and I found myself going further into it than I'd planned because she was actually following. She asked me what I thought about Lennox Falls so far, and I told her it was surreal being here in person after hearing about it so much during our late night chats. She looked at me sideways when I said that.

"You remembered that?"

"I remember everything you told me," I said simply.

She looked down at her plate and I studied her. I thought about last night. The party, our dancing, the way she'd moved. The way she'd looked at me before she looked away. I'd had her in my orbit for almost a week now, but always with other people present. Always with somewhere else to be, or some reason to keep the distance managed. It dawned on me that this was the first time in six years that it was just us.

I'd missed her. I'd been telling myself seeing her again was curiosity, unfinished business, or just the natural pull of proximity. But sitting there, in quiet of a room that was just the two of us, I knew I'd missed her, *specifically*. Six years and my feelings were still there. All of them.

"I had a good time last night," I said.

"Me too."

"Yeah. Your family…" I shook my head. "They're something else."

"They are definitely that." She laughed, relaxed and unguarded. But then, I watched something shift in her. Some internal gear changing and her laugh settled. Her hands went still in her lap. She was working up to something. I could see it moving across her face. A slight change in her breathing, the way her eyes went somewhere just past me, her shoulders drawing in. She was building toward something.

"I owe you an apology," she said quietly. "For how I left things. The way I just… went quiet. You deserved so much better than that."

I looked at her and nodded.

"It was never you," she continued. "I need you to know that. I've regretted it every…" She stopped and swallowed, took a breath then started again. "There's something I need to say to you. Something that —"

Her breathing started to change. Not a full panic attack, but maybe the beginning of one. Her breath went shallow and her shoulders pulled in and her eyes went somewhere slightly distant while the rest of her kept trying to hold herself together.

Does she still have them?

The thought saddened me. Years later and she was still dealing with this. Whatever this was, I could feel the weight of it from across the couch, it had been sitting in her chest long enough that her body reacted.

Something happened to her. Something she'd been holding for a long time. Maybe something someone *did* to her? I felt a protectiveness rise up from nowhere . I thought, *what happened, what can I fix* maybe the instinct of a man who had spent his whole life making sure the women around him were okay.

But underneath that, was something else. Something I was less proud of but am not going to lie about. This was the first time we'd been alone. Just us in a room and Ari playing and nobody watching. And whatever she was about to put on this table between us was going to change the temperature of the room. I could feel it. The kind of thing that didn't get said and then walked back.

And I wanted the room first. I wanted to sit there and breathe her in without anything else in the way. I wanted just that before whatever she was carrying arrived. Was that selfish? Yes. Did I care? Not enough to stop myself.

And she was breathing wrong. She was trying her hardest to control it, but she definitely needed to slow down and collect herself before she said anything else.

"Hey." I reached over and covered her hand with mine. "Simone."

She looked at me with wide eyes.

"You don't have to do this right this second," I said quietly. "And I'm not sitting here holding anything against you. Whatever happened, whatever the reason… I promise you that." I paused. "And I want to hear it. Whatever you've been holding, I want to hear it. We've got the whole night. Let's finish eating first. Breathe a little."

She looked at me for a long moment. Something running behind her eyes that I read and chose not to read at the same time.

"You're making this very hard," she whispered.

"Making what hard?"

"Thinking clearly." Her voice was calmer now. "You look at me like that and I forget everything else."

I didn't say anything, because I was doing exactly that. Looking at her like that, taking her in — and I couldn't stop. Six years and she was sitting two feet away from me with Ari Lennox playing low through the speaker. I thought I'd filed her away. That what we had was a moment in time and a chapter I'd moved past. And then I walked into that club and she was there and my heart turned on me.

La La La La shifted on the speaker. A smooth, atmospheric, neo-soul rhythm, with Ari's voice dropping into something sultry. And suddenly I was back in Culver City, on the floor of my apartment with cushions and blankets piled around us and candles burning low and this same voice playing all night while we forgot that anything else existed outside of us.

We looked at each other, and everything I thought I'd buried was right there in her eyes too, warm and unguarded, looking back at me like she'd been carrying the same thing I had and was just as undone as I was.

We didn't need to say anything. The slow melodic tempo of *La La La La* kept playing and I reached over and tucked a piece of her hair back. My hand barely grazing her face.

"Raschad," she breathed my name a little unsteady.

I leaned in, and she met me halfway. Our kiss wasn't careful. It was years of wondering, of missing, of distance coming undone. My hands came up to her face as I kissed her deeper and she made a sound that I felt in my spine. I pulled her onto my lap, as the song kept playing and the world around us faded away.

She wrapped both arms around my neck, pulling me deeper into our kiss, melting into me. Our kiss intensified, deeper, wetter, and more desperate, both of us knowing where this was heading, and neither of us resisting.

My shirt was somewhere on the floor. I don't even remember taking it off. All I remember is the heat of her skin, and the sound she made when I sucked that spot just beneath her collarbone.

"Mmm," she moaned, eyes half-lidded, and lips swollen.

I scooped her up and she wrapped her legs around me as I carried her to the bedroom. I laid her down gently on my bed and began to undress her layer by layer. Every inch I revealed felt like unwrapping a present.

When I looked at her lying there, naked and breathtaking, I felt like I was inside of a dream. "I've thought about you often," I whispered, eyes tracing her body, as my hands trailed down her sides. "Your body... your mouth... your laugh... your heart. I've missed you."

"Raschad, I've missed you so much," her eyes were glistening and she pulled me down onto her kissing me until we were both breathless again. Her sounds against my lips made my heart race, as she slipped her hands under my waistband, tugging at my belt.

I kissed her shoulders, her collarbone, the hollow of her neck. Kept moving down her chest, her ribs, to the soft warmth of her stomach, and the curve of her waist. She arched her back, sweet sounds falling from her mouth like a melody.

Then I saw it. A fine line running vertically from just below her ribcage down past her navel. Thin and faded, the kind that came from skin that had stretched and settled. The mark of carrying a life.

Growing up in a house full of women, I knew what it was. Tamika and Alyssa had both gone through pregnancies so I'd heard more than any brother needed to hear about what carrying a baby did to a body. They'd compared notes a few summers ago, when I'd gotten us a house at the Jersey Shore, the first real family vacation we'd ever taken. Alyssa was standing at the edge of the pool pointing out the faint line still running down her stomach, Tamika complaining that hers still hadn't faded years later, called it a *linea nigra*.

Simone had carried a child. For some reason, the visual reminder of that made my heart go tender in a way I hadn't expected. I traced her line gently with my thumb without thinking. Then I bent down and pressed my lips to it, slowly moving upward.

I felt her tense. Her breathing changed, and her eyes shifted, as she moved to cover herself. I stopped her gently, taking her wrist. I kissed her palm and intertwined my fingers between hers.

"Don't hide. You're perfect, Simone."

Then I bent down again and kissed softly at the start of that line, right above her pelvis, three kisses as I moved upwards, then I began to lick, slowly, trailing that faint, faded mark with my tongue, from the bottom curve of her stomach all the way to the curve just beneath her breasts.

She gasped and shivered. Then bit her lip like she didn't know whether to cry or moan. I looked up at her as I kissed just under the swell of her breast.

"You're so damn beautiful," I whispered. "Every inch of you." Then I took her breast into my mouth and worshipped it.

She whimpered, but it wasn't the sound of pleasure. Something else was happening. I looked up at her and could see the way her lips trembled, how her eyes were distant and glassy. Like her mind had slipped somewhere else.

I sat up slightly, giving her space and placed my hand on her cheek. "Simone? What is it? Talk to me."

"I-I can't." Her voice cracked as she sat up, pulling the cover up over herself. "I'm sorry. I thought I could, but..." She shook her head and turned her face away, blinking hard.

"Hey. Hey..." I cupped her face gently, coaxing her to look at me. "You don't owe me anything, alright? Not your body. Not a thing. It's okay."

Tears slid down the sides of her face, and I wiped them away.

"I just..." she choked. "I'm sorry. I didn't mean to let it get this far..."

"You didn't do anything to apologize for."

She looked at me then, and I saw fear there. Not of me...I hoped... but of something else entirely. I watched her blink back more tears, and my heart twisted.

"Are you still having them?" I asked. "Panic attacks?"

She nodded once, barely. She just wasn't ready.

I kissed her forehead. "Okay. Listen, we don't have to rush. Just... let me hold you." I moved up beside her and pulled her back against my chest, my arms around her. Her hands had found my forearms and gripped them.

"I'm sorry," she whispered. "I'm so sorry, I —"

"Don't." I pressed my lips to her temple. "You don't have to apologize for that."

"It's not you," she said urgently. Wanting me to understand. "You didn't do anything wrong."

"I know."

It took every ounce of strength I had to stop. My body was damn near trembling, every nerve on fire, but when she whispered "I can't," I knew there was something deeper happening. Something I needed to respect even if I didn't understand what had shifted. So I held her. Stroked her hair. Let her breathe until her heartbeat slowed against my chest.

"You good?" I finally asked softly.

She nodded against my shoulder. "Just got… overwhelmed."

I understood that. This thing between us, it was intense even for me. Heavy with history and possibility and feelings neither of us had probably planned on. She tilted her face up to look at me. Her eyes were clearer now, but there was still something unresolved swimming behind them.

"Raschad. We need to talk. I just —" She stopped, and whatever it was still wouldn't come. "I need a minute. Just a minute."

"Okay. Bathroom is there," I pointed. "Take your time."

She untangled herself and moved toward the bathroom. She paused at the door with her back to me, her hand flat against it, forehead almost touching the wood, and then she went in and closed it behind her.

I sat on the edge of the bed and listened to the music, still playing like the playlist didn't know the night had shifted.

I ran my hands over my face and exhaled. She'd been trying to tell me something. Early in the evening, before the food was finished, before our kiss… she'd been circling something real and I'd reached over and taken her hand and said let's have this moment first. Because I'd wanted the moment. Because six years had passed and she was here and whatever weight she was carrying had felt like something we could face together once we'd had this.

I'd been wrong about the order. I understood that now, sitting there listening to her run the water on the other side of the bathroom door.

Something had happened to her back then. Something she'd been carrying alone, something that had been too heavy to say out loud at the table or on the couch or in any of the moments she'd opened her mouth and then closed it again.

I thought about the way she'd looked when I'd stopped her. Not fully relieved, something more conflicted than that. Like I'd done her a kindness and a harm at the same time.

I should have let her finish. But my wanting had been louder than my listening and I'd made a choice with the wrong thing. I sat there on the edge of the bed, staring at the bathroom door, and waited.

Then I picked up my phone from the nightstand. I'd put it on Do Not Disturb earlier. I had four missed calls from Tre. Two from Zion. A chain of texts.

I called Tre back, and he picked up on the first ring. "Yo. Finally."

"What's going on?"

"SZA's people just called. She's in the area already, they want to meet to review the track tonight. Like right now."

I looked at the bathroom door.

"Tonight? I was kinda in the middle of—"

"This is SZA, man. It's now or never."

I closed my eyes for a second. *Of all the times.*

"Alright. Give me an hour," I said. "I'll be there."

"Bet."

I hung up and stared at the bathroom door, shaking my head. Then got up and started getting dressed.

simone

I SLIPPED OUT OF BED AND PADDED BAREFOOT INTO THE BATHROOM, closing the door quietly behind me. And then I stared at myself in the mirror. My lips were swollen. My hair was a mess. My eyes were red from holding back tears that still wanted out.

My reflection looked haunted. Not because of what we'd almost done. But because of what I still hadn't said. The ghost of his touch still lingered on my skin. My chest. My belly. There. Right there where that faint line marked proof of everything I'd kept from him.

He touched me like he never forgot. And when he kissed that line on my stomach... when his lips and tongue traced it... I almost collapsed because he didn't know what that line really meant. Didn't know it marked the life we'd created together. Didn't know it led directly to his son.

And now that made this all *so* much worse. I pressed both hands against the sink and let my forehead drop forward, breath catching hard in my throat.

You should've told him. Right then. When he was soft and open and looking at you like he already saw everything. But the words got stuck. Again.

Not even a whisper. Because the truth would've shattered that beautiful moment. And I needed it. I needed to feel adored and wanted. Without consequence.

But now? Now it was just another reason to hate myself.

I was even more scared than I'd been before, because now the stakes were even higher. This wasn't just attraction anymore. This was deeper. This was still *real*. I was falling for him all over again. And I was about to break his heart in a million ways. He didn't deserve any of what I was about to put him through.

I wiped under my eyes, trying to steady my hands. He thinks I'm just another woman he wants to take his time with. But I've already stolen time from him. Years of it.

I took a breath, splashed water on my face and straightened my spine. *Okay. No more hiding.* I said to myself in the mirror. *You're going to put your clothes on, walk back out there, and tell him everything. Right now. This can't go on any longer.*

I took a deep breath, splashed more water on my face, and prepared myself to finally be brave enough to tell Raschad the truth.

I opened the door, my heart was beating out of my chest, and there he was, sitting at the edge of the bed, looking at his phone with a frown.

He looked up, and the conflict on his face told me before the words did. "Tre and Zion have been blowing up my phone. I had it on DND." He let out a breath. "Last minute session. SZA. If I don't go now…"

The timing was almost funny. Almost. I had just looked myself in the mirror and said *no more hiding.* I had just talked myself into being brave. And the universe had other plans.

"Go," I said. "You have to, that's important."

"Simone… what you were going to tell me?"

"It can wait."

"Are you sure? Because I feel like —"

"Raschad. This is what you've been working toward. Don't miss it because of me."

He searched my face for a long moment.

"Come to my office on Monday. We will talk then. I promise."

He nodded slowly. "Monday. I'll be there."

"Monday," I confirmed.

He nodded again, still looking at me like he was trying to solve something. Then he kissed me.

"Thank you," he said against my lips. "For understanding."

I kissed him back and tried to memorize it. The last kiss he'd ever want to give me.

"Go make something great," I said. "That's what you're here for."

We gathered our things and left together, him walking me to the elevator, neither of us saying much. The hallway was quiet. At the elevator he turned to face me.

"Hey." I put my hand on his chest. Just to have one more second. He looked down at my hand, then at my face. I pulled him down and kissed him goodbye. I meant for it to be quick. I meant to be composed about it. But his hands came up to hold my face and the kiss opened into the kind of thoroughness that said *I know you, I've always known you, I'm not done knowing you.* I felt my eyes fill and blinked the tears back, not wanting to break this, not wanting him to pull back and see them and have to explain.

He felt it anyway, and pulled back just enough to see my face. His thumbs moved across my cheeks and his expression did something complicated. Confused.

"What is this, Simone?" he asked quietly.

I shook my head and forced a smile even though my face was doing everything it was doing. "Nothing. Go. They're waiting."

"Simone."

I pressed my palm flat against his chest, feeling his heartbeat under my hand. "You're gonna be late. Monday."

He looked at me for a long moment. I watched him want to stay. Watched him weigh it. What was in front of him and what was behind him, the thing I wasn't explaining and the people waiting on him across town. His hands were still on my face.

"Monday?" he asked.

"Monday," I said. The only promise I had left to give him.

He kissed me once more then he stepped back "I should have let you talk earlier. I'm sorry for that."

I shook my head slightly.

"You're going to be okay," he said, like he was telling himself as much as me.

I nodded and kept my smile steady. Then we left.

I HELD IT TOGETHER UNTIL I MADE IT TO MY CAR, THEN I LET MYSELF come apart. I'd been ready. I'd finally been ready to tell him. And the universe gave me an out. Another excuse. Another delay. But this time, I wasn't taking it.

Monday. I'd said Monday. Which meant I had two days to prepare for him to hate me. Two days before everything fell apart. I drove home in silence, hand resting on my stomach where he'd kissed the permanent reminder of the secret I couldn't keep anymore.

Monday. No more running.

zhaire nova wade

raschad

It was Monday morning and I was at WadeHouse early. The SZA session had started Saturday night and ran straight through Sunday. By the time we wrapped it was late evening and the track was locked. The session was one of those where nobody wanted to call it done. I'd driven home, showered, slept, and was back at WadeHouse Monday morning before most people had their first cup of coffee.

Simone was expecting me at noon. I had time, so I posted up in Studio B working on a track I wanted to revisit. Not long after I got there, Zion and Tre came in, and the three of us posted up in Studio B recapping the weekend and listening to new beats.

That's when Julian walked in with Simone's son.

"No school today," he said, settling into one of the chairs. "Aunt Lorraine is on her way to pick him up. We're just killing time until she gets here."

"Hey, little man. What's up?" I said to him.

"Hi, Mr. Raschad!" He made a beeline for my keyboard, fingers already moving across the keys, tapping out a rhythm. The kid had feel. Natural.

"You said you'd show me how to make the drum sounds," he said, looking up."Remember? You said next time."

"I remember, Questlove Jr.," I said with a grin. "Deal's still good."

"Can you show me now?"

"Zhaire." Julian tossed him a look. "No. Time to go. Aunt Lorraine texted, she is here to get you."

Zhaire groaned, half-pouting. "But I'm being good! I don't wanna go with Aunt Lorraine. I wanna stay here!"

"Zhaire," Julian warned.

"No!" he whined and crossed his arms, plopping down on the floor.

Julian cut him off with a voice like stone. "Zhaire Nova Wade. You heard what I said. Up. *Now.*"

The room stilled and my heart dropped out of my chest.

Nova?

The name hit me deep inside, my body responding like a five-alarm fire. My ears started ringing, my breathing sped up, and my heart began to race, as I sat very still and *really* looked at him.

Zhaire. Nova. Wade.

I didn't move. Didn't speak. Just sat there while the name rearranged itself over and over inside my head. I opened my mouth but nothing would come out. I stared at him intently. He was tall. I'd clocked that before but I'd filed it away the way you file away things that don't require your attention. Now I was pulling it back out. Tall. Long limbs he hadn't grown into yet. Knees poking out when he sat cross-legged on the floor.

I knew that build. I'd lived in it.

"How old are you, little man?" My voice came out too careful.

"I'm five!" he replied proudly.

Five. I recalibrated fast, the way you do when numbers stop making sense and you need them to. Zion must have seen something shift in my face because he said unprompted: "He's always been tall for his age. Ninety-ninth percentile every checkup. People think he's older until he starts talking."

I nodded, but I don't know what my face was doing. My eyes moved across Zhaire's face slowly, piece by piece. The set of his jaw. His wide, watchful eyes. The dimple sitting in his right cheek.

He looked like Simone. He also looked like… *me.*

I pressed my palms flat against my thighs to keep my hands from shaking, as the math started in my head.

Six years back. California.

Minus nine months.

Five.

I don't know why I hadn't run those numbers before. Why I hadn't thought to ask how old he was before. Maybe because it wasn't in the realm of what I thought was plausible. Or maybe because on some level I hadn't wanted to look too directly at the question of what happened after she'd disappeared on me. But now every number was pointing the same direction. The timing. Her ghosting me with no explanation. And now this boy, sitting on the floor of a recording studio in Lennox Falls, wearing my face.

"Bye, Mr. Raschad." Zhaire said sadly, still pouting as he stood at the door.

"Huh? Oh, later little man." My voice was barely there.

He took off running behind Julian and I sat completely stunned and still while the room moved around me. Tre's hand landed on my shoulder at some point and I heard him say something I didn't catch. I said something halfway coherent back — *must be something I ate — pick back up tomorrow — yeah that's cool* — and then suddenly I was in the hallway and I didn't remember standing up.

I walked, not even knowing where to. My feet moving faster than my mind. I'd come back to Lennox Falls because of the WadeHouse deal. That was the practical answer. But I'd known what else was here. *Who* else was here. And I'd told myself at first, that I could handle being in proximity to Simone Wade without making it into something it wasn't. But then I saw her, and realized that something in me had been waiting six years to understand what happened, and maybe to get back what we'd had with better timing. Fate had put me here, I thought. Dropped me exactly where I was supposed to be. A second chance. That's what it had felt like. A door reopening.

I stopped walking and I thought about the first time I met Zhaire the other day. How quickly he'd come to me. How easy it was to sit with him, talk to him. How he'd hugged my leg. I'd thought that the warmth I felt was about Simone. That being close to her world was making everything feel more significant than it was.

But that wasn't it. That feeling wasn't about her. It was about him. Maybe my body had known something my mind hadn't let in yet. Some recognition underneath the surface, pulling toward this kid the way you pull toward something that belongs to you.

I hadn't been brought here for a second chance with Simone.

I'd been brought here for my son.

My son.

I didn't expect my world to tilt on its axis on a random Monday. I didn't expect to see my child's whole damn life laid out in front of me in the form of a middle name. I damn sure didn't expect to feel something inside me crack so violently I swear I could hear it.

I leaned against a wall, trying to catch my breath. My hands were shaking. "Shit," I gasped trying to steady my breaths. Then I looked up and found myself standing outside of Simone's office.

I took a deep inhale and long exhale, straightened up, didn't knock, and pushed the door open.

Simone looked up from her desk when I walked in. The moment she saw my face I could tell she knew. The way her face changed, not surprise, or confusion. It was recognition. Like she'd been waiting for this exact moment and realized she had run out of room to keep running from it.

I couldn't speak at first. So I just stood there, staring at her.

"Hi… y-you're early," her voice was barely anything.

I closed the door behind me, but still couldn't find words. Just stood there with this revelation sitting on my heart like a cinder block.

She stood up and cleared her throat. "There's something I need to —"

"Zhaire Nova?" I heard my own voice like it was coming from somewhere outside my body.

She gasped and her eyes got wide, then filled with tears.

"Zhaire… *Nova*, Simone?"

She didn't move or speak.

"Simone?" That was all I had. Just her name and this sudden wave of grief.

Tears began to slide down her face. "I was going to… I was going to tell you, I—"

"When? *When* were you — he's five, Simone. He is FIVE years old. When were…" I stopped and my throat closed on whatever came next. I pressed both hands against the back of my head and stood there trying to breathe. "When were you going to tell me?"

"I…" Her voice broke. "I was scared, I —"

"You were *scared*?" I laughed, broken and hollow and nothing like a laugh. "Unbelievable. You were scared? Okay. For *five years?* You were scared for five years?"

"How many more years would you have been scared, huh? Until he was ten? Fifteen? Would you have let him graduate high school without his father? Go to college? Get married? Have kids of his own, never knowing me?"

"No, Raschad, no. I would have, I —" she started moving closer toward me.

"Don't!" I held up a hand and she froze in place. "Just… give me a second."

I turned away from her and faced a wall, bent over with my hands on my thighs. One breath. Two. Trying to find some ground underneath me because the floor kept shifting.

I stood straight and turned back around. "I *held* you," I said, stepping forward. "Touched every inch of you. Kissed you like you were mine again. And all the while, you were sitting on… *this*? Letting me fall for you again while you dragged this *lie* behind you like it wasn't going to cut me to fucking pieces!"

She began to sob, but I shook my head. "No, don't cry now. Not now. You don't get to be a victim in this."

"I don't even know what I came here for anymore," I mumbled more to myself. "I thought maybe… *maybe* you were gonna tell me something heavy. I didn't know it was going to be my entire fucking LIFE, Simone!"

She stepped forward, reaching for me. "Raschad. Please let me explain."

I flinched back like her touch was poison. "There is no explanation. *Nothing* you could possibly say explains what you've done." I turned away again, rubbing both hands down my face, pacing and trying to steady myself.

"You were never going to tell me, were you?" The realization hit me like a freight train. "If I hadn't gotten injured. If I hadn't come to Lennox Falls for this production deal. If I hadn't happened to walk into that club, you would have kept this secret forever."

No denial came. "Answer me, Simone!"

Her face crumpled. "I wanted to… kept planning to, but I just —"

"But you DIDN'T! Five years, Simone. No, SIX years! Six and you never reached out. Never called. Never texted. Nothing but silence. So *when*?"

"I don't know!" she cried. "I don't know. Every day I thought about it. Many times I tried, started to. But it just kept getting harder and I'd freeze. I just... kept putting it off."

"*Putting it off*? Like this is some doctor's appointment you kept rescheduling? This is our *child*. My *son*. And you kept '*putting it off*'? That's supposed to make fucking sense to me?"

"I know it's not good enough. I know. But I wasn't... I didn't decide you'd never know. I just couldn't make myself tell you. And then more time passed, and it got harder, and I..." She cried harder. "I'm a coward. I'm a coward and I robbed you both and I don't know how to fix it."

"Do you have a goddamn time machine, Simone? Huh? Do you? You can't fix it. You can't give me back years with him. You can't fix shit!"

She closed her eyes and quickly nodded, then covered her face, trying to wipe away the tears that kept coming.

"Jesus, Simone. How could you do this? I can't believe you'd do this. This can't be real." I shook my head, still in disbelief. I began to feel lightheaded and dropped down on the chair in front of her desk, bent over with my elbows on my knees and my head in my hands. Silent tears streamed down my face and I couldn't decide if they were angry tears, heartbroken tears, regretful tears, or all three. If I had thought my heart was broken all those years ago when she'd disappeared on me, I realized then that I never really had a clue what true heartbreak was.

The two of us sat there for what felt like minutes, not looking at each other, silently crying. Destroyed.

"You just… decided you didn't need me." I said finally. "You didn't even give me the chance to show up. You didn't give me the dignity of *trying*."

I stood and started pacing again, then turned back to face her, eyes blazing. "And then you had the nerve to let me be in the same room as him. Like I wasn't looking my own blood in the eyes. Do you understand how fucking *cruel* that is?"

Her hand covered her mouth, as confusion flickered in her eyes. "What do you mean?" her voice was shaky. "When did you —"

"Julian brought him by the studio. I sat there talking to that little boy about Transformers, promised to teach him beats. He called me 'Mr. Raschad'. My *son* calls me Mr. Raschad, hugged me and I didn't even know who he was to me."

"Oh God!" Her hand went to her mouth, tears streaming again in full force. "I didn't know. I didn't know you met him. I'm so sorry, I didn't —"

Something ignited in me. "You didn't know because you've been so busy managing all of this. Managing me, managing what I know, managing what he knows, that you lost track of your own —" I stopped. My voice was climbing and I was trying to hold it but it kept slipping. "Do you understand what that is? That is my son. That is my SON and he looked me in the face and I smiled at him and I didn't…"

"I-I know, I'm —"

"You know? You *have* known! From the second you found out you have always known *everything* and I have known NOTHING and that is…" I broke off, my eyes were burning. "That is not something you do to a person."

She was crying with her full body, trying to speak but barely able to. "I panicked," she finally got it out. "When I found out I was pregnant, I just… I panicked. You had just left for Spain. You had everything mapped out. Your whole plan, everything you'd worked for your whole life and you were finally… it was right there. And I thought about telling you and I just —" She pressed her hands together. "I didn't want to derail that. Everything you'd planned for."

"I would have made a NEW plan, Simone! People do that. People find out they have a child coming and they adjust. They figure shit out. That is something human beings DO."

"I know," she looked down. "I was scared."

"Of what!"

She didn't answer fast enough.

"Simone. You have said that word four or five times now. You were *scared*. Scared of WHAT? Say the actual thing!"

"That… that you'd resent me," she said quietly. "That you'd feel obligated. To me. That you'd come back because you felt like you had to and spend the rest of your life…" She stopped and swallowed. "I didn't want you to be here because you felt trapped."

"So you made the decision for me."

"Everything you'd worked for was finally happening. Spain, then the NBA, take care of your family. An entire roadmap and it was happening for you. And I just… I didn't fit in that. Not without disruption. You would've stayed. Thrown the whole thing away."

"I would've figured it out! Maybe I don't go to Spain. Maybe I play domestically. Maybe I work my way up differently. Maybe the timeline changes. Maybe I don't make it to the NBA until later. SO WHAT?"

"You had too much to lose."

"Don't tell me what I had to lose! Yes, I had people depending on me. My mother. My sisters. But *you* were on that list too, Simone. Back then? I had *you* to lose. Now I find out I had my *CHILD* to lose! And you just… took yourself off the list. Took our SON off the list!"

I swallowed against tears. "You didn't give me the chance to figure out a single thing. *You* made every decision. *You* controlled the whole situation. *You* chose *FOR me*, Simone! You didn't have that right. You didn't! And you chose wrong."

"You shouldn't have had to choose," she cried and something moved through her face. "It just didn't make sense. You blowing up your life over me."

I looked at her. "You decided what you were worth… and you didn't ask me." I said quietly. "You decided what I could handle and you didn't ask me. You made every call and you act like it was protection."

I looked away, drew in a slow breath and let it go. Then looked at her straight. "That's not protection. That's control."

Then it hit me. "Does your family know? Am I just the clown in this whole setup? The dumbass everyone laughed at and watched in silence?" But even as I asked it, the pieces clicked. No. The way she panicked when she first saw me, pretending like we'd just met in front of her brothers. No. And they wouldn't have brought Zhaire around me if they knew. Julian wouldn't be that stupid. None of them would.

She shook her head. "No. I never told them."

I really looked at her, tears streaming down her face, her shoulders shaking, trying hard not to hyperventilate. And for a split second, I felt something twist inside. Damn. She carried this alone all this time. Six years of keeping this secret, not telling a soul. Not even her own brothers. But as quick as the thought hit me, I shook it off. She didn't deserve my sympathy.

"Who does Zhaire think his father is?"

"He hasn't asked yet," she whispered. "He has three active uncles, he's never felt that lack."

That stung like salt in a wound. "'Never felt that *lack*'? How could he miss what he was never allowed to have? But there IS a lack, Simone. I would have been *everything* to that boy."

She nodded her head but didn't speak.

"You *robbed* me. And you didn't just take *him* away from *me*. You took *me* away from *him*. My mother. My sisters. My whole damn family. People who would've loved him, spoiled him, shown up for him. But you decided half of him didn't matter! That *I* didn't matter. You act like love from your side of the family replaces *me*. But I would've shown up. I would've *been* here. I would've been *so* much to him. To *you*. I never had a choice."

I swallowed hard before continuing. "You didn't protect him, Simone. You controlled the narrative so you wouldn't have to compromise. You made me the villain without ever giving me a chance to prove different. And now? Now I gotta carry this because you decided I wasn't worth the truth. Wasn't worth anything *period*."

I closed my eyes trying to fight back the piercing headache that had surfaced. "You had him without me. You're raising him without me. And now you want me to what? Just accept that and say 'okay, thanks for telling me'? Nah, Simone. Nah."

"I'm so sorry." she whimpered.

"Stop saying that!" My hand came down flat on her desk. She flinched and I hated that I caused it. I paused for a second, then kept going, because I didn't know how to stop. "You keep saying '*sorry*' like it's a word that fixes this. You remember what I told you? About my father? Do you?"

My voice was coming apart at the seams and I couldn't hold it together anymore. "I am a man with a five-year-old son who doesn't know who I am. You made me into the *one* thing I swore I would *never* be. A deadbeat dad."

I leaned forward and pressed both hands flat on her desk with my head down. That's when I saw her hand go to her chest. Her breathing changed, getting shorter and shallow, and she was sweating.

Now? Right now? Part of me wanted to step away. Wanted to tell her she didn't get to use this to get out of the conversation. Didn't get to make me stand there feeling like the one who did something wrong for making her so upset. But then I really looked at her.

This wasn't performance. *Damn it.*

"Simone." My anger shifted without permission. Still there, burning underneath everything, but something else moved in front of it.

She shook her head, waving me back, while gasping. "It's..." she couldn't get words out, and her other hand found the edge of her desk and gripped. "...Okay," she spit out, then dropped down in her chair, still trying to catch her breath.

I crossed to the other side of her desk and crouched in front of her chair, in her eye line. "Look at me." My voice was uneven. "Look at me right now."

Her wild, red and wet eyes found mine, as she gasped for air.

"In through your nose." I demonstrated, even though my own hands weren't steady and my chest felt like it was caving in. "Out through your mouth. Come on. Breathe with me. In. Hold it. Out."

She tried, hitched, then tried again. I stayed in front of her, breathing slow and steady, holding the line for her even though nobody was holding it for me. When her breathing started to find a rhythm I stood up and stepped back. I pulled out my phone with shaky hands and typed into the group thread I had with her brothers.

> Simone needs you. Now. Her office.

I sent it, put my phone away, and looked at her one more time. I knew I couldn't stay there. I was the reason she was breaking and she was the reason I was shattered and there was no version of this where I stayed in that room and kept it together much longer.

The door burst open less than a minute later. Tre came in first, took one look at Simone's tear-stained face, the look on mine, and my position standing in front of her, and his expression turned murderous.

"What the fuck did you do to her!" He grabbed my shirt, yanking me away from her.

"Tre..." Simone's voice was weak, still trying to catch her breath. "Don't..." she gasped. "He..."

I didn't fight back. Didn't even try to defend myself, because part of me wanted him to hit me. Wanted the physical pain to take away from what I was feeling inside.

Julian and Zion rushed in behind him, both of them taking in the scene. Simone barely breathing, me in Tre's grip, the tension thick enough to choke on.

"Let... him... go," Simone gasped out, struggling to stand. "He didn't... it wasn't... it was me."

Tre's grip loosened, confusion crossing his face. Simone's breathing was getting worse again, as she plopped back down in her chair.

"Let him go, Tre," Julian said firmly, moving toward Simone. "Can't you see she's having a panic attack?" Julian crouched in front of her. "Simi. Three things you can see. Focus. Name them for me."

I watched them move around her like a system, filling in every gap. Zion looked at me, his face unreadable. "What happened?"

I looked at Simone and she shook her head barely. I said it anyway.

"Zhaire is my son." My voice came out hollow, scraped clean of everything. "Your sister… I just found out."

The room went completely silent except for Simone's labored breathing and crying. Julian's head snapped toward her. Tre's mouth fell open. Zion looked like the floor had opened up under him.

"What?" Julian's voice was barely above a whisper.

Simone's breathing spiked back up immediately, panic flooding back in at the look on her brothers' faces, her secret detonating in real time in front of her. Zion refocused on her fast. "Breathe. We'll deal with this later. Right now you just breathe."

I needed to go, so I moved toward the door.

"Ra... schad." Her voice was barely anything behind me.

I stopped with my hand on the door handle, not turning around for a long moment. Then I did. I looked at her falling apart, her brothers on either side of her, the room full of wreckage and I only had one thing left to say.

"You named him Nova." My voice was hoarse and wrecked and I let it be. "You gave our son my name. A name that means new beginning." I exhaled and it shook. "And then you didn't give me the chance to be there when he took his first breath."

The sound that came out of her wasn't a word.

"Damn," Tre said quietly.

Julian closed his eyes, as Zion pulled Simone in closer.

I walked out and made it to the stairwell before my knees went. I sat down on the cold concrete steps, put my head in my hands, and sat there.

I have a son. Who loves action figures and has a drummer's ear and my dimple and long limbs. I let silent tears fall. For Zhaire. For myself. For every first I didn't get to have. For my mother who didn't know she had a grandson. For the man I had promised myself I'd be and the years that promise had already been broken without my knowledge or consent.

And for her. Even then, even after all of it, for her too.

I don't know how long I sat there. I had a son. His name was Zhaire Nova. And I was going to have to figure out how to be his father. Whatever that looked like. Whatever it took.

I was going to show up.

brothers & sisters

simone

My brothers took me home. I don't remember the drive, but I remember Tre's hand on my back in the parking lot. I remember the click of a seatbelt as Julian strapped me in. I remember the window being cold against my forehead and the sound of Zion on the phone, low, telling someone something I couldn't process.

At my house, Julian poured me a glass of water and set it on the table in front of me. I didn't touch it. Zion heated something, leftovers, I think, and the smell made my stomach turn. He put the plate away without commenting.

They sat with me in silence for a half an hour, maybe longer. I was on the couch with my knees pulled up, in a daze. Julian on the armrest. Tre next to me. Zion across from me.

Eventually Julian broke the silence. "We need to hear it from you, Simone."

I looked at the ceiling, then the floor, then my hands. "It's true," I said. "Raschad is Zhaire's father."

Even though Raschad had said it to their faces, hearing me confirm it changed something in the room. Julian let out the longest exhale I'd ever heard, and Zion leaned forward, elbows on his knees and both hands pressed to his face.

"Okay," Julian said. "Explain. When?"

"San Diego. That conference. That's how we met."

I walked them through all of it. How it started. The calls, every day for months. My trip to LA. Falling. Finding out I was pregnant the week he left for Spain and making the choice I made. I didn't skip anything. By the time I finished the room was very quiet.

I looked at their faces and the expressions they wore broke my heart. Disappointment. Disbelief. Judgment. My voice cracked and the tears started to fall again. "I-I promise you I didn't plan to keep it from him forever. I never meant for it to go this long. But then Zhaire was born. And the choice I'd made was just... done. It was done. And what I hadn't said was the size of his whole life. And I couldn't. I didn't know how to undo it. Every day it got bigger. Every day it got harder to say. And the longer it went…"

"The harder it got," Tre finished my sentence. "Six years though, Simi? We been dapping this man up for months. Working with him. Making plans with him. I had him at my birthday party. You should have *at least* let us know."

"*The longer it went, the harder it got,*" Julian repeated, turning it over.

The three of them looked at each other. I caught it, and it hit me like a truck because I knew exactly what that look meant. I knew whose name was on it.

"Don't," I said. "Don't."

"Nobody said anything," Zion said quietly.

"You didn't have to."

We all heard it. Felt the echo. *The longer it went, the harder it got.* That wasn't just my story. That was our father's. The man who left and never came back. Not because he stopped loving us. But because his guilt compounded. Every month that he didn't come home made the next month harder to face. At some point his absence became its own wall and he convinced himself the damage he'd done was too far gone and that we were better off without him. That he doesn't deserve to be in our lives. At least that's what Uncle Reggie, his brother, tells us. So he stays away. Refuses to see us and 'interrupt our happiness'.

"Simone." Julian's voice was low. "You understand what you did? You decided for him what was best for him. He didn't get a voice. You decided your fear and guilt wins over facing it. And you let time do the rest of the damage."

His words sliced through me. Not because they were cruel. Because they were true.

"That man probably feels like a fool right now," Tre added, quietly. "He's been looking us in the face for months. Laughing with us. Building something with us. And now he's sitting somewhere probably wondering: *did they know?* For all he knows, we were all in on it. The whole Wade family, smiling in his face."

"He doesn't think that." I retorted.

"You don't know what he thinks, Simone." Zion stood up. "He opened up to us. Real shit. His dreams, his family, his goals. He trusted us. And now he finds out we're connected to the biggest lie of his life."

"He knows you didn't know. I told him you didn't, in the office, before —"

"Damn." Tre cut me off, realization hitting fresh. "Zhaire got that man's whole face. Blind man could've seen that from a balcony. How we not see that shit?" He looked at Julian and Zion.

"Nobody saw it." Zion said.

"Because we weren't looking!" Tre was up again, pacing. "I damn near put that man through a wall, Simone. And this whole time —" He stopped, rubbed his face. "I gotta apologize to him." He looked at Julian and Zion again, "We gotta go talk to him."

"Please don't talk to him," I said, my heart racing again. "Any of you, not yet. *Please.* Just let me handle this."

Julian scoffed but didn't respond. Zion shifted in his chair and cleared his throat. Tre looked at me like I'd lost my mind. None of them said they wouldn't. They just let it hang there, and I knew, they were gonna do what they wanted to do.

"He might not want to talk to me again. Maybe ever." I admitted more to myself.

"Can you blame him?" Zion asked.

"No."

"Give him space," Julian said. "Let him come to you."

"What if he doesn't?"

"He texted us," Julian said, letting that sit. "The man just found out you've been hiding his son, and his first instinct was to make sure someone came to take care of you. If I didn't it know before, that tells me who he is. He's going to do the right thing, Simone. But *you* don't get to direct or rush anything. *You* don't get to manage it. You're gonna have to sit with the discomfort and let him process."

The room went quiet again and the hard part was done. My brothers were still here. Albeit, looking at me with disappointment, but also with love.

And that's when it hit me. Not shame... I'd been living in that forever. The thing underneath. The thing I'd been pushing down since Raschad walked out of my office because if I let myself feel it I wouldn't have been able to talk, and my brothers needed me to talk.

But they were done asking questions. And the room was quiet. And in the quiet, the grief rushed in. Because he was gone. Not just angry. *Gone.* The way he'd looked at me. Not even rage. Worse. Like I was someone he didn't recognize. Like I was a stranger he couldn't stand to look at.

"I love him," I said, barely audible.

"Yeah? That man might've loved you too," Tre said. "It was all over his face whenever y'all were in the same room. I just thought he was feelin' you. Turns out he was staring at his legacy." He paused and looked at me. "Might not love you anymore though."

"Tre!" Zion spat. "Do you always have to?"

"I'm just being real."

"You're being an asshole."

"I feel for you, Simone. I do." Tre continued. "But somebody needs to keep it real with you. You talkin' about love when you just cut that man clean open."

I nodded in agreement, wiping away tears.

"Enough." Julian cut his eyes at Tre, then looked at me. "You're worried about the wrong thing right now, Simone. This is not about your relationship with Raschad. Whatever that was, is, could've been — I don't know. None of us do. But right now? That's not the priority. The priority is his relationship with *Zhaire*. And how the two of you navigate being parents. *Together*. All the other stuff? Right now, it's irrelevant."

It stung. But the sting was the point. Julian was right. So was Tre in his less diplomatic way. I'd been sitting there crying about a man who might not love me anymore when the real conversation was about my five-year-old son who didn't know his father existed.

"What do I do?" I asked.

"You give Raschad space. You let him come to you. And when he does, you talk about Zhaire. Not about your feelings. About your son. What he needs. How you're going to tell him. How you move forward." Julian answered.

Zion looked at Julian, then back at me. "Simi, I know this feels like the end of the world right now. But it doesn't have to be the disaster you think it is. It's out now. That's the hardest part. What comes next is just work. And we'll help you through it."

Tre nodded. "Raschad is a good man. A real one. Let him breathe. Then figure out together what Zhaire needs."

Julian stood and looked down at me. And underneath the disappointment and the quiet judgment, I saw the same thing I'd seen when I was twelve and he was nineteen and our world had collapsed, and he'd looked at all of us and said: '*We're going to be okay*'.

"You're going to be okay, Simi," he looked at me with love and compassion. "Not today. Maybe not for a while. But you're going to get through this."

I nodded.

"And Simone?"

"Yes?"

"No more secrets. Not from us. Not ever again."

"No more secrets." I conceded.

Just then, my front door opened. Taryn walked in, took one look at the room — my brothers' faces, me wrecked on the couch — and nodded once.

"Oh good. You're alive."

Zion turned to her. "T, you knew?"

She looked at him "I did."

"And you didn't think to tell me?"

"No." She set her purse down. "She swore me to secrecy. What was I supposed to do?"

Zion studied her. "Uh, tell your husband?"

"Please don't be upset with her." I said. "She tried to get me to tell him countless times. This is my fault. Mine alone."

Zion stared at her as she held his gaze without flinching. Then he just shook his head, pulled her toward him, and kissed the side of her head. "We'll talk about this later."

Tre leaned back in his chair and shook his head. "Man gets married and turns weak. You used to stand on business, Z."

"Shut the fuck up, man," Zion snapped.

Taryn whipped around in Zion's arms. "Don't be a hater, Tre."

Julian's voice cut in, "Alright. Can we keep the focus on Simone?"

Taryn's attention turned to me, she stepped out of Zion's arms and sat down, putting her arm around me.

"I know you're hurting," she said, "I'm sorry, Simi. But I'm proud of you for facing it. The hardest part is over with now."

I leaned into her. Let myself break again, the kind of crying that happens when the height of the crisis has passed and the grief is just beginning, and one thought kept echoing in my mind:

This was hard. But would it be the hardest part? Somehow I wasn't so sure.

raschad

I'D DRIVEN TO MY EXTENDED STAY FROM WADEHOUSE ON AUTOPILOT. Got inside, sat on the bed, and hadn't moved since. My mind was running in a loop. The same thoughts cycling through on repeat, each pass scraping a little deeper. *I have a son. He's five. She knew. She knew the whole time. His name is Zhaire. He has my face. She named him after me. She kept him from me. I have a son.*

After what felt like hours of that, I realized I needed to talk to someone before I drove myself crazy.

I needed my sisters.

I opened our "Fab 5" group chat and hit FaceTime without texting first. Tamika answered first, peering over her reading glasses. Red pen in hand. "This better be good, Nova. I have thirty-two essays to grade and if this is you making us listen to another damn beat…"

Jordan popped in next. Satin scarf on, lounging. "It's a Monday. What's going on?"

Then Alyssa, with Micah's voice in the background. "Mommy, who is it?"

"Uncle Nova." She looked at the camera. "You've got ten minutes. Bedtime negotiations start soon and that child does not play fair."

Jada hopped on last, gnawing on a carrot stick. "Everybody's on? Is it serious?"

Four faces. Four women who'd raised me alongside my mother. Who'd cornrowed my hair and dragged me to events, and taught me, by showing me every single day, what it looked like when women held everything without breaking.

Jordan leaned in. "Okay wait. Why you look like that? What happened?"

Tamika set down her pen. "Nova, you alright?"

I swallowed. "No. I'm not."

Alyssa squinted. "Did somebody die?!"

"No." I replied quickly. "No, it's not that."

I looked down and rubbed the back of my neck. "I found out something today. Big. And I… I don't know what to do with it yet." I swallowed and took a deep breath.

"I have a son."

The call exploded. Mouths dropped and eyes widened.

Jordan's eyebrows were damn near in her hairline. "I'm sorry… WHAT?"

Jada tossed her carrot down like it had offended her." Wait, hold up. I *know* you're fucking lying."

Alyssa gasped, then just stared, processing it.

Tamika leaned back "A son? Since when?!"

I took a breath and let it all out. I told them the entire backstory. San Diego, the girl I met. How hard I fell. How she vanished on me without a word. How I found myself in her city years later. WadeHouse. Her brothers. Seeing her again. Feeling everything come back. How I'd met my son in a recording studio and didn't even know it.

Jordan snapped her fingers. "Ohhh wait. *That* girl? I remember you were down bad. Playing *End of the Road* on repeat in the dark."

I shook my head. "Yeah. That girl."

"I remember that," Tamika added. "You were dragging around like somebody died."

"I haven't seen you like that over a girl since then. Not once… until now," Jordan said, squinting at me. "This makes two strikes. Do I need to fly down there and beat a bi—"

"J0rdan" I cut her off, shaking my head. "Nah."

"She kept him from you," Jada said flat. "For *five* years. Yeah, she might need her ass beat for that, I'm sorry."

Jordan shook her head. "That's wild. That's just… that's wild."

The call was quiet. Then Alyssa, who'd been the quietest of all of them, absorbing rather than reacting, chimed in:

"You can't get those years back, Nova" she said. "And sitting in that hotel room listening to Jordan and Jada rant about wanting to fight the girl isn't going to add any new ones. The question isn't what she took. It's what you do now."

Jordan sucked her teeth. "I guess, so." Then she raised her eyebrows with skepticism. "Wait a minute. How do you even know he's yours?"

I looked straight at my camera with conviction. "He's mine. No doubt about it. Something in me just… knew. Like my whole body recognized it before my mind could catch up. And he looks just like me. I mean…*just* like me. Tall for his age. Same dimple. Same eyes. That's my twin right there." I realized suddenly that I was describing him with pride, and we hadn't even been properly introduced yet.

Alyssa pressed her hand to her chest. "Oh my God."

Jada exhaled. "Woooow."

I sighed. "I don't even know what I'm supposed to do now. Where do I even fit in his life? How do I start from nothing?"

"It's not easy." Alyssa answered. "But it is simple. You already know how to love a child. You've been practicing on your nieces and nephews since they were born. Now go do it for yours."

"That's right." Tamika added. "You start showing up now. Be the father you needed. You'll be surprised at how well kids adapt, especially at that age. Yes, you've missed some years, but he's still young. Just be there."

Jada nodded. "And you will be. You always show up. That's who you are, Nova."

Then Alyssa looked straight at the screen, eyes soft. "That girl doesn't know it yet, but she hit the jackpot in the 'baby-daddy' department."

They all laughed and that got a small smile from me.

"Wait. What's his name?" Tamika asked.

I swallowed. "Zhaire. Zhaire Nova Wade."

A beat of silence stretched between us.

"Hold up." Jada whispered. "*Nova?*"

"You are LYING!" Tamika gasped, hand over her mouth.

"She named him *after* you," Jordan said slowly.

"Oh my God." Alyssa's eyes were wet. "Even when she was keeping him from you, she still..."

She didn't finish. The contradiction hung there. A woman who'd left me off the birth certificate but carved my name into my son's identity.

"Send us a picture," Jada said after a moment. "We need to see him."

"I don't have one. I found out a few hours ago."

"Get one. Tomorrow. First thing." Jada demanded.

"And when you officially meet him, tell Little Nova he's got four aunties ready to love him *down*," Jordan added.

"Did you tell Mama?" Tamika asked.

I flinched. "Not yet."

All four of them groaned at the exact same time.

"She gon' want him baptized, fed, and enrolled in Sunday school by yesterday," Alyssa muttered.

"Whew. Good luck with that," Jada laughed.

I laughed too then let out a breath. The ache in my chest hadn't gone away. But it felt lighter. Like I wasn't carrying the whole thing by myself. "I needed this," I said.

"That's what we're for." Tamika said

"We love you." Jada added

"Even when you FaceTime us with trauma on a Monday night," Jordan added. "You still our favorite baby brother."

Alyssa caught my eye with her lawyer face on, "It will all work out, Raschad. If you want to talk through the next steps, the real ones, not the emotional ones, call me."

"I will. Love you guys," I said.

"We love you too!" they said back in unison.

The call ended and I lay back on the bed, thinking. My son was somewhere in this town. Sleeping in a bed I'd never seen. Living a life I'd never touched. He called me *Mr. Raschad* and I'd promised to teach him how to make drum sounds on the keyboard. He'd held me to it like I was someone worth holding to a promise.

He didn't know I was his father. Didn't know the promise already meant more than either one of us understood. But I knew. And tomorrow, I was going to have to figure out what came next. Whether I was ready or not. Everything about my life had just changed.

i need a lawyer

raschad

———

I CALLED MY SISTER ALYSSA AT ONE IN THE MORNING. I'D BEEN IN THAT room for almost two days. Since the day my life rearranged itself. I hadn't slept more than two hours at a stretch. Hadn't eaten anything that registered. I'd stare at the ceiling the way I used to stare at hotel ceilings before games, mapping the cracks, running plays, except the play I was running now was every moment of the last six years, rewound and examined and shredded for clues I'd missed.

The night at my place. She'd been trying to tell me and I'd said *not now*. Because I still wanted her. I said tomorrow and she said okay and I kissed her and I told myself whatever it was could wait.

It couldn't wait. And now the woman who'd stirred up so many feelings in me, who I'd realized I wasn't over, who I foolishly thought I could have a do-over start with, is now a woman I can't think about without fire in my chest.

Alyssa answered on the second ring. I knew she'd be up. I could hear a TV in the background, low volume.

"Hey," she answered. "What are you doing up?"

"I need a lawyer," I said.

She muted the TV "What kind of lawyer?"

"Family. Custody."

"Raschad…"

"She kept my son from me for five years, Alyssa. Five years. His first word. His first steps. First day of school. All of it. Gone."

"I know."

"I'm not even on his birth certificate. My son exists, he's walking and talking and going to school, and my name isn't on a single document that says he's mine."

The silence that followed had a different quality. I heard Alyssa exhale slowly. "Okay. I hear you. And I'm going to help you. But Nova, I need you to slow down."

"I don't want to slow down."

"I know you don't. That's why you need to," she paused. "Before we talk about lawyers and custody and any of that… answer me something. Does Zhaire know yet?"

The question stopped me. "No. He doesn't know."

"So right now, to your son, you're what? Someone who works with his uncles?"

"Yeah. Something like that."

"Okay. So the very first thing, before lawyers, before custody agreements, before any of it, is that child finding out who you are. And that has to happen the right way, Raschad. And *not* in a courtroom. Not because a legal document forced it. *The right way.* Which means you and Simone need to be on the same page about how and when to tell him."

I didn't say anything.

"Have you talked to her?"

"I can't even look at her."

"I understand. But you need to. You two *have* to talk. Not about your feelings… not yet. About Zhaire. About next steps. About the fact that he has a father and he doesn't know it yet and every day that goes by without him knowing is another day of the exact thing you're angry about continuing."

"What am I supposed to say to her?"

"You say: how are we going to tell our son? That's it. One conversation. One topic. You don't have to forgive her to have that conversation. You just have to be in the same room and agree on how a five-year-old boy learns that the man he just met is his daddy. One thing at a time, Nova."

I pressed my hand over my eyes. She was right. "And then what?"

"Then you figure out your situation. Are you staying there? Is this temporary? If not, then where will be your home base. Kids need routine and permanence. Especially a kid who's about to have his whole world rearranged."

"I'm staying."

"You're sure?"

"At least part time. I'm sure. And WadeHouse is here, if that's even still a thing anymore. Either way, he's here. So I'm going to have to be here too in some capacity."

"Then find a place. A real place. Somewhere your son can visit, sleep over, feel at home whenever you are in town."

"And the legal stuff?"

"The legal stuff will come. The birth certificate. Voluntary acknowledgment of paternity. She'll sign it if she's cooperating, and from everything you've told me, she will. That establishes you as his father on paper. Your name. Your rights."

"And custody?"

"Nova." She said it gently, which was how I knew I wasn't going to like what followed. "You're jumping ten steps ahead and you're reacting out of raw emotion right now. You're hurt. You feel betrayed and I get it. Custody agreements, visitation schedules, decision-making authority — all of that framework will come. And I'll help you with every piece of it. But the question right now is whether that framework gets built through healthy cooperation, or through war."

"Meaning?"

"Meaning you and Simone need to try to sit down like two adults who both love this child and agree on a plan. Simple, binding, no battle. But if you come at her off the rip with lawyers and legal threats? You are going to put that woman on the defensive. And a mother who feels threatened? Who thinks you might be trying to take her child? That's a different person than one who's offering you access and giving you her schedule to work with you."

"She doesn't get to feel threatened. She's the one who —"

"I *know* what she did. And if this ever goes to court, that works in your favor. But court is the last resort, not the first one. The first move is a conversation. The second move is a plan. The third move is putting that plan on paper. If you handle this with a *clear* head, you may never need a lawyer other than for simple paperwork. Don't lead with a weapon when the door is still open. Walk through it first. See what's on the other side."

I was quiet, my room hummed around me. "You're right, Alyssa. You're right. I know."

"Now," Alyssa said. Her voice shifted, the lawyer stepped back, my sister forward. "How are *you*, Nova? Not the legalities. You."

"I'm fine."

"You're not fine. You're in a hotel room at nearly two in the morning calling me because you can't sleep. Talk to me for real."

I rubbed my face. "I'm angry."

"At Simone."

"At everything. At her for keeping him from me. At myself for not seeing it sooner. For not trying harder to reach her years ago. At — I don't know. Whatever put me in that building with her and made me think..." I stopped.

"Made you think what?"

The silence stretched. Alyssa waiting patiently for me to answer.

"I was falling for her again, Lyss. That's the part I can't get past. It's

not just the five years I've missed with Zhaire. It's… six years ago, she
gutted me. She disappeared. No explanation. No goodbye. I spent months
calling a woman who wouldn't pick up the phone, lying awake trying to
figure out what I did wrong, and I had to just accept it. Move on. Tell
myself she didn't want me."

"And then you came to Lennox Falls."

"And then I came to Lennox Falls. And she was here. And I felt *everything* again. *Every* single thing I thought I'd buried. And I let myself
think…"

I took a breath. "She was lying to me the entire time. Every conversation, every look, every kiss, she was carrying this secret. She let me
walk right back in without telling me I had a son. So it's two betrayals,
Lyss. The first time she broke my heart as a man. This time she broke it
as a father. It's all one wound."

"It's not, though." Alyssa said quietly. "And you need to separate
them. Because the anger you feel about having your heart broken?
That's about you and Simone. That's personal. That's heartbreak. And
you're entitled to every ounce of it. But the anger about Zhaire? About
the missed years, the secret? That's about your son. That's parental. And
those two things require *different* responses."

I nodded to myself, didn't argue.

"Your relationship heartbreak doesn't belong in the co-parenting
conversation. If you walk into a room with Simone carrying both, the
fury of a man who was left, and the fury of a father who was denied,
she won't be able to see or hear anything except rage. And you need
her to *hear* you, Raschad. You need her functional and clear-headed,
not defensive and afraid. Save the heartbreak for a conversation that's
about you and her. Deal with the parenting stuff from the parenting
part of you. They're different rooms. Don't open both doors at the
same time."

I almost smiled, feeling calmer and more clear-headed. This was
why Alyssa was my go to for the tough conversations. "When did you get
so wise?"

"Somewhere between law school and my life exploding and having
to figure out how to raise my son in the wreckage." She deadpanned.

"Micah's good?" I asked. Needing something that wasn't about me.

"Micah's Micah. He's good. He's resilient. Kids are more resilient
than we give them credit for. Zhaire will be too. Watch."

"I hope so."

"I know so. He's probably got the Carter stubbornness. None of us
have escaped it." She laughed. "Did you get a picture yet? We've all been
waiting."

That reminded me that Julian had texted me yesterday. Not a long message, just Julian being Julian.

JULIAN

I know you're still processing. Take whatever time you need. When you're ready to talk, you know how to find me.

Do you need anything?

Right now? A picture of my son.

He sent a photo two minutes later. No caption. Zhaire mid-laugh, wearing a bowtie that was slightly crooked, his face tilted up at the camera. My face. My jaw. My eyes.

I stared at that photo for an hour. Zoomed in on his hands, long-fingered, too big for his body. My hands. Looked at his dimple. Studied the way he stood, weight on one leg, chin tilted.

I hadn't sent it to my sisters yet. Wasn't ready to share him. The photo felt private. It was the first image of my son that I owned. The first proof that existed on my phone that he was real.

"Yeah," I said to Alyssa. "Julian sent me one."

"Who's Julian?"

"Her brother. Well, one of her brothers. She has three."

"Oh. Send it."

I sent it and waited. The silence on her end lasted long enough that I knew she'd seen it.

"Raschad." Her voice was thick. "He looks *just* like you."

"I know. I told you."

"Mama is going to lose her mind."

"I know. Don't tell her yet."

"I won't. But you better call her soon, because if she finds out from anyone else that she has a grandson she didn't know about, the battle won't be with Simone. It'll be with Valencia Carter, and that's a fight nobody wins."

I laughed. "I love you, Lyss."

"Love you too, Nova. Now stop calling me at two in the morning. Micah wakes up at six-thirty regardless of what time his uncle decides to have a crisis, and I need to be functional."

"You know you were already awake."

She laughed. "First thing tomorrow, call your business manager. Get a financial infrastructure started. Trusts, insurance, all of it. That's not a custody move. That's a father move."

"I will."

"Okay."

"Call your son tomorrow. Well, his mother. Call her."

She hung up. I sat there for a minute, then I opened my laptop, and began searching for realtors in Lennox Falls. Scrolled apartments, condos, rental homes, anything available immediately. Then I texted my business manager:

> Need to meet this week. Setting up a trust and financial protections for my son.

DRE

> Son?? WTF?

> I'll explain when we talk.

Alyssa was right. Tomorrow I was going to find a place to live. Then I was going to have the conversation. I was going to meet my son. Not as "Mr. Raschad", as his father.

what i want to tell my son

raschad

THE NEXT MORNING, I DECIDED TO GO INTO THE STUDIO, HOPING LAYING some beats down would distract me. I'd been posted in Studio B for hours, letting chords loop and layers build without meaning. Just noise filling the space.

The door opened without a knock. I turned and was surprised for a second when I saw them. Julian. Zion. Tre. All three of them. No one said a word.

Julian was holding a drink carrier with four drinks, like this was a casual lunch drop. Zion had an unreadable look in his eyes. Tre had on sunglasses and his hoodie up.

I sat up straight. "You come here to check me?"

Julian's voice was calm. "No. We came to talk."

I scoffed. "About Simone?"

Tre flopped into the side chair next to me and stretched his legs out. "Nah, about the weather. Of course about Simone."

I exhaled. "She send you three to come talk to me?"

Julian gave me a look. "She asked us not to."

"So why are you here?"

Zion looked me dead in my face. "Because she's our sister. And we do what we want."

I braced for it. "Look, I know you're mad. I slept with your sister. I didn't say anything because it was years ago, and she's grown, and that was her business to tell. But you are her brothers. So…I get it."

Julian shook his head. "We're not here for drama."

Zion added, "We're here because... you're family now. You're Zhaire's father. That makes you our family too."

I looked at them carefully, wondering if this was a setup.

Tre grabbed one of the drinks. "And we're here because this whole thing is a damn mess."

I leaned forward, elbows resting on my knees, my voice was low. "She should've told me. Why didn't she tell me?"

"You're right," Julian said with no hesitation. "She should have."

Silence stretched, then Tre let out a long breath. "I ain't even gonna hold you. When she told us, I damn near fell out the chair."

Zion nodded. "We had no clue. Six years, she never once said your name. Not once."

"That's wild to me," I said.

"Wild is one word," Tre muttered. "Triflin' is another."

Zion shot him a look. "Tre, chill. You always gotta be extra. Damn."

"What? I love her to death, but come on now." Tre shrugged.

Julian sat forward. "It was wrong. But understand... this wasn't about you, Raschad. Wasn't some bitter baby mama drama. Simone's got a heart of gold, but she gets too deep in her own head sometimes. Overthinks to the point of paralysis."

Zion nodded. "She's not vindictive or calculating. She was scared, and she let it get out of control. The longer she let fear rule her, the stronger hold it took of her."

Then Julian added, "I understand that none of that changes how you feel. If I had a child somebody had kept from me?" He shook his head. "I'd be fucked up too, no matter the reason."

"I am fucked up," I admitted. "She took that from me, man. I missed everything."

Julian's voice turned even more serious, and I could see he was choosing his words carefully. "I'm going to tell you something we don't talk about much with anyone."

The room shifted and Zion and Tre went still, like they knew what he was about to say.

"Our mother... she died when she was pregnant. She was seven months along at the time."

"Complications," Zion added. "One morning she was fine. By the afternoon she was gone."

I remembered parts of this story from conversations I'd had with Simone years ago. But hearing it from them, I could feel their grief was still as fresh. "I'm sorry," was all I could think to say.

Julian nodded. "When Simone told us she was pregnant, all we could think about was Mama."

"She was terrified. *We* were terrified too, but tried hard not to show her." Tre said quietly. "Every appointment, every cramp, she'd panic."

Julian added, "That's why we never pushed her about who the father was. We were so focused on making sure she had the best doctors. The safest pregnancy and delivery. That she stayed stress-free. Everything else was secondary."

"She barely even slept the last couple months, especially when she got as far along as Mama was when she passed," Tre remembered. "Would call us in the middle of the night in a panic if she felt the slightest discomfort, or if she hadn't felt the baby kick in a while."

"Eventually, we started rotating shifts," Zion continued. "One of us was always with her. Always. We weren't taking any chances."

Tre nodded. "By the time she went into labor, we'd all been on baby-watch-slash-security-detail for months."

I stared at the floor, thinking about Simone, terrified, carrying our child while reliving her mother's death. "I would've been there for her," I said, my voice barely above a whisper. "She was carrying *my* child. Scared she might die. And I was in Europe living my life."

"That's not on you, man," Tre said. "You didn't know."

"*She* knew." The grief in my voice was raw. "She knew and *chose* to do it without me."

Zion leaned forward, quiet for a moment before he spoke. "Simone was twelve when we lost our parents. Only girl in a house full of boys. We were all broken by it, but we were nineteen, seventeen and sixteen. We were young men. We could lean on and guide each other in ways she couldn't access." He paused. "We also had more years with our parents. We did our best to show up for her, and we did. But we weren't her mother. We weren't her father. There's no substitute for that."

"She developed panic attacks that same year," Julian added quietly. "We didn't even know what they were at first."

Zion nodded. "But the thing about Simone is she never wanted us to know how bad it was. That's who she is. She shrinks herself. Tries to take up as little space as possible. Never wants to be a burden. Never wants to add weight to something she thinks is already heavy. Convinces herself she's protecting people when really she's just protecting herself from being too much for someone."

He looked at me directly. "I'm not saying what she did to you was right. It wasn't. But I want you to understand who did it. Not a cold, calculating woman who didn't care about you. A girl who lost everything before she was old enough to handle it."

I felt tears building, but I forced them back. I understood what they were trying to explain. But it didn't erase the hurt. "I get it," I said finally. "And I don't... I don't hate her. But it still hurts like hell."

"We know," Julian said.

"I don't even know what to do with this. With any of it."

"Start by showing up. For Zhaire." Julian said. "You don't have to be perfect. Just be present. That boy is smart. Sensitive. Got a good heart."

Zion nodded. "We've helped raise him so far. But we *never* pretended to be his father. We're his uncles. His father? That's you, man."

I swallowed hard.

Tre patted my shoulder. "We know what it's like to lose time with people you love. We're not tryna see Zhaire lose any more time with you over grown folks' mistakes."

I looked at each of them, men who'd helped raise my son, who could've easily seen me as a threat, but didn't.

"Alright," I said finally. "I hear you."

Tre grinned. "Good. But yo, I'm still tripping on how we didn't see it. Like, we really sat there playing spades with you while your carbon copy was asking us for a juice box."

That pulled a dry laugh out of all of us. For the first time in days, I felt something other than anger and hurt.

After they left, I sat alone in the studio and pulled up my phone and started a list.

What I Want to Tell My Son.

I stared at the blank screen, typed, deleted and typed again.

- *I'm sorry.*
- *You matter to me already.*
- *I should have been there.*
- *I'm not going anywhere.*

I stared at the note for a long moment. Then scrolled to Simone's contact. Part of me wanted to text instead, but this was too important for that. I hit the call button and she answered on the first ring.

"Hello?" Her voice was soft and hoarse like she'd been crying.

"You got a minute?" I kept my tone flat.

She took a shaky breath. "Yes. I do."

"We need to talk about Zhaire."

"Yes. Okay."

"I want to be there when you tell him. We do this together."

"Yes." Her voice cracked. "Yes, I agree. Thank you for —"

"When?" I cut her off sharply.

"Is today okay? After school at my place. I'll prep him first, then you can come by. Around four-thirty?"

"Four-thirty is fine. See you then."

"Raschad, I'm s—"

I hung up. No goodbye, no small talk. I wasn't ready to hear more apologies. Wasn't ready to let her voice try to soften me. That woman had carved out her own space in my heart without asking and I'd been building futures in my head with her in them. I gritted my teeth, swiped a hand down my face. "Man, what the fuck," I muttered.

I still couldn't believe I'd looked her in the face so many times...and she never said a word. That love I had? I knew it was still there. Still humming under my ribs like it didn't just get betrayed. But I couldn't reach for it now. I didn't even want to. But I knew I was going to have to be around her. A lot. Because I wanted to know him. Needed to be there.

I picked up my phone again and looked at that list. Soon, I'd get my chance to be the father I should've been from day one.

daddy

simone

I'D BEEN PACING THE LIVING ROOM, STRAIGHTENING PILLOWS THAT DIDN'T need straightening, wiping down surfaces I'd already cleaned. It had been three days since I'd shattered both our worlds with the truth, and now Raschad and I had to tell Zhaire. Together. The little boy who had no idea his entire universe was about to shift.

When the doorbell rang at exactly four-thirty, my heart slammed against my ribs. I opened the door to find Raschad standing there, hands shoved deep in his pockets. He looked exhausted, tense… and still angry.

"Hey," I said softly.

He nodded once. "He here?"

"In his room. Playing." I stepped aside to let him in. "Raschad, I need you to know how sorry—"

"No." His voice was quiet but firm. "We're not doing that. We're telling him, and then we're figuring out how I can be in his life. That's it."

I swallowed hard, nodding. Zhaire appeared in the hallway then, juice box in hand, one sock half-off his foot. When he saw Raschad, his face lit up.

"Hi Mr. Raschad! You came back! Did you come to teach me drums?" He bounded over, completely oblivious to the weight in the room.

Raschad's entire expression softened, the hardness melting away as he crouched down to Zhaire's eye level. "Hey, little man. I brought you something first." He pulled out a box from the bag he was carrying. "Remember we talked about Starscream? The one that turns into a jet?"

Zhaire's eyes went huge. "NO WAY! Really?!" He threw his arms around Raschad's neck without hesitation. "Thank you, thank you!"

Raschad's eyes fluttered shut for just a second as he wrapped his arms around Zhaire and hugged him back. "You're welcome," he said, voice slightly thick. "Your mom and I want to talk to you about something. Can I sit with you?"

Zhaire's smile faltered slightly. "Am I in trouble?"

"No, baby," I said quickly, settling on the couch and patting the cushion beside me. "Nothing like that. Just something we should have told you before."

He climbed up next to me, automatically curling into my side the way he did when he sensed grown-up energy. Raschad sat on the coffee table across from us, elbows resting on his knees, close enough to touch but careful to give Zhaire space. I could feel the weight in my chest as I brushed Zhaire's twists back from his forehead.

"Zhaire," I started, keeping my voice calm, "you know how some of your friends have a dad, or how some live with their mom and dad?"

He nodded, working the corner of the Starscream box.

"Well…" My throat caught, but I pushed through. "You have a dad too. You've always had one." I tipped my head toward Raschad. "This is your daddy."

Zhaire's head jerked up, eyes darting between us. The box slid onto the cushion beside him, forgotten.

"For real?" He said it like he wasn't sure if he should be excited or nervous.

"For real, little man," Raschad said, then his voice shook. "I'm your dad."

Zhaire blinked a few times, mouth pressing into a little line as if he was working out a problem. He was quiet for a moment.

"Is your name still Mr. Raschad?" he asked without looking up.

Raschad smiled. "Um…My name's Raschad, yeah."

That earned him a quick glance before Zhaire went back to working the Starscream box open. "'Cause I call Uncle Tre '*Uncle Tre*.' And Uncle Julian '*Uncle Julian*.' And Uncle Zion is just '*Uncle Z*.' And Auntie Taryn is *Auntie Taryn*. And Mommy is '*Mommy*'…" He trailed off, frowning like he'd hit a puzzle he couldn't quite finish.

He looked back up at Raschad for a long moment. Raschad tilted his head, a small smile at the corner of his mouth. "What do you want to call me?"

"I don't know." Zhaire shrugged, eyes darting between the two of us. "Noah calls his dad 'Dad.' Kai says 'Daddy.'" He gave the Transformer one last twist. "Do I say Daddy? Or Mr. Raschad?"

"Whatever feels right, Zhaire. No rush."

Zhaire nodded slowly, serious now. "Okay." Then he went right back to making robot-fighting noises.

Suddenly he tilted his head. "Will you live here now? With us?"

Raschad shook his head gently. "Not in this house. But close. I'm looking for a bigger place so we can make a nice room just for you when you hang out with me."

Zhaire's eyebrows shot up. "I get two rooms?"

"That's right."

A smile spread across his face. "Cool!" He hopped down from the couch, then settled on the floor, legs crossed, sipping juice while he put his Transformers through some kind of high-stakes battle.

Raschad slid off the coffee table and eased down to the rug beside Zhaire, long legs folding awkwardly.

"You got room for me in this battle?" he asked.

Zhaire smiled and handed him the half opened Starscream box. "You can be Starscream."

For a few minutes, it was nothing but the clack of plastic and Zhaire's "pow! pow!" sound effects. My heart started to settle just watching them. Raschad, so careful not to crowd him but still leaning in, mirroring his moves like he'd been doing this for years.

Zhaire's concentration was fierce, tongue caught between his teeth. Then, out of nowhere, he glanced up again. "I think... I like Daddy."

His words hit me hard. Raschad blinked, setting his transformer down. "Do you mean... you want to call me Daddy?"

Zhaire nodded, like it was the simplest thing in the world. "Yes."

"I'd like that, Zhaire. I'd like that a lot."

He didn't touch him, didn't scoop him up, just sat there, eyes glassy, letting the moment settle between them while Zhaire went right back to saving the universe.

"So I have a daddy just like Noah and Kai?" he asked, naming his friends from school.

My heart sank. He'd been aware all along that something was missing.

"Yeah. Just like them." Raschad's voice was soft.

"And you know what? You look just like me when I was your age. Same eyes, same smile when you're being silly."

Zhaire studied Raschad's face, then broke into a huge grin. "I do look like you! Mommy always says I have big pretty eyes!" He pressed his arm against Raschad's arm, "And we got the same color too."

Raschad laughed, and I saw him quickly swipe at his eyes. "And you know what else we have that's the same?"

"What?"

"Our middle names. Mine is Nova, and yours is Nova too. My family calls me Nova sometimes."

Zhaire's eyes went wide with delight. "We have the same name?!

That's so cool!" Then, quietly: "Does that mean we get to play together all the time now? And you'll teach me drums like you said?"

"Yep. We're gonna spend lots of time together. I'm gonna teach you drums, and basketball, and anything else you want to learn."

"What's your favorite color?" Zhaire asked suddenly.

"Blue. What's yours?"

"Red! And yellow! And sometimes green!" Zhaire bounced in his seat. "I like chicken nuggets. Do you like chicken nuggets?"

"I do," Raschad answered. "I like to dip mine in honey mustard."

He gasped. "I like honey mustard! Do you like to play games?"

"I love playing games. I play games for a living too, in the NBA."

Zhaire's eyes got big. "Like on TV?"

"Yeah, like on TV."

"Oh yeah, I forgot! Mommy can I go?"

"Go where?" I asked.

"To the TV to see his game?"

I caught Raschad's amused look. "Soon," he answered. "I'll check the schedule and talk to your mom about it."

"Really?"

"Really."

"Wanna see my Lego spaceship?"

"Absolutely."

They headed toward Zhaire's room, hand in hand with Zhaire tugging him along, and for the next few hours, I let them be. I brought them snacks, listened to their laughter echoing from the bedroom and later from the backyard where they kicked a soccer ball around. When it started getting dark, I called them in for dinner.

"Time for your bath, sweet p," I told Zhaire after dinner.

"Can he help me get ready for bed too?" he asked, looking between us with hopeful eyes.

"If he wants to," I said, glancing at Raschad.

"I'd love to," he said softly.

After Zhaire's bath, we both tucked him in, Raschad sitting on one side of the bed while I sat on the other. Zhaire said his nightly prayers, adding at the end: "And thank you, God, for my Mommy and my new Daddy. Amen."

I had to step out of the room for a moment to compose myself. When I came back, Raschad was in the kitchen, staring at his hands.

"We need to talk about logistics," he said, all business.

I nodded, bracing myself.

"I want to be involved. *Really* involved. Not just weekend visits." He leaned against the counter, arms crossed and focused. "I need you to put together some information for me. His school schedule, his activities, routines, medical stuff, teacher's names. Everything."

"Of course," I said quickly. "I can get all of that together."

"I understand that your brothers take him to a lot of things. Games, practices, whatever. I'd like to start doing that whenever I am in town. I want to be the one picking him up from school sometimes, taking him to his activities."

The reasonableness in his tone made it harder for me, because I knew I didn't deserve it. He wasn't trying to hurt me, he was trying to be a father.

"We should figure out a schedule that works," he continued. "Something consistent so he knows when to expect me. I don't want to just pop in and out of his life."

"You're right. That makes sense."

He was quiet for a moment, then: "And I need you to start thinking of me as his father. *Really* thinking of me that way. If he needs clothes, if there's a field trip, if he wants something, if he's sick, I want you to let me know. Don't just handle it yourself. I want to provide for my son too."

"I will," I promised. "I want you to be involved, Raschad. I want him to have you."

He nodded once, then moved toward the door. "I'll call you tomorrow. We can start working out details."

As he reached for the handle, he paused without turning around, and cleared his throat. "Despite it all, I... know you're a good mom. I want to be a good father to him too. I hope we can keep this cordial and not difficult so that I can do that."

And then he was gone, leaving me with words that somehow hurt and healed at the same time. I stood in my kitchen, hands shaking as the intensity of the evening settled over me.

He could have made this so much harder. He had every right to. He could have threatened to sue for custody, drag me through court, make demands, spit venom about what he'd missed. But he didn't. Even angry — and he was definitely still angry — he'd tempered it around Zhaire. Held back even when it was just us.

In a few hours, he'd shown me exactly the kind of man and father he was. Patient. Loving. Reasonable. The way he'd held Zhaire when our son hugged him, the way he'd got down on Zhaire's level, followed his lead, and listened to every word about Transformers like it was the most important conversation in the world.

This should have been Zhaire's life from the beginning. Bedtime prayers that included thanking God for his daddy. His father teaching him things, picking him up from school, showing up to games. Instead, I'd kept them apart because I was too scared to trust that this good man would stay. Even his parting words, asking to keep things cordial, acknowledging I was a good mom… that was grace I didn't deserve. He was thinking about what was best for Zhaire, when he had every reason to think about revenge.

raschad

I SAT IN MY CAR FOR TWENTY MINUTES BEFORE I COULD EVEN TURN THE key. My hands were trembling. Actually shaking, like I was coming down from an adrenaline high.

Daddy.

The way he'd said it. No hesitation. Like he'd been waiting his whole life to have someone to call that. And he had been. Five years of being aware something was missing but never asking about it. Five years of seeing friends with their dads and just accepting that wasn't his reality. I pressed my hands against my eyes, trying to hold it together, but my tears came anyway.

That little boy had hugged me and looked at me with eyes that were mirrors of my own and called me Daddy without an ounce of doubt. Had thanked God for his "new daddy" in his bedtime prayers like I was an answered prayer instead of a stranger who'd missed his life.

How the hell do you process instant love like that? Because that's what it was. The second I saw him light up over that Starscream figure, the second he'd thrown his arms around my neck, the moment he'd decided on my name, I was gone. Completely, utterly, irrevocably in love with that kid.

My son.

My son.

I kept saying it, making sure it was real. Zhaire Nova was my son. A bright, beautiful, perfect little boy who talked a mile a minute about Transformers and built Lego spaceships… he was mine.

I couldn't get back the years I'd lost, but I could make damn sure I didn't lose another day. I picked up my phone and scrolled to my sports agent, Reid's number. Held it there for a long moment. Then I put the phone down. Not tonight. There was too much in my mind to make a decision this size from a parking spot.

But I already knew. The knowing had been building since I walked into that house, since he grabbed my hand and said *come on, Daddy*. I already knew.

I'd make the call tomorrow.

My phone buzzed with a text from my mother:

MA

How did it go?

I'd called her just a day ago, too shattered to hold it in anymore. She'd cried. Then she'd gotten angry. Then she'd started planning, asking when she could meet her grandson, offering to come help however I needed.

I typed back:

He's perfect, Ma. Called me Daddy.

Three dots appeared immediately, then:

MA

Oh Nova. I'm so proud of you. And I can't wait to meet my grandbaby.

Soon. We're gonna figure out a schedule. I'm gonna do this right.

MA

You will. You're going to be an amazing father.

I read her message twice. Then I just sat there in the dark, still not ready to drive yet, and go back to an empty room. I wanted to believe her. But how do you make up for years? And how do you build a relationship with a woman who broke your heart, but who you have to work with for the next thirteen-plus years?

The truth was, I was terrified. Terrified of messing this up. Terrified that Zhaire would figure out I had no idea what I was doing. Terrified that the pain I felt would somehow leak out and hurt him. I didn't know how to be a father yet. But I was going to learn. Show up every day and figure it out, because Zhaire deserved nothing less.

I finally started the car, but before I pulled away, I looked back at the house one more time. My son was in there. Best damn day of my life. And the hardest.

But mostly the best.

15 /

plans change

raschad

I WAS STILL LIVING OUT OF THE EXTENDED STAY, A WEEK LATER. I'D barely left that room other than the four times I'd been with Zhaire. After school pickup twice, dinner at a place called Clucky's that he declared had the best chicken nuggets, an afternoon at the studio where I kept my promise about the drums, and an afternoon at the park where I learned that he had opinions about the right way to go down a slide and was not open to debate about it.

Besides that, I stayed in. Ordered food. Didn't answer most calls. And did a lot of thinking. Not because I had nowhere to go, I had three places — my condo in New York, my condo in LA, and my main home in Jersey. But I stayed in the extended stay in Lennox Falls because leaving was a decision I wasn't ready to make yet. Zhaire was here, and somehow, I understood that the next chapter of my life was going to be mapped out in this room, and I hadn't finished the work.

That was always my first response to hard things. Not action. Stillness. I'd learned it from watching my mother solve problems at the kitchen table with a notepad and the quiet of a woman who'd been through enough to know that moving too fast was how you made things worse. She'd think things all the way through first. *Then* she'd move. And when she moved, she didn't second-guess herself. I was her son. So I sat. And I thought.

The first question I asked myself: *what do I actually want?*

The answer came before I finished asking it. My son.

That was first. That was the whole thing. Everything else was logistics.

I wanted to know him. Not a scheduled version, every other weekend and on FaceTime in between. Not a relationship that existed in the margins of both our lives. I wanted to be there for the ordinary things. School pickups and homework and the kind of nothing that added up to everything over years.

I knew what it looked like when a father didn't do that. I'd made a promise to myself before I was old enough to fully understand promises. I was not going to be him. Not in any version of any plan I made in life.

Zhaire's whole life was in Lennox Falls. Which meant the question of where I was going to live had already been answered. I needed a real place here. Something permanent with space for him to move in, a room that was his, something he could count on being there. Kids needed that, they needed to know the geography of love was stable.

I opened my notes app and started laying it out:

- *Real estate: Lennox Falls and greater area.*
- *Purchase: 4 beds minimum, yard, 3 car garage. Close to Simone so pickups/drop-offs don't feel like travel.*
- *Interim: find a rental home that meets close criteria while I house hunt.*
- *Music production: WadeHouse. Build portfolio.*

I still had Jersey. I wasn't giving that up. My mother was there, my sisters were there, my whole origin was there. Zhaire would know that world too. He'd come with me, meet his cousins, eat my mother's food, understand where his father came from. That mattered. But Jersey wasn't going to be where I lived most of the time anymore. Keep the roots. But I was planting something new down here.

My phone had been buzzing for days. I'd answered maybe a quarter of it. My agent. A couple teammates. My sisters, increasingly less patient each time. I scrolled through what I'd missed, near the bottom, from two days ago, a text from Julian.

JULIAN

I'd like to be useful to you if you're open to it.
Separate from everything else. When you're ready,
let's talk. What you want to build here, long term.
Numbers, structure, next steps. No rush.

I set my phone down and thought about that for a minute. I'd been paying attention to how Julian operated and there was consistency in what I saw. He didn't make things about himself, and he gave advice without making you feel like you'd needed it. We'd had three or four conversations about money and investments since we'd first met. Not the surface-level stuff people say to athletes about diversifying portfolios. Julian talked to me like I was capable of understanding the actual mechanics. How he structured things, what he thought about long-term, the difference between money that sat and money that worked for you, showing me angles I hadn't considered.

I added to my notes:

Sit down with Julian. Properties, investments, business ˙

I thought a lot about my career and what came next for me. What I knew was that I had money and a career and a future I'd built and none of it had given me the one thing I would have traded all of it for without blinking. Years with my son.

I called my agent Reid at nine in the morning. He picked up on the first ring, which meant he'd been waiting.

"Finally," Reid exhaled. "I've been trying to reach you for a week. Got your clearance the other day, team doctors signed off. You're officially good to go."

"Reid. I'm retiring."

He went silent. "Uh…say that again?"

"I'm retiring."

He cleared his throat. "Raschad. You're thirty years old. You just made All-Star. You're cleared to play. Do you understand what you're saying right now?"

"I understand exactly what I'm saying."

"New York still wants you. LA and Chicago have been checking in. They're interested. I can have a contract on your desk by Friday. A good one."

"I know."

"Then walk me through this. Because I'm not following."

"I have a son," I said. "He's five years old. I just found out about him. And I'm not going to spend the next four years on a road schedule seeing him a couple days a month."

Reid went quiet. When he spoke again his voice had shifted. "How many guys in the league have kids, Raschad? How many have families? You can do both. Players do it all the time."

"I know they do. I've watched how that goes. I've had teammates miss first steps on FaceTime. Miss school plays because we were in Denver. Miss birthdays because the schedule said otherwise. And most of them will tell you it's fine, they make it work, the money provides." I paused. "I'm not saying they're wrong for their families. I'm saying that's not what I want for mine."

"You're overcorrecting. You just found out about him and you're emotional right now, which is understandable. But this is a permanent decision made from a temporary feeling."

"It's not temporary."

"Four more years, Raschad. Maybe five. Another All-Star run if you stay healthy. We're talking legacy contract territory here. Forty, sixty million minimum. You understand that number? You have a child now, more than ever you need —"

"I have money," I said. "I have properties. I have investments. Dre's been building the infrastructure for years. My son is not going to want for anything. That's not the issue." I kept my voice even. "The issue is that I have a five-year-old boy who just learned my name last week. And the NBA road schedule is eighty-two games plus playoffs, two hundred days a year on the road. I'm not doing that to him. Not for money I don't need."

Reid was quiet for a long moment. "You've thought about this."

"I've thought about nothing else for a week."

Another pause. "The timing is terrible. Training starts in six weeks. The league is going to —"

"I know the timing. I'm not asking about the timing."

He exhaled. Long and slow. "Broadcasting."

"You've been trying to have that conversation with me for two years. Now we're having it. Find out what's actually available. Commentary, studio, whatever the real landscape looks like. And put it out quietly that I'm available. No press release yet. Just start the conversations."

A long pause. I could hear him moving through it, past the argument and into the work.

"I want it on record that I think this is a mistake," he said finally.

"Noted. Appreciate you, Reid."

"Yeah, yeah." The shift in his voice told me he'd accepted it. "I'll call you Friday."

I CALLED MY MOTHER THAT NIGHT.

"Hi, Nova! How's my baby doing?"

"Hi, Ma. I'm doing alright."

"Well, I meant little Nova, but I'm glad to hear you are doing good too."

I chuckled, "Oh, I've been demoted already, huh? Zhaire is good. I've been spending time with him this week. He is an incredible kid, Ma. Gonna have my hands full with him though, but in a good way."

"Aww, that makes me so happy to hear, Nova. So happy."

I paused. "I called to tell you something."

"Okay. What is it?"

"I'm retiring."

She was quiet for a moment. "Are you sure?"

"Yeah."

"This was your dream, Raschad."

"My dream was to take care of you," I said. "I did that. My dream was to make the NBA. I did that too. I did everything I said I was going to do." I leaned back against the headboard. "Now I have a new dream."

"What's that?"

"Being the father I never had." I said it quietly. "Being there. Not missing anything else."

She took a breath. "You are not him, Nova."

"I know."

"I'm not finished." She continued. "Your father didn't love baseball more than us. He just loved himself, and only himself. Period. I was young and I loved him and I told myself that's just how it was with men like him. So I put up with a lot. Accepted a lot. So I have a hand in putting us in the position we were in. Because of who I chose and what I chose to put up with."

She said it plainly, without self-pity, the way she said everything hard.

"Ma…"

"I'm not looking for you to tell me I'm wrong. I'm just telling you what's true." Her voice was steady. "When he finally stopped coming back altogether, I made a decision. I wasn't going to chase him. Wasn't going to beg him for a dime or a phone call or a visit or an explanation. I picked up and I kept going, cause that's what you do."

"But hear me good, Nova. Your father didn't leave because he played baseball. He left because he didn't care enough to stay. That's the truth of it. No amount of road trips or away games made him who he was. He was already that man before he ever picked up a bat. The baseball just gave him somewhere to go."

I nodded even though she couldn't see me.

Her voice was even. "You could stay in the NBA for ten more years, Raschad. Travel three hundred days a year, gone more than you are home. And even then you *still* would not be him. Because you are not built that way. That is not your character. That has never been your character."

I didn't say anything.

"So I want to make sure, that you are retiring because you want to be present for your son. Not because you are afraid of becoming a man you were *never* in danger of being. Those are two different reasons. And only one of them is the right one."

I really thought about it. "It's the first one," I confirmed. "I want to be there. I want the ordinary stuff. The pickups and the homework and the nothing. I don't want to miss anything I don't have to."

"Then that's the right reason," she said. "And I am proud of you. Always so proud."

"Thanks, Ma. Love you."

"Love you too," she said. "Now bring my grandson to meet me soon, okay?"

"Yes, ma'am."

AFTER I HUNG UP I SAT IN THE QUIET FOR A WHILE, LOOKING AT MY notes. My plans weren't perfect, nothing was ever perfect from the front end. The details always showed up when you were already moving. But it was solid. Something I could build from.

I thought about what I'd told Simone in her office the day I found out. *Plans change.* I'd shouted it like an argument, or a correction. But sitting here now, I let myself sit with the honest version of that.

If she'd told me, I wouldn't have gone to Spain. I knew that about myself without having to think about it. I would have stayed and figured out a different path. Maybe the timeline shifted. Maybe I came to the NBA later, through a different door. Maybe the money looked different for a few years. But, I would have figured it out. That was what she hadn't trusted. Not just that I'd stay, but that I'd adapt. She'd looked at the plan I laid out in Cali and seen rigidity where there was actually just direction.

She didn't understand that my plan was always going to change. Life was always going to require a new version. The only question was whether we made a new one alone or together. She chose alone for the both of us.

But I know I would have done it anyway. Whatever path I'd have taken with a child and a woman and a whole different set of variables, I would have gotten here anyway. Maybe not on the same timeline. Maybe not the same numbers. But I would have found a way to take care of them and still build something solid. That was not a question.

And now, here I was having accomplished what I set out to do by this point in my life. My mother was retired, resting the way she deserved to rest. My sisters were taken care of. Everything I'd promised myself at thirteen… I'd done it.

Simone didn't get to take credit for that. It worked out because *I* worked. Because *I* adapted and refused to quit every time my plan required a new version of itself. That was me. That had nothing to do with her decision to shut me out.

She was still wrong. You don't get to make that call for somebody else and call it love.

I'd planned my whole career year by year. And none of it had prepared me for a five-year-old who FaceTimed me from his tablet at seven-thirty at night, to tell me good night and say his prayers with me and his mother. That wasn't in my plans.

But it was the best curveball I'd ever been thrown.

16 /
bag lady

THIS CHAPTER HAS A SOUNDTRACK

Heartbreak Anniversary by GIVEON | *Cranes in the Sky* by Solange | *A Song For You* Donny Hathaway | *20*

Something by SZA | *Bag Lady* by Erykah Badu

simone

I'D BEEN WATCHING OUT THE WINDOW FOR TWENTY MINUTES. I'D PACKED Zhaire's bag twice. Repacked it because I'd forgotten his nightlight and then stood in the hallway holding it for a full minute trying to remember what I was supposed to do next.

It was going to be Zhaire's first overnight with Raschad. Two nights actually. I'd thought I was ready for it. We'd agreed on it two weeks prior, calmly and practically, the way we'd been agreeing on everything since he'd found out. Raschad had been showing up consistently, Zhaire was calling him Daddy like he'd been doing it his whole life, and an overnight was the natural next step. I'd said yes without hesitating because it was the right thing.

But knowing something is right and being ready for it are not the same thing. I understood that now, staring out the window for the sixth time.

I heard the car door, then heard Zhaire's shout excitedly from his room: "Daddy's here!" Followed by the thunder of small feet down the hall.

I opened the door before Raschad could knock. When he came up the walk, he looked up. Our eyes met for half a second. Then his gaze moved past me to Zhaire, who had materialized at my hip, and his whole face changed. Opened into something warm and loving as he focused on our son.

"Hey, little man."

"Hi!" Zhaire launched off the front step and Raschad caught him and swung him up, as I stood in the doorway holding his overnight bag, watching the two of them like I was on the other side of a window.

"Hi," I said.

He didn't respond. Just set Zhaire down and crouched to retie a lace that had come loose.

I stepped forward and held out the bag. "I packed his dinosaur book and the Starscream, he won't sleep without it now." I managed a small smile and kept my voice even. "His nightlight is in the front pocket. He needs it on or he'll wake up around two." I unzipped the pocket to show him. "His vitamins are in the small bag inside, give them with food in the morning."

"Okay."

"Oh, and he had a runny nose yesterday, probably just the weather, but there's children's Tylenol in there too, the dye-free kind, he doesn't like the cherry."

"Okay."

I stopped. He was watching Zhaire, who was explaining something about a Transformer with great urgency. Raschad was listening to every word. Present and attentive, just not to me. I was the logistics. The handoff point. I could feel the effort of his not-looking directly at me. His jaw flexing, and the careful way he was holding himself together in front of our son.

"He brushed his teeth already," I said, quieter. Running out of things to say. "And he ate, so he shouldn't be hungry but he'll ask for a snack before bed anyway."

"I got it."

I swallowed. "Okay." I held the bag out further. "I think that's everything."

He took the bag. "Zhaire." He straightened. "Say bye to your Mom."

Zhaire turned and crashed into me, arms around my waist, face against my stomach. I held him tighter than I meant to and pressed my lips to the top of his head. "Be good," I said. "I love you, okay?"

"Bye, Mommy," he pulled back and reached for Raschad's hand. "Can we get pancakes tomorrow?"

"We'll see," Raschad said as they turned toward the car.

"Bye," I said.

He opened the back door and buckled Zhaire in. Closed the door, rounded to the driver's side, then paused with his hand on the door. He looked in my direction, but more past me, not at me.

"I'll have him FaceTime you before bedtime." Then he got in the car and pulled away.

I stood in the doorway, watching until they turned the corner. Then I stood there a little longer because I didn't know what to do with my body.

When I finally went inside, I turned off the lights, and sat down on my couch. My house had a somber silence to it then. Zhaire was a kid who generated noise constantly. Singing to himself, asking questions, moving around. And now there was none of that. Just the refrigerator hum and my own breathing.

I sat there for a while without doing anything. Then I picked up my phone. I needed music. The kind that was going to hurt, not comfort music. I needed to wallow in my self-inflicted misery. I found *Heartbreak Anniversary*, pressed play, lay down on the couch and pulled a blanket over myself.

I played it twice, thinking about the way Raschad couldn't look at me when he picked up Zhaire. I thought about the effort that took to train your face that completely. I recognized that effort. I had been doing it too at every exchange. Composed co-parenting on the surface while losing it underneath.

Raschad's version of it was different from mine though. His was a man protecting his son from the sight of his father falling apart. Mine was a woman hiding the fact that she deserved exactly what she was getting.

Nothing about how he was regarding me was unfair. I knew that. He looked through me and I deserved that.

Cranes in the Sky came on. I almost skipped it. Then I didn't. Solange's voice named every way a person tries to run from something internal and kept failing. I had tried all the ways. Tried to work it away. Stay busy enough that there was no space for the truth to find me. Kept moving, kept lying to myself, kept being useful to everyone around me, and called that living. I hadn't been living. I had been running and hiding.

I skipped to the next song before it finished. Then I thought about my mother. She would have known what to say. If she were here she would have sat at the other end of this couch with her feet tucked under her and looked at me for a long moment without speaking and then told me the true thing. But she hadn't been here since I was twelve years old.

I wondered sometimes what would have been different if she'd lived. If I had grown up with my mother instead of with her ghost. If I had watched my father stay instead of leave. If I had learned something different about what love looked like when it got hard. Maybe I would have made the call to Raschad back then. Maybe I would have known, and believed, that being chosen was something I was allowed to have.

I scrolled through my music. Past everything recent, until I found Donny Hathaway. Mama's favorite artist. She had all his albums and played them constantly, singing along to every word of every song. I remember she used to say he sang like a man who had felt everything twice: once when it happened and again when he understood it.

I pulled up *A Song For You* and stopped. I remembered asking her once why this song made her cry every time. I couldn't have been more than ten or eleven. She'd looked at me for a moment, then at my father, and said: *because it's the truest thing anyone ever said about loving someone.*

I pressed play and Donny's voice moved through the room and my tears came before he got to the second verse.

I missed my mother.

I thought about one of the things Raschad had said to me in my office. *I would've made a new plan, Simone.* The thing that undid me, was that I believed him. I had always believed him. I hadn't kept the secret because I didn't trust him to stay. I had kept it because I didn't trust that I was worth staying for. I had been so certain he would eventually arrive at the correct conclusion: that I wasn't worth the disruption, that I wasn't enough to build a new plan around, that I chose to save him the trouble.

I had protected myself from watching him figure out I wasn't enough.

My tears came harder, when *20 Something* came on and somewhere in the middle of it I stopped being quiet about it. The ugly tears. I cried for Zhaire fifteen minutes away in a house that wasn't mine. For Raschad looking at me like a stranger with access to his son. For my mother and the mother-daughter conversations I would never get to have. For the twelve-year-old me who watched my father leave, and developed anxiety, and built walls out of my pain calling it self-preservation.

I cried for the version of Raschad, Zhaire and I that never got to exist. The one where I made the call and said the words. Where he made a new plan and we were a family, building something together.

I would never know what that looked like.

I pressed my face into the cushion as the music moved through the room like a storm, and cried some more.

I don't know how long I was there. The sun had gone down and the room had gotten darker. The music had been on long enough to stop being something I'd chosen.

I heard my front door open and looked up. Taryn stood in the doorway looking over at me across the room. She didn't say anything for a moment. Just stood there taking in the whole picture, and then she tilted her head listening to what was playing.

She flipped on a bunch of lights and I flinched as light flooded the room.

"Taryn?"

She looked at me, taking inventory, then she looked toward the speaker. "Sad music? Alone? In the dark?" She squinted. "What is it with you Wades and the self-pity playlists? Your brother had the same energy before his court date. DMX *Slippin'* at seven in the morning.... Tupac's saddest." She shook her head and sucked her teeth. "At least this is a vibe. A sad vibe, but still a vibe."

She sat down on the coffee table directly in front of me and crossed her arms. "I have been trying to reach you. You're not answering your phone. Wanted to see how the first overnight is going." She looked at me from top to bottom and made a face. "I see, not so well."

"Yeah." I replied.

"How long have you been lying here?"

"I don't know."

She listened for a moment. "How many times has this played?"

"I don't know. I'm fine, Taryn."

"You are aggressively not fine. Get up. Go take a shower."

"Taryn, just let me be."

"Simone. I'm going to say something and I need you to actually listen, okay?" Her face was serious in the way it only got when she'd been rehearsing something.

I nodded.

"You did a wrong thing," she said. "You know that. He knows that. We all know that. That's done." She looked at me intently. "But I've been watching you for these past few weeks, and I need you to know the difference between acknowledging what you did, and deciding you deserve to drown in it."

Tears streamed silently down my face, and I nodded again as she snatched tissues out the box on my table and handed them to me.

"You are punishing yourself like punishment is the same thing as accountability. It's not." She leaned forward. "Accountability is *I did this, I understand why it was wrong, I'm going to do differently.* Punishment is sitting alone in the dark, crying, listening to the same song until it stops meaning anything. That doesn't help you, babe."

My eyes kept filling, as I blew my nose.

"You were not evil. Not calculated. You were *scared.* That's not an excuse. It's a reason." She paused. "You made him pay for a crime your father committed. And you have to live with that. But living *with it* doesn't mean *you* actually stop living."

"I can't look at myself right now, Taryn." I cried.

She moved from the coffee table, sat next to me, wrapped her arms around me, and squeezed. "I know what this feels like."

I looked at her.

"I know what it is to be your own worst enemy and call it self-protection."

"It's not the same thing." I shook my head.

"No. What you did was bigger. I'm not saying it's the same. I'm saying I know the *root* of it. And I know it doesn't grow from a bad person. It grows from a traumatized one." She let go of me. "And traumatized people can heal. Bad people don't usually try."

Taryn pulled out her phone, and tapped a few times, and then held it out to me. It was a playlist on the screen titled "*You Don't Have To Carry This Alone*".

"Zion made this for me," she said. "I was in a spiral. Getting in my own way. All the stuff from my childhood that I kept dragging into rooms it didn't belong in." She nodded at the phone. "He didn't say much. Just sent me this and said *you don't have to carry this alone.*"

I took the phone and looked at the songs.

Be Good to Yourself (BGTY) by Ledisi
Bag Lady by Erykah Badu
I Am Light by India.Arie
Crown by Chika
Golden by Jill Scott
Masterpiece (Mona Lisa) by Jazmine Sullivan

"I haven't needed it in a while," she said. "I'm sending it to you. Swap this out for the woe-is-me concert you have going on in here." She paused. "I added a song to it for you, too."

I scrolled to the bottom, to the last song.

My Life by Mary J. Blige

She stood and went to my kitchen. "I'm making you something to eat. You're going to shower. And then you're going to sit with those songs and remember who you are and what you are worth." She looked back at me from the kitchen. "And tomorrow you're going to get up and be Simone 'muthafuckin' Wade again. Because Zhaire needs his mother in good spirits. And frankly so do I."

I got up and went to my room to get ready to take a shower. I got my phone and opened the playlist she'd shared and pressed play. Then sat on the edge of my bed and listened to Erykah Badu singing about a woman dragging so much baggage behind her she couldn't run to catch her bus. I thought about every bag I had picked up, and refused to put down. My mother's death. My father's leaving. Zhaire's birth. The six years of secrets. The guilt I carried that felt even heavier now than it ever had before.

I had missed so many buses, with my arms full, watching them pull away.

I listened to the rest of the playlist as I showered then lay back down on my bed. By the time Taryn knocked on my bedroom door holding a plate with a look that said *don't even think about saying you're not hungry*, something in me had shifted. I felt a little lighter.

"Thank you," I said. "For the food. For the playlist. For being here for me."

She sat cross-legged at the foot of my bed like we were sixteen again. "That's what I'm here for," she said. "Now eat."

a plan that included—

simone

I'D BEEN STARING AT RASCHAD'S CONTACT FOR TEN MINUTES, THUMB hovering over the keyboard like it might bite me. It had been a month since we told Zhaire. A few weeks of Raschad calling every night at bedtime, FaceTiming through Zhaire's tablet, reading him stories over video chat when he couldn't be there in person. Having to introduce him to Zhaire's teachers, add him to the approved pickup list, and stand there awkwardly while Ms. Peterson tried to hide her surprise that Zhaire's father was suddenly very present and real. Everyone he'd get introduced to, giving surprised looks and what felt like whispered stares.

A few weeks of learning how to share space with someone who felt both familiar and like a stranger.

"Girl, you're gonna wear a hole in that phone screen."

I looked up to find Taryn perched on my kitchen counter, nursing her coffee.

"I don't know the protocol here," I admitted, setting my phone down. "Like, I don't know how to include him in everything else. I don't want to overstep or overwhelm him, but I also don't want to keep him at arm's length."

"What you mean?" Taryn hopped down.

"Like, family stuff. Zhaire asked yesterday if Daddy was coming to Sunday dinner, and I realized I don't even know how to navigate that."

"Girl. Why are you making this harder than it has to be? Invite him."

"But what if it's weird? What if my brothers —"

"Simone." Taryn didn't let me finish. "You can't keep trying to control how this unfolds. Either you're gonna include him or you're not. And if you're not, then what was the point of all this?"

I picked up my phone again, heart racing. "So I just... text him?"

"You just text him."

I typed slowly, deleting and retyping three times:

> Hey. We do Sunday dinner often at my place. Me, my brothers, and Taryn. Sometimes my extended family. Would you like to come this Sunday? 5 PM. This time it is just my brothers, Taryn and I. Zhaire would love it.

I stared at the message for a full minute before hitting send. Three dots appeared immediately. Then disappeared. Then appeared again. Then nothing for what felt like forever. Finally, my phone buzzed:

RASCHAD NOVA

> Ok. I'll be there.

Relief flooded through me so fast I had to sit down.

"Did you do it?" Taryn asked.

"I did. He said yes."

"Of course he did."

I opened the family group chat, typing quickly:

> Heads up, Raschad's coming to Sunday dinner this week

The responses came rapid-fire:

JULIAN

> Good.

ZION

> I'll bring the dominoes and some decent liquor, since all you have is fruity wine.

TRE

> Bet. Can I ask about his NBA groupie stories or is that off limits? Asking for a friend.

"They actually seem excited."

"Why wouldn't they be?" Taryn shrugged. "They already work with him, hang out with him. Zion told me they've been inviting him to some of their gym sessions. They don't let just anybody into their workout routine."

I hadn't realized that. The gym was their thing, their sacred brother time. If they were including Raschad...

"They really are trying," I said softly.

"They love Zhaire, and they can see Raschad's a good man. Plus, having his daddy at family dinner? That's what Zhaire needs."

I stared at my phone. For the first time since this whole thing started, it felt less like I was managing a crisis and more like we were building something.

"I just hope it's not awkward," I mumbled. "Other than five minute drop off and pickup and text messages, Raschad and I haven't been in the same space for a long period of time."

Taryn smirked. "Oh, it's definitely gonna be awkward. But that's what makes it interesting."

THROUGH THE FRONT WINDOW I WATCHED RASCHAD PARK HIS CAR. HE sat there for a full minute before getting out. The moment Zhaire saw Raschad's car in the driveway, he was already running for the door before I could catch him.

"Zhaire! Shoes!" but he was already down the front steps in his socks, launching himself at Raschad's legs before he was all the way out of the car.

"You came!"

"Of course I came." Raschad scooped him up and walked inside.

"He's been watching for your car for an hour," I said as they walked toward the door. "And he saved you the good chair."

"The good chair?"

"Next to his. The one that doesn't wobble."

He looked at me over Zhaire's head and for a second it wasn't careful, or managed. Just the three of us like it was the most natural thing.

Taryn approached first, pulling Raschad into a hug before he'd cleared the doorway. Zion and Tre dapped him up. Julian shook his hand and said *"Family dinner. You're family"* when Raschad thanked us for having him.

Zhaire pulled him to the table before anyone could say anything else. "I made you something!" He ran to the counter and came back with a piece of construction paper with stick figures under a yellow sun. Raschad the tallest, Zhaire smaller with a huge smile, and me in what I think was meant to be a purple dress. All three of us holding hands.

I watched Raschad look at it. He crouched to Zhaire's level and listened to every explanation — which crayon he'd used for the sun, why he'd drawn the tree on the left, how long it had taken him to get the hands right.

"You can put it on your fridge," Zhaire said.

"I definitely will." He cleared his throat.

I stood at his elbow without meaning to. "He's been working on it all day," I said quietly. "Wanted it to be perfect."

Raschad looked at the drawing again. "It is."

We filed into the dining room, and Raschad took in the full spread on the table.

"This looks great," he said.

"Simone doesn't play about Sunday dinner," Tre said, settling into his usual spot. "She's been guilt-tripping us into this for over ten years now."

"It's not guilt-tripping if y'all actually want to be here," I shot back.

"Daddy, you want some juice?" Zhaire asked, already picking up the pitcher. "It's the good kind. Not the kind that tastes like water."

"I'd love some," Raschad said, and I watched him accept the slightly overfilled cup Zhaire handed him without flinching, even though juice was definitely going to spill on his shirt.

"Zhaire," I started, but Raschad caught my eye and shook his head slightly.

Juice sloshed over the rim as Zhaire climbed back into his seat, leaving a small purple stain on Raschad's cream top. He didn't even look down.

"Thank you, Zhaire."

"You're welcome!" Zhaire replied proudly.

"Should we say grace?" Julian asked, and we all joined hands around the table. "Zhaire, you want to do the honors?"

"Yes!" Zhaire squeezed his eyes shut tight. "Dear God, thank you for the food and for Mommy and Daddy and Uncle Julian and Uncle Zion and Uncle Tre and Auntie Taryn and for Daddy being here for dinner. And please don't let Uncle Tre tell embarrassing stories. Amen."

"Amen," we all said, laughing.

Tre protested. "My stories aren't embarrassing. They're educational."

"So Raschad," Tre started, that mischievous glint in his eye, "now that you're officially part of Sunday dinner, you gotta know the rules."

"Oh God," I muttered.

"Rule one: no phones at the table unless someone's bleeding or the house is on fire."

"That's actually reasonable," Raschad said.

"Rule two: if you don't clean your plate, Simone takes it personally and guilt-trips you for a week."

"That's not true."

"It's true. And rule three," Tre continued over my protest, "whatever happens at Sunday dinner stays at Sunday dinner. Including Zion's secret addiction to reality TV."

"I don't have a secret addiction."

"You watched three hours of *Married to Medicine* yesterday," Taryn said without looking up from her plate.

"That was research. Understanding social dynamics."

We all stared at him then laughed.

"Anyway," Zion said, clearing his throat, "the real rule is just show up and eat. Everything else works itself out."

"Daddy, when you get your new house, can we get a dog?"

I looked up. "New house? You don't like where you're at?"

"That's a rental. I got a six month lease, to give me time to find a permanent home to buy."

Taryn set her fork down. "So you're actually moving here. Permanently."

"That's the plan."

"Can we get a dog though?" Zhaire pressed, undeterred.

"Z's been asking for a dog for two years," Zion said.

"And what do you tell him?" Raschad asked me.

"That dogs are a big responsibility," I said. "And that our schedule is already crazy enough."

"Maybe now that there's two of us..." Raschad said carefully, "it might be easier to manage."

"Two of us," I repeated softly.

"If that's something you'd be okay with," he said.

"Yeah," I said.

Zhaire whooped. "So I can get a dog?"

"We'll see," Raschad and I said at the same time, then looked at each other.

"Jinx!" Zhaire shouted.

"This boy," Julian shook his head.

The conversation flowed easier after that. Stories about Zhaire's latest adventures at school, Tre's dating disasters, Julian's new workout obsession. Raschad fit in naturally, asking questions, laughing at the right moments, adding his own stories when prompted.

It wasn't until Taryn started clearing plates that Zhaire asked the question that stopped everyone cold.

"Daddy, do you remember when I was a baby?"

The table went silent. Completely silent.

Raschad's smile faltered for just a second before he recovered. "No, lil man. I... I wasn't around when you were a baby."

"Oh." Zhaire tilted his head, processing. "How come?"

I felt my chest tighten. This was the conversation I'd been dreading.

"Sometimes," Raschad said carefully, "grown-ups make things more complicated than they need to be. Your mom and I... we lost touch for a while."

"Okay. Wanna see my baby book?" Zhaire said, like it was the simplest thing in the world.

Before anyone could respond, he was already scrambling down from his chair and running toward the living room.

Raschad looked confused. "His what?"

"Baby book," I said quietly. "Photo album."

I watched the realization hit him. Pictures of all the moments he'd missed.

Julian stood abruptly. "Zhaire you want dessert now?"

But it was too late. Zhaire came bounding back, thick photo album clutched to his chest.

"Come on, Daddy!" He grabbed Raschad's hand, tugging him toward the couch.

I stayed frozen at the table, watching them settle on the sofa. Taryn's hand found my shoulder, squeezing gently. I could see Julian and Zion exchanging worried looks.

"This is me when I was born," Zhaire said proudly, opening to the first page. "Mommy says I was really loud."

Raschad stared at the photo, swallowed hard and smiled. When he spoke, his voice cracked. "You were beautiful."

"And this is me eating! And this is my first Halloween! I was a pumpkin!"

Page after page of memories Raschad had never seen. I felt tears building behind my eyes as I watched his face, trying to hold it together as Zhaire chattered excitedly about each photo.

"And look! This is when I learned to walk!"

It was a video screenshot still of Zhaire taking his first wobbly steps toward Julian's outstretched arms.

Raschad stared at it, not saying anything.

"Uncle Julian caught me," Zhaire explained.

Zion appeared beside me, touching my arm gently. "You okay?" he whispered.

I nodded, not trusting my voice.

"Do you cry, Daddy?" Zhaire asked innocently.

"Sometimes."

"Good. Uncle Tre says real men cry. But I'm not supposed to tell anyone he cries. Don't tell him I told you that."

Raschad's laugh was shaky but genuine. "Your secret's safe with me."

They continued through the album, Zhaire narrating every milestone with five-year-old enthusiasm, completely unaware of the weight each page carried for the adults watching.

"Mommy!" Zhaire called suddenly. "Tell Daddy about my first haircut!"

I nervously started to stand, but Tre appeared from nowhere, dropping onto the couch next to them.

"Hold up, hold up," Tre said dramatically. "Can we talk about this haircut situation in these pictures? Z, my man, you were looking like a little linebacker with that cut."

Zhaire giggled. "Uncle Tre, that's not nice!"

"I'm just saying, good thing you grew into those ears."

"Uncle Tre!" Zhaire protested, laughing now.

I caught Tre's eye and mouthed "thank you." He winked.

They stayed on that couch for another twenty minutes, Zhaire narrating, Tre providing color commentary that kept things light, closer to a comedy than a memorial of moments lost. By the time Zhaire declared he was done and ran off for his Legos, the energy in the room didn't feel as somber.

We moved to the kitchen for dessert. Julian cut the pie while Zion poured drinks, and at some point the dominoes came out, because they always did.

"So, Raschad, when does preseason start? October, right? You heading back to New York soon?" Tre asked

"I'm not going back," Raschad said matter of factly.

Everyone went quiet.

Julian leaned forward. "What do you mean? I thought you were cleared."

"I am cleared to play." Raschad picked up his water and took a sip. "I'm retiring."

"Retiring? Are you serious?" Tre's voice cracked upward.

"Deadass," he said.

"Bruh, you're thirty. You've got years left. Why would you—"

"Because I have a son, who I'm just getting to know, and who's just getting to know me." Raschad said simply. "I've missed five years already. I'm not tryna miss hundreds of days of his sixth year."

Zhaire looked up from his Legos. "Are you talking about me?"

Raschad looked at him and his face softened. "Yeah, little man. I'm talking about you."

"Cool." Zhaire went back to his Legos not understanding that his father had just walked away from a career, a contract, a life... for him.

But I understood. Everyone in the room did. Julian sat back in his chair and looked at Raschad with an expression of respect.

"That's real," Zion said nodding. "That's real, man." He reached across the table and clasped Raschad's hand.

Tre was still processing. "Man." He shook his head, stood up and gave Raschad a hug. The kind with the hard clap on the back, and grip that says *I see you.* "That's king shit. For real."

Raschad accepted the quiet acknowledgment from a table full of men who understood, in their bones, what his decision meant.

And I just sat there. I sat there with my hands in my lap and my heart disintegrating and a smile on my face that I was holding up with every muscle I had because if I let it slip, the thing behind it was going to pour out of me like water through a broken dam, and I would drown this room in guilty grief.

He gave it up. He gave it up. For Zhaire. Without hesitation. Without resentment. Without anyone asking him to. He just gave it up.

The thing I'd been telling myself since the start. The thing that had become the foundation of every justification, every excuse, every reason I gave Taryn and myself and the universe for why I couldn't tell him, slapped me dead in the face.

"Excuse me," I said. "I need some air."

I walked onto my back deck where the evening was warm and the sky was turning purple and orange at the edges. I made it to the railing before my tears came.

The sliding door opened behind me. I knew Taryn's footsteps. She stood beside me and didn't say anything for a minute. Let me cry.

"He really did that," she said finally.

"He didn't even hesitate." I nodded, wiping my face with the back of my hand uselessly, as more tears replaced the ones I cleared.

"He would have done it back then too," she said. "You know that now."

"I know." My voice was barely there. "Now he's retiring in his prime anyway because of me." I leaned on the railing. "I took years with his son, now I took this from him too."

"Do you hear yourself?" She sighed. "You're doing the thing where you decide that you don't count. That you being a factor in someone's life is automatically at a cost to them. Like the idea that he would choose his son… would have chosen *you*… is something that should make you feel guilty." She touched my arm. "Simone. He's not *losing* something. He knows what he's gaining."

I shook my head. "You don't know that."

"He just said it in front of your whole family and didn't flinch. I think he knows." She looked at me for a long moment. "The question isn't whether you were worth it. You were. The question is when you're going to start believing that."

The screen door opened again and Taryn looked over her shoulder, then back at me and squeezed my arm once, then went back inside, as Raschad stepped onto the deck.

I wiped my face again, faster, as if clearing the evidence would undo the fact that he'd just watched me flee the room because he'd announced he was retiring from the NBA. I stared at the railing, at my yard, at anything that wasn't him.

He stood a few feet away, in the space between the door and where I was, and let the distance be what it was.

"You okay?" he asked.

I laughed a broken laugh that said *no, I am the furthest thing from okay, I am in ruins, but thank you for asking.* "I'm fine."

"You don't look fine."

"Raschad, you just…" My voice broke and I pressed my fingers to my eyes. "You just retired. From the NBA. You had years left. You could go back and play and —"

"And what? Be all over the country months out of the year while my son is here?" He leaned against the deck post with his arms crossed. "That's not a hard decision for me, Simone."

"It IS a hard decision. That's your career. That's everything you've worked for since you were —"

"It's not everything I've worked for." His voice was calm. "Basketball was one plan. It was a good plan. And I executed it. I made the money. I took care of my family. And now I'm working for something else. Now I have a new plan."

"A new plan."

"Music was always the next step. Broadcasting too. I just moved the timeline up." He shrugged like it meant nothing. "I'm going to be fine. I was always going to be fine."

His words landed like rocks being thrown at me, because the implication, the thing underneath the thing he was actually saying, was so clear it might as well have been written on the sky in letters visible from space:

If you had told me six years ago, I would have been fine then too.

He didn't say it. But it was in the air between us.

"You would have left Spain." I whispered.

He looked at me and for the first time in weeks, I saw something that wasn't anger, or hurt. It looked like exhaustion. "Yeah," he said. "I would have."

"But then you wouldn't have been drafted. You wouldn't have played for the Knicks. Your mom, your sisters, all of that."

"I'm not going to stand here and act like I understand your thought process." He cut me off. "Because I don't. I don't understand how you could decide that I was better off not knowing my own child. I would have figured it out, Simone. A new plan that included Zhaire. A plan that included—"

He stopped himself and swallowed whatever word was next. I knew what it was. I could feel the shape of it. He cleared his throat. "I need you to know I'm not doing this for you," he said, as if he were worried I caught what he stopped himself from saying. "I'm doing this for Zhaire."

I nodded. Because what right did I have to want it to be about me too? What right did I have to want anything from this man?

"I know," I said.

"You should go back inside," he said. "Zhaire's going to wonder where you went."

He went back inside and the sliding door closed behind him. I stayed where I was with the evening settling into darkness, thinking about the undeniable evidence of a man who just walked away from everything and called it an easy decision.

I thought about the word he hadn't said. *A plan that included— and* then swallowed it back down. And then: *I'm not doing this for you,* like a wall going up between what could have happened and what was actually true.

He was right to put the wall up. I hadn't earned what was on the other side of it. But I'd heard it anyway and I was going to have to figure out how to carry that. The thing he almost said, the name he almost put in the sentence, alongside everything else I was carrying.

I wiped my face and took a deep breath, then went back inside to my family.

sit in it

simone

THE ISAIAH AND NIECY WADE FOUNDATION ANNUAL GALA WAS THE biggest event WadeHouse put on each year. Julian started it about ten years ago. A fundraiser to pour back into the Lennox Falls area the way Lennox Falls had poured into us.

I took over running the event for the last five years when Julian looked at me across a planning table and said *you're the only one of us organized enough to do this right, Simi,* which was true but also very convenient for him. In the beginning it was a small banquet hall and DJ. Once I took over, it filled the old converted tobacco warehouse with hundreds of guests, a jazz ensemble, silent auctions, and so much Black excellence in one room you felt it in your chest when you walked in. One of the centerpieces of the night had become the bachelor auction. Three years running now. Tre had suggested as a joke in year one and it had quickly become the most talked-about part of the whole gala.

My team and I worked on the logistics for several months. Which meant by the time I was standing in the venue at ten in the morning, overseeing the set up of decorations and tables and silent auction displays, I'd had months to prepare for every variable.

Every variable except one.

Andre, my Marketing and Ops Manager, had come to me two weeks earlier, practically vibrating with pride.

"I got him," he said, grinning. "I told you the bachelor auction was going to take off even more this year."

I hadn't even needed to ask who. He'd seen Raschad around the offices and decided to pitch the bachelor auction to him, without thinking through the implications. To be fair, he didn't really have all the facts. All he knew was that a retired NBA player, slash new WadeHouse producer moved to town, and that meant more donations from eager socialites ready with their checkbooks.

"He agreed, Simone. Do you know what this does for the room? The auction numbers?" Andre asked excitedly.

I looked at him for a long moment. "Does he understand what that segment of the night is? That we parade these men out in front of hundreds of people like a live highlight reel?"

Andre waved it off. "I led with the philanthropy angle. It's straightforward. He knows it's all in good fun. For the foundation."

I took a very slow breath, "Okay. That's… great."

Because what was I going to say? Tell Andre to go and uninvite the father of my child from a charity event because I couldn't handle another reminder of what I'd ruined and could never have? Tell Raschad himself that I'd rather he not participate in something that raised money for my parents' foundation?

No. So here I was, morning of, clipboard in hand, with nervous energy in my stomach that had less to do with pulling off a flawless event and everything to do with surviving a night in the same room as the man I can't stop loving.

The cruel irony of the last two months was that he kept giving me more reasons. Every moment I watched him with Zhaire made getting over him harder. I'd hoped that him being angry with me would do something useful. Dull the feeling, maybe. Redirect it.

It didn't. If anything, watching him choose his son every single day, without hesitation, without resentment, just confirmed what I already knew about who he was. Which made tonight as complicated as I'd feared.

But I'm a professional. It would be fine.

I'D GONE HOME AT FOUR TO GET READY. ENOUGH TIME TO SHOWER, DO my makeup, pin my hair up with a few loose pieces framing my face, and slip into my dress. A floor length, black asymmetric with off-shoulder neckline, cutout with mesh detailing and a high slit. I put it on now, gave myself one look in the mirror, and went back to work.

I was on my way back from checking the auction registration table when I saw Raschad. Midnight blue suit, tie loosened, like he'd made his concession to the dress code and then immediately negotiated his way back out of it. He was talking to someone near the entrance, at ease in his body the way he always was, and the room had already started to orient itself around him the way rooms did when someone like him walked in.

He looked good. That wasn't new.

I was still staring when he turned, and his eyes moved across the space and found me. He didn't move, or look away. This was the first time in two months that he had actually looked *at* me. Not past me, not the quick glance-then-away that had become his default with me. Not the careful not-looking I'd felt every time we were in each other's presence. *At me.* The way he used to.

His expression did something quiet. Not a smile exactly, more like recognition without surprise. He gave me a slight nod. I nodded back.

Then two men materialized at his shoulder, dapping him up, pulling him into that back-slapping shorthand men do. His attention shifted and he turned toward them, laughing at something, and just like that the moment was over.

Forty minutes later and Raschad already had a small orbit forming around him. Men who wanted to talk basketball. Women doing the thing women did when they'd decided; circling, angled in, laughing too deliberately. He was gracious about it, receiving attention with contained courtesy that gave nothing away.

I looked at my phone to check the time.

"Simone." Diane, a committee member who knew everyone's business and filed it accordingly, approached me. "Raschad Carter. So he lives in town now? How long has he been in Lennox Falls?"

"A couple of months."

"Mhm." She glanced across the room at him, then back at me. "And y'all are just… I mean, is there something…" She made a vague gesture that covered everything she wasn't saying directly.

I looked at her. "He's my child's father," I said. Which was true and answered nothing and everything.

"Right, right," she nodded, recalibrating. "Okay so I have to ask. Is he actually single or is that like —"

"I couldn't tell you his personal situation," I cut her off. "Excuse me, I have work to do." I gave her a fake smile, and moved on.

Taryn was at my side before Diane had cleared ten feet. "What did that heffa want?"

"To know if she had a clear path."

"And you said what?"

"I told her I couldn't tell her."

Taryn looked at me for a long moment. "Simone."

"I don't have a claim on him, Taryn."

She took a sip of her champagne and said nothing.

By the time the dinner was done and formal programming had moved into the hands of the MC, I was finally, technically, off duty. I found my seat at a table with Taryn and my cousins Zenobia, Marlowe and Kendra, tossing back a glass of wine. Around me, Lennox Falls'

finest were doing what they did every year at this point in the night…
loosening up. The real event was about to start.

"You okay?" Taryn asked, studying my face.

"I'm good," I said. "Tired. But good."

We turned back toward the stage. The MC was good at his job. He set up each bachelor, starting with Julian, which had become tradition. Julian walked onto the stage in his tux with his signature composed and measured expression. I had told him on more than one occasion that he should smile. He had explained to me, that he was smiling.

"There he is," Taryn said. "Same expression."

"Every year. It's his philanthropist face. He's very committed to it."

The bids opened faster than last year. Word had gotten around. Two businesswomen from the development community started off bidding. Then a woman from Raleigh I recognized from last year, joined in, raising her paddle. And then, from the table Julian had specifically avoided since he arrived, Sabrina West raised her paddle with the calm of someone announcing a foregone conclusion.

"Twelve thousand."

Last year she'd bid ten on him and won.

"Twelve thousand going once…twice… sold."

"She escalated," Taryn whispered in my ear.

Sabrina smiled at the room, satisfied, as Julian stepped off the stage. He glanced toward her table with his neutral face fully deployed and then looked away.

Tre was next, turned it into the production he always turned it into as the DJ dropped a snippet of one of his records. Bids went past last year's final number before the third paddle went up. He grabbed the mic and sang an a cappella snippet of one of his throwback hits *Sex in the Backseat* and a group of women squealed, practically tossing their panties at him. I covered my face. Taryn cackled.

"Tre has absolutely no shame," Zenobia shook her head.

"None," I agreed. "Not a drop."

Khairos went after Tre, his first year in the lineup, after Tre had spent two months convincing him. My cousin walked out looking like mischief, flexing his muscles, working the stage. The paddles flew up in a fast frenzy, and he walked off looking pleased with himself.

"The men in our family are too much," Marlowe laughed.

"For real, something else." Taryn agreed.

"You married into it," Kendra joked.

"No one put that in the vows," Taryn retorted and we all laughed.

The MC paused and I felt the room shift before I understood why.

"Up next" he said, dropping his voice, "a very special addition to this year's lineup. NBA All-Star player, music producer, *and* Lennox Falls' newest and most sought-after resident…"

My hands went still in my lap.

"…Raschad Carter!"

The room came apart. I don't have a better word for it. Raschad walked out in his midnight blue, tie completely off now, first few buttons undone, exposing the start of some of his tattoos.

"Oh," Taryn said, very quietly.

"Don't," I said.

"All I said was 'oh', Simi. I am simply observing that the room is…"

The first paddle went up before the MC had given a starting number. A thousand from a woman near the center who had been quiet all night and was apparently done with that. Fifteen-hundred from another. Then the echoes began.

"Twenty-five hundred…"

"Bid," Taryn elbowed me.

"I'm not bidding."

"Simone!"

"He's not mine to —"

"Four thousand!"

I looked toward a woman in a white dress. Honey-brown skin, hair in perfect waves, a smile that went straight to the stage with the patience that said she had more ceiling than everyone else in the room.

"I will proxy bid for you right now." Taryn turned to face me fully. "I'll use my paddle. Or I can walk to that bid station and have them do it. No one will know it's you. Just say the word."

"Taryn, stop."

"You cannot sit here and let these bitches walk out of here with your baby daddy," she hissed.

"He is not mine to bid on, T. Drop it."

"Seventy-five hundred from the lady in white!"

"He has your child's face. You can absolutely bid on him."

The organized group in the back rallied. Ten thousand, eleven thousand, and the woman in white answered each one with ease.

"Fourteen thousand."

A murmur moved through the room. Real money now, past where most people had budgeted for a charity date. The back table held a brief, visible conference. Paddles stayed down.

"Fourteen thousand going once…"

Taryn and my cousins looked at me. I looked at the table.

You gave up that right. You made a choice and this is what it costs. Sit in it. I told myself.

"We have a winner! Congratulations and thank you to the gorgeous lady in white."

I clapped and smiled. Because I was the event director and the foundation would benefit from it. I clapped and smiled and kept my face exactly where it needed to be, and beside me Taryn stopped clapping before I did and just looked at me, as I kept looking at the stage.

Near the stage, the woman in white moved through the crowd toward him. She reached him, shaking his hand, then going in for a hug. Then she held out her phone. He glanced at it, said something, and she typed.

He didn't look toward my table. He had no reason to.

Then, another woman put her hand on his arm and tilted her head toward the dance floor. He smiled and shook his head once. She accepted it gracefully and moved away. He stood alone for exactly two seconds before another woman approached him. Then two more after that, approaching with the ease of women who knew that a charity auction was one kind of access, and proximity and a phone number was another.

I stopped watching and looked down at my glass. Somewhere between the raised paddles and this moment I'd finished my second or third drink and hadn't noticed. I turned the empty stem in my hand, reminding myself what I'd been saying since the day he walked out of my office, broken and betrayed. *This is the least of what I deserve.*

This was gonna be his life here now. In this town. In Zhaire's town. In *my* town. I hadn't fully thought through what that meant until right then, watching yet another woman laugh at something he'd said and lean into him like it was the most natural thing, with my heart feeling things I had absolutely no right to feel.

"I hear you're the one who pulled this whole thing off. Amazing job." I turned around and Nasir Torres was standing there smiling at me. I'd clocked him earlier at the table Khairos, Raschad and Tre were sitting at, and hadn't thought much past that.

"Thank you." I said.

"You always run it like this? From the back of the room, watching everyone else enjoy themselves?" he asked.

"Someone has to, I guess."

"And you like that. Watching." He said it like an observation, not a question. "You look like the most relaxed and unassuming person in here, and also clearly the most essential. That's a skill."

I smiled. It wasn't a line exactly, it was actually kind of accurate, which was more disarming than a typical line would have been.

Taryn appeared out of nowhere, which meant she'd been watching this from a distance and decided to get closer.

"Nasir Torres," he said, turning to her briefly.

"Oh, I know who you are." She smiled. "Taryn Wade. Her sister-in-law." She gestured at me. "Don't mind me. I'm just standing here."

He looked back at me. "I saw you when I walked in," he said. "Thought about coming over then, but talked myself out of it twice."

"What changed your mind?"

"It's late enough in the night that I'd rather just ask the thing." He held my gaze. "You want to get lunch sometime? Just lunch."

I looked at him. He was confident but not pushy. "I appreciate that," I said. "But… I'm just not really in a place for it right now."

He nodded. "Alright. I'll ask again another time." He said it like a statement of fact then he moved back into the party.

"Simone, why!" Taryn was in my ear. "He is cute and confident. And he didn't pout when you said no. He just —" She made a chef's kiss sound. "Said he'd ask again. Like it was already decided."

"Go be with your husband, Taryn."

"I'm going." But she didn't move. "I'm just saying. When you're ready to stop moping around and get your groove back. That's a man who knows what he wants." She wiggled her eyebrows at me and finally peeled away toward Zion.

THE NIGHT WAS WINDING DOWN AND THE CROWD HAD THINNED. THE JAZZ ensemble was still playing low, and I was doing my last sweep of the room when I heard Raschad behind me.

"Hey."

"Hey," I said.

He gestured around the room. "You… put on a really great event," he said. "What your family does for the community, it's really impressive. Inspiring."

"Thank you." I paused. "And thank you for participating. I know Andre didn't exactly give you the full picture when he asked."

"No. He did not." He gave a halfway smile. "I wasn't sure how it was going to feel. Being here like this." He glanced around, then back at me. "But it was good. It wasn't —" He stopped. "It was fine."

It wasn't fine. Neither of us thought it was fine. But it was the word he landed on and I understood why and I let it be what it was.

"I'm glad," I said.

He looked at me again. "I, uh, didn't get a chance to say it before." He paused. "You look… amazing tonight."

Something happened in me that I was completely unprepared for. It wasn't that no one had complimented me tonight. Many had. But this was different. This was Raschad, standing two feet away from me, looking at me like he was actually *seeing* me, saying something that had nothing to do with Zhaire or logistics or co-parenting arrangements. Just me.

Don't, I told myself. *Do not do this.* But my body had already done it. The warmth moving through me, the involuntary pull toward him, the part of me that wanted to close the space between us and put my arms around his neck. I wanted to say: *I've missed you. Every day. And watching you be this man, this father, this person… it only makes it worse.*

I could say none of that.

"Thank you," I said. "You do too. Navy is a good color on you."

"Thanks. Goodnight, Simone."

"Goodnight."

19 /

growing pains

raschad

I LOVE MY SON. THAT'S THE BEGINNING AND THE END OF EVERYTHING. From the second I realized he was mine, that was it. That was my boy.

Every day since, I've felt like a different man. Nothing else hits the same for me. No contract, no applause, no possible championship, nothing compares to hearing him call me "Daddy."

But damn if it isn't hard.

Half the time, I feel like I'm walking on glass around Simone. Asking permission to do the simplest shit. Can I let him stay up late? Can I take him for ice cream after practice? Can I sign him up for rec league basketball?

Because I should've been there to help build his routines and decide what matters. Instead I'm the guest in my own kid's life.

Simone spent five years being his everything. That kind of habit is hard to break. But every time she corrects me: "*He doesn't like syrup on his pancakes*"; "*He needs nightlights on*"; "*He only likes beef sausage*", I'm reminded that I was almost cut out of my own legacy.

I'm tired of asking how to be a father. Zhaire is mine, just like he is hers. I get he needs routine, but don't I deserve a shot to figure out some of this on my own? To help him try new things? To build my own routines with him? I'm trying not to lose my shit. Trying to focus on the blessing that I even get to be here now. But every time I have to stand back and ask permission, it cuts me all over again.

So I'd been swallowing it and letting the small shit slide. But tonight? Tonight did me in.

I'd brought Zhaire home from practice and he was riding that post-soccer high, talking a million miles a minute about how he and his teammate practiced how to tag to score. All I wanted was to enjoy time with my son. So on the way home, I asked him what he wanted to eat and picked up wings and fries.

When we got to Simone's house, while he was in the bathroom, I decided to lay out his food for him before I said goodnight.

Simone came in with her arms crossed. "He doesn't eat fried food this late. It makes his stomach hurt."

I could feel the pressure building behind my eyes. "It's just wings, Simone."

She sighed. "I know, but he has his routine."

I gripped the back of a kitchen stool, trying to stay calm. "Simone, I'm his dad. I think I can decide if the kid can have wings one damn time."

Her voice sharpened. "I'm not trying to argue, but this is what I mean, you just jump in, you don't consider how I've managed things."

I lost it. "Managed things?" I barked. "You mean how you kept him from me for five damn years? Yeah, I guess you're a pro at managing things, Simone."

Her face crumpled, "That's not fair."

I stepped closer. "What about any of this is fair? You get to make every choice for him, then what? Hand me a script so I don't fuck it up? I'm his *father*. I shouldn't have to run my decisions by you every damn second!"

"I'm trying to help you understand —"

"Understand what? That you don't trust me with him? That after years of doing this without me, you can't stand the thought of letting me figure some shit out on my own?"

"That's not what I'm saying."

"It's exactly what you're saying. Every pickup, every meal, every bedtime, you've got some note, some rule, some way I'm doing it wrong. I'm not your goddamn babysitter, Simone."

Zhaire poked his head out from the hallway, his eyes wide and worried. "Daddy?"

My heart dropped. I took a breath, trying to get it together, but I couldn't. I took the wings and tossed them in the trash.

"Daddy's gotta go home now, Z. FaceTime me tonight before bed, okay?"

"Okay," he replied, voice small.

I gave him a hug, then looked past Simone. "I'm out," I said flatly. "I'll text you later to set up my days for next month."

She started to say something, but I couldn't hear it. I slammed the door on the way out, breathing hard like I'd just run a marathon, wondering how something so small as a plate of wings could hurt this damn bad.

simone

ZHAIRE HAD GONE TO BED WITHOUT EATING ANYTHING, REFUSING THE leftovers I heated up for him, looking disappointed like it was his fault somehow. That gutted me.

I tried to clean up the kitchen, put away the plates we never used, but my hands wouldn't stop shaking. Julian showed up maybe forty minutes later because he'd left his portable charger here and texted that he was stopping by to get it on his way home. He lived five minutes up the block from me.

He came in, took one look at my face, and knew something was wrong.

"What happened? Are you okay?"

I shook my head, "Define okay."

He raised an eyebrow, then poured himself a glass of water and waited me out. Julian was like that, quiet and unmovable.

Finally I broke. "I don't know what to do. It feels like every time we get close to figuring this out, it just blows up. Like I can't win."

I ran it down for him, the wings, the routine, Raschad snapping, the things he'd said. Julian just listened, not interrupting.

When I finished, he set his glass down. "You know he's not wrong, right?"

I blinked. "What?"

"He's not wrong, Simi." Julian repeated. "You've been Zhaire's everything for five years. That's beautiful. But that boy's got his father now, and you have to let that man be a father in the way that works for him."

"I'm trying. I really am, Jules. But... what if he does it wrong? What if he gets hurt because I didn't explain something properly? I mean —"

"Stop. You know Raschad. You know what kind of man he is. We can all see it. You know he would die for that kid as quick as any of us would."

I swallowed. "I know."

"Then *trust* him," Julian said. "Trust him the way you'd want him to trust you. You two aren't going to figure this out overnight. But you can't treat him like a guest in Zhaire's life."

I closed my eyes, feeling every single word sink in. "How?" I whispered. "Honestly half the time I don't even realize I'm doing it. I don't realize I'm doing anything that pushes his buttons."

Julian smiled at me. "Do you know why I knew you'd be an exceptional VP of Operations?"

"Why?"

"Because you're organized. Meticulous. A perfectionist. You see the whole picture and every detail inside it and think through it twice. You anticipate problems before they happen and you fix them before anyone else can be impacted."

He paused. "You are exceptional at what you do, Simone. But sometimes, those same qualities in other areas of your life can make you an over-thinker. And to be honest? A bit controlling."

I opened my mouth, ready to defend myself, but I had nothing.

"I'm not finished." He held up a hand. "You know I love you. We all love you to death. And as your brothers, we've always let you get away with being bossy because you're our baby sister. We were never going to push back on you for it." He leaned forward. "But Raschad is not your brother. He's Zhaire's father. And whatever this is between you two? It's going to require compromise. Flexibility. And it requires you to let him be the man that he *is*. Not a version of him that fits inside your system."

I looked at the table and nodded.

"And you know me. If I thought for one second he wasn't worthy of it. That he was the kind of man who needs to be managed or watched or corrected, I would be the first one laying down laws. You wouldn't even have to do it. But he is not that man, Simone."

Julian's voice went quieter. "Boys need things from their fathers that they can't get from their mothers. Before he came, we were that for Zhaire. Now his actual father is here. You have to give him room to be that. Even when it doesn't look exactly the way you'd do it."

I pressed my lips together and nodded again.

"You're a good mom, Simi," he pulled me into a hug. "Let him be a good dad."

Then he left. Without his charger.

WHEN RASCHAD CALLED TWO DAYS LATER ASKING IF HE COULD KEEP Zhaire for an entire week since his school was closed additional days around the Labor Day weekend, I felt my heart race with the familiar panic, when things I hadn't planned for catch me off guard.

Julian's words played in my head, so I pushed it down, and heard myself say, "That sounds good. He'd love it."

The surprise in Raschad's voice was clear. "You sure?"

"Yes. Of course. It'll be good for you both."

Tuesday he came to pick up Zhaire, I got up early, heart pounding, and packed Zhaire's suitcase without fussing. No bullet-point schedule. No sticky notes. No reminders about what Zhaire eats or what bedtime should look like. Just clothes, a toothbrush, pajamas.

Raschad pulled up around ten, the rumble of that engine sending the usual weird rush through my body. Zhaire jumped up and ran to the door, swinging it open.

"Ready for our boys-only week, lil man?" he asked.

"Yeah!"

Raschad looked over at me, probably waiting for my usual barrage of instructions.

"He's all set." I said handing him his suitcase. "Just... text me if you want to. You don't have to."

His eyebrows shot up, surprised. "You okay?"

I nodded. "Yeah, I'm fine. He's with his dad. I know he's good."

His face softened. "Alright," he said quietly. "I'll update you during the week, and Zhaire will FaceTime at night before bed."

"See you Saturday? His game."

"I'll be there," I said.

I stood in the doorway and watched Raschad carry that Spider-Man suitcase down the walk and I thought: Julian was right. Zhaire needs this. And maybe so did I.

raschad

IT WAS DAY FOUR OF THE WEEK I HAD ZHAIRE. SATURDAY MORNING, AND Zhaire climbed into my bed at six AM, lying there quietly for exactly two minutes before he started narrating everything he was going to do on the soccer field that day.

We pulled into Lennox Falls Community Park and I found the Wade family section by sound before I found it by sight.

The air was cool for a Fall morning. Zhaire gave me a hug and ran on to the field to join his teammates. I went to the family section, already loud and impossible to miss, and worked my way toward it. Aunt Lorraine, Simone's father's sister, who I'd met the week prior, was in her fold-out chair in a rhinestone shirt that said *Zhaire's Grandauntie* across the front, next to her cousin Khaz, along with a couple of cousins who's names I was still learning. Taryn was two chairs in, already leaning forward with her elbows on her knees like this was the World Cup. Simone was on the end.

She looked up when I got close, and there was that beat of adjustment, the air between us doing what it did, the managed politeness that had replaced whatever we used to be. She moved her bag off the empty chair beside her and I sat down. We didn't say much. Zhaire was on the field ready for the game to start, so we both stared at the field.

That was where we were. Over four months in and we weren't exactly enemies. But we weren't exactly fine either. Just two people who were prioritizing Zhaire above everything else. It was working for the most part, but I wasn't going to pretend it wasn't hard.

"He was up at six," I said, nodding towards Zhaire.

"He actually FaceTimed me at five-fifty, to remind me he has a game today," she smiled. "I told him not to wake you up."

I laughed, shaking my head. "He waited until exactly 6:02."

"THAT'S MY BABY! RUN, ZHAIRE, RUN!" Simone jumped up suddenly screaming.

"THAT'S TRAVELING!" Aunt Lorraine shouted from her chair.

"Mama, that's basketball," Khaz said patiently.

"Same rules apply!"

"They really don't."

"DEFENSE, ZHAIRE!" Taryn yelled.

I sat there, trying not to laugh. Zion was on the field with Julian and Tre, all three in matching *Wade Athletics Youth League* shirts. Julian was pacing the sideline with a clipboard. Zion was out there with him, crouched down next to a kid showing him something about his stance. Tre was on the opposite end of the field, just vibing with kids.

"This is nice," I said quietly.

"What is?"

"All of this. Family, showing up for little league soccer game. It's nice."

Zhaire had gotten the ball at midfield, hesitated for exactly one second while he clocked the defenders, and then cut left, cut back right, and was through the gap before the other team had caught up with what happened.

He scored. Arms up, jumping, the whole celebration. Then he turned to find the stands. He found me, and his face broke open into huge grin. I was already standing holding up both hands, pointing at him. He pointed right back at me.

"Awww," Simone and Taryn cooed at the same time.

"TOUCHDOWN!" Aunt Lorraine shouted.

"Auntie, that's not it." Simone laughed.

I was still watching Zhaire celebrate his goal with his team, when Julian materialized at the sideline in front of me.

"Carter." He nodded at me. "You played professional basketball."

"Yes."

"You know what a defensive scheme looks like."

"I do."

He held out a second clipboard he'd been holding and a rolled up t-shirt, handing them both to me.

"What are you doing sitting over here? These kids are running no structure on the left side and it's driving me insane," he said. "You want to help fix it or do you want to keep sitting in that chair?"

I took the shirt and unrolled it to see *Wade Athletics Youth League* printed on the back. I looked at the field, where Zhaire had circled back toward the center line and was now looking at me again. I took the clipboard, tugged the shirt over mine, got up, and stepped onto the field. I heard Aunt Lorraine say something satisfied that I didn't fully catch.

Tre came jogging over from the other end, grinning. "Knew he was gonna do that." He jerked his head toward Julian. "He's been waiting."

"Why didn't he just ask me?"

Tre shrugged. "That's not how Jules does it."

"Daddy!" Zhaire had broken formation and was running toward me at full speed.

"Zhaire, we're mid —" Zion started.

But Zhaire was already there, arms around my waist. I put my hand on the back of his head, and the field kept going around us, kids running, whistles blowing, Aunt Lorraine shouting something about traveling that still didn't apply to soccer, the whole enormous warm chaos of his world, and for a moment I just stood in it.

"You good?" Zion said, coming up beside me, quiet.

"Yeah. I'm good."

"Good." He clapped me on the shoulder. "Because Julian's trying to explain a 4-3-3 formation to five and six-year-olds and he needs someone to tell him that's not going to work."

"I got it."

He was already heading back toward his side. "Glad you're here."

AFTER THE LAST WHISTLE, ZHAIRE GRABBED MY HAND AND STARTED pulling me toward where the family was gathering, snacks materializing from bags.

"Are you gonna coach the next game?" Zhaire asked me.

"Every game," I said.

He nodded like that was the correct answer, then moved on, already telling a cousin how he made a goal as though they hadn't been watching it in real time. In the middle of his village, completely at ease like a kid who had never once had to wonder whether the people who loved him would show up.

I stood at the edge of it and watched him work the crowd and thought: whatever I still had to work through, this was what I was here for. This was the thing that didn't have a complicated answer.

"So, how's your boys week been so far?" Simone was suddenly standing next to me.

I kept staring at where Zhaire was. Not because I was really watching him. But because looking at her directly was still something I was rationing. I'd figured out early that it cost me something every time I did it. Something I wasn't ready to keep spending.

It wasn't just anger anymore. It was simpler and harder than that. She looked like herself. She looked like the woman I'd spent six years trying to forget and clearly hadn't. And every time I let myself really look, I felt it all over again. Had to start that work over again. So I didn't look.

"Good. Real good. We stayed busy. Park, movies, mini golf. He cheated at mini golf."

She laughed.

I kept my eyes on Zhaire. "Kept kicking his ball when he thought I wasn't looking."

"Sounds about right." She was still smiling. I could hear it in her voice.

"Then we got ice cream and he asked for candy on top of it. I told him 'no', too many sweets would give him a tummy ache. He looked at me completely serious and said, '*Daddy, candy goes in your mouth, not your tummy.*'"

She laughed again and this time I made the mistake of looking. She was turned slightly toward me, one hand pressed to her mouth trying to hold it in, eyes bright. And for a moment she wasn't the woman I was angry at, or the person I was carefully managing my proximity to. She was just Simone.

I looked away and cleared something in my throat. "I had nothing to say back." I said, shaking my head.

"He's something else," she said, catching her breath.

"Yeah." I said it quieter. "He really is."

We were both quiet for a moment, watching Zhaire. Two people watching the same kid and feeling the same thing about him. I didn't know what to call it. Whatever it was, it was the closest thing to easy we'd had since before all of this happened.

"I'll drop him off Tuesday. Since Monday's a holiday."

"Tuesday's fine," she said.

I nodded and should've left it there. I looked at her again anyway. And there was that same pull. The one that didn't care about betrayal or anger or what actually made sense. The one I'd been trying to starve out, but kept showing up anyway.

I stepped back, putting space where it needed to be.

"Alright," I said. "See you then."

when is my son's birthday?

simone

THE BASS WAS STILL THUMPING THROUGH THE WALLS WHEN I STEPPED into Studio B, looking for Raschad. He was at the board with Tre and a sound engineer, all of them nodding to a beat, lost in the music. I hated interrupting him here, but Zhaire's birthday was next month, and I couldn't keep putting this conversation off.

When the track ended, Tre noticed me first, raising a brow. "Yo, Simi. You good?"

I nodded, but my stomach was already knotting up. "Can I talk to him for a sec?"

Tre looked back at Raschad, who had gone still the moment he saw me. These days, my showing up like this usually meant something needed to be discussed.

He stood up, pulling off his headphones. "What's up?" he asked guardedly.

"I wanted to talk about Zhaire's birthday," I started. "It's next month, and I figured... maybe you'd want to help plan something?"

His expression didn't shift. "He's turning six."

I nodded. "Yeah. I was thinking something simple. A few friends, family, cake, maybe a bounce house..."

"When's his birthday?"

His question was so quiet I almost missed it. But something in his tone made me freeze.

"What?"

He looked at the floor instead of at me. "What day is my son's birth-day, Simone?"

Everyone in the room went still and my heart started to race. "N-November twenty-second," I whispered

He just stood there. Silent. "November twenty-second," he repeated finally. His eyes got glassy, and he blinked hard. "Five birthdays. And I didn't even know the date."

My face crumpled. "I'm sorry. I —"

He held up his hand, cutting me off. "Don't. Don't apologize. I can't hear that shit."

I swallowed, lips trembling, as he looked away, staring at the sound-board, the walls, anywhere but at me.

"I'll think about it," he managed. "Planning something with you. You'd know better than me anyway. I'll hit you up."

And before I could say another word, he walked out of the studio, the door closing too softly behind him for how loud everything else felt.

———

THE NEXT DAY, I HEARD ZHAIRE'S EASY LAUGH FLOATING UP MY WALKWAY, with Raschad behind him, to drop him off.

They reached the porch, and I opened the door, giving my son a wide smile. "Hey, sweet potato!"

"Mommy!" He gave me a hug, squeezing me tight.

Raschad hung back, one foot still on the bottom step, eyes guarded.

"Thanks for keeping him. This project has been a lot. Meetings after meetings." I said trying to catch his eyes.

"Yeah," he nodded, eyes drifting toward the street. "No problem."

Zhaire darted inside, already talking a mile a minute about some video game Raschad had bought him. The second he disappeared, Raschad shifted and rubbed the back of his neck.

"I was thinking," he started, tone flat, "since his birthday is the week of Thanksgiving... I might want to take him out to New Jersey. Let him meet my family. Celebrate out there."

My stomach dropped. "New Jersey?"

"Yeah," he didn't soften it. "Jersey."

I hesitated. "But... the holidays, I mean... I've never spent them without him. Ever."

He looked at me with fire in his eyes. "Oh, really? You never missed a Thanksgiving?"

I flinched.

He let out a cold laugh. "That must be nice."

I swallowed, trying to keep my voice from breaking. "It's not that I don't want him to go, Raschad. It's just..."

"Just what?" he snapped. "You don't trust me with him?"

I shook my head, tears stinging. "No, it's not that. I trust you. I do. I just... I've never been without him during the holidays. Or his birthday. It feels…"

He cut me off, voice sharp enough to slice. "Yeah, well, I've done it for years. Maybe it's your turn."

His words landed hard enough to knock the breath out of me. He saw it, and then something shifted in his face. He took a deep breath in and out.

"I'm sorry," he exhaled again, dragging a hand over his face, then sighed. "Look… come too. Really. If you want. I'm sure he'd be happier with both of us there."

I hesitated. "Your family… I mean…"

"They're good people, Simone." he cut in. "They'll be fine. And I'll talk to them. All they want is to meet their nephew and grandson."

I nodded, biting my lip, trying to hold back everything in me. "Okay. I'll think about it."

He leveled his eyes at me, no escape. "Simone. Whether you come or not, I *want* Zhaire with me. You *gotta* give me that. Let me show him where I came from. Meet my people. *His* people. Let me show him that part of me."

He leaned in, his voice a quiet plea and looked me dead in my eyes. "Don't deny me that too."

I just nodded, my heart pounding, wondering how in the hell I was going to survive it.

Two days later, I dropped Zhaire off with Raschad for his weekend, then headed straight to Zion and Taryn's place. Julian and Tre were there too, half-watching a game and half-listening to whatever I was about to dump on them.

Zion muted the TV. "What's up, Simi? You look tore up."

I sat down hard. "Raschad wants to take Zhaire to New Jersey for Thanksgiving. For his birthday."

They all went quiet. Taryn whistled low.

I rubbed my temples. "He wants to introduce him to his family, show him where he lives, where he grew up. Celebrate both occasions." I paused. "And he invited me to come too. I guess, to make it easier… on me. Y'all, I can't even think straight about it."

Zion spoke first. "You trust him with Zhaire, right?"

"Of course," I shot back. "It's not that."

"Then what?" Tre asked.

I sighed. "It's me. I've never been away from him on his birthday. Or

Thanksgiving. Or any holidays. But the thought of going with them? Being in New Jersey with his people? It feels... I don't know. Like I'd be on trial."

Julian leaned forward, elbows on his knees. "Nobody will be putting you on trial, Simi."

I laughed. "Julian, come on. Those are his sisters. *Four* of them. And his mother. You know they're gonna have a million questions, and every single one of them is going to look at me like I'm the woman who ruined their brother's life."

Taryn shook her head. "Girl, listen. They probably will have questions, but who cares? If Raschad invited you, then he's telling them to chill. Plus…" she paused dramatically, "I will be there with you."

I squinted. "You?"

"Oh, absolutely," Taryn grinned. "That man got four sisters? I am not about to let you get jumped by a bunch of women in their own damn house. We will hit a swap meet as soon as we land. Get a taser. You know they won't let me fly with mine."

Zion side-eyed her. "You and that damn taser."

Taryn rolled her eyes and the room cracked up, my tension breaking for a second.

Julian leaned back, serious again. "Simi, I understand. I do. But Zhaire deserves to know that side of his family too. And you being there will help him feel comfortable in a new environment. It'll help you too."

I pressed my lips together nervously. "I don't know if I can handle it. I don't know if I can look them in the eyes."

Zion reached over and squeezed my hand. "You don't have to face the music all alone. We got you. Always. And if you want, hell, we can rent a house out there too, make it a whole Thanksgiving family vacation. Let Zhaire see everybody on both sides loving him at once."

Tre nodded. "We can roll deep, Simone. Just say the word."

"Okay. Let's do it." I said.

"I just hope they can cook," he muttered, "because we're gonna be missing Aunt Lorraine's spread for this."

We all laughed in agreement and I left there grateful down to my bones that no matter how messy I'd been, these people still had my back.

Later, I called Raschad. He answered on the second ring.

"Hi."

"Hey," I said. "Um, I wanted to let you know... we're coming. To New Jersey. For Zhaire's birthday and Thanksgiving. If that's okay?"

Silence stretched on the line. "We?"

I took a breath. "Me. My brothers. And Taryn. I talked to them about it, and they all want to be there for Zhaire, to celebrate. If that works for you."

He didn't answer right away. When he spoke, his voice was softer than I'd heard it in weeks. "Yeah. Yeah, that's... that's really good, Simone. He needs his whole family there."

"You sure it won't be too much? Too many people?"

"Nah," he said, and I could hear the relief in his voice. "I have plenty of room at my spot. My family's loud anyway. You'll all fit right in."

"I'll start looking at flights," I said finally.

"Already on it. I'll text you the details once I get everything booked."

"Raschad?"

"Yeah?"

"Thank you. For inviting me."

"Thank you," he said quietly, "for saying yes."

is that me?

simone

—

Essex Heights hit my senses all at once. Mature oak trees lining every street, colonial houses with wraparound porches, and a North Jersey mix of suburban charm with city proximity. Even in late November, the Garden State lived up to its name with its natural landscaping.

Zhaire pressed his face to the window as our car service wound through tree-lined streets. "Mommy, is this where Daddy lives!"

I smiled. "Yes, we're close. Pretty cool, huh?"

Taryn sat beside me, scrolling her phone. She'd insisted on coming a day early to help me prep for tomorrow's lunch when I'd meet Raschad's family. My brothers had already headed to Julian's condo in New York, twenty minutes across the bridge. They'd come in for Zhaire's birthday party and Thanksgiving, but tonight was just us.

"OK, Simi, game face on," Taryn said, not looking up from her phone. "We're in Raschad Carter territory now."

The driver turned onto a street where the houses got bigger and more spread out. When we pulled into Raschad's driveway, my stomach flipped. This was real. Raschad's house was gorgeous. A sprawling colonial mansion, three-car garage with stone accents and big windows. Professional landscaping. Off to the side down a hill, I could see a basketball court in the yard.

Raschad stepped out of the house before we knocked, grabbing bags. "Go on in," he said, nodding toward the door.

Zhaire darted straight past us, running into the front room. "Daddy! This is so cool!"

Inside felt like a real home: hardwood floors, family photos, a few trophies and plaques on built-in shelves, but also lived-in touches, throw blankets, books, a guitar leaning against the wall.

Taryn stepped in behind me, looking around appreciatively. "OK, Raschad! I see you out here."

"Thanks," he replied.

I swallowed, taking it all in. Everything he'd built, everything I'd never seen.

Raschad caught my eye, smiling. "Wanna see Z's room?"

I nodded, my heart pounding. He led us upstairs, pushed open a door, and I lost it. Optimus Prime comforter. Bumblebee curtains. Giant Transformers posters. A desk with art supplies already set out. A bookshelf with picture books arranged by height.

Zhaire gasped, hands flying to his cheeks. "This is MY room?!"

"Yeah, man. All yours."

He turned to me, softer than I'd seen him in weeks. "I wanted him to feel at home."

I couldn't speak, just kept nodding.

Zhaire jumped on the bed like he was on a trampoline, beaming. "Mommy! Daddy! Can you both tuck me in tonight?"

"Of course," I managed.

LATER, HIS HOUSE FELT CALM AFTER A WHIRLWIND OF LUGGAGE, DINNER that he'd prepared, and Zhaire exploring every inch of every room in the house. Raschad had retreated to his back patio with a drink. Tomorrow, his sisters and mother would come over for an early dinner, and my official introduction before Zhaire's birthday party the next day.

I was putting my clothes away in one of the guest rooms when Taryn appeared in the doorway, bonnet on.

"Girl." she flopped dramatically across the foot of the bed. "Now I see why you be crying in the dark… in the shower… in the car… at the Piggly Wiggly. This man is a *catch*, Simone."

I tried to smile, half-laughing. "Taryn, please."

She held up a finger, dead serious. "No, listen. Did you see him? Fine, soft with his son, making sure you got a place to stay, baby's room all decked out. *And* he cooked for us? *Chile.*"

I groaned. "You are not helping."

"Listen, one the sexiest things to see is a Black man loving on his kid. You are literally sitting here watching everything you want unfold, but out of reach. That's a hard pill, sis, I know it is. *BUT…*"

She tapped my knee, voice turning fierce. "You are not gonna fumble this twice. You. Are. Getting. Your. Family. Back. Period."

I swallowed, heart cracking all over again. "It's already fumbled, Taryn. He's not a man who forgives like that. There won't be a second chance to fumble."

Taryn made an '*are you serious*' face at me. "Simone. That man put you in a guest room in his house."

I blinked. "Okay?"

"He could've told you to stay at a hotel. He didn't have to do any of this." She gestured at the room, the house, the whole night. "He cooked. He set up a room for you. He said goodnight to you like it was a normal thing."

"That's just…"

"That's not nothing, Simi. I know he's hurt. I know it's complicated. And I'm not saying he's going to wake up tomorrow like none of the past happened. But a man who was truly done? Doesn't do all this. He sends you a hotel address and keeps it moving."

I didn't say anything.

"He's struggling," she said simply. "And he's still upset. But we've been watching him around you for months now, even Zion agrees; that is not a man who is done. That's a man who doesn't know what to do with what he still feels. I think it's just going to take time. And I think you need to stop deciding the ending before the book is finished."

She stood, stretching. "Now get some rest. Tomorrow we gotta face four sisters of judgment and I need you functional."

"Goodnight, T." I smiled.

She winked, heading for her room.

raschad

My house had an anxious energy the morning my family planned to arrive for a late lunch. I could hear Simone in the kitchen, rummaging through the cabinets with Taryn. I walked in and leaned against the counter, arms crossed, watching Simone move around the kitchen like she was trying to earn her keep.

"Simone, for the last time," I said. "You don't have to make anything. You're a guest."

She looked up at me with anxiety written all over her face. "I can't just stand around and do nothing."

"She really can't," Taryn said from the spice rack, not looking up. "I've been trying to get her to sit down for years. Save yourself the energy."

I sighed, shaking my head. "My sisters are bringing half the menu and I ordered catered platters. There will be more than enough food. Sit down."

She ignored me, already reaching for a mixing bowl. I walked over and took it out of her hands, gently, and looked at her. She let go without arguing, and for a second neither of us moved.

She looked at me, "Okay," she said quietly.

"Okay," I said looking at her. I set the bowl down and stepped back.

Taryn had gone very still at the spice rack. When I glanced over, she looked away quickly and started reading the back of a spice jar, pretending she'd absolutely not been watching.

"This cumin expired in 2023," she said.

"I don't cook with cumin."

"Then why do you have it?"

"I don't know, Taryn."

She set it down. "Just asking."

Zhaire came tearing through the hallway, eyes wide with excitement. "Daddy! When are they coming? Do they have kids? Do they have toys?!"

Taryn smiled, bending down to his level. "Baby, you about to meet four aunties, a grandma, and new cousins. You better get ready."

He giggled, "I'm ready!"

The doorbell made us all pause. I straightened up and took a deep breath. This was it. The moment I'd been wanting and dreading for weeks.

"That's them," I said, heading for the door.

Simone froze, swallowing hard, and I could see her chest rising and falling faster. Taryn nudged her, voice low but encouraging. "Chin up, Queen. Let's go."

As soon as I cracked open that door, the energy hit me like a wave. Loud, warm, heavy with that Carter family vibe mixed with the smell of baked goods, perfume, and a hint of shea butter. Home.

Jordan was first through the door, arms stacked with foil-covered pans, talking before she even crossed the threshold. "Nova! You better have cleared counter space, boy!"

My third sister, bold since birth and never met a room she couldn't command. She pushed past me into the foyer, already surveying the space like she was planning to rearrange it.

My oldest sister Tamika followed behind her, with my thirteen-year-old twin niece and nephew, and eleven year old niece, balancing her lemon pound cake like precious cargo.

"Let me through before I drop something," she said, kissing my cheek as she passed.

Then came Alyssa, balancing a covered pan in one hand, holding my nephew Micah's hand with the other as they stepped inside. "Nova, take this," she passed me the pan. Micah's eyes were already eyeing the house like he was planning his next move.

Jada slipped in last, quiet as always, carefully holding bags of sodas. My youngest sister, still the baby girl even though she was a year older than me, soft spoken, but with more steel in her spine than people gave her credit for.

And behind them came my mother. Valencia Carter, the matriarch of our whole tribe. She stepped through the door, clutching her purse and an old leather photo album.

"Look what I brought," she announced, holding up the album with tears already threatening to spill.

"Hey, Ma," I pulled her into a hug.

The kids immediately swarmed me, just like always.

"Uncle Nova!"

"Uncle Nova, look at my new shoes!"

"Uncle Nova, I lost another tooth!"

I smiled as I hugged them one by one. Zhaire stood next to Simone, wide-eyed by the sudden invasion of his quiet house. I waved him over to me.

"Everyone," I announced proudly, "This is my son, Zhaire."

The reactions were immediate. Tamika's face transformed, her usual composure cracking as her eyes filled with tears. "Oh my God, Raschad, he looks just like you."

Jordan practically squealed, abandoning her pans to rush over and cup his face in her hands. "Baby, you are a carbon copy! Y'all see this?!"

Alyssa smiled wide. "So this is my adorable nephew I been hearing about," she said, dropping into a crouch so they were eye level. "I'm your Auntie Alyssa. And this..." she hooked an arm around Micah peeking out from behind her hip, "...is Micah. He's your age. Same grade, too."

Micah smiled, and Zhaire's shoulders relaxed.

Jada, soft and wide-eyed, whispered, "He's perfect."

But it was my mother who broke me. She stepped forward, and crouched down, her voice trembling with emotion.

"Little Nova," she breathed. "Come here, baby."

Zhaire looked up at me, uncertain for a second, and I nodded. He stepped right into her arms, this sweet, trusting boy who'd never met a stranger. She held him like he was made of gold, tears sliding down her cheeks, rocking him slightly back and forth.

"Lord, it's like seeing my baby all over again," she exclaimed.

When she finally pulled back, she wiped her face, trying to compose herself, but her hands were shaking as she opened that old photo album, taking Zhaire's hand and walking to the sofa.

"Look here, sugar," she said, flipping to a page with a cracked corner pointing to a picture of me when I was about seven. "Do you know who this is?"

Zhaire squinted at the photo, then looked up at me, then back at the picture. "Is that me?"

We all laughed, big, glorious laughs that filled the whole house and reminded me why I'd missed this so much.

Ma beamed. "No, baby. That's your daddy. But you two could be twins."

Zhaire studied the photo more carefully, his little brow furrowed in concentration. "Daddy, that's really you?"

"Yeah, that's really me."

He smiled a thousand-watt smile "Cool! I look like you when you were little!"

"Exactly like me," I said.

"You wanna see my room?" he asked Micah, suddenly remembering he had an audience of potential playmates. "I got Transformers and Legos and a race car track!"

Micah exploded with excitement, following him upstairs like Zhaire was the Pied Piper. The rest of the kids disappeared with them upstairs in the stampede.

As their voices faded up the stairwell, I became aware of the adults still standing around, and the woman who'd been watching all of this in careful silence.

Simone stood near the kitchen with Taryn. Chin up. Hands still at her sides and I could see her pulse in her throat. I took a breath and stepped into the center of the room. My sisters had arranged themselves in something like a receiving line, all of them studying Simone with varying degrees of curiosity and judgment. I could feel the protective energy radiating off them, and could sense Jordan already working up to say something that would probably start a fight.

"Alright," I told them, my voice carrying over the sudden quiet, "I want you to meet Simone."

Jordan squinted past me at Taryn. "That her?"

Taryn put both hands up. "Nope. I'm security, thank you kindly."

The room cracked, tension breaking just a hair as everyone chuckled.

I found Simone's eyes and held them for a second, trying to tell her *I got you*, then turned back.

"This…" I said, standing next to her, "is Simone. Zhaire's mother."

Every eye in the room locked on her, but no one made a sound at first.

"I'm Jordan." My sister tilted her head finally, voice dropping into something that was almost polite but wasn't. "So *you're* the one who decided my brother didn't deserve to know about his own child?"

"Jordan!" My voice hit the floor.

She looked at me, eyebrows up. "What? I'm stating facts."

"No, you're starting shit, and we're not doing that." I stepped closer to her, making sure she understood this wasn't negotiable. "We talked about this before you came. This is about Zhaire. You want to love on him? That includes respecting his mother."

Jordan scoffed and pressed her lips together. Then backed down. Barely.

Tamika stepped forward, extending her hand to Simone with that natural leadership she'd always had. "I'm Tamika," she said, controlled but not unfriendly. "The oldest." She cleared her throat. "Welcome to the family."

Simone shook her hand. "Nice to meet you. Thank you."

Alyssa nodded from where she stood. "I'm Alyssa."

"Nice to meet you," Simone managed.

Jada gave a small wave, but genuine. "Jada."

Then my mother moved, crossed to Simone, looking her over. "So you're the woman who's been raising my grandbaby, huh?" she said.

"Yes ma'am." Simone gave a weak smile.

Ma studied her for a long moment, then she extended her hand. "Valencia Carter."

"Hello, Ms. Carter." she shook her hand.

They held each other's gaze, taking measure. Then Simone did something I didn't expect. She looked around the room, meeting each of their faces in turn, and spoke.

"I understand why you all might be upset," she said. "Every one of you. I get it. No one can be harder on me than I already am on myself." She paused. "I'm not running from what I did. If you want to talk... have questions, I'll answer them."

The honesty in her voice, the way she owned it without making excuses, seemed to shift the room. It shifted something in me too. Taryn reached over and squeezed her arm.

Tamika's expression softened just a fraction. "You got spine," she said. "I'll give you that."

Alyssa smiled at her. "We appreciate that."

Jordan sucked her teeth, rolled her eyes, and sat down. She wasn't done. Anyone who knew her, could see that.

. . .

THE DINING ROOM TABLE LOOKED LIKE A MAGAZINE SPREAD. AFTER WE'D all filled our plates and the kids had eaten, they scattered back upstairs and it was just the adults again, looking at each other in the quiet that follows when there's no longer any reason to wait.

I looked around the table. Tamika folded her hands real calm. Jordan leaned back in her chair, ready to battle. Ma, quiet but sharp, had one hand still resting on Zhaire's empty seat like it was her anchor.

I had to grip my knee to fight the urge I had to reach out and squeeze Simone's hand under the table next to me, as I watched her square her shoulders, breathing deep like she was about to face a firing squad. I had to remind myself that we weren't *that*, yet every part of me wanted to shield her. That feeling made me so damn conflicted and mad I nearly choked on it.

Tamika leaned forward, her tone measured. "Simone, you said you'd answer questions. So let's get it done, so there's no mess later on Zhaire's birthday."

Simone nodded, lifting her chin. "That's fair."

"So." Jordan set down her fork. "Nova tells us you run a music company with your brothers?"

"That's right," Simone said, sitting up straighter. "WadeHouse Music. It was started by my parents, but we've been growing it together."

"Must be nice," Jada said, "having that kind of family support."

"I'm grateful for them," she replied simply.

"Mmhm." Jordan took another bite, chewing slowly. "And where was that support when you were deciding not to tell our brother about his child? You run a whole record label, hold down a brand, manage artists with bigger egos than God." She tilted her head. "But you couldn't tell my brother about his son?"

The table went dead quiet.

"Jordan…" I started.

Simone flinched, just a flicker, then steadied. She held up a hand, stopping me. "No. It's okay."

She looked at Jordan directly. "You're right that I could have. *Should* have." Her voice was calm, but I heard the edges in it. "It wasn't about being able to. It was about being… terrified. Being young, and thinking if I told him, he'd resent me, or give up everything he was working towards. The honest answer is that I panicked and I told myself I had good reasons. It was a mistake. A horrible life altering mistake. One I've been paying for every single day."

Jordan stared at her, that wasn't the answer she'd been loading up for.

Tamika looked like she'd been deciding whether to say what she was thinking. "You know... I remember when you disappeared on him. Back then. He was a wreck for months. All he'd say was you were his person. And then you were just gone." She paused. "Finding out it was *you* who had his child? Who broke his heart and then broke it again on a whole different level —"

"Come on, Mika." I shook my head, cutting her off.

Jordan shook her head and chimed in. "She's just saying, the only two times we've ever seen our brother truly broken and hurt were both over you. So forgive us for feeling some type of way about it."

Simone's eyes went glassy, locking on mine like she might apologize again without words. I cleared my throat and looked at the table to cut the awkwardness.

Jada spoke up for the first time since grace, her voice cutting through the moment like a blade. "So what made you decide to tell him now?"

"He started working with my brothers," she said carefully. "Fate, I guess. I'd been trying to find the courage to tell him for years, but fear and guilt paralyzed me. But when he was suddenly there, right in front of me..." She took a breath.

"How convenient," Jordan muttered, rolling her eyes again.

"Jordan," I glared at her. "That's enough."

"No, it's okay. Y'all have every right to be angry." Simone looked at each of them. "I hurt your brother, and I kept his son from him. I made a choice that affected all of you, not just him, and I know sorry doesn't fix it. But I am so very sorry for that."

Alyssa leaned in, genuinely curious. "Walk me through it. Your thought process. Not the cleaned-up version."

Simone exhaled slowly. "I wasn't angry at him. I wasn't trying to hurt hurt. I kept thinking about the plans he had made. How specific they were. How much work had gone into it... and I thought... if I call him, he wouldn't go. His dream is over. And he'd lose everything he'd worked for someone he'd only known for a few months."

"So that's what you mean by you were scared?" Jada said softly.

"*Scared* sounds manageable. What I had was —" she took a deep breath. "Suddenly I was pregnant by a man who was about to be on another continent, and every rational thought I had just dissolved. And what was left was one thing: *do not burden him. Do not be the reason he ends up somewhere he didn't choose.*"

The table was quiet. Then my mother, who had been quiet the entire time, finally spoke. "Since he was seven years old, Nova carried notebooks full of plans, reorganizing them every time something changed. When he was thirteen and realized that his talents were great enough to take him further in life than the average person, he looked at me and said *don't worry, Ma, I got us.*" She paused. "My illness was real. It was the hardest thing this family has gone through. But if Raschad had come home... we would have figured it out. God has never left this family without a door open somewhere."

She looked at Simone directly. "My son did not need to be protected from his own life."

Tears were sliding down Simone's face. "I know, I'm sorry," she said again. "I'm so sorry."

Taryn had been uncharacteristically quiet through all of this, and finally spoke up. "Y'all mind if I say something?" She sat forward.

"There is a thing that happens," Taryn said carefully, "When you've grown up with loss, you start doing this..." she tapped her temple "... preemptive math. You calculate the damage before it happens. You figure, if I stop it now, then when it all goes to hell, there'll be less of me missing."

She glanced at Simone sideways, ready to say the thing Simone wouldn't. "Simone has been doing that math her whole life. Since she was twelve years old and she watched her mother die, and then her father walked out, leaving four kids to figure it out alone."

My sisters and mother shifted in their seats at that revelation.

"I've known Simone for over fifteen years," she said. "I watched her raise that boy with nothing but love and sacrifice and sheer stubbornness. Was she wrong not to tell Raschad? Hell yes. But is she a good mother?" She looked around the table. "The best. That kid is happy and healthy and kind because of her. Judge her choices all you want. Please don't question her as a person, or her love for that child."

I watched my sisters' faces listening to Taryn, and saw some of their anger started to give way to something else. Understanding, maybe. Or at least the possibility of it. Even Jordan's expression was softening, though she was clearly fighting it.

I'd known all of it already. Her brothers had told me things. She'd told me things, years ago. I'd been wrestling with it since the day I found out. And because of that, my anger had never been clean. If she'd been bitter, or calculating, or done it clearly out of spite, it would've been easier for me. I could've held onto the rage without it costing me anything.

But she wasn't any of those things. She was a woman who loved me and who I loved, who made the worst possible choice out of her fear. And I understood her, while hating that I did. The real thing was not being able to stop feeling what I felt about her. My heart had been trying to give her back to itself since the moment I saw her again in Lennox Falls. My head kept reminding my heart what she'd done to it. The two of them had been at war for months and neither was winning.

I looked at her next to me, holding herself together in a room full of people who had every reason to hate her. I looked away before I felt any more of it.

Alyssa reached over and squeezed Simone's hand. "I understand," she said quietly. "To let what's happened to you quietly run the math on what you let yourself have. It can make you lead with fear and call it logic," she paused. "It doesn't make it right. But I can understand how it can happen."

My mother looked at Simone. "You understand," she said, "That boy is precious to us. We don't know you yet. But we love him and we love Nova." Her eyes didn't move from Simone's face. "So if you're going to be in our lives, you better understand, this family protects what it loves."

"I understand," Simone said. "And I hope you'll let me show you who I am."

Ma studied her for a long moment, taking her measure. Then she nodded once, sharp and decisive. "We'll see."

My house took a while to empty the way Carter gatherings always did. Nobody actually leaving for thirty minutes after they said goodbye. One more story, one more round of hugs, Ma making sure every person walked out with leftover food containers whether they wanted it or not.

Zhaire came downstairs right at the end, half-asleep in his pajamas and I watched my sisters absorb him. Micah had him in a headlock for a goodbye, that Zhaire was loudly protesting and clearly enjoying. When the last car finally pulled away, my house went quiet all at once.

I drifted back to the kitchen. Simone had started putting away the few remaining glasses on the counter. I leaned against the opposite counter and watched her.

"Your family is…" she started, then stopped, like she couldn't find a word big enough and wasn't willing to settle for a small one.

"I know," I said.

She nodded and put up the last glass. "Thank you," she said finally. "For tonight. For trying to shield me when you didn't have to."

"Jordan needs checking sometimes."

"Still." She looked at me. "You didn't have to."

I looked away. "You held your own," I said. "Better than I expected."

I felt more than saw the small exhale that moved through her. I looked at her then, the way I'd been avoiding most of the night. She was exhausted. The careful mask she'd worn through hours of my family's scrutiny had slipped, and underneath it she just looked tired.

I pushed off the counter. "Go get some sleep. Party starts at three tomorrow."

"Okay." But she didn't move right away. "Raschad..."

I stopped.

"I know you're still angry," she said. "I'm not asking you not to be. I just —" She pressed her lips together, choosing carefully. "I'm not going anywhere. Whatever this looks like going forward. I'm not running."

I looked at her for a long moment.

"Good," I said simply.

I stood there longer than I should have, because part of me wanted to say more. But I knew better. I gave another nod and headed upstairs, not letting myself look back.

little nova

simone

Pulling up to Valencia's house felt like arriving at a festival. Cars lined around the block, and music floated down the sidewalk. The smell of ribs and smoked wings was thick in the crisp November air.

Her house sat at the end of a quiet street, a wide ranch-style home with a wraparound porch. I'd heard him mention once, back in the day, that his plan was to get his mother out of the apartment she'd been in for years, into something with space and a yard and no stairs. He'd done that.

The Carters did not come to play. A huge bounce house dominated the front yard. A candy bar with gold favor bags was lined up along the porch railing. An ice cream truck parked at the curb, with kids already lined up in, despite the cold winter air.

"HAPPY 6TH BIRTHDAY ZHAIRE NOVA" was spelled out in large colorful letter cutouts in the front yard.

Zhaire jumped out of the SUV and spun in a full circle, eyes wide, taking in all directions at once.

"Mommy! Mommy! It's like a theme park for me!"

"Yeah, birthday boy," Raschad said, meeting us at the car. "Your village showed out."

Zhaire gave him a huge hug, then yelped and bolted across the lawn, immediately swallowed by a group of cousins, yelling his name and handing out high-fives.

Taryn got out of the back seat in awe. "Wow, this is some set up."

We walked around the side of the house to the back yard. My brothers had gotten there earlier, offering to help Raschad and his family set up. Julian was posted up by the grill in the back with Tre and Zion, all three of them wearing matching *Uncle Crew* shirts that made me smile. Taryn went over to Zion, giving him a hug and a kiss. I hugged my brothers one by one.

Alyssa came out the back sliding door of the house carrying a tray, moving with efficient purpose. She set it on the table near the grill and reached past Julian for the tongs without looking up. "These done?"

Julian checked the rack. "Just pulled them."

She looked up at him when he answered and smiled. "Perfect. Thank you."

Julian nodded once. "Of course."

She took the tongs from him, transferred the wings, and headed back toward the house as Julian cleared his throat and moved the remaining wings to the other side of the grate, methodically.

Tre watched him do it. "You already did that side."

Julian looked down. "Oh."

Valencia stepped off the porch with her arms already open. "Where my baby at?!"

Zhaire heard her voice from across the yard and went straight to her, wrapping both arms around her waist.

My heart swelled. Zhaire had never been deprived. But this was different. Loud and extra and over the top. Raschad appeared beside me, watching our son get passed from family member to family member.

"He deserves every bit of this."

A group of kids tore past us screaming "Little Nova, come on!" and I choked up at that, *Little Nova*. They'd all already claimed him, like he'd always been amongst them. This was what he was supposed to have all along.

Everywhere I looked for the rest of the afternoon, someone was loving on my son. Valencia had him on her lap at one point, showing him something in that photo album again. Jada painted his face at his request. Tamika's twins had adopted him as their little brother by hour two, and Micah hadn't left his side since they'd been introduced. Cousins he'd never met were calling his name like they'd known it forever. My brothers and Taryn wove through it all like they'd known the Carters for years.

Eventually, Jordan started corralling everyone for photos, fussing about hair and who was blinking.

"Alright, Carters front and center! Nova, get in here. Little Nova, you're in the middle. Ma, right here…"

They arranged themselves, everyone finding their place. Raschad stood in the center with Zhaire in front of him, Valencia on one side, his sisters filling in around them, as one of his Raschad's Uncles took a few pictures.

Suddenly, Jordan looked up at me taking my own pictures with my phone. "Simone! Get over here!"

I shook my head, stepping back. "I'm good. This one's yours."

"Girl, get —"

"It's okay," I said. "Really. Go ahead." I meant it. This was their moment. Their first photos with a grandson and nephew they hadn't known existed months ago. I didn't belong in the frame for that one.

I saw Raschad move, stepping out of the frame, crossing the few feet between us. Then he held out his hand. I looked at it for a second, then I took it. His grip was warm and firm, and I forced myself not to think about what it felt like as I let him walk me into the frame.

Zhaire grabbed my other hand the moment I was within reach, positioning me on his left, Raschad on his right.

The flash went off.

"Okay just you three now," Alyssa said as they all dispersed.

"Ready?" She said holding out her phone, next to Taryn who had hers out.

Zhaire grinned up at both of us. "Ready!" He grabbed both our hands, and the flash went off again, and for those few seconds, we looked like what we were supposed to be.

raschad

THE PATIO WAS DARK AND COLD, MY MOTHER'S YARD BELOW STILL holding the ghost of the afternoon. Simone was out there when I came down, leaning against the railing.

"This really was the best birthday he's ever had," she said, without turning around. "Your family went all out."

I stood beside her and looked out at the yard. The deflated bounce house. The scattered juice boxes. The chalk outline of something one of the kids had drawn on the patio. Five years of birthdays I hadn't seen, and now this one, every detail had been everything I wanted it to be for him. Which made the ones before it hurt more, not less.

"Would've been nice to be there for more of them." I said without thinking.

She stilled.

"Sorry. That came out wrong."

"No," she said quietly. "It didn't."

We let that sit. I hadn't meant to say it. Or maybe I had. That was the thing about grief and regret and anger you kept putting in a drawer. It didn't stay there. It just waited until your guard was down.

We hadn't really talked about it. Not since that first day in her office when everything was raw and I was in shock, saying every true thing I had at the time before fully processing it all. After that it became about Zhaire only for me. Pickups and drop-offs and games and Sunday dinners and a birthday party in New Jersey. All of it carefully arranged around the thing neither of us had touched since.

And now I'd let another snippet of evidence of my resentment slip, and she'd absorbed it the way she absorbed everything... quietly, without deflecting. I didn't know if that made it better or worse.

She turned to face me, and I could see in the low light the sadness on her face.

"Is this what it's going to be like, always?" Not accusatory, just genuinely asking.

"I don't know yet," I said honestly. "I'm still working through it. Trying."
She nodded.

"We should get Zhaire," I said finally. "He's probably crashed somewhere inside."

"Yeah," she pushed off the railing. "Probably."

Neither of us moved right away. The yard was quiet except for distant voices from inside. I thought about everything that had been in that yard and our six-year-old who had no idea how much his existence had cost both of us and given back to both of us in the same breath.

"He had a good day," she said finally.

"Yeah," I said. "He did."

Then she pushed off the railing and I followed her inside.

ALYSSA FOUND ME IN THE KITCHEN TEN MINUTES LATER. "YOU OKAY?"
"Tryna be."

She tilted her head toward the back porch. "Come on."

We sat on the steps, the string lights above us.

"Talk," she said.

I stared out at the yard. "I keep thinking about everything I missed. I see him now, laughing, running around with his cousins... and these small moments when it's Simone and me and Zhaire... and it guts me. Because this was supposed to be my life all along, Lyss. Ours."

She nodded, letting me get it out. "I know. I know, Raschad."

"I would've married her." I said it. The truest version. "If she'd just *told* me. I loved her. I *knew* back then she was it. And she just —" I stopped. "I look at him and it makes me love her more. That's the worst part for me. Every time he smiles it's like he's chaining me right back to her. And I hate that."

Alyssa's eyes glistened and she was quiet for a moment. "That dream you're grieving… it's not gone, Nova. She's here. Zhaire's here. You can still build it." She paused. "Just forward, not back."

"How could I ever trust her again?"

She exhaled. "I can't answer that. But what I don't want is for you to let pain and resentment cost you the next five years too," she pulled me into her side. "You got this far in life because you are driven and persistent and headstrong. But love doesn't move like a contract, Nova. You have to soften up or you'll lose what's still right in front of you."

I leaned into my sister, listening to the sounds of the of the night settle around us."It's easy to say. Feels impossible to do."

simone

Thanksgiving - two days later

VALENCIA'S HOUSE SMELLED LIKE GOOD MEMORIES. KIDS WERE YELLING somewhere in the back, and music played low from the living room, as Zhaire shot past us as soon as we walked in, already calling Micah's name.

My brothers and Taryn were already there, playing dominos with Tamika's husband and Raschad's uncles. Taryn caught my eye from across the room and raised her glass in a small salute.

Valencia came out of the kitchen wiping her hands on a dish towel. She hugged Raschad first, long and tight, and then turned to me, with her hand on my arm, briefly. "Glad you made it."

Dinner plates came out fast. Zhaire was wedged between me and Raschad already eyeing the mac and cheese.

Valencia clapped her hands. "Before we eat," she said, "I want to go around. Say what you're thankful for."

She looked around the table. "I'll start. I'm thankful for this table. For every person at it, old family and new." She folded her hands. "And I'm thankful to be three years cancer free."

Her daughters reached toward her at once. One of the grandchildren asked what cancer free meant and got shushed from three directions.

Valencia smoothed her napkin and nodded. "Okay. Next."

His sisters went in a wave. Jordan loud and laughing at herself mid-sentence. Tamika steady and deliberate. Jada soft-voiced. Then Alyssa looked down at her plate for just a second before looking up.

"I'm thankful that I don't look like what I've been through," she said. "That my son is happy and healthy and doesn't carry what I've been carrying." She stopped and shook her head slightly. "And that I can finally feel the fog lifting. That's everything, actually."

Tamika's hand moved to her arm, and Jordan gave her a hug. Nobody said anything. The table just held it for a moment and moved on.

Tre stood. "I'm thankful for this food," he said. "Especially this stuffing. Especially these greens." He pointed his fork at Valencia. "And for the woman who made them." He added another roll to his plate. "I'm also thankful Julian talked me into coming because I almost stayed in the city and that would've been a personal tragedy."

Everyone laughed.

"Sit down, Tre," Julian said.

Tre sat down, still grinning.

Taryn went next. "I'm thankful for not having to fight anybody." She laced her fingers through Zion's on the table without looking at him. "And I'm thankful Zion Wade doesn't know how to take no for an answer."

Zion shook his head, and brought her hand to his lips, "I'm thankful she didn't mean it," he said.

Then Julian stood up, and when he spoke he looked at Raschad directly. "I'm grateful for the man that you are," he said to Raschad. "For the way you've handled something that many men wouldn't have. My nephew knows his father. That matters more than I can say."

Raschad nodded once and looked at the table.

Then Julian turned and looked at me. "And I'm grateful of you, Simone. Proud of you for showing up. For being brave enough to let people in. I know what that cost you."

I nodded too because it was all I had.

Raschad went next, his hands on the table, looking at Zhaire. "I'm thankful for my son," he said. "For this chance. For every person at this table who made these last few days possible." He exhaled. "Every piece of this moment right here."

I was next. "I'm thankful for grace," I said. "For second chances. And for family."

Zhaire sat up straight and looked around with great seriousness. "I'm thankful for my daddy." He began counting on his fingers. "And my Mommy. And Uncle Julian and Uncle Zion and Uncle Tre and Auntie Taryn and Grandma Valencia and Auntie Jordan and Auntie Mika and

Auntie Lyssa and Auntie Jada," he paused. "And Micah. My new best friend."

Micah pointed at him from across the table. "That's me."

"I know." Zhaire said flinging his arms wide. His fork flew, hit the centerpiece, rattled the gravy boat, and clattered onto the table in the half-second of silence before the whole room erupted in laughter.

I covered my face, laughing and crying at the same time, and under the table Raschad's hand found my thigh, and squeezed once. I didn't look at him. I just left my hand over my face and let it land.

————

The morning after Thanksgiving, Raschad's house was a swirl of suitcases and a thousand goodbyes. Zhaire was refusing to leave without one more round on the backyard trampoline, and Raschad was letting him, standing on the porch like he wasn't ready for this to end either.

Tamika found me by the front door. "Simone." She held out her phone. "Put your number in."

I typed it in, and handed it back. She looked at it, then turned and held it up so her sisters could see the screen.

"We're making a group chat," she said. "You're in it."

Jordan leaned against the doorframe, arms crossed, but her edge from three days ago was gone. "Look. We're not exactly on your side." she paused. "But we're not against you either. But hurt him again, and we will fight you… and Taryn." She laughed. "We want what's best for Little Nova." She shrugged, like that settled it.

Alyssa stepped forward. "Ignore her." She squeezed my arm and whispered. "Don't waste this. Give him time."

"And don't be cheap with the photos," Jordan added, pointing. "We are not trusting our brother to keep us updated."

I laughed, eyes stinging. "I promise."

Taryn appeared with her sunglasses. She looked at his sisters, then at me, then back at his sisters. "It was lovely meeting all of you," she said. "I'm glad nobody made me use my taser." She opened her arms toward Jordan. "Come here, bully."

Jordan barked a laugh and hugged her.

Raschad stood on the sidewalk after loading our luggage in the car he'd called for us. He caught my eye over Zhaire's head as I buckled him into the car.

"Travel safe. Text me when you get to the airport and when you land." he said.

"Okay." I said. "Thank you for everything. It was a great time."

He nodded, then leaned down and pressed a kiss to Zhaire's forehead. "Be good. I'll call you tonight."

"Okay, Daddy." Zhaire was half paying attention, playing a game on his tablet.

I straightened up and Raschad was still standing there, close enough that I had to tilt my chin up slightly.

"Text me when you land," he said again.

"I will."

WE PULLED AWAY AND BEFORE WE TURNED THE CORNER, MY PHONE buzzed.

> TAMIKA
>
> Safe travels back.
>
> JORDAN
>
> Do NOT play with us about pics.
>
> ALYSSA:
>
> See you again soon.
>
> JADA:
>
> Bye Simone. It was good finally meeting you.

I looked out the window at Essex Heights moving past. Maybe we really could build something new. Or maybe we were still standing in the middle of everything we hadn't finished breaking.

23 /

we made him

THIS CHAPTER HAS A SOUNDTRACK

The Line by dvsn

raschad

ZHAIRE HAD BEEN EYEING THE BIG-KID SIDE OF THE PLAYGROUND SINCE we got there. The park was emptier than it usually was on a Saturday. Cold enough now that most parents had moved their kids indoors.

The park split the equipment by age, with a shorter section with chunky plastic steps and low slides for littler kids, and a bigger structure on the other side with monkey bars, a rock wall, and a climbing net that went up about ten feet. A group of nine- and ten-year-olds were scaling it like it was nothing.

Zhaire wanted to be over there. I could see it every time he drifted toward the dividing line, craning his neck.

"Z. Stay on this side. That's for older kids."

"But I'm tall enough!"

"*This* side."

He gave me a look that was pure Simone. The *I hear you but I disagree* face. Then he turned and ran back toward the slides.

Simone was already there when we arrived, sitting on a bench, at the edge of the playground. I walked over and sat on the opposite end of the bench.

"He ate?" she asked.

"Turkey sandwich, grapes, juice."

"Okay."

That was us for the most part. Logistics, schedule updates, the minimum required information about a shared child.

"I was thinking about signing him up for actual drum lessons, I found a music school that does beginner lessons on Tuesdays. What do you think?" I said.

"His swim lessons start back up next month on Tuesdays. He's been going since he was four."

She meant it as information. But *since he was four* ate at me. I tried to brush it off.

"I didn't know that."

"I'll send you his schedule of upcoming seasonal activities. Swimming Tuesdays, karate and soccer you already know. Flag football starts in—"

"Going forward, I'd like to be part of those decisions. Not just cc'd after the fact." I cut her off.

"Of course. I'm just telling you what's in place."

"What's 'in place' might need to change, Simone." I said firmly. "My input needs to be taken into account."

She set her phone down. "I hear you. I've just been doing this a certain way for a long time. Adjusting the routine takes time."

"Five years isn't a routine. It's a whole life I wasn't part of." There it was again, the truth slipping past my filter.

"I know," she said quietly.

"I'm not trying to argue. I just need you to understand this is still —"

Then a sound. A loud thud, heavy and wrong, followed by a scream that went straight through my spine. We both turned to see Zhaire on the ground at the base of the big-kid climbing structure. The one I'd told him to stay away from. He'd climbed it while we were talking, not paying attention.

He was on his side holding his left arm against his body, mouth open with a silent scream with no sound because he couldn't catch a breath. His arm was wrong, bent in a way that arms shouldn't bend.

We both ran. I got there first and dropped to my knees.

"Zhaire. Hey. Don't move. Don't move. I'm right here."

"DADDY, IT HURTS." He screamed. The sharp, throbbing kind that came in waves. When he tried to shift the arm, more screaming cries ripped out of him.

Simone was on her knees beside me, hands hovering, afraid to touch and make it worse. "I know, baby. Don't move your arm. Just stay still."

"We need to go," I said. "Now."

I scooped him up, slow and careful, supporting his injured arm against my chest so nothing shifted. He screamed again and cried when I lifted him, then settled into hard sobs against my neck, with the arm secured between us.

"I'll drive," Simone said. "I know where the pediatric ER is."

I got in her backseat with Zhaire on my lap and she bolted out of the parking lot, neither of us caring about the speed limit. Zhaire cried in waves, screaming when the car hit a bump, whimpering in the spaces between, shaking against me. I held him steadily, kissing his head often.

"It's okay, big man. We're almost there. You are so brave."

I caught Simone's wild eyes in the rearview. Two parents in the same nightmare.

THE ER TOOK HIM STRAIGHT BACK. THEY GAVE HIM PAIN MEDICATION first, something through an IV that took the edge off. Zhaire grabbed my hand when the needle went in, as I put my face in front of his and asked him about Bumblebee until it was over.

An hour or so later they wheeled him away for X-rays. He had a buckle fracture, common in kids his age, the doctor said. No surgery needed, but the bone would need to be set.

Conscious sedation was needed for the bone-setting making him drowsy the doctor said but he wouldn't feel pain, and wouldn't remember it. Watching his eyes go heavy and feeling his grip on my hand loosening, as his body went slack was the worst part. Simone bit her lip, biting back her emotions, as she stroked his hand on the other side of him. They set the bone and put a splint on, bright blue because the tech had asked his favorite color before the sedation kicked.

After that, it was waiting. Zhaire drifted in and out of sleep groggy, confused, asking for water, then falling back asleep. At some point he wanted out of the hospital bed and ended up draped across both of us on the sofa, his head in Simone's lap, his legs across mine. Neither of us moved at all.

Julian showed up at some point, took one look at us and sat down without a word, staying for an hour. When the doctor cleared us to leave, it was dark out. Nine hours had passed since the park.

I drove to Simone's as she sat in the back with Zhaire, who was out cold from the meds, his blue splint glowing faintly every time we passed under a streetlight.

At her house, I carried him to his room and laid him down, the two of us working together to change him into his pajamas. We tucked him in from opposite sides of his bed. Both bending to kiss his forehead at the same time without coordinating it.

He stirred, eyes half-open and looked at me, then looked at her. "Mommy. Daddy," he murmured.

"Yeah, baby," Simone whispered. "We're here."

He smiled, small and drowsy, then was out.

I STOOD IN HIS DOORWAY FOR A MOMENT AND WATCHED HIM BREATHE. Simone appeared beside me and I'd felt her shaking when our hands brushed at the door. The tremors of a body that had been running on adrenaline and primal fear and the agony of seeing your child in pain. I could feel her warmth. She smelled like hospital soap and the faintest trace of perfume. We stood there together. Watching our son sleep. Not speaking.

Eventually, we closed his door and went to the kitchen. Simone grabbed two waters from her fridge, handing me one.

I connected to her speaker. dvsn's *Sept. 5th* album came on, the last thing I had been listening to, low enough to fill the silence and distract my mind.

Simone took a swig of her water and exhaled, letting out a long, shaky release. "He's okay," she whispered.

"He's okay." I repeated.

She closed her eyes and I saw her start to crack. She'd been trying to stay strong all day, but now it was just us. And the door was closing on the day and her body was finally allowing itself to feel what it had been postponing for hours.

A single tear slid down her cheek, and then another, then her shoulders began to shake, and I went to her without thinking. Both my hands finding her face, fingers catching tears before they reached her chin.

She looked up at me and her eyes were open and unguarded in a way I hadn't let myself see in months. The air between us dissipated. Months of careful choreography and deliberate distance, dissolved like it had been made of smoke and the first honest breath blew it apart.

I kissed her. Or she kissed me. Or we both moved at the same time the way gravity does when two people have been fighting it for too long and the fight finally runs out of fuel.

I kissed her again. She kissed me back like she'd been saving it. We continued kissing each other like the world was ending. Desperately gasping for air in between. Her tears were salt on my tongue, as her hands came up to my chest, gripping.

"Raschad," she whispered against my lips, and the way she said my name unraveled me even more.

I lifted her up and her legs found their place around my waist. We stumbled toward her bedroom, hands grabbing, pulling, neither of us thinking beyond our need, and the chance to feel whole again.

When I laid her down on her bed, I moved feverishly as I undressed her, relearning every curve and every sensitive spot. When I traced the faint stretch marks on her stomach, reminders of carrying my child, I slowed down and pressed soft kisses along them.

She helped me out of my clothes, her hands shaking with emotion, and when our bare skin finally connected, we both moaned at the contact.

I hovered over her, then lifted one leg up, gripping under her thigh, and eased inside her as deep as I could sink, then began moving in and out of her slowly as she gasped and moaned and gripped my back. I bent down and sucked on her breasts as I continued to grind into her.

Being inside her again felt like coming back home after years of traveling. She was warm and slick and her grip had me dizzy. She still fit me perfectly, her body welcoming me like no time had passed. We continued to move together slowly, savoring every sensation, every kiss, every whispered word.

I pulled back to look at her. "*We* made him," I whispered, moving deeper inside her as I stared into her eyes. "Right here, Simone," I pressed my forehead to hers and looked down to where we were joined.

"You and me. Together," I grunted, pushing deeper and harder as I blinked back tears. I thrusted with every word, "*Right. Here. We. Made. Him.*"

She let out a whimper, mixed with a moan. The reminder of what we'd created together out of love, making tears well up in her eyes, fall out the sides and disappear into her ears.

She nodded, understanding what I was trying to say. Despite everything, what we'd had was real. That what we'd made was a perfect symbol of that.

"I'm sorry. I'm sorry" she cried between thrusts and moans.

"Why, Simone?" I held choked back, "You should've told me. I woulda taken care of you. I woulda—" Pleasure began to tear up my spine in a sharp interruption of my thoughts and I began to push harder into her.

"I-I love you," she gasped, her body arching beneath mine.

I didn't say it back. Not because it wasn't true. But my mouth wouldn't form the words because giving them to her felt like giving away the last thing I was still holding for myself.

So I kissed her again instead, and I let myself feel all of it. How nothing in seven years had come close to this. Not a single woman, not a single night, not a single body beside mine in the dark. I'd tried. Dated. Been with women who were beautiful and willing and kind. And every time, there was a moment where I'd close my eyes and the wrong face would appear behind my lids. This face. The one looking up at me with tears and love in her eyes.

I still love her.

The thought didn't arrive. It had never left. It had been sitting in my chest for years like a tenant who refused to be evicted. And right then, with her body wrapped around mine and her breath on my neck and the way she fit against me so perfectly, I knew I could never get over her.

Suddenly, as the emotion built between us, so did something else in me. The abandonment, the pain, the confusion, the hurt and the betrayal. Every missed moment, I should have been there and wasn't.

My brain caught up to my heart. To my hurt. To every stolen moment. Every lie by omission, and regret and pain filled my veins.

I pulled out of her, and flipped her over, planting her on all fours. She gasped, gripping her comforter to find something to hold herself steady.

"Raschad…" she moaned as I grabbed her hips, then drove back into her, the slap of skin on skin echoing through the room.

Her mouth fell open in a broken cry of ecstasy, tears dripping onto her bed, and she didn't resist, she took it.

She choked on a moan, voice wrecked. *"Oh God. R-Raschaaad."*

"Don't hold back," I gritted out, forehead tipping forward against her back.

She arched back, pushing against my thrusts, taking it all, moaning in surrender. Like she understood. And I hated that she gave herself so willingly like that to a man who was barely holding it together. Maybe because she thought she owed it to me.

I slid my hand up her back, curling around her throat in a gentle pressure. I slammed into her again, and she sobbed out a cry, half pleasure, half pain, her body taking every wild thrust.

I was losing it. My rhythm turned relentless.

"Raschad —oh God—oh God! Yes! Yes!" she cried out.

Her body clamped around me as she climaxed, milking me, *owning* me, and I couldn't stop it, couldn't slow it, couldn't *breathe*. Couldn't hold it. Not with her crying out for me like that.

I drove in one last time, until I could go no deeper, and let go, my whole body seizing, emptying, falling apart with a groan so guttural it sounded like mourning.

Maybe it was.

I grunted, then stilled, struggling to catch my breath. Then stayed there, shaking and undone. I pulled out of her, my body jerking as reality crashed back in. She turned toward me, but she didn't reach out. Understanding was in her eyes. Love had collided with pain and neither had won.

Her shoulders shook with quiet sobs, but she didn't hide her face from me. She was beautiful. Even wrecked and crying, she was the most beautiful thing I'd ever known. And it killed me. That she would let me break her apart, then hold the pieces for me like they were mine to claim.

"Raschad," she whispered, and there was no confusion in her voice. Just recognition of what had just happened between us.

"I'm sorry. I can't do this," I croaked out.

Her face crumpled, tears running fresh, but she nodded. She didn't ask why. Didn't pretend she didn't understand. She just pulled the sheet around herself and watched me.

I stood, finding my clothes and pulling them on. Every muscle in my body was screaming at me to stay. To crawl back into bed with her and pretend everything was fixed.

"We can't be together, Simone," I said, my voice hoarse. "This… this can't happen again. Whatever just happened between us…"

Her mouth trembled, but she didn't speak.

"I want to forgive you. God, I wish I could. I hope I can find a way someday, but right now I just can't."

She nodded.

"When I look at you, I see the mother of my child. Someone I once loved." I said like it didn't still live in my heart.

"But I also see betrayal. I still see years I can't get back. I loved you once, Simone. But I can't go there again… I can't trust you."

"I know," she said again, her voice breaking.

I took a deep breath. "But Zhaire… he deserves two parents who can stand in the same room and not burn down the walls with pain."

She nodded again.

"Let's focus on being the best parents we can. Show him what a healthy relationship looks like… even when it's not a romantic one." I took a breath. "That boy deserves the world. And I'm gonna give it to him. I won't let my hurt touch him."

I paused, the weight in my chest so heavy I could barely breathe.

"I'm not saying I hate you, Simone," I added, softer now. "I don't. I could never. But whatever we had? Whatever it could've been? I just can't give you that. Not with resentment sitting in my chest like a rock."

"I'm sorry," I said again and turned and walked out, the sound of her muffled crying chasing me all the way to the door, tearing me to pieces with every step.

I stepped out into the night, breathing cold air, trying to stop shaking, knowing I'd left the best thing I ever loved behind me. But I couldn't go back. Trust wasn't a switch you could flip. You couldn't just decide to give it back. It came back on its own schedule or it didn't come back at all. And my wounds were still open.

part two

INEVITABLE

three and a half feet

simone

six months later

ON PAPER, RASCHAD AND I WERE DOING WELL. ZHAIRE WAS THRIVING, IN first grade with loud confidence. We had a good rhythm. Drop-offs, pick-ups, shared calendars, and co-signed forms. Side-by-side seats at games with smiles that could fool anyone who wasn't looking too hard.

On paper, we were a co-parenting success story. But paper doesn't feel anything.

I watched Raschad from across the basketball court, coaching Zhaire's rec league team during their game. His voice carried across the gym and wrapped around me in a way that made it hard to focus. I hated how my body still answered to him, even when my heart was trying to play it safe.

One year. That's about how long it had been since the day Raschad found out that Zhaire was his son. We had built something careful in that time. Delicate and disciplined and measured down to the inch.

Three and a half feet. That was the gap. Three and a half feet of polite, professional space that Raschad maintained between us at every pickup, every drop-off, every little league game where we sat on the same bleachers but might as well have been in different stadiums.

Three and a half feet, and one year. An eternity.

Across the gym, Raschad caught my eye and my heart fluttered. He smiled. I forced myself to smile back. *Co-parenting. That's all.* The timer blew on the fourth quarter, shrill enough to make me wince, and Zhaire came running off the court smiling wide.

"Mommy! Did you see my baskets?"

I hugged him, breathless and sweaty. "Of course I did, superstar." I pressed a kiss to the side of his face. "You were amazing."

Raschad was only a few steps behind, his shadow falling over us. "That was a solid pull-back shot at the end, lil man."

Zhaire beamed up at him. "You taught me that!"

"Ready to go?" Raschad asked, eyes darting to mine for half a second.

We walked to our cars in silence. When we stopped at my car, Zhaire gave me a hug. "See you later, Mommy!"

"Later, sweet potato." I kissed him, then went back to Raschad.

He looked at me, and gave me the smallest nod. Three and a half feet away.

"See you Wednesday, Simone."

"See you Wednesday."

I got in my car and drove away.

A YEAR AGO, THE SECRET OF ZHAIRE HAD BEEN THE HEAVIEST THING I'D ever carried. But the secret was out now. And the thing I'd expected, the complete collapse of my world, the moment where everyone looked at me and saw nothing but the liar I'd been for years, hadn't happened. Not in the way I'd feared it.

What happened was worse. Because the secret being out hadn't exactly freed me. It had just changed the shape of my cage. Before, I carried the guilt of what Raschad didn't know. Now, I carried the guilt of what he did. I carried the memory of his pain and the knowledge that I'd caused it. Every day. Every time he walked into my house and couldn't quite look me in the eyes. Every time he said *see you Wednesday, Simone* in that even, measured, careful voice that was worse than yelling, because yelling meant he still felt something, and his politeness meant he'd decided I wasn't worth the energy of emotion at all.

That was my new weight. Not the secret. The consequence.

I told everyone I was fine. My brothers would ask and I'd say fine. Aunt Lorraine asked how I was *really* doing and I said fine. I was fine at work. Fine at pickups. Fine at drop-offs. Fine at family events. Fine fine fine fine fine.

Fine was the word I used to lock the door.

But behind the door was this: I hadn't let anyone touch me in almost seven years. Not touch me the way that meant something. Not since him, before Spain, before everything fell apart. And yes, there had been that one night months ago, after Zhaire's accident, when the dam broke and I'd let myself have the thing I'd been starving for. One night that ended with him standing by my bed saying *this can't happen again* in the gentlest, most devastating voice I'd heard.

That night made everything worse for me. Because before that, I could pretend I'd forgotten what it felt like to be touched like that. After that I couldn't pretend anything. It was like being given a cup of water after years of thirst, and then the cup is snatched away after just one sip. It made my drought feel worse. A reminder of what I couldn't have.

I now had the vivid memory of his hands and his voice and the warmth of being wanted... then rejected... and I had to carry that alongside the three-and-a-half-foot gap and the *see you Wednesday's*, and the door he kept closed.

I wasn't a woman. I was a mother.

I didn't have needs. I had responsibilities.

I wasn't desirable. I was functional.

And the part of me that remembered what it felt like to be wanted, I'd put it in a box on the highest shelf and told myself it was fine.

Fine.

I'd decided it was punishment. Because I didn't deserve it. The quiet, foundational belief that lived underneath everything else was that I didn't deserve to be wanted. My mother was gone. My father hadn't wanted me enough to stay. And I'd done something terrible. I'd kept my child from his father for years. And the punishment for that, the correct, appropriate sentence, was to be alone. To raise my son. To be good at my job. To hold everyone else together.

To be fine.

The other truth was I was waiting. And he hadn't asked me to wait. He had been very clear about what he could and couldn't offer. But I'd been waiting anyway, calling it accountability, calling it time to reflect, calling it anything that made it look like a choice I was making rather than a hope I couldn't put down.

I was holding my breath, because I still loved him. More now than I did then. Which felt like another kind of punishment. Because he could have made my life very small. He had every justification. He had the grievance. Instead he had simply decided to be the man he was. Every day without ceremony. So, I hadn't just fallen back in love with the Raschad I remembered. I'd fallen in love with the man he was today. The man I'd gotten a taste of seven years ago, and had spent every year since trying to convince myself I'd imagined.

I hadn't imagined him.

At night, I would sometimes put on his song *Ghost*, wrap myself up in the UCLA sweatshirt I refused to part with, and sit in the quiet of it. Letting myself have the feeling I kept locked during daylight. The song asked the question I was too scared to answer six years ago.

Were you real? Did you feel it too?

I felt it. I still felt it.

TARYN NOTICED FIRST. THE BENEFIT AND THE CURSE OF BEING MARRIED to my most emotionally attuned brother. She noticed the way I deflected when conversations turned to men and dating. The way I changed the subject when she talked about her and Zion's life. The way I'd have to use the bathroom, or grab a snack when a scene came on during a movie or TV show that was too close to the thing I'd been denying myself.

She waited. She showed up. She let me be fine until one night Raschad called to ask if I'd given Zhaire his allergy meds, and I put on a voice so bright and so steady that when I hung up Taryn just looked at me from across the couch and said "Okay. That's enough."

Zhaire was at Raschad's for the night. Taryn had come over without asking, found me on my couch in sweats watching reruns, existing in the hollow space that forms when you're used to a child filling your home with life, and then suddenly he's not there fifty percent of the time. That was where we were when my phone buzzed.

After I hung up she sat down and tucked her legs under her the way she did when she was settling in for a conversation.

"Talk to me," she said.

"I'm fine."

"Simone."

"I'm *fine*, T."

"You're not fine. You haven't been fine in months. And I love you too much to let you keep pretending."

I didn't answer, just stared at the TV.

"This is my life," I said finally. "This is what I live in. And I know I caused it. I know I'm the reason. And so I take the forced smile and the pickup nod because it's what I deserve. Because what I did was unforgivable. And if this is my punishment—"

"Simone. Stop it. Listen to me and don't just let it pass through you and come out the other side as *I'm fine.*"

"Okay."

"Yes. Keeping Zhaire from Raschad was wrong. We've beat that with a dead horse already. But you have been punishing yourself for *years*. You were young and you were scared. And you should have told him. But you didn't. You can't unmake that choice. You can only decide how long you're going to let it define you."

"It does define me."

"No. It doesn't. It's a thing you did. It's not who you are."

"And what you're doing," she continued. "The not dating. The not living. The not letting yourself be a woman with needs and desires and a right to happiness, is not healing. That's hiding. And it's been going on so long you can't even see it anymore."

"You haven't been on a date in seven years," she looked at me.

"I haven't wanted to."

"That's a lie. You haven't *let* yourself want to."

The silence that followed was long. Taryn let it breathe in the quiet while the truth of what she'd said settled. "You're allowed to be happy, Simone," she said. "You're allowed to want things. You're allowed to put on a dress and go out and feel beautiful and desired and alive. Not because you've served enough time. Because you're a human being. A young, beautiful, brilliant human being who has spent years acting like wanting to be desired is a luxury she doesn't deserve."

"What about Raschad?"

"What about him?"

"If I start... dating. If I move on. He_—"

"He'll what? Be upset? He's had a year. He's had a year to let it go, to try, to open that door, and he hasn't. And that's his right. His healing is on his timeline. But your healing can't wait for his, Simi. You can't put your entire life on hold waiting for a man to decide if you're worth it or not."

"I love him."

"I know you do. And maybe one day, y'all will figure it out. Maybe you won't. But either way, you have to start living again. For *you*."

She paused. "You know... Nasir asked about you again."

I closed my eyes. "Taryn."

"He asked Zion last week if you were seeing anyone."

"I'm not interested."

"You don't have to marry the man, damn. Just... go to lunch. Have a conversation with someone who looks at you like a woman and not a co-parenting schedule. That's all."

I didn't say yes. But I didn't say no. Taryn didn't push after that, just let it sit there like an open door.

no strings

raschad

ONE YEAR OF BEING SOMEBODY'S FATHER WILL REARRANGE YOU IN WAYS you don't see coming. I think about Zhaire first thing every morning. What time he needs to be picked up. Whether he mentioned anything about a quiz that week. How I need to take him to get new sneakers. My whole internal calendar has reorganized itself around this kid and I don't have a single complaint about that.

That part settled faster than I expected. The first few months were figuring out the mechanics; his schedule, learning how to read him, learning which moods needed space and which ones needed engagement. Now it just is. I can't remember what mornings felt like before I had somewhere to be that mattered like that. I watch him and think: *I almost missed all of this.* But I no longer stay in the thought too long because there's nothing useful there. He's here. I'm here. That's what we have.

That wound has mostly closed.

Zhaire is good. Settled and already telling stories about his life that include me in chapters I wasn't actually present for. He has absorbed me into the fabric of his life and I have done the same with him. So that has healed in the only way it was ever going to; by showing up until the showing up became the whole story.

The other thing. The thing she did to me as a man who was in love with her? Still felt raw some days. She broke my heart. Twice. Same woman. Different ways. And the second time was worse because I was older and I knew better and I walked into it anyway.

I've forgiven her. I can be in the same room with her and be friendly and co-parent. I made that choice deliberately and I've held it. She'll never know how much I've held it. How much I've chosen not to say. How many conversations I've redirected, and swallowed the thing that was still sitting right there, because the time wasn't right, or Zhaire was in the next room. I'd decided early that I wasn't going to let my hurt and anger become anyone's problem.

But that doesn't mean the hurt is gone. It just means I've decided not to lead with it. I don't wake up in it, but if I sit still long enough and let myself actually feel it, it's there. Waiting.

And buried with that is the thing that's harder to hold; I still want her.

I know that because I've spent the past six months trying not to and failing privately every single time. Other women have been good. Fine. Better than fine in some cases. But every time there's the same flat line afterward. The same absence of the thing I'm looking for, that I know I'm only going to find in one place. But I have made a deliberate decision not to go back to that place.

I think about that night after Zhaire's accident often. The way something just gave. All that compressed weight and relief and desire finally having somewhere to go. And it was exactly what I knew it would be. Which is why walking away took more from me than anything I've done in a long time.

But I knew what I was walking away from. And I have been living with that knowledge every day since, chasing the echo of it in rooms that aren't her, coming up empty, and getting angrier about it.

I know what I want and exactly why I can't have it. She didn't lock this door. I did. Because a man with *any* self-respect draws a line after something like that and holds it.

I'm holding it.

But I'm pissed off about being right. We were supposed to be something. I knew it in San Diego. I knew it watching her in that club trying not to look at me. I know it every time Zhaire draws a picture of his family with all three of us in the same house like it's already true.

We were supposed to be that.

And because of what she chose and what I've decided I cannot risk again, we're not that. And I wake up in this house I bought in this town that has started to feel like home, and some mornings the grief of that is the first thing I feel.

Then I get up and move on. Because that's what I do.

I DIDN'T EXPECT TO LOVE LENNOX FALLS. I'VE PUT MONEY INTO TWO commercial properties in the area already, and I'm looking at a third. I own my own home here now, and am out of the rental. Being here doesn't feel like a temporary situation anymore. Jersey is still home and always will be. But Lennox Falls is becoming something too. Choosing a place rather than being from one.

Growing up with all women, I know what it was to be surrounded by people who loved you, yet still feel like something was missing. The architecture that comes from men who've been through versions of what you've been through and survived it. I have that now with Julian, Zion, and Tre.

Julian talks to me like someone whose future he's actually invested in. He asks questions about where I'm going and offers guidance from his own experience without making it a lecture. Zion can sit in a hard conversation and not flinch and not let you flinch either. And Tre is one I didn't see coming. The one who showed up in the margins and became essential without either of us announcing it. Tre and I have developed a rhythm that I've come to look forward to. He knows how to be out. Clubs, lounges, Tre's house when he wants to keep things in his own environment. The one who checks in and makes sure I'm living, and keeps the weight from getting too heavy by sheer force of his personality.

They're Simone's brothers. But they've also become mine.

The broadcasting thing is moving faster than I expected. Conversations with my agent have turned into actual meetings with networks. But this was the year that music stopped being a side thing. I stopped calculating how many years I had left in basketball and started calculating what the music could become if I gave it everything.

Tre and I had been in the studio constantly. He had a way of making work feel like something else. Not transactional the way it was with many producers. Collaborative. Thinking out loud with someone who was thinking in the same direction.

We'd started on a track for one of the WadeHouse artists, abandoned it by unspoken agreement, and both of us moved toward something new at the same time. He went to the keys. I pulled up a beat I'd been sitting on for a month and played them simultaneously.

It fit.

"That's it," Tre said. "The bass and your high end. Play it again."

I played it again. He was already moving toward his notebook, then pointed at me. "That chord progression you're running underneath. Keep building that. I want to write into it."

We built it together from there. Him writing toward the track, me building the track toward what he was writing, calling adjustments back and forth until the two things became one thing. Somewhere in the middle of it I started talking about carrying weight without realizing it. About setting something down that had been yours. Tre listened without interrupting. Then he picked up his pen and wrote more.

What came out was the second verse. A line buried between lines that were purely fun. We kept working until four in the morning.

"That's the song," Tre said when we played it back.

"Yeah," I said. "That's the song."

"I know a vocalist. He can handle this."

"Get him in."

Tre stretched and cracked his neck. "You know what this is actually about?" Tre said.

"I know what mine is about," I said. "Don't know about yours."

He laughed. "Yeah."

We packed up and headed out, and somewhere on the drive home I thought about what I'd told him in that room. How I'd talked around it without ever saying her name, and how Tre had heard everything I didn't say and written it anyway.

No Strings dropped six weeks ago. It's been on urban radio every day since. Sitting at number two on the R&B charts. Climbing streaming numbers that Zion texted us about twice a day in disbelief. It started showing up in clubs, on social media, the kind of organic spread that happens when a song finds the people.

My phone has been busy. The WadeHouse partnership is looking like exactly what Julian said it would look like when he laid it out over lunch in Tribeca.

I built the right thing. I know that now in a way I only suspected a year ago.

The irony is not lost on me that the song everyone is calling a breakup anthem, a liberation record, a vibe for anyone who's done with the whole serious relationship thing, was made by two men who are anything but free. Whatever Tre carries I've never asked about directly and he's never offered. But I know the difference between a man writing from observation and a man writing from experience. Those buried lines in the verse didn't come from just me.

NO STRINGS
written and produced by: R. Carter & Tre Wade
performed by Nishad
(c) 2026 WadeHouse Records

VERSE 1
Come through, you know the move
Low lights, not setting the mood
Hands in your hair, you right there
Don't say nothing, just arch it there

Pull me closer, just like that
Don't stop baby, throw it back
Keep it moving
No confusion
No one losing

CHORUS
No strings, just skin, no label
Mine for right now
that's fine for right now
Pull up, vibes are set
No candles, you already wet
Don't gotta say what it is
Both know what it is
No strings, just skin, no label
No strings

VERSE 2
Two glasses, you already sipping
Body talking, you know I'm listening
Dress hit floor by the second verse
Said you not staying, climaxed with a curse
Love make you stupid
Done with all that
Ain't tryna be your regret
Got enough of my own
Gave it all, and got a lesson
Scars don't lie, so no stressin'
Keep it light, wounds sting
No strings

CHORUS
No strings, just skin, no label
Mine for right now
that's fine for right now
Pull up, vibes are set
No candles, you already wet
Don't gotta say what it is
Both know what it is
No strings, just skin, no label
No strings

operation shut shit down

raschad

I'D STOPPED BY THE STUDIO TO CHECK ON SOMETHING, AND ENDED UP still there at nine at night. That was WadeHouse. You came in for one reason and the building held you past it. Tre and Zion had been in Studio B most of the afternoon. Khairos popped in and claimed the couch at some point. Julian had checked in on his way home and ended up staying. The studio had morphed into an unofficial man cave.

I knew Simone was still in the building. I'd seen her when I came in, working on logistics, and donor reconciliation for an upcoming community event. We'd passed in the hallway around six and done the thing we'd gotten good at. *How was Zhaire's morning. Does he have practice tomorrow. Taryn is gonna keep him tonight. Yes I got the school email.*

I'd come back down to Studio B and stayed.

"*No Strings* is doing something," Tre said, not looking up from the board. "Like actually doing something."

"Numbers have been good," I said.

"Good?" Zion looked up from his phone. "It's number two. Nishad's trending every day."

"Women are in the comments like it's a confessional," Tre said. "Nishad's about to have a moment."

"That's what's up. That's what we made it for."

"Yeah, but R. Carter credit on a number two record?" Zion said, "Your name as a Producer is in rooms it wasn't in before. That's something to celebrate."

"I know. Appreciate it."

"Enjoy it," Tre said. "You built something real this past year." He spun around in his chair. "And you are still out here living like a damn monk."

"I'm not living like a monk."

"When's the last time you went out?" Khairos asked. "Not studio. Not dad activities. Actually went *out*. Matter of fact... when's the last time you got some?"

Silence.

"That's what I thought," Tre said.

"What happened with Dominique anyway," Khairos asked. "The auction girl? Didn't you go on a few dates?"

"It ran its course."

Tre shook his head. "Head on speed dial and he talking about it ran its course."

"We're still cool. It's just not gonna go anywhere."

"Because you didn't want it to," Tre said.

I didn't respond.

"We gotta get you to expand the radius," Tre said. "This weekend. You, me, Khairos. We're going out. And we're not taking no for an answer this time. You act like you have a one every other month quota or some shit."

He looked at Zion and Julian. "I'd invite y'all but Zion went and got boring since he got married, and Julian… well you've always been boring. No excuse there."

He and Khairos fell out laughing and I just shook my head.

"Just don't spread yourself thin," Julian ignored Tre, looking at me. He'd been so quiet I'd half-forgotten he was there. "You've got a lot moving at once. Music. Fatherhood. The broadcasting thing. Stress relief is one thing. Distraction is another."

"That's wisdom," Khairos said.

"I occasionally have it," Julian replied.

"I know where my head is," I told him.

"'*Stress relief*'. I like that Jules." Tre leaned forward. "Beautiful women. Good drinks. Good food. No complications. Like our song says…" he spread his hands, "No strings!"

"Why are you like this?" I laughed.

"Because I care about your development," Tre said solemnly, "And I want you to have a life."

"I do have a life."

"You have a schedule," Tre corrected. "Zhaire, studio, fly to New Jersey, back to Lennox Falls, repeat. That's a very responsible timetable." He said it without judgment. "I'm saying expand the radius."

I was mid-thought when the door shifted. I looked up and Simone was in the frame. Bag on her shoulder, clearly done for the night. Her face did the thing it did when she was composing herself quickly.

"Hey." She gave the room a smile that was warm and even. "Sorry, I didn't realize everyone was in here. Julian, I'm heading out."

"Financial forecast done?" Julian asked.

"Close. Donor numbers are looking good. Really good, actually."

She crossed to Julian, handing him a folder. "Can you sign this before you leave tonight? Leave it on my desk."

He took them from her as she looked over at me. "Hi. Um, so I think it's our turn to bring the snacks for Zhaire's game tomorrow."

I nodded. "Yeah. I'll grab Gatorades. You want me to get those fruit packs he likes?"

She nodded. "Perfect. Thanks."

She was already moving. Her eyes had done the sweep of the room at Tre, Khairos, Julian, Zion, and found somewhere neutral to land that wasn't the couch where I was sitting.

"Good night, y'all." And with that, she turned and left, the door clicking shut behind her.

The room breathed and Tre turned back to the board slowly. Khairos set his phone down on his chest. Julian read over the papers she'd given him, and Zion stared at me while swirling his drink. Nobody said anything for a moment. Then Tre pushed back in his chair, stretched, and stood up. "I'm gonna get some water. Anybody want anything?"

"I'm good," I said, as everyone else shook their heads no, knowing he wasn't getting water. He walked toward the door and out into the corridor, hands in his pockets.

simone

I HADN'T MEANT TO STOP IN THAT DOORWAY. THE DOOR WAS CRACKED and I heard their voices, and by the time I understood what I was hearing I'd already heard it.

I knew what that room was. I'd watched Julian and Zion and Tre talk in it for years, knew what men sounded like when they thought it was just them. I had just never been on the outside of it listening to them talk about Raschad's options before.

I was almost to the elevator when I heard Tre.

"Simi!"

I didn't turn around immediately. I heard the studio door, and him walking behind me, and then he was there, beside me, leaning against the wall as I waited for the elevator.

"I wasn't eavesdropping," I denied quickly.

"Door was open," he said.

"Yeah."

He didn't say anything else for a moment. Just stood there with his hands in his pockets, looking at me, all the way through the maintenance version to whatever was underneath.

"You two made that song," I said.

He blinked.

"A *literal* song. About —" I lowered my voice. "About *sex*. About no strings and no labels and *women*. You and Raschad sat in that studio together and *that* is what you came up with? Now it's on the radio and I have to hear it every time I get in my car."

"You know what that song is actually about?"

"I know exactly what that song is about."

"No." He said it simply. "You know what it *sounds* like. That's different. Songs aren't always what they sound like on the surface," he said. "Trust me on that."

"Well *not* to mention." I kept going. "I had to sit in a room and watch women throw money and numbers at him, and now you and Khairos are in there talking about how he should keep getting head from his auction winner? '*Head on speed dial*'? *Expand his radius?* Really Tre?"

"So you *were* listening."

"Like you said, the door was open."

He didn't argue with that. Just nodded, but didn't apologize for it.

"You're my brothers. Khairos is my cousin. And y'all are in there helping him plan hookups."

"Your cousin likes him. Your brothers like him." He said it plain. "We don't like him because of you, Simi. We like him because he's a good dude and he's handled a bad situation better than most would've."

"So you're just going to *encourage* him to —"

"Yeah," Tre cut me off. "Probably."

I looked at him, surprised and confused."Whose side are you on, huh?"

"Yours," he said. "Same as always."

I scoffed. "It doesn't look like that from where I'm standing."

"I know." He pushed off the wall and faced me. "But here's what it looks like from where *I'm* standing. That man went through something. He's *still* going through it. He gets to work through his feelings, which sometimes might look like going on dates and going out and..." He tilted his head. "...all the stuff you overheard in there. That's real. I'm not going to pretend it's not happening to make you feel better."

"I know he gets to do that. But it's hard to hear." I said.

"I've seen up close what it looks like when a man's in pain and covering it." He said it to the floor. "Let him work through it."

"And by the way, when's the last time *you* went out?" he continued.

I didn't respond. He already knew the answer.

"He's living his life, Simone. And while he's doing that? *You* need to be living yours."

I nodded, "Taryn told me the same thing."

"She's right. And here's the thing," he said. "I think you two will probably find your way back. I actually believe that. But not now and not like this. Not while he's in his process and you're standing in the hallway listening through a cracked door." He paused. "Live your life Simi, because you're disappearing from it."

He put his hands on both my shoulders. "I want there to still be a you, a *better* you, for him to come back to. If that's what y'all decide. That's all."

The elevator opened and neither of us moved for a second.

"You really think we can get there?" I asked.

Tre looked at me long enough to make sure I knew he meant it. "I mean, I don't have a crystal ball or nothing but, I do know he cares about you. Even after everything. That is a man who does care. So, yeah, I don't think it's impossible."

He held the door open, and bent down and kissed my cheek. "I love you, baby girl. And I'm sorry if I hurt your feelings. But... you know I'm right."

I rolled my eyes at him and gave him a peck back on his cheek. "Night, Turncoat." I grinned.

"Take your ass on home." he laughed at me as the elevator doors closed.

Of all my brothers. Of course it was Tre that Raschad would get closest too. I almost laughed.

I PULLED UP IN FRONT OF ZION AND TARYN'S PLACE, MIND STILL ROLLING over every word I'd overheard. It shouldn't have affected me like it did. I'd been around men my whole life and knew how they talked. By the time Taryn flung open her door, I'd forced my face into something that looked like being unbothered.

"Zhaire is asleep. You might as well just let him stay the night," she fussed.

Her house smelled like sugar cookies and *Martin* was on, yelling about Tommy not having a job. I dropped into her couch and told her about the conversation I'd overheard.

"They care about him," she said.

"They're supposed to care about me."

"They do care about you." She said it simply. "Tre told you that himself. That's not them choosing a side."

"He's slept with his auction winner apparently. Probably still is." I said flat. Like if I said it that way I could keep it at a distance. "He's out there doing what people do when they've moved on and my family is cheering him on."

She guzzled the rest of her drink and slammed her glass down on the coffee table. "I *told* your ass not to let those heifers bid on your baby daddy!"

I laughed despite myself, wiping under my eyes. "It's fine."

Taryn narrowed her eyes. "Don't you dare *fine* me, Simone Wade." She snapped her fingers in my face. "It is not fine. Okay? He wanna play? You can play too. Miss 'head doctor' Dominique is not the only bad bitch in Lennox Falls."

"Taryn. How many glasses of wine have you had?"

"No! I'm serious. It is time for you to dust it the fuck off. You are Simone *Motherfucking* Wade. You hear me? We outside this weekend. Shutting shit down."

She shifted toward me. "You made a choice that hurt him. That doesn't mean watching him date other people feels like nothing. The question is what you're going to do about it."

"What am I supposed to do about it?"

"The same thing he's doing. *The fuck?*" she looked at me like I had no sense.

"We've had plenty of girls' nights, Taryn. You and me, the whole crew."

"That's not what I mean and you know it." Taryn tilted her head. "You've gone out *with me.* Behind me, practically. You dance with whoever gets close enough, you laugh, you have a good time, and then you come home alone and that's exactly what you planned to do when you left the house." She paused. "When is the last time you went somewhere with the *intention* of being seen? Of even just, kissing somebody, Simone."

I looked at my glass.

"You've been celibate for *years.*"

I rolled my eyes. "We're not doing this."

"We are doing this." She pointed at me. "You haven't dated. Haven't let anything start. And yes, you've been out, but there's a difference between going out and *going out.* One of those is you existing near other people. The other one is you actually showing up for your own life."

Something in my face must have moved and Taryn stopped.

"What was that look?"

I looked at the table and exhaled. "Six months ago, after Zhaire's accident. It just happened. All that tension, the whole day just exploded."

Taryn stared at me. "You slept with Raschad?"

"Yes."

"And you didn't *tell* me!"

"I was embarrassed… because of how it ended. Afterward he said it couldn't happen again. That we needed to focus on co-parenting. That he'd probably always —" My voice caught. " That without trust it wasn't possible. And then he left."

"He *LEFT*?!" Taryn repeated.

"He left." I stared at the table.

"Okay. Okay," she said, more focused. "So that's why you have hope, Simone. He gave you a reason to and then took it back and left you holding it."

I didn't say anything because she wasn't necessarily wrong. She stood up, and there was a new energy in her now, decisive, almost amused in the way she got when she'd made a decision. "Oh, okay, okay. We're going OUT Saturday."

"Taryn, please."

"Nope. Not a suggestion anymore. Operation Shut Shit Down." She pointed at me. "He is out there living his damn life. Making songs and shit. Meanwhile you are sitting around, giving him absolutely *nothing* to react to." She tilted her head. "That ends Saturday. Not to make him jealous — okay, a little bit to make him jealous — but *mostly* because you deserve to walk into a room and be wanted and you have forgotten what that feels like."

"He may come back. I think he will. But he might not. Not the way you want. You cannot make your life about a door that might not ever fully open."

"He's a Leo," I said. "Leos don't forgive betrayal. Once you break that…"

"Simone." Taryn rolled her eyes at me. "I love you. But astrology is not going to tell you how this ends."

"It gives me a framework —"

"It gives you somewhere to hide." She said plainly. "Think about when this started. When did you go from casually interested in horoscopes to checking transits at two in the morning?"

I didn't answer.

"You got pregnant. That's when. You needed something that made the world feel like it had a logic to it." She paused. "I get it. But you've been using them to explain things instead of living through them. His birth chart doesn't know how this ends."

I thought about it. She wasn't wrong.

"Seven years of not dating. Not going out. Not letting anyone look at you the way you deserve to be looked at. You built a whole life around protecting a secret, and the secret is out now. He knows. He's here. Zhaire has his father." She spread her hands. "The secret kept you frozen and now it's gone and you're still frozen, and at some point you have to decide that's a choice, not a consequence."

"So, it's decided. We are going out Saturday," she said again.

I thought about Tre at the elevator. *I want there to still be a you to come back to.*

I raised an eyebrow. "Outside?"

"OUTSIDE." She practically yelled it. "He wanna play? You can play, too. There are men lined up waiting. You just been keeping it on the top shelf like a collector's item."

I laughed so hard I nearly spilled my wine. "You are so dramatic."

"And you are so *overdue*," she shot back.

I laughed again, then sat with it for a moment. Taryn was right. Tre was right.

Saturday, I thought. Okay.

who'd you wear this for?

THIS CHAPTER HAS A SOUNDTRACK

Heart of a Woman by Summer Walker

simone

"Okay, so listen," Taryn said, digging through a drawer full of lashes, "I know exactly where we're going. That new spot on Oak Street? It's Black-owned, live DJ, sexy lighting, and I heard the drinks don't taste like watered-down sugar water."

I laughed. "Do you even know the name of it?"

She waved me off. "Details, details. We'll find it. The point is, *we outside*." She gave me a look so serious I had to laugh. "Raschad is living rent-free in your head, and it is time for eviction. Mmkay?"

"Mmkay," I mimicked laughing.

"Nope," she announced, pointing at the blue dress I was about to step into. "Too soft. We are not giving church usher tonight. We are giving main character energy."

She rummaged through my closet. "This," she said, yanking out a slinky silver dress I hadn't even remembered buying. "This right here is a problem."

I looked at it, skeptically. "Taryn, I bought that years ago. That barely covers my *ass*."

"Exactly!" she grinned. "Your ass needs to be *seen*. Let the streets remember."

I sighed, then caved, taking the dress from her. When I slipped it on, it clung to every curve like it was painted on me, hugging my hips, dipping low at the front.

Taryn whistled, fanning herself. "Whew! Oh, you about to cause a *collision* with that on."

I tried not to blush. "It's a little... much."

"Nope. It's just the right *much*." She adjusted my straps. "Now, makeup, lashes, hair laid, and perfume."

Forty minutes later, I was dabbing on lip gloss when my doorbell rang.

Taryn smirked. "You want me to get it?"

"No," I sighed. "It's Raschad. He's just here to pick up Zhaire."

I walked to the door, heels clicking on hardwood, dress hugging my thighs so tight I had to remind myself to breathe. The second I opened it, Raschad's face changed. He froze, eyes sweeping over every inch of me slowly.

His mouth opened, then closed, then opened again. "Uh."

I fought a smirk. "Hey."

He cleared his throat, trying and failing to look casual as he stepped inside. "Where you two going tonight?"

Before I could answer, Taryn popped up behind me, grinning. "Out. *Way out*, Raschad. Your son is getting a sleepover with you, and his mother is getting a *grown woman* night."

He cut her a look, then looked back at me. "How long you think you'll be out?"

Taryn stepped in again before I could reply. "Late. Real late."

Raschad flexed his jaw, the tiniest bit. "You... uh... you look nice," he managed.

I tilted my head, letting the dress do all the talking. "Thank you."

Taryn was thriving on the awkward. "She looks better than nice, Raschad. She looks like a whole *schnnack*! Doesn't she?"

He shot her a death glare, but she ignored it, going to grab Zhaire's little overnight bag from the couch.

Raschad looked back at me, eyes dark. "Just... be careful, alright?"

I nodded. "We will."

Taryn wiggled her eyebrows behind him, practically dancing from the mess she'd stirred up. He shook his head, muttered something under his breath, and went to scoop up Zhaire, who was bounding toward him.

When they left, Taryn turned to me, laughing and clapping her hands. "Girl! Did you see his *face*? You just shook his entire soul. I know that's right!"

I smiled, letting some of that pride settle into my bones. "It's not about him."

Taryn side-eyed me. "Mmhm. Now let's go make these men sweat."

At the club, Taryn and I pushed our way through the line. "VIP," she yelled over her shoulder, flashing the promoter a smile. We

WERE INSIDE IN SECONDS, LIGHTS STROBING, THE SMELL OF HOOKAH, coconut oil, and cologne thick in the air.

The DJ dropped a track that sent the whole place into a slow grind.

"Okay, this is a vibe!" Taryn shouted, as we went to the bar.

I tugged at the hem of my silver dress, hyper-aware of how much skin it showed. For a second, I felt the instinct to shrink, and cover. Then I caught my reflection in a mirrored wall, and paused. I looked good. Period.

Taryn handed me a shot. "We toasting to liberation tonight, Simi."

I laughed. "Liberation from what?"

"From any man who can't figure out what the hell he *got*," she fired back, raising her glass. "Now drink!"

I clinked her glass and knocked it back, the burn settling warm in my chest. It was easy after that. Easier than I expected. Men looked, not subtly, some not politely. They looked.

One stepped in close behind me on the way to the dance floor, hand hovering at my waist.

"Damn," he said low. "You came outside tonight."

I turned just enough to meet his eyes. "Clearly."

He grinned, and leaned in a little more. I stepped back, just out of reach, but still smiling. "Careful now," I said. "You're getting bold."

Taryn whooped beside me. "Oh, she back!"

Taryn and I hit the dance floor, and I didn't hold back. Didn't dance like I was waiting for the night to end. I was in it. I let the music carry me, hips rolling, arms up, hair brushing my shoulders as I turned. A man stepped in front of me, catching my rhythm easily. I let it all go. I wasn't a mom. I wasn't thinking about Raschad. I was just Simone. And that felt good.

"Where you been hiding?" he asked.

I laughed. "Not hiding. Just selective."

"Lemme get you a drink."

"Maybe later."

Taryn pulled me back in to dance, eyes bright. "You see that? You still got it."

At some point, I was laughing with Taryn when a voice slipped through the music.

"Simone?"

I turned, blinking against the club lights. Devon, Raschad's friend, who plays pickup games with him and my brothers.

"Hi, Devon!" I smiled genuinely. "What are you doing here?"

He gave me a friendly dap-hug and stepped back to take me in.

"Okay… yeah. You look… wow."

Taryn smirked. "She does, right?"

He chuckled. "Y'all both do. Out celebrating?"

"Just living." I said.

"I can see that," he said, glancing behind me.

A man had already stepped back toward me, waiting for his opening. Another hovered near, watching. Devon clocked it.

"Looks like ya'll got options tonight," he said.

I smiled, shaking my head. "We're good for now."

He nodded slowly. "Aight. I'ma let y'all enjoy," he stepped back, still watching for a second, then pulled his phone out as he turned away.

Taryn leaned over. "Oh, he's definitely snitching."

I shrugged. "Let him."

Taryn cackled like she'd been waiting for that. "*Exaaaaactly.*"

raschad

M*Y* *PHONE BUZZED JUST AFTER* I'*D PUT* Z*HAIRE TO BED.*

DEVON

Yo, not tryna start shit, but your girl out here looking like a problem. Line of dudes tryna shoot they shot.

I read it twice. Three times. My first reaction was to laugh, dead in my chest, like *that's crazy.* My second was a tight, hot burn that crawled up my throat. She wasn't my girl. We weren't together. I had no claim. But damn if I didn't feel every muscle in my body lock up at the thought of some random clown putting his hands on her.

I stared at the text for a minute, my heart spiking. *Not my girl,* I told myself. But my brain refused to listen.

She's out there, this late, looking like that?

My chest started burning as images hit me, fast. Simone laughing; Simone dancing with some asshole grinding on her ass; Simone in that dress, legs wrapped around some other man.

Nah.

I was up before I even knew it, pacing my living room, clenching and unclenching my fists. I told myself I wasn't going to be that toxic, jealous, controlling "baby daddy." I told myself she deserved to have her fun, and to move on.

But then I thought about her dating, getting serious with someone, bringing them around and Zhaire being there, hearing another man's voice in his mama's house.

Nah. That wasn't happening.

I shook my head, grabbed my keys, checking for my copy of Simone's house key. We had keys to each other's spots in case of emergencies since Zhaire was back and forth between us so often.

I walked down the hall, and tapped on Zhaire's door. "Aye, you left your Beyblades at your mom's right?"

Zhaire looked up at me, groggy and confused. "Daddy, you told me to leave them there. I'm sleepy."

"Yeah, but I thought about it and you might wanna get 'em back. Just in case."

He shrugged, "Okay."

simone

IT WAS A LITTLE AFTER MIDNIGHT WHEN ZION'S CAR PULLED UP OUTSIDE the club. Taryn had texted him somewhere around our third lemon drop, or he'd texted her, she wasn't entirely sure of the order of events at that point. Either way, there he was, waiting right out front, in a no parking zone with his hazards on.

"My husband," Taryn placed her hand on her chest like she'd spotted a vision.

"Your designated driver," I teased.

"Same thing."

We climbed in, Taryn in the front, me in the back. Zion looked at Taryn and leaned over and kissed her hard. She came up from it slightly dazed.

"Hi," she smiled at him.

"Hi, baby." His eyes cut to the rearview at me. "You good? Had a good time?"

"Yep. Life-changing," I said.

He pulled into traffic, and his hand found Taryn's between the seats. The radio was low and Summer Walker's *Heart of a Woman* played. Taryn turned it up and started singing, giving it everything she had. Full commitment with zero accuracy. She has never once landed a note in her life and has never once let that stop her. By the second bar she was eyes closed, one hand raised, fully in it.

Zion was smiling wide. The chorus hit and I joined in from the back-seat, which only encouraged her. She went for a run that had no business existing in any key, and held it.

"Okay, T." Zion's voice was easy. "It's dark out here, baby. We're not trying to crash."

Taryn dropped her hand and turned to him. "I was feeling that part."

"I know you were." He brought her hand up and kissed her knuckles.

When he pulled up to my place, Taryn turned around and pointed in my face. The lemon drop point.

"You still got it, Simi," she said, very seriously.

"I know."

"Say it."

"I still got it."

"Louder."

"Goodnight, Taryn."

I caught Zion's eye in the rearview. "Thank you, Z."

He gave me a nod. "Get inside safe."

My feet hurt, my head was light, and my voice was half-gone from laughing so much. It felt good, though. *So* good. I climbed the steps to my place, fishing my keys out of my clutch, only to pause when I noticed the faint glow of the TV behind my curtains.

Weird. I thought I'd turned it off.

I unlocked the door and stepped inside to find Raschad stretched across my sectional, remote in hand, and a half-empty juice pouch on the coffee table next to Zhaire's Beyblades.

He looked up, eyes tracking every inch of me. "You good?" he asked, nonchalantly.

I blinked. "What are you doing here?"

He scratched at his jaw. "Oh. Zhaire forgot something, so... I brought him back over."

I looked around. "Where is he?"

"In his room. Knocked out," he answered casually, like this was normal. Like I was supposed to accept him in my house at almost one a.m., posted up, watching ESPN highlights.

I crossed my arms. "*Okaaay.*"

Silence stretched between us, thick. His eyes did another slow drag down my body and back up.

"You had fun?" he asked.

I tilted my head, catching the tension wrapped around his words. "It was a good night."

"Cool. Cool." He paused. "You, uh... you looked good tonight."

"You already told me that."

"Yeah, well. Still true."

He shifted, eyes still skating over every exposed inch of me, then he cleared his throat. "It got late. He fell asleep. So I figured we'd just... crash here."

I narrowed my eyes. "You *figured?*"

He didn't even blink, his stare dropping to my thighs, up over my neckline, then back to my face. "Yeah."

I tried to laugh it off. "Well, damn, what if I had brought a date home?"

He sat up, elbows on his knees, voice dropping to a place so low it vibrated through me. "Did you?"

"Did I what?"

His nostrils flared. "Bring a date home."

I swallowed. "No. Obviously." I fanned my hands in the air behind me at an invisible person.

He nodded, his eyes still locked on me so hard I wanted to wrap my arms around myself to hide. But I didn't. Instead I lifted my chin. "Why do you care?"

He let out a harsh breath. "You know why."

"Say it," I pushed, my heart thudding. "If you got something to say, say it."

His gaze snapped up, possessive. "Because I'm a jealous mother-fucker, Simone. That's why."

I licked my lips and felt my hands tremble. "Jealous of what?"

"I don't want..." His eyes went molten, "I don't want another man touching you."

I inhaled deeply. "You don't get to say that, Raschad. Not when you —"

But he had already stood up, walking toward me, tall, ravenous and determined. "I *do* get to say it," he whispered when he got to me, stepping so close I had to look up.

Heat surged through me, sharper than the liquor still humming in my veins. "That's not fair," I said. "You don't want me, but you don't want anybody else to want me either?"

He looked surprised. "Who said I don't want you?"

"You did," I whispered. "Every time you push me away."

He towered over me now. "Don't get it twisted, Simone. I *always* want you."

My heart clenched, a wildfire sparking under my ribs. "Then why?"

"Because wanting you and being able to have you? Aren't the same thing. You know that," he ground out.

We stared at each other in silence.

"But right now..." he ran a finger down my arm. "Tonight? The way I'm feelin'? I don't give a fuck."

Before I could process what he was saying, his mouth was on mine, kissing me like it was his last chance. His hands caught my waist, palms warm through the fabric, fingers digging in making me melt into him.

I should have pushed him away. Held the line *he* drew. But the second he kissed me, my knees buckled, and I knew in that moment I wanted nothing more than to be devoured.

It was raw. Desperate. Teeth clashing, tongues tangling, months of suppressed emotions crashing between us. He spun me around, pressing me against the wall, hands sliding up my thighs, pulling the hem of my dress higher and higher, until I could barely catch my breath.

He growled low as I reached behind me and clawed at his pants, then he spun me back around as I dragged his shirt over his head, my nails raking up the ridges of his abs, feeling him twitch under my touch.

"Who'd you wear this for?" he rasped, lips moving down my neck, biting, sucking, probably leaving marks.

I met his eyes, dazed. "I wore it for me."

He growled low, nose brushing mine. "Lies. I think you wore it for me."

Before I could deny it again, he grabbed the back of my thighs, lifted me like it was light work, and carried me toward my stairs. My arms locked around his shoulders, the world spinning, and I felt him thick and hard between us, pushing against me with every step.

He pushed my bedroom door open, kicked it closed, then set me down, ripping the dress off me, tearing it away, leaving me in nothing but a black thong and a strapless bra.

"Raschad, my dress."

"I'll buy you a new one," he said as he lay me down on my bed, then leaned back to look at me.

"How are you this fine?" His chest was heaving, as he licked his lips. "It's not fair."

His hands slid between my thighs, palm flat, firm and warm against me, and my breath left my body in a single rush. He watched my face while he touched me, his palm rubbing gently against my clit.

"*Raschaaad...*"

"Relax. Breeeathe."

I couldn't breathe. He was kissing down my neck while his hand kept moving and I was losing track of everything. My name, the room, the months of distance between us, all of it dissolving under his hands.

"Tell me you want this," he demanded, licking and sucking my nipple while his hand picked up pace.

I gasped, head falling back. "I want it."

"You wanna come?" he murmured against my chest.

I nodded. Could barely even manage that.

"Say it."

"Yes." Barely a sound.

He pulled back to look at me again with almost a smile at the corner of his mouth. "Tell me how you wanna come? On my face? Or on my dick?"

I gulped, couldn't answer, my brain short-circuited. "Raschad," I finally replied, shocked and even more turned on at the same time.

He sucked my neck and I moaned. "I'm waiting for your answer."

I swallowed. "Y-your —" I couldn't finish the sentence, but reached down and gripped him through his pants.

He grinned. "Good choice. Turn around."

I did, heat slick between my thighs, my mind spinning from how fast and unstoppable he was. He pulled my panties down, then dragged a hand up the back of my thigh, over my ass, gripping tight enough to leave prints.

I whimpered, breath stuttering.

"You want me to stop?" he asked, voice low, warning.

I shook my head. "No."

"Good."

He shoved his sweatpants down enough to free himself. I barely had time to think before he pushed inside me, letting me stretch around him until the burn turned to bliss. We both moaned, the sound of it shattering the air.

He held me still, forehead to my shoulder. "Simone," he choked, "you feel so good, baby."

He started to move, hips rolling relentlessly, each thrust hitting a spot that made me lose my mind even more. My hands braced against the bed, knees weak, mouth open in a silent cry. He leaned over me, one hand tangling in my hair, the other snaking around to play with my clit while he fucked me from behind.

"Who's the only one who gets this?" He thrust into me harder.

"Youuuu," I moaned, eyes rolling back.

"You're mine, Simone. Always been mine like this. That right?"

"Y-yeeeess."

"*Shit,*" he panted. "You got no business feeling this *good*, Simone."

I fell apart so hard I thought I might break, my body convulsed, as I cried out his name. He kept going, chasing his own high, pounding into me so deep I could feel it in my belly.

Then he stilled, letting out a raw, tortured groan, shuddering against me, arms wrapped so tight around my waist I couldn't move. The moment hung there, breathless, hearts pounding, bodies shaking.

He stayed close, head to my shoulder, breath against the back of my neck, his hands almost cradling me. I closed my eyes and didn't let myself think past the moment. Just our bodies still tangled, slick with sweat, and the sheets twisted around us.

***

THE NEXT MORNING, I WOKE UP AND HE WAS ALREADY GONE FROM MY bed. I lay there for a moment and let myself feel it. Last night kept coming back in pieces, his hands on my waist, the way he'd kissed me like he was furious and starving at the same time. The things he'd said. *I'm a jealous motherfucker. I always want you.* The way he'd held me after, tight enough that I could hardly move, his heartbeat going hard against my back.

He'd come back. Not in the way that counted, I wasn't confused about that, but something in last night had told me things I'd been afraid to believe. That the distance he'd been keeping was deliberate. That he'd been choosing it, working at it, the same way I'd been working at accepting it. That underneath the co-parenting and the careful professionalism, none of it had gone anywhere for him either.

He hadn't moved on. He was just holding.

I pressed my face into his pillow, breathing in the faint smell of him, and let myself have thirty seconds of pure, uncomplicated hope. Then I got up.

I smelled bacon before I reached the bottom of my stairs. Raschad was in my kitchen, in joggers and no shirt, moving around with a spatula in one hand and Zhaire's juice already poured in his favorite cup waiting on the counter.

He turned when he heard me, with a half-grin. "Mornin'."

"Hey, Morning." My voice was hoarse.

Zhaire came barreling down the hall a moment later, sliding on the hardwood. His eyes lit up when he saw both of us.

"Daddy! Did you sleep here?"

Raschad caught my eyes for half a second. "Yeah, lil man. Like a sleepover."

Zhaire's whole face went bright. He accepted this completely, grabbed his juice off the counter, and climbed up onto the barstool like it was any other morning.

I moved to the counter and started cutting fruit, falling into the rhythm of the morning. Raschad plated the bacon, and asked Zhaire if he wanted his eggs scrambled, getting a very serious *yes, scrambled* in response.

I watched him at the stove for a moment. His muscular back, and the tattoos decorating his body. His easy domestic confidence, tilting the pan and moving around my kitchen like it was his. Zhaire was telling him something about a YouTube video he'd watched, as Raschad listened intently, asking follow-up questions, fully engaged with him.

I sat there taking the moment in. The three of us in my kitchen on a Sunday morning. Bacon, eggs and fruit. Sunlight coming through the window over the sink. *This was what it could be*, was the thought I couldn't stop. The possibility of it sat right there in the room with us, unbearably clear. This man, this child, this kitchen. Waking up to this.

I wanted it so badly it was almost embarrassing.

Soon, Zhaire finished eating, declared he was going to play with his Beyblades, and disappeared down the hall. The kitchen was awkwardly quiet. I kept my hands busy rinsing plates, not looking at Raschad, giving both of us a moment to locate ourselves.

He moved to the counter and leaned against it. I shut off the water and turned around, and looked at him.

"So," I said.

He exhaled through his nose. "Yeah."

"What does last night mean?"

He took another breath. "I don't have a clean answer."

"I'm not asking for clean. I'm asking for honest."

He looked at me for a moment. "Last night wasn't an accident. I wasn't confused. I knew what I was doing."

"Okay." I nodded. "So what does it mean going forward?"

"I don't know yet."

"You don't know yet," I repeated.

"I'm still working through things. You know that."

I kept my voice even. "I don't know what working through things is supposed to look like for *me*, Raschad. For the past several months, it's looked like me holding still while you do what you want. I've done that. I've respected it."

I paused. "But last night you were in my living room at one in the morning. You waited for *me*. You…" I let the rest sit between us. "But you're telling me you're not ready. What am I supposed to do with that?"

"I couldn't sit with it," he said. "The thought of you coming home with somebody. I know how that sounds. I'm not proud of it. But I'm not gonna pretend either."

"You couldn't sit with it. But I'm supposed to sit with knowing you've been out here '*no stringing it*'? Living your life."

"That's not the same thing," he retorted.

"How is it not?"

"Because…" His voice dropped, "I didn't do anything wrong. I didn't create this. I didn't make the choice that took years from me." His eyes found mine and held them and my breath went short. "*You* did that. Not me. So yeah, maybe my version looks different than yours. Maybe it should. Maybe I've been out here living because *you* left me nothing else."

His words landed like something thrown. My heart was going fast but I didn't move. For a moment everything he'd been holding since that day in my office. The version of this conversation that hadn't fully happened yet. The anger that he'd been trying to keep swallowed, all of it was right there on the surface in his eyes. Then he looked away. Took two breaths and when he looked back he was controlled again.

But I had already felt the temperature of it. And the guilt in my chest pressed. Because maybe he was right. I had never once tried to argue my way out of that truth. I owned it. I would own it for the rest of my life.

"You're right," I said quietly. "I created this. And I carry that every day. I'm not standing here asking you to forget it." I looked at him. "But Raschad, I've been punishing myself for years. I know what I took from both of you."

I stopped and steadied myself. "I'll never forgive myself for that. Never. But I cannot let that guilt be the reason I stay stuck in my own life anymore. I can't."

"I'm not trying to make you stuck," he said.

"Aren't you?" I kept my voice even and measured, because I needed him to actually hear me. "You're telling me you don't know. Not yes, not no. You need more time. Okay. I could work with that, if we were working *toward* something. I could keep waiting. I *would* wait."

My voice almost broke but I held it. "But that's not what this is. You *don't* know. And while you don't know, you're living. You're going out. You're writing songs about sleeping with women. Your version of not knowing looks like a full life." I paused. "Mine looks like work, home,

Zhaire. Work, home, Zhaire. Because every time I think about anything else, I think about you."

I shook my head. "I can't keep thinking about you when you're not thinking of me back. I want joy in my life too. My version of waiting can't look like what it's looked like to you anymore, Raschad. Not to make you jealous. Staying frozen while you decide if you can *really* forgive me? That's not healthy for me."

He stared at me, not responding. So I kept going. "I can't fix it. I can't give you those years back with Zhaire. So maybe, we should just call it what it is. Unforgivable. It's just something you won't ever get over."

He looked at me for a long moment. "That's not it," he said finally.

"What?"

"The years with Zhaire," he said it quietly. "That's not what I can't get over."

I didn't move, confused. "What do you mean?"

"Zhaire is good." His face softened. "He doesn't know what he missed and I don't think about what I missed much anymore because what I have with him now is..." He paused and shook his head slightly. "That's not my pain, Simone. Not really."

"Then... what?" I asked.

"You left me," he said simply. "Not Zhaire's father. *Me.* I let you in." His jaw worked. "I don't do that. I don't. But I did it with you. And then you were gone." He looked at me, then looked away. "With Zhaire, I can look at now and see what we have. I can hold that. But the other part..."

He exhaled. "I loved you. I let you all the way in and you —"

"Mommy," Zhaire appeared in the doorway with a Beyblade in each hand. "Daddy said he'd battle me but I need you to be the judge because last time he said he won but he didn't win."

I looked at my son, then at the man across from me, who had already pulled himself back, the moment closed.

"We'll be right there, baby," I said.

"Yes! Get ready to lose Daddy! Come on!" He disappeared back down the hall, already narrating the terms of the battle to himself.

The kitchen was quiet again. Raschad looked at me. I looked at him. The thing he'd started to say was still in the room, unfinished and waiting.

Neither of us reached for it.

"Go be with your son," I said quietly.

We stared at each other for one more second, then he nodded and went, and I stood there alone thinking.

I had been carrying the wrong thing. I had thought I knew what I'd done to him. I had been so sure I knew the shape of it, the parental debt that couldn't be repaid. The one I'd decided could never be settled. I had organized my guilt around that. Built my penance around that. But that wasn't what was still sitting between us. It was simpler than that. And so much harder.

He hadn't finished. But I understood enough. We fell in love and then I'd just... left him. There was nothing I could say to that that wouldn't fall short.

28 /
breaking point

THIS CHAPTER HAS A SOUNDTRACK

Breaking Point by Leon Thomas

simone

FIVE WEEKS SINCE THAT MORNING IN MY KITCHEN. HIS SENTENCE STILL floating there. *I loved you and you…*

He never came back to finish it. I'd given him five weeks and he hadn't knocked on my door or made a call that wasn't about our son. And I understood that. But understanding it didn't make the incompleteness of it easier to carry. I didn't know how that sentence ended. I had guesses — *left me, broke me, betrayed me* — but I didn't know for certain, and not knowing the shape of it meant I couldn't fully measure what I was asking him to recover from.

What I did know was what I'd told him. My waiting was going to look different.

Taryn and I were at lunch after shopping, talking about everything and nothing, when I told her. "Nasir asked me out again," I said.

"I know. Zion told me. He heard it from Tre, who'd heard it from some mutual friend. Men are such gossips. What did you say?"

"Nothing yet. If I say yes, it feels like giving up on that sentence. Like I'm deciding it doesn't matter how he was going to complete it."

"And if you say no?"

"Then I'm staying frozen. Waiting on something that might not come. While he goes on about his life."

"Simone," she leaned forward. "You looked him in the eyes and you told him your waiting was going to look different. Did you mean it when you said it?"

"Yes."

"Then mean it now. Nasir seems like a decent man, and he's been patient if not persistent. Go eat a nice lunch or dinner with someone who wants to be there."

I sat with it. "Okay," I said.

"Okay?"

"Yes. I'll say yes."

She nodded once, "Great! Now tell me what you're wearing. Do we need to hit another one of these boutiques?"

I STOOD IN MY CLOSET AND FELL APART A LITTLE. NOT DRAMATICALLY. But I was standing there deciding what to wear on my date with Nasir, realizing how completely I'd edited myself out of my own life.

I had clothes. Plenty of them. Things I put on to feel good and look good. But I hadn't dressed for the purpose of going out with a man since years ago when I went to a beach party, to meet someone who would change my life.

Seven years. I'd been invisible on purpose for seven years. Not because men hadn't looked, or asked. But I'd trained myself not to receive it. To deflect and exist in public as a mother, a sister, a professional, never as a woman who wanted to be wanted.

And now I was standing in my closet trying to get dressed for an early evening dinner date and the muscle had atrophied. The instinct had gone dormant. I was staring at rows of clothes that covered every version of myself except the one Nasir was meeting this afternoon.

After what was probably an hour, I finally settled on a maxi sundress. Rich copper, fitted at the waist, flowing at the hem, low neckline to tease a little cleavage. I held it against myself in the mirror. "That's me," I said to myself.

I showered, did my hair and makeup, got dressed, and I looked in the mirror. I saw her. The woman underneath. The one I'd been burying. She was still there. Under the guilt and the control and the years of *I'm fine*. She was still there. She was beautiful. And she was done being invisible.

I picked up my bag, head out my door and paused. I was nervous. Like the first day at a new job. I took a deep breath. *You got this*, I told myself, then nervously set out toward my first date in seven years.

MY DATE WITH NASIR WAS EASY. I WAS ACTUALLY SURPRISED AT HOW EASY it had been to sit across from a man and just *be*. No calibration of what I was letting show. No inventory of distance. He asked questions and listened to my answers and laughed at the right moments and at no point did I have to manage anything.

Two hours at a table in the back of the restaurant. He talked about a case he'd been working, the kind he actually cared about. I talked about the back-to-school drive our foundation was hosting soon. At some point he said something that made me laugh so hard I had to set my glass down. He looked pleased.

"There you are," he said.

"What do you mean?"

"You're relaxed," he said. "You were a little in your head at the beginning."

"Was I that obvious?"

"A little," he admitted. "But I'm patient."

He was. Nasir was patient and warm and genuinely interested in what I said, in what I thought. He was good company. I liked him. I just didn't feel anything that started in my chest and moved outward. I looked at him across the table and thought *my cousin Marlowe would love him.* I put the thought away and smiled at something else he said.

When the check came he suggested we go for a walk. There was a fall festival down by the lake with local vendors, and activities. I said yes.

"This has been nice," Nasir said, as we walked. "I was starting to think you were avoiding me."

"Just busy with work and Zhaire. Single working mom life."

"I respect that." He smiled. "But you need to have some fun too though."

"Agreed. That's what I'm trying to do, these days." I smiled.

He took my hand, lacing his fingers through mine naturally like it was something we'd done before. It felt fine. His hand was large and his grip was firm and there was nothing wrong with it. It didn't feel wrong, but it didn't feel right, but I filed the thought away because I had promised myself I wasn't going to spend this afternoon comparing.

We walked around a bend in the path and I could hear the basketball court before I saw it. The percussion of a game in progress, sneakers on concrete, and trash talking. Nasir was mid-sentence about something, and I was nodding and present and doing fine, when the energy around us shifted. Not unlike the way air shifts before a storm.

And then I saw the court. I clocked Julian and Zion first, facing off at each other. A few other guys I didn't know. Then Tre, animated, calling somebody out. Khairos was chugging water on the sideline. And then… Raschad.

We had maybe four seconds before the path curved into full view of anyone facing our direction. And my first thought, before anything else, was go to *the other path.* The one that branched left a few feet back and wound around the far side of the park. Longer, less direct, no basketball courts. I could say *oh, let's go this way,* and make it sound like I just wanted to see the fountain, and we would just —

I stopped that thought and made myself keep walking.

You're allowed to be here. You made childcare arrangements and you put on a nice outfit and you came outside. That is not a crime.

But my heart had already decided it was a crisis. *You don't owe him an explanation. You're on a date. You're allowed.*

We kept walking and the court got closer. I don't know what made him look up. The game was live. Raschad had the ball, ready to pass, but then he turned his head toward the path. He went still for a second. I watched him see us. Walking together. Holding hands.

Not *see*. Register it and process it. His chin lifted slightly and then, slowly, all of the game around him stopped mattering. He bounced the ball once. Twice. A third time, slower. Then he held it in both hands, and passed it sideways without looking.

"Carter," somebody behind said, confused.

He didn't turn around, he just started walking off the court towards us. Not fast. An unhurried stride, which was somehow more alarming than if he'd jogged. The game paused behind him. Someone called his name again. He ignored it. Everyone on the court just stood there and watched, the way you watch something that might resolve itself or might not.

Nasir finally noticed and I felt the slight change of his posture beside me. He didn't let go of my hand.

"That your brothers and…?" he asked.

"Yes," I said and released Nasir's hand, but then he placed his hand at my back.

And then suddenly Raschad was in front of us. He looked at Nasir first. *At* him the way you inventory someone. Slowly, starting at his face, moving down, moving back up. Taking his time. Not hostile exactly. Nasir held it without flinching, which I both appreciated and knew was not going to help anything.

Then Raschad looked at me. I could see the calculation in his eyes as he looked at my hair, then his eyes rolled slowly down my maxi dress, then back up again. I could see his Adam's apple bobbing up and down as he swallowed. But he didn't say anything, making the silence heavy.

I broke first. "Hi, Raschad."

He let another second pass, not saying anything. "Where's Zhaire?" he finally spoke.

I felt anger starting to claw its way up my throat. The question was perfectly reasonable and absolutely *not* reasonable at the same time, and we both knew it.

"With Taryn." I kept my voice even. "Why?"

"Just asking." His eyes flicked back to Nasir, briefly, and then back to me. The controlled thing he was doing with his face slipping at the edges. "So what's this?" He lifted his chin toward the two of us.

Beside me, Nasir's shoulders settled and he straightened. "Raschad. Good to see you man."

They knew each other. Not deeply, but enough to have been at the same club, or gym, and through Tre. Not enough for it to have ever been personal. Until now, maybe.

Raschad's eyes moved from Nasir's face down to his hand on my back, then back up. "Torres," he replied flatly. "Didn't know you two were like that."

"We're —" Nasir started.

"On a date," I said, lifting my head. If he wanted to play territory, I wasn't going to make it easy.

Raschad's eyes swept over Nasir again slower. The sizing up of a man who stood six-six and had spent his life making other men feel small without trying.

"Right," he said finally with an edge that prickled my skin. He looked at Nasir. "How long you been... dating?"

"Man…" Nasir started, and I heard the shift in his voice. Amusement, almost.

"Raschad." I said it carefully, trying to keep the temperature where it was. "We're just—"

"I asked the man a question, Simone. Let him answer." His eyes were still on Nasir.

Nasir smiled, but not warmly. "First date." He let it sit. "But not the last I hope." He pressed his hand on my back pulling me in slightly.

I looked at him. *Why did you have to say it like that.* I thought. He didn't notice. Or he noticed and didn't care.

Raschad stepped closer, heat in his eyes. "Simone. Let me talk to you for a second."

I started to answer, when Nasir's hand moved from my back to my waist, deciding he wasn't going to be dismissed from his own date.

"We're in the middle of something," Nasir said pleasantly. "Whatever it is, can't it wait?"

Raschad looked at his hand and chuckled.

"Nasir," I said quietly. He squeezed my waist once, gently, like he was telling me *I've got this*, and I felt my stomach drop.

"You know what this is," Raschad said to him, the volume dropping on his voice. "*Who* she is?"

"I know you co-parent." Nasir said it straight. "That's what I know."

"That's what you know? Move your hand, bruh." Raschad said, very quiet.

Nasir didn't move it. "Why don't you go finish your game, man? She's fine. Y'all can chat later."

Raschad looked at me, then reached over and lifted Nasir's hand off my waist, like he was picking lint off my dress. His hand replaced it, palm flat against my stomach, and he shifted me one step back.

"Watch out, Sim."

Then he turned back and caught Nasir clean across the jaw. Nasir stumbled back a few steps, caught himself, and came forward with one shot to Raschad's ribs, then a hit to the side of his face. Raschad grabbed him by the shirt and punched him in the side of his head. Then they were locked up. Two men grabbing, grappling, neither one willing to be the first to let go.

Julian was there in seconds, I didn't even see him cross the distance. He had Raschad from behind, arms locked under his. "CONTROL YOURSELF." He kept repeating. "Calm down."

Zion materialized between them, as Tre nudged Nasir back by the shoulders. "Hey, hey, come on, man."

"Muthafucka is crazy!" Nasir shouted in genuine disbelief.

"He's leaving," Julian said flatly. "Raschad. We're going. Now."

I was shaking. Families were staring. A kid had stopped mid-stride on a nearby path. And then, before I'd finished a single thought, before I knew what my body was deciding, I moved toward Raschad.

I was in front of him before I understood what I'd done. My eyes moved over his face, down to his ribs where Nasir had connected. The cut at the corner of his mouth. His breathing, still ragged. I was looking for damage, making sure he was okay.

I registered where I was standing about two seconds after I'd gotten there. Raschad looked at me. Julian looked at me over his shoulder. Raschad's chest was still heaving and his eyes on mine were suddenly too much.

His face fell. "Simone, I'm sorry."

"Don't." I couldn't get out a full sentence for what I meant. *Don't apologize right now because I don't have anywhere to put it. Don't look at me like that. Don't make this harder than you've already made it.* All of it at once. None of it sayable.

I looked at him for one more second, long enough to confirm he wasn't seriously hurt. Then I made myself turn around. Tre had stepped back, giving me room. Nasir was off to the side, working his jaw carefully.

"Hey." I came to him, touching his arm lightly. "Are you okay? I'm so sorry. That should've never happened."

"I'm fine." He looked at me. Then, briefly, at where Raschad was still being held back by Julian. Then back to me. "Let's walk."

We moved through the park together, past the staring faces. I kept my eyes forward. I could feel exactly where my brothers and Raschad were standing, watching us leave without having to turn around.

Nasir's car was at the far end of the lot. We didn't talk all the way there. Both of us processing what happened. When we stopped at his car, he turned to face me, not saying anything right away. He just looked at me for a moment, keys in his hand.

"I'm really sorry," I said again. "That was completely —"

"I need to say something." He turned his keys over once. "I like you, Simone. I have for a while. And I'm not trying to be harsh with you." He paused. "But that man just punched me in the face. In a public park. In the middle of the day."

"I know. There's no excuse for —"

"And the first thing you did was walk straight to him. Not to me. To him."

I didn't say anything.

"I'd be lying if I said it didn't tell me everything I needed to know," he met my eyes.

"It's complicated," I said, the most useless thing I could offer.

"Clearly," he almost laughed. "Look, I'm not interested in being somebody's placeholder while they figure out if they want somebody else."

"Nasir —"

"I hope you figure it out," he said. "I genuinely do."

I nodded. "You're right. Listen, I'll get a ride with my brothers," I said before he could ask. "You don't need to worry about that. Go home. Take care of your face."

He looked at me for a second, and nodded once. "Take care of yourself."

"You too."

He got in his car and I stepped back, as he reversed out of the space, and then he was gone. I stood there for a moment. One date. That was all I'd asked for. Three hours and a walk in the park.

I pulled out my phone and opened the family group chat.

> Can one of you give me a ride home? I'm at the east parking lot.

Three dots appeared immediately. Then:

ZION

Raschad rode with Tre and me

TRE

Jules got you

JULIAN

Main entrance. Two minutes.

Moments later, my phone buzzed again.

RASCHAD NOVA

We need to talk. Tonight.

There's nothing to talk about.

RASCHAD NOVA

There's everything to talk about. I'm coming over.

Don't.

raschad

———

TWO HOURS LATER, I WAS AT SIMONE'S DOOR.

"I told you not to come here," she answered her door with an atti-
tude and wouldn't look at me.

"Since when do you get to tell me what to do?" I stepped past her
into the foyer. "We need to talk."

"About my dating life? Because that's none of your business."

"It *is* my business."

Her eyes flashed. "You keep me at arm's length. Make it crystal clear
you can't be with me. So I *finally* listen. I *finally* start to move on. And
somehow that's about *your* ass?"

She was right, I had no right to feel what I felt. Hot, irrational,
possessive jealousy over a woman I refused to be with, but couldn't stand
the thought of her being with anyone else. But I wasn't gonna admit
that.

"Everything you do is about me."

"Not true."

"What about Zhaire?" My words came out before I could stop them.

"You gonna bring random men around my son? Let him get attached to someone who might not stick around?"

I saw the direct hit in her eyes. The way she flinched like I'd slapped her.

"That's not fair and you know it!"

"Fair? I'm still getting to *know* my son. Still building that relationship *you* kept from me. And now you want to date? Holding hands and shit like it's serious? And then what? Confuse Zhaire by bringing another man into the picture?"

The pain on her face told me I'd hit exactly where I was aiming. And I hated myself for it even as I kept going. "You want to introduce chaos into his life because you're lonely?"

"Fuck you! Stop. Just shut up." Her voice was a blade and she took a shaky breath. "You don't get to do that. You don't get to use our son as a weapon because *you're* scared of losing me to someone else."

"I'm not!"

"Yes, you are! You're using Zhaire to manipulate me into staying alone while *you* date and *you* fuck whoever *you* want! That's exactly what you're doing."

"I would *never* bring a man around Zhaire until I was sure about him. I would *never* let our son get attached to someone who I didn't think was going to be permanent. I'm a better mother than that, and you know it."

I did know better and knew it was a cheap shot.

"I'm not going to stay alone because you're threatened by the idea of another man in our life. If you don't want that to happen, then figure your shit out, Raschad! Decide if you want to try to be together or not. But don't you *dare* hide behind Zhaire to keep me on hold."

The challenge hung in the air. But facing the real issue was more terrifying than any argument. So I deflected. "You don't even want that man. Be for real. He could never make you feel what I make you feel."

"You're right," she said, and for a second I thought she was agreeing with me. "Nasir will never make me feel the way you do. He'll never make me question every decision I've ever made. He'll never break my heart every single day just by existing. Because I could never love him the way I love you. And maybe that's better. Loving someone who can't love me back is worse than not loving anyone at all."

I couldn't say anything to that.

"So what do you want from me, Raschad? You want me to stay alone forever? Is that to be my punishment? Because I did that already. Six years of it. Isolated myself. Didn't date. Didn't let anyone in. Didn't let anyone touch me."

"What?"

"Before you came back." She said it small like it cost her something. "I hadn't been with anyone since California. Until that night. Zhaire's accident. No one but you since."

The admission hit the air and just sat there.

"That… that was six years— Simone, you're telling me…"

She looked away like she was embarrassed to admit it. She hadn't been with anyone after me, for six years, and when she finally was… it was me again. I was the only man who had seen her like that… touched her in years.

If I wasn't already possessive and conflicted before, knowing this had my head completely fucked up. The word echoed in my head, primal, irrational, and completely at odds with everything I'd been telling myself for a year. *Mine.* She really was *always mine*. But I couldn't say that.

"And what about you?" her voice cut through my spiral. "You're really going to stand there and act like you've been celibate since the last time we…" she raised her eyebrows.

I didn't answer. Didn't deny it.

"So it is true," she said softly.

"That's different and you know it."

"It's the same thing, Raschad!"

"It's not, because they don't mean shit to me."

"So what? Keep me on ice while you sleep with other women but lose your mind if I do the same? You gonna fight every date I have, huh? What's your plan, Raschad? Keep passing time until you're done punishing me?"

"I don't —" I stopped.

"You don't what? You don't know? You don't have an answer?"

"I'm not punishing you Simone. It honestly feels like you're punishing *me*."

"I'M NOT PUNISHING YOU! I'M TRYING TO *SURVIVE* YOU!" The words tore out of her, raw as tears fell. "Do you know what it's like to love someone who looks at you and sees the worst thing you've ever done? Every single time. You look at me and you're still deciding. Still measuring. And I have given you space and time and grace." She took a breath. "But I am *drowning* in the space you put between us. And I can't keep loving you in a place where you won't have the courage to love me back."

"Courage?" My voice broke open. "You want to talk to me about *courage*? I moved across the country and gave up my career without a second thought. I moved to a town where I knew *nobody*. I sit across from you, the woman who kept my child from me for FIVE YEARS, and I co-parent. I show up! You want to talk about courage?"

"But not with me," she said quietly. "You have the courage for everything except me."

I scoffed "And you're surprised by that?"

She looked up at me with wet eyes, hurt and confused. I stood there looking at her and felt the thing I'd been holding for a year shift loose in my chest.

"You want to know why?" My voice didn't sound like mine anymore. "You want to know the reason?"

"Yes," she nodded.

"Because you're the only person who can *destroy* me!" It came out from somewhere I didn't know I had access to. "Everyone else, every*thing* else, I can survive. I HAVE survived. But you? If I let you in again and you keep something else from me. Betray me like that again? If you get scared and you shut me out the way you shut me out for *years?*"

"I wouldn't —"

"You DID! You already did it Simone! Broke my heart TWICE! And I'm supposed to just trust that it won't happen again? Trust the woman who looked me dead in my face and knew what she was keeping from me and let me go? Who let me fall deeply and completely in love with her, then just said, '*fuck that shit*'. And poof! Disappeared. *No* explanation, *no* conversation, *no* goodbye. Nothing! Do you understand how that crushed me? Do you even get that?"

She flinched, full body, and began to cry. It almost stopped me. But everything underneath a year of polite smiles was finally surfacing, and pouring out. My eyes were burning, blurring. I blinked and felt it on my face, hot tears I'd been holding since the day I knew Zhaire was mine.

"You knew where I was," I said barely audible. "You had my number. You could've called me any day for five years and you *CHOSE,* every—single—day, *not* to. And I understand your fear and trauma and all that. I really do, Simone. But understanding why someone stabbed you doesn't make you not bleed."

Simone slid down on the wall. We hadn't moved far from her front door that whole time. She sat on the floor in the entryway of her house, in a sundress she'd put on for another man, and she came apart.

"I... know." She gasped between her words. "I know what I did to you. I have known every single day. I wake up and I know it. I go to sleep and I know it. I look at Zhaire and I see every moment you should have been there and I KNOW." Her tears were streaming. "His first word was *mama* and I cried for two hours. Not because I was happy. Because you should have been there to hear it. He walked for the first time and I recorded it and I actually almost sent it to you. But I couldn't... didn't. And I have hated myself for it."

She wiped her face with both hands. "I know what I did when I left you like that. I let you call. I let you text. I let you wonder. I let you think you'd done something wrong when you hadn't done anything. I know how it looked. What it probably felt like. Like you didn't matter. Like none of it mattered." She shook her head. "But you *did* matter. None of that was about you. I didn't *plan* to leave you in the dark with no good-bye. I know how that sounds… but I never meant for it to be permanent. I never meant to never tell you about Zhaire. I just… didn't know how to come back, and every day made coming back harder."

"Why?" My voice cracked. "WHY couldn't you just —"

"Because my mother was dead." It ripped out of her. "And when I found out I was pregnant, I didn't feel joy. I felt terror. I saw my mother's lifeless body. I saw her coffin. I thought I was going to die the same way she did. And telling you meant making it real. Meant admitting it was happening. Meant needing you and what if I needed you and you didn't come? Or what if you came and then I died and…"

"And *after* that?" I asked. "Once he was born, Simone?"

She didn't answer right away. I waited.

"Do you remember how I told you my father left?" She said finally. "My mother died and it hollowed him out. It turned him into a ghost in our house first, and then finally an actual ghost. Every month he didn't come home made the next month harder for him to face. His guilt compounded. Until coming home felt impossible. Until he convinced himself we were better off without him showing up after all that time. He's still gone. Almost twenty years."

I looked at her.

"I spent years being angry at him for that. And then I spent the last few years being confused by how much I understood it."

She looked up at me. "Shame is a coward. Makes itself at home between the thing you did and the person you know you should be. And the longer you let it stay, the more of your home it takes up, until you're living in the corners of your life trying not to disturb it."

"I didn't think I was like my father, but I inherited his avoidance. The way the longer something goes unaddressed the more impossible addressing it feels, and the more impossible it feels the easier it is to keep not addressing it."

"My father's grief became guilt became shame became absence. Then I did my own version of it. My fear became a secret became a lie became years of silence. I told myself I would tell you eventually. 'Soon' I'd told myself so many times."

Her hands pressed flat against the floor. "Zhaire was born and the choice I'd made was just… done. I couldn't find the door back in. I'm not saying that to excuse it," she said. "It doesn't. You asked me why and that's the real answer."

I stood there absorbing what she'd said. My father had abandoned me too, and I'd always said that I would not be like him. And here was Simone telling me that she didn't want to be like her father. I kept turning that over in my head.

"Okay," I said, scraped clean of everything except what it was. Not absolution, just: *I heard you.*

"My father wasn't in our lives." I said, calmly. "I made myself a promise so early I can't even remember when I made it, that I would never be that man. That whatever else I did or didn't do, my kids would know me. Would have me. Every day." I looked at her. "That was one thing I was always certain of."

She was very still.

"And you made me him anyway." My words came out flat, not to wound her. Just true. "You made the choice. For both of us to become our fathers. Except I didn't even know I was doing it."

She pressed her lips together. "I know," she said, barely audible. "I know that. There is nothing I can say to that. There's no version of I'm sorry that's big enough for that."

Then she said, softer: "He looks for you first."

I looked at her, confused.

"Zhaire. In any room. He finds you first." She took a deep breath. "He doesn't remember a time without you. Like… cognitively he knows there was a before, but in his body? In the way he moves through the world? You have always been there. You are so essential to him that he can't imagine the shape of his life without you in it. Neither can I." She said it steadily. "I can't give you back what I took. I can't give you the first word or the first steps or the birthday parties. I know that. But you've made up for it. Every single day. And he feels it. He feels all of it."

"You are nothing like your father, Raschad." she said. "You never were."

I looked at the floor. "I don't need…" I started.

"I know you don't need me to tell you. I'm saying it because it's true and you deserve to actually hear it."

The fight had gone out of the room, but not resolved or fixed. Nothing between us was fixed and we both knew it. But there was a feeling, like air in a pressure cooker that had finally been allowed to release.

I was on the floor too. I didn't remember sitting down. But I was across from her, knees up, both of us in her hallway with tears and the truth between us, instead of buried under a year of being careful.

"I'm tired," I said.

"Me too."

We just sat there. Both of us wrung out on the floor. We hadn't gotten to the other side of it. But we were done trying, at least for the night.

"I don't know where to go from here," I said. "I don't know how to fix this. I don't know if it can be fixed."

She wiped her eyes. "I grieve you, Raschad. Every day. Grieving what we could've been. And I can't even mourn it properly because you are right here. Present and absent at the same time." More tears fell. "Losing someone who's gone is one thing. Losing someone who's standing at your door every other morning, that's a different kind of torture."

I closed my eyes.

"I still love you," she said, quietly. "I have always loved you. Even when I was scared and alone. Even when I was avoiding. Even now, when you look at me like I'm your biggest regret."

I opened my eyes and stared at this woman who'd given me the greatest gift and the deepest wound of my life. Who'd loved me enough to name our son after me but kept us apart. Sitting on the floor of her hallway, giving me the one thing she had left.

I didn't have an answer to her admission. I had a thousand things in my heart and not one of them could find its way to my mouth. The hurt and the love were tangled together and I couldn't separate them.

I stood up. "I need to go," I said.

She nodded and just sat there on the floor. I walked to the door and opened it. "Nasir. He didn't deserve that. I'll reach out to him."

"Okay."

"And Simone?"

She looked up at me. "Yes?"

"You're not my biggest regret. My biggest regret is not fighting harder to reach you back then. If I hadn't given up... things would be different."

I leaned down and kissed the top of her head. Heard her breath catch.

Then I left.

blanket fort

raschad

IT HAD BEEN A WEEK SINCE I'D PUNCHED A MAN IN THE MIDDLE OF A park. I was wrong. Embarrassingly wrong. And I'd known it before my fist even landed. I'd apologized to Nasir the next day, and he accepted it with more grace than I deserved. So that part was done. Easy.

What I'd been sitting with since was harder. Because you didn't go after a man over a woman you keep saying you're just co-parenting with. You can't do that and then go back to pretending the line you'd drawn was real.

I wanted Simone. I'd stopped arguing with that part. That part I was sure of. But wanting didn't mean going back. Going back meant trusting her again, and there was still a voice in my head that kept saying *a man who goes back to that is a fool*. Kept telling me that I'd spent a year rebuilding something that looked like dignity and if I walked back through that door, I would be giving that away.

I couldn't tell if that voice was protecting me or just afraid. Couldn't stop hearing it. Couldn't stop thinking about her either. So I'd been living in the purgatory of showing up to studio sessions, calls, dinners and doing all of it with half my mind somewhere else. She was just about all I thought about now.

It had been raining all week. By Thursday afternoon the weather alerts were warning of a tropical storm system pushing inland from the coast. Wind advisories, possible flooding, the kind of thing that made the whole studio stop and check their phones between sessions.

"Alright, I'm out," Tre said, standing and stretching. "Gonna go stock up before the shelves get wiped. Ya'll need anything?"

"Going to get Taryn," Zion said, already reaching for his keys. "Head home and stay put."

Julian looked up from his phone. "I'll check on Simone and —"

"I've got them," I said.

Everyone looked at me. Julian set his phone down slowly. "You sure?"

"Yeah."

Tre tilted his head. "How things been, by the way? Since you tried to dogwalk Nasir."

"We're good. I apologized. He was decent about it."

"Mmhm." Tre nodded. "And Simone?"

"We're good."

Nobody pushed it. Julian picked his phone back up. Zion headed for the door and I started looking up the nearest hardware store and making a list of supplies; *candles, batteries, bottled water, backup charger, something to tie down yard furniture.*

"What are you looking for?" Tre asked, reading over my shoulder.

"Hardware store. She's probably got nothing prepped."

"Look at Raschad. Showing up with tropical storm prep like a knight in shining armor." Tre shook his head, grinning. "Nothing says '*sorry for beating up your date*' like candles and a backup generator."

Zion laughed from the doorway. Julian kept his eyes on his phone but I saw the corner of his mouth curve. I didn't argue with any of it. Because the honest version was that I didn't just feel responsible for Zhaire, and by extension for her. I also wanted to show up, because I still felt bad about what I'd done. And maybe, I wanted to see where her head was after the way things ended that day. We hadn't been in the same space alone since. Just the quick handoffs.

I wanted more than sixty seconds.

"Moreau's Hardware Store on Main Street is still open, five miles east," Tre said. "Get extra batteries. Her flashlights are probably dead."

"Thanks."

He grabbed his jacket and slapped my back. "Go be her hero."

"Shut up," I chuckled.

I went to the store, stopped home to pack a bag, then headed out into the rain to Simone's.

SIMONE OPENED THE DOOR BEFORE I FINISHED KNOCKING. I DON'T KNOW what I was expecting, but I wasn't expecting this. No makeup, skin glowing, hair in a bun. She was barefoot. Her hot pink toenails contrasted against the hardwood floor. Depending on how she stood it was genuinely unclear if she had shorts on.

She was wearing a hoodie. Oversized. Swallowing her. Clearly worn from years of washing. UCLA was across the front in letters that had started to crack at the edges.

My hoodie.

I recognized it before my brain caught up with what I was seeing. I knew this hoodie. I'd worn it a hundred times before that weekend. I'd put it on her shoulders on that beach in San Diego because she was cold and I wanted an excuse to be closer to her.

She'd kept it.

Seven years. She'd kept it and she still wore it and she had no realization she was standing in front of me with it on. She hadn't put it on for me. She didn't even know I was coming. She'd put it on because it was comfortable. Because it was hers, or had become hers. And somehow that got to me more than if she'd done it on purpose.

I forced myself to look at her face instead of the faded letters across her chest. I was not going to say anything. She hadn't thought about it. And if I said something, she would know that I knew, and then we'd both be standing in this doorway holding something we hadn't agreed to hold tonight.

"Raschad," she said, surprised.

"You..." I caught myself and cleared my throat. "You look comfortable."

She blinked. "What?"

"Nothing. Did you see the weather alert? They upgraded the storm."

She looked past me at the sky. "Oh. I was inside working, I didn't realize it got that bad."

"Well, good thing you got me."

She looked at the bags I was carrying. "You didn't have to."

"My son is here," I said. "The mother of my son is here." I met her eyes. "Where else would I be?"

She gave a small smile, stepped back and let me in.

Zhaire materialized, already at full volume. "DADDY! The sky was green!" He grabbed my hand and pulled me toward the window to show me personally.

I'd been inside maybe fifteen minutes when a lawn chair hit her back door hard enough to make us all jump.

"Oh! The furniture." Simone said, already moving.

"Stay inside, I got it." I was already heading for the back door.

The wind had picked up seriously in the last hour. I went around her yard gathering, chairs, a side table, little potted plants, and moved most of it to her shed and garage. Securing what I couldn't relocate. By the time I came back inside I was soaked.

She was standing in the doorway with towels. "Thank you," she said. "Go shower. I'm gonna cook something while we still have power."

I grabbed my bag, showered fast, and came back out to the smell of whatever she'd been making. She was mid-stir, her back to me, head tilted the way it did when she was concentrating.

Suddenly the power went out.

"No, no, no!" She grabbed the pot off the burner. "I was almost done, I just needed fifteen more minutes"

"Simone."

"The chicken's not finished, and the rice is—" she sighed.

"It's okay." I was already at the cabinet, getting containers. "We stick it in the freezer. It'll keep, as long as the power is not out more than a day."

"I brought stuff that doesn't need to be cooked." I nodded toward my grocery bags. "We're fine."

She exhaled and watched me transfer food to containers with more calm than she currently had. Zhaire appeared in the kitchen holding a flashlight pointed directly at his face.

"We're camping!" he announced.

I caught her eyes and she pressed her lips together, fighting a smile.

WE PLAYED UNO BY ELECTRIC LANTERN LIGHT WHILE THERE WAS STILL some grey coming through the windows. Zhaire had learned the basics but compensated for gaps by making up his own rules. Draw Four cards were immune to challenge if the player was wearing socks. Skip didn't apply when the power was out. And wild cards could be played twice if you said the right word, which he declined to specify in advance.

"Draw four," I said laying my cards in front of Simone.

"Raschad!"

"And I'm stacking." I put another one down. "Draw eight."

"YOU CANNOT!"

"Yes he can, Mommy," Zhaire said. "Those are the rules."

"Whose side are you on?"

He considered it. "Daddy's," he said finally. "Sorry, Mommy."

I belly laughed as she threw cards at me, trying not to laugh herself, as Zhaire sat there looking pleased. I looked at them both and thought, *I want this every Saturday.* But didn't say it.

It got fully dark out of nowhere as the storm ate up the evening. I set up the candles I'd brought, enough to light the living room.

"If the power doesn't come back on, we should all stay in the same room tonight," I said. "Easier to manage the light we have."

"Where will we sleep?" Zhaire asked immediately. Zero interest in actually sleeping.

"We'll figure it out. Here might be best."

"Can we build a fort?"

I looked at Simone and she nodded.

"Yeah," I said. "We can build a fort."

He lost his mind with excitement. Simone gathered sheets and blankets and we built a fort with couch cushions and chairs. Zhaire and Simone supervised with the intensity of project managers while I handled the structural work.

"It needs another anchor on that side."

"It's holding."

"It's going to —"

"Yes! This is like CAMPING!" Zhaire announced already crawling inside. "Come on!" He poked his head out at us.

We got in with flashlights and the electric lantern.

"Music," Zhaire said, reaching for my phone.

Simone raised a brow. "You're letting him run it? I'm not trying to hear Bruno Mars all night."

"He's been expanding his range. Right, Z?"

He nodded and scrolled, then hit play and Wale came through my phone speaker. She was quiet for a moment, then looked at me. "You've been teaching him."

Zhaire was already bobbin' his head. He started rapping along, not all the words, the shape of them, filling in the gaps with sounds that were in the right vicinity.

"Daddy put me on this one," he said, not looking up from his dancing.

Simone laughed under her breath. "'*Put me on?*'" she looked at me sideways. "Raschad, you got our six-year-old talking like he's a teenager from Jersey."

"He's got range." I smiled.

"He asked his teacher '*what's good*'. A sixty-year-old white woman from Athens."

"That's a respectful greeting." I chuckled.

"And *then*," she continued, "His friend Kai's mom called me the other day complaining that Zhaire has Kai saying *deadbutt*. I asked Zhaire what that means and he said he can't say '*a-s-s*' so he says *deadbutt*. I *know* that's gotta be you."

I fell out laughing. Full on tears, I could hardly get it together to speak.

"What does that even mean Raschad?"

"*Deadass*. He's saying *deadass*, Sim. Means 'seriously' or 'true'. Gotta give him credit for self-censoring. That boy's a genius. He really is." I was still laughing.

She shook her head, still smiling. "You also got him saying *'facts'* and *'son'*. You know he called Julian *'son'*? Julian couldn't speak for thirty seconds. Poor man short circuited."

I put my hand over my face shaking my head. "In my defense," I said, "I've got to balance out all the country twang he gets from *y'all*." I drew the word out.

She squinted. "We do not have a twang."

"He told me he was *'fixin to'* watch his show the other day, and told Micah on FaceTime that he *'might could'* visit this summer. Got my son sounding like someone's grandaddy."

"*'Might could'* is —"

"It's not a sentence, Simone."

"And how about when he said *'bless your heart'* to that little girl having a tantrum at the park? That came from somewhere."

She pressed her lips together. "That might have been Aunt Lorraine."

"Uh huh."

We both looked at Zhaire, moving through the fort and cycling through songs on my phone.

"He's going to be fine," I said.

"Yeah." She said smiling. "He really is."

Neither of us looked away from him for a moment, letting him have the fort, the music, and the Saturday.

Zhaire went down fast. One minute he was keeping time to the music, the next he was knocked out. The fort was quiet, the only sound was the rain now beating against the windows. We sat there for a while in the quiet of it. The storm easing. The house settling. Power still out. Zhaire asleep between us, breathing hard.

I looked at Simone. Then I said it.

"I owe you an apology," I said.

She looked at me.

I kept my voice low so Zhaire stayed down. "For the back and forth. For reaching for you and then pulling away. That wasn't fair and I knew it and I did it anyway."

She was quiet for a moment. "You were hurting."

"That's not an excuse."

She looked at Zhaire. "I'm not without fault. I'm sorry too," she said quietly. "I know that doesn't —"

"It does," I said. "I hear it now in a way I couldn't before."

I looked around the fort. At Zhaire sleeping peacefully. At Simone lying next to me in the low gold light, still absentmindedly in my UCLA hoodie. Then I thought about the last time I'd been in a blanket fort. In a different city. In an apartment with too-thin walls.

"You know what this reminds me of?" I asked.

She smiled, but her eyes did something complicated. "Your apartment. In LA."

"Yeah."

"Best concert I've ever been to," she said.

"Same." I said.

We smiled at each other. I used to think about that time with a weight on it. The last time I saw her. The "before". But in that moment, that wasn't what it felt like anymore. It just felt like good memories.

"Seven years ago," I said. "On a fort of pillows and blankets."

She looked at me, knowing what I meant.

"And now here he is," I looked at Zhaire. "Asleep in one."

Her eyes went shiny and she pressed her lips together hard. I reached over and pulled Zhaire's blanket up where it had slipped. Smoothed it down and pressed a kiss to his temple.

When I straightened she was right there. Closer than I'd registered. Close enough that I could see the wet edges of her lashes in the candle-light. I wanted so badly to close the gap, find her lips, and stay there. But I'd already proven I could want her and still hurt her. Still confuse the line by stepping into something I wasn't ready to stand in all the way. And I was determined not to do that to her again.

I looked at her for a long moment. "I'm going to check the doors," I said. "Make sure everything's locked up."

She nodded, but didn't speak.

I got up and moved through the dark house with my flashlight. Checked the back door, the front, the garage and windows. Stood at the back for a minute looking out at the rain. The yard furniture where I'd stacked it against the house was still holding.

When I came back she had dozed off, asleep on my side. I sat back down and carefully slid into the open space between them, and lay back.

Zhaire was on my left. Simone was on my right. The storm had gone somewhere else and taken its noise with it. I stared at the ceiling of the blanket fort and didn't try to organize what I was feeling into anything useful. His weight on one side. Her warmth on the other. Both of them breathing peacefully. Me there content in a way that felt like something I hadn't known to want until I was already in it. I didn't move. And a question started circling that I didn't have an answer to yet.

What exactly are you protecting yourself from?

I lay there holding both of them in the dark and let it sit there unanswered.

raschad

TRE'S PENTHOUSE TOLD YOU IMMEDIATELY HE WAS SUCCESSFUL. FLOOR-to-ceiling windows, the city laid out below, a chef's kitchen built for someone who actually cooked, even though Tre didn't. We'd started the afternoon in his home studio. A full setup, not a hobby situation, then drifted out when the session wound down. Now it was just the game on low, wings and Zhaire on the floor with his tablet. This was what a lot of Saturdays looked like now.

"How's things with Simone?" Tre asked, eyes still on the game.

"Fine." I replied.

"Fine like actually fine, or fine like you're not trying to talk about it."

"Fine like it's better. We're good."

Tre nodded and let the game run for a minute. "I can't make the Knicks game."

I looked at him.

"Something came up." He said to the television. "Take Simone."

"I'll see if Julian or Zion —"

"Don't take them. Take Simone."

"She's not into sports like that."

"She'll be fine." He leaned back. I'm just saying… take her to the game. It'll be a good time. Make it a family outing. Your son wants her there."

He glanced at Zhaire, who I'd thought was completely absorbed in his tablet.

"Can Mommy come with us?" Zhaire looked up long enough to make eye contact with Tre and then went back to his tablet. Tre looked at Zhaire, then looked at me and grinned.

"You think you're slick," I said.

"I'm just a man who can't make a game." He pointed at Zhaire. "That right there is your closer. I had nothing to do with it."

"Weren't you the one telling me I need to *expand my radius*?"

"That was before I saw you throw hands in front of impressionable youth at the park." He said flatly. "My assessment of the situation changed. I was steering you wrong. My bad."

"Take her." he turned back to the screen.

Family outing, I thought to myself. That's what it was. "I'll ask her," I said.

Tre turned the volume up on the game.

THE ARENA HIT ZHAIRE BEFORE WE WERE THROUGH THE DOOR, WITH THE low roar of twenty thousand people settling into the Spectrum Center, and bass from the speakers doing pregame. We were still in the concourse and he stopped walking and looked up.

"It's loud."

"Gets louder."

He grabbed my hand and Simone's on the other side of him and started moving faster. Simone had worn jeans and a simple top, with her hair in a ponytail, and she still looked like someone you'd turn to look at twice.

We came out at floor level through the tunnel and Zhaire stopped again staring at players moving through warmups twenty feet away. We were in the first row, basically on the sideline. Zhaire looked at the court, looked at me, then looked at the court again.

"They're tall like you."

"Most of them."

"Is that your team?" he pointed to a few Knicks players.

"Used to be."

"Do you know them?"

"Most of them."

We were in our seats maybe five minutes before a player from warmups jogged over to the sideline and spotted me. Jerrod Webb, we'd played together for three seasons.

"Schad." He dapped me up over the sideline. "Didn't know you were coming through."

"Last minute. Got my son here."

Webb looked at Zhaire, who was sitting straight up in his seat like he was in an important meeting. "Little man. You look just like your pops."

Zhaire looked at me to confirm this was a compliment. I nodded. He looked back at Webb. "Thank you."

Webb laughed. "He's got your whole energy too, bro." He dapped Zhaire up, which Zhaire accepted with seriousness. "You gonna be a baller like your dad?"

"I play soccer and football and basketball and do karate," Zhaire said. "I'm keeping my options open."

Webb looked at me. I looked at the court trying not to laugh.

"Keeping your options open," he laughed. "Okay. I respect that." He jogged back toward the warmup line, shaking his head, still laughing.

The game started and the jumbotron caught us sometime in the first quarter. I felt Zhaire go still before I realized why. Then I looked up and there we were, the three of us, on the big screen. The PA came through: "In the building tonight, All-Star, and Knicks veteran, Raschad Nova Carter, here with his family."

I looked at the camera and waved, Simone smiled, and Zhaire looked at himself on the jumbotron, looked at me, then back at the screen. Then he waved, big and wide like he was waving at someone across a very large field who might not see him. The camera stayed on us. Some of the arena laughed, and Zhaire stood up and waved again. Even bigger.

"Zhaire." Simone tried to get his attention.

He pointed at me, then pointed at himself. Then gave a thumbs up. The arena lost it. I put my hand to my face and shook my head. Simone's head dropped to my shoulder she was laughing so hard.

"That is all you," she said, barely holding it.

"That is not me. He invented that himself."

Zhaire was still looking at the jumbotron even though the camera had moved on, his hand still up, waving at nothing.

"Zhaire" I said. "Camera's gone."

He lowered his hand "Did everyone see?"

"Everyone saw."

He nodded and sat back down, focused back on the court like nothing had happened.

After the final buzzer I took them down through the tunnel. The locker room was loud the way it always was after a win. Music and the loud voices of twenty-some-odd men who'd just executed for two and a half hours and could finally stop. A few guys called my name when I came through, dapping me up.

Zhaire stayed close to my side, taking everything in. Webb found us near the equipment area. He had a ball already signed by half the roster, and crouched down to Zhaire's level.

"We got something for you, Mr. *Keeping my options open*." He laughed about it again.

Zhaire looked at the ball. "Those are everyone's?"

"Almost. Go around and get the rest, they'll sign it."

Zhaire looked at me. "Go ahead," I said.

He was already moving. Simone had stayed a few steps back the whole time, watching. Every time someone acknowledged her she smiled and stepped back further, making herself peripheral on purpose, I noticed.

One of the younger guys on the team, Reeves, spotted her from across the room. Then he looked at me. "Schad." he came over. "That you?" He gestured toward Simone.

Before I could figure out what to call her, running through every label with none of them landing right, *my ex* too final, *my son's mother* too removed from what she actually was, Zhaire appeared at my elbow.

He looked up at Reeves, then at where Reeves was looking at Simone, looked back up at Reeves again and declared loudly; "That's my mommy," he pointed at Simone. "And that's my daddy." He pointed at me without looking at me, eyes still on Reeves. Case closed.

Reeves blinked, then recovered. "My bad, my bad."

Zhaire looked at him again, "All good."

The locker room erupted in laughter.

"He's all you, Schad," Webb said. "I'm telling you."

I shook my head and laughed. A few feet away Simone looked up from her phone at the sudden noise. She caught my eye with a raised eyebrow *what's funny?*

I shook my head. *Nothing.*

She narrowed her eyes slightly, knowing it was something, then let it go and turned back to watching Zhaire work the room with his ball and his pen.

Webb leaned over to me, "For real though. He said that like he meant it."

"He did mean it."

My son had looked at a grown man who was looking at his mother and said *that's my mommy and that's my daddy* like those two things belonged together. Like the arrangement was obvious and settled and not up for discussion.

I looked across the room at Simone, who was crouching down now to look at the ball with Zhaire, her face close to his, as he pointed at the signatures.

She was ours. And my son, six years old, had just said it out loud in a room full of professional athletes with more clarity than I'd managed in a year. *All good.* The flat look. The case-closed energy. He'd picked that up from me. Been watching, absorbing, filing away, and when the moment came he deployed it perfectly.

I'd never been more proud in my life.

THE THREE OF US CAME OUT OF THE ARENA INTO THE PARKING GARAGE, with Zhaire holding the ball with both arms, recapping his experience at rapid speed, when I said absentmindedly:

"I wish he could've seen me play." Not really to anyone.

"I've got footage," Simone said, reflexively.

I looked at her.

"From your seasons with the Knicks. And the Spain ones too." She continued simply, not making it a thing. "I have them."

Zhaire stopped walking and turned around. "Can I watch them!"

"Whenever you want."

He turned back around satisfied, two steps ahead of us, back into his narration about the locker room. I was still looking at her.

She met my eyes for a second. "I also saw you play live. Once."

The garage was quiet except for Zhaire's voice ahead of us.

"Here," she added.

"When?"

She named the season. Almost a year before I found out about Zhaire. I looked at her again, stunned. She was watching Zhaire, her expression the careful one she wore when she'd said something she thought might cost her.

What I felt first wasn't anger that she'd been that close and chickened out, adding another year to the time I wouldn't know my child. What moved through me first was sadness. For her. I could imagine her in those seats, and feel the panic moving through her body. She had been that close and something in her had come apart before she could get to me. She'd gone home and another year passed and everything had gotten that much harder to say.

And then, underneath the sadness, another realization: She had tapes. Of my Knicks games. Of my Spain games. Of seasons I played thinking she'd moved on, thinking our time together had meant nothing to her. That *I* had meant nothing to her.

She'd been recording me. She'd been watching me. For five years, she had been sitting in front of a screen watching me play. Saving my games. She had bought a ticket once and sat in an arena to watch me with her own eyes.

The secret was real. The distance was real. The five years were real. But somewhere in those years, in the dark of whatever room she was in, she had been *with* me. Not the version of her I'd built in my head; the one who'd looked at the test and decided I wasn't worth a phone call. A different one. The one who couldn't say my name out loud but couldn't stop watching me either.

I'd been somebody to her the whole time.

It didn't undo what she'd done. It didn't make the years shorter or any of the nights I'd spent furious and hurt at her less hurtful. But it changed the shape of it for me a bit. She hadn't thrown me away. She had carried me, while her secret got bigger and bigger and she got smaller underneath it.

"I'm glad you were there," I said.

I meant it. She had tried. And standing there two years later with our son carrying a signed ball, that mattered.

simone

—

By six-thirty in the morning the Ironwood Community Center was alive with volunteers. Aunt Lorraine and her church ladies had been in the kitchen since five-thirty, the smell of eggs and grits wafted in the air, and thirty-plus volunteers in red *WadeHouse Cares* t-shirts moved across the gymnasium and grounds with focused energy. Stations were going up, signs being hung, and five-hundred backpacks had been stuffed and stacked by grade level. I stood with my clipboard in the middle of it and let myself take it in before the day took over.

It was the morning of our WadeHouse Annual Back to School Drive. My mother started it with a folding table and donated notebooks the year I turned seven, and she ran it every June for five years until she died. Now I ran it. School supplies, fresh cuts from volunteer barbers, free health screenings with local pediatricians, fully stuffed backpacks, breakfast and lunch because nobody was leaving hungry. Three-hundred-fifty area kids were registered, and I expected another hundred or more walk-ins. I'd spent months on the logistics and had every detail mapped out so the day itself could feel easy. That was the point. The families shouldn't feel the labor behind it. They should just feel seen.

My mother's original sign was leaned against the back wall where I'd put it. Painted on plywood in her handwriting over twenty years ago.

WADEHOUSE BACK TO SCHOOL DRIVE
— ALL FAMILIES WELCOME.

The paint was chipped along the bottom edge from being dragged across parking lot asphalt. I brought it every year and set it up where I could see it. Nobody else paid attention to it.

Khairos appeared at my elbow with a headset on, looking like Secret Service. "Barber station's short a chair. Creston guy can't make it."

"Call Demarcus at Fly Cutz. He owes Julian a favor."

"On it." He was gone before he finished saying it.

Then Tre walked in with sunglasses on and a coffee in his hand. "Balloon arch outside is crooked. Left side."

"Fix it then." I squinted at him.

"I'm a music producer, Simone."

"Tre."

"Okay, I'll fix it." He took a long sip and drifted toward the back. "DJ's here, by the way."

Julian came in next, wearing a button-up. I pointed at the table of folded volunteer T-shirts without saying a word. He made a face, then picked up a shirt and went to change.

Zhaire came bouncing through the doors at seven-thirty already in his red shirt, vibrating.

"Mommy, can I do the stickers?"

"Yes. Every kid gets one when they check in. Stay at the table, okay?"

"I know, Mommy."

Raschad came through the doors thirty seconds behind him, slower, also with a coffee in his hand. He met my eyes across the gym and lifted his cup in a quiet hello, before someone grabbed him for help with boxes.

I went back to my clipboard, then I touched the corner my mother's sign on my way to meet the DJ. *Mama. Here we go.*

Doors opened at eight-thirty and the line was already down the block. The gym was filled with excited energy. Strollers and grandparents and teenagers trying to look like they were only here because somebody made them, whose eyes went wide when they saw the sneaker wall.

I worked the room not from behind a table, engaging with everyone I could, making sure everyone felt welcome. Charity could feel clinical if you weren't careful. My mother always treated every family like they were doing her a favor by showing up, and I did the same.

"Mrs. Johnson. We've got you in the system." I crouched in front of her smallest, a girl with braids and enormous brown eyes. "What's your favorite color?"

"Purple."

"We've got a purple one with your name on it. Come on."

By noon outside had come alive. The food trucks were running, kids were on the blacktop cycling through activities while they waited, and the energy from inside the gym had spread to the whole property. I went out to check the rotation and spotted Raschad.

A group of teenage boys had found him, phones out excitedly, the indifference they'd been practicing all morning fell away entirely. One of them was mid-sentence about something I couldn't hear, pointing at the basketball court.

I watched Raschad look at the court, then back at them. He said something and they all erupted, excitedly running to clear the younger kids off the court.

Zhaire materialized at my hip from nowhere. "Daddy's gonna play?"

"Looks like it."

"Can I watch?"

"Okay, go sit with Uncle Reggie." I pointed to my father's brother sitting on a bench along the court.

He was already running, and shouting. "That's my DAD!" As Raschad was warming up at half speed and letting one of the nine-year-olds who didn't want to leave the court yet score on him, acting like he'd been beaten clean.

The teenagers thought that was hilarious. The tallest one, sixteen maybe, came at Raschad first. He was good, looking like he'd been playing seriously for years. Raschad wasn't being soft about it then. He was playing, not full speed but close enough. When he posted up the tall one and scored on him with a move so casual it was almost rude, the whole court reacted.

"Okay," the kid said, nodding slow. "Okay. I see. I see."

Raschad smiled. "You're fast though. You play for your school?"

"JV. Trying to make varsity."

"Move your left hand higher when you push off your first step. You're telegraphing." He demonstrated. Just his hands, quick. "Try it."

The kid tried it the next possession, got into the lane easier, and looked up surprised.

"Yeah. There it is."

From the bench: "*GO DADDY GO GO GO*"

I smiled and realized I had been watching for too long and needed to get back to work. I had stations to check and a volunteer question in my earpiece I hadn't answered. I stood there for one more moment, watching my son cheer his father on as he played with teenagers who forgot to play it cool. *He fit here.*

Later, I was at the registration table with Marlowe going over walk-ins when Raschad came in with Zhaire for water. He stopped at the cooler next to me, filled a cup, drained it, and filled another.

"You eat today?" he asked me, without turning around.

"I had coffee."

"That's not eating."

He filled another cup and set it on the registration table next to my clipboard. "What do you want from outside? There's a hot dog truck and I think an empanada spot."

I looked up. "You don't have to…"

"Simone. You've been running around all day. You need fuel."

"The empanadas."

He paused for a moment and grinned, then nodded and walked back out without another word. Ten minutes later, he was back with chicken empanadas, and hot sauce packets. Placed them next to my clipboard and had already moved to the sneaker wall by the time I noticed.

Taryn silently watched the exchange, gave me a look and a smile, then was suddenly very busy with the registration list. I picked up an empanada and ate it with a small smile on my face.

By afternoon the crowd outside had changed and Taryn came to find me.

"The ratio of children to non-children has adjusted significantly."

I looked through the propped-open doors. There were women on the blacktop who hadn't come with kids, dressed for a Saturday that hadn't started as a back-to-school drive.

"It's a public event," I shrugged.

Through the doorway we could see a group of men and women who had circled Raschad, phones out.

"Some of them are fans," Taryn said. "And some of them are floosies."

He took photos, signed what people put in front of him, but he didn't stop working. Photo, sign, back to boxes. Back to the shoe station. He was genuinely there, with the attention happening around him without consuming him.

"He's still working," I said.

"He is."

She showed up at three. Dominique. His auction winner from months back, and according to Tre's commentary, *'head on speed dial'*. I watched her walk across the gym in a skintight thigh-high dress and chunky heels that did not belong on a gymnasium floor. She scanned the room, spotted Raschad and Zion bringing in more boxes of sneakers, recalibrated, then started toward him.

I should have walked away, instead I casually made my way toward the sneaker wall instead, clipboard in hand. By the time I was close enough to hear, she had her hand on Raschad's upperarm.

"I didn't know you'd be here," she was saying. "Thought I'd come support."

She did a survey, eyes moving across the event, taking inventory. They landed on me, briefly. Scanned me up and down and moved on.

"This is incredible," she said to him. "Whoever put this together —"

"Simone did." He gestured over at me. "My…"

He stopped and tried again. "Simone. She put all of this together. Worked on it for months," in a tone that almost sounded prideful, if I didn't know any better.

Dominique turned the full focus of her fake smile in my direction. She was beautiful, and she wore it the way women wore things they were used to having work for them.

"It's incredible," she said to me. "Truly. Must have been a lot of work. You look… exhausted."

I held my smile in place. "It's been a long day."

"I can see that," she looked me up and down. "Well… you should be proud."

"I am." That was all I had. Anything more and I'd say or do the wrong thing in front of people who knew me as my mother's daughter.

"Dominique." Taryn appeared at my side. "Didn't know you had kids."

"I don't."

"Oh." Taryn looked around the room with manufactured puzzlement. "You bring a niece? A nephew? Somebody's child?"

"I was in the area. Came to offer support."

"Right." Taryn smiled. "How generous. Of your Saturday afternoon."

The two of them held an icy stare. Then Taryn's eyes flicked down Dominique's dress and back up. "That your go-to uniform? You know, for when you're *offering support.*"

"Taryn." Zion's hand eased across her back. "Don't," he whispered in her ear.

"I'm having a conversation."

"You're having a Taryn conversation." He looked at Dominique with straightforward pleasantness. "Enjoy the event." Then to Taryn: "Come help me with something."

She let herself be steered, but not before she turned to me and said, low in my ear: "I don't have to fall back. Say the word."

I shook my head. She held my eyes for a second, then let Zion move her along. I gave Raschad a quick glance, then walked away to check on the barber station. I did not look back.

raschad

I WATCHED SIMONE WALK AWAY. DOMINIQUE WAS STILL TALKING, BUT I'D missed the last three sentences.

"...and I was thinking, if you're free next week, there's a —"

"Dominique."

She stopped.

"I'm not available. Any week I haven't been for a while."

"Oh."

"And the way you spoke to her? Don't ever do that again."

Her smile faltered. "Raschad, I don't know what you think I —"

"I was standing right there."

"I was complimenting the event."

"You weren't."

She stared at me, her smile was gone, then slowly came back, tighter.

"Okay."

"Take care."

She held my eyes one more second, then nodded and walked away with her heels scraping across the gym floor. When I turned back, Simone was at the barber station, looking at me. She didn't smile or nod, just looked at me with that quiet processing she did with her face, then turned back to the volunteer she'd been talking to.

Tre materialized at my shoulder with an expression that said he'd heard every second of it. "Don't," I said.

"I didn't say anything."

"You're making a face."

"I have a very open and nonjudgmental face." He fell into step beside me.

"So. Since you've apparently cleaned house, you wouldn't mind if I —"

"Tre."

"What?"

"I never slept with her."

He stopped walking. "What?"

"Took her out twice. She offered. I tried to want it. Didn't." I kept walking. "I don't give a fuck what you do with Dominique."

He shook his head, half laughing. "I been out here lying on you."

"You been out here entertaining yourself." I started walking again.

"Aight. So she's fair game."

"Knock yourself out." I stopped again. "Real talk though? When you gon' slow down, bruh?"

I'd been watching Tre do this long enough now, his easy pivots to whoever was next, the way he moved through women like he was already on his way to somewhere else. Close as we'd gotten over the past year, he'd never once slipped and said anything real about any of them.

"Slow down from what?"

"From whatever it is you're doin'."

He grinned. "I'm livin'."

"Mm." I kept walking.

He fell back in step. "I'm good, bruh."

"Aight."

"I'm serious. I'm good."

"I heard you." I let it go.

THE DAY WOUND DOWN AS WE BROKE DOWN STATIONS, STACKED CHAIRS, and boxed up what was left for donation, loading them into trucks. By eight-thirty the gym was echoing. Julian found me with a stack of boxes in my arms.

He nodded at the boxes. "Need a hand?"

"I got it."

He held the door open and walked alongside me without saying anything else, and when I set the boxes down he was already back on his phone, firing off texts.

"Good day," he said, not looking up.

"Yeah."

We ended up beside each other at the edge of the gymnasium watching Simone thank the last few volunteers.

"She really built something amazing with this," I said to him.

"She did." Julian watched her. "Our mother started with school supplies. Simone's the one who said why stop there? Kept adding to it. Shoes. Haircuts. Doctors. Coordinating all of it herself."

We watched her stand, say something to a little girl that made her smile, and move on to thank the next staging family without breaking stride.

"Our mother would've loved today," Julian said.

He looked at me directly then. "I appreciate you being here," he said. "Really. You rolled up your sleeves and you worked. Even with all the extra attention, you don't let that distract you." He paused. "You fit. That's not nothing."

Before I could think how to respond to that, he was already walking away, back on his phone.

I walked with Simone to her car. I had parked right next to her. Zhaire was asleep against my shoulder, face paint destroyed, sticker sheet still clutched in one limp hand.

She looked up at me from her phone, "Four hundred and seventy-one families," she said proudly. "Final count."

"That's a lot of kids walking into school feeling ready."

"That's the whole point." She exhaled.

I shifted Zhaire on my shoulder. "You want me to keep him tonight? Let you sleep in tomorrow."

She looked at Zhaire, then back at me. "You sure?"

"He's already out. He won't even know."

She hesitated, but she definitely needed the sleep."Yeah. Okay. Thank you."

I got him buckled in, and when I straightened she was leaning against her car, arms crossed loosely, tired from a day of giving everything she had.

I looked out at the parking lot for a moment. "I've been to a lot of events. Charity stuff, league stuff, high production, big budgets." I paused. "What you did today was different. The way those families were treated. The way nobody felt like a number." I looked at her. "You're really good at this, Simone. Genuinely good."

She held my stare for a second, then looked down. "Thank you."

"I mean it." I cleared my throat. "Hey, uh… about earlier, with Dominique. I'm sorry about that."

She shook her head. "Doesn't matter. Not my business."

"It is though. But… it doesn't matter the way you probably think it does. I just want you to know, nothing happened. There's nothing there."

She was still for a moment, then nodded once.

"Let me get you out of here," I said. I opened her car door and she slipped in.

"Goodnight, Raschad," she said.

I nodded, and it was already in my head before I'd decided. I had half a second to push it down. I didn't.

"Goodnight, Peach."

I closed her door. Through the glass I watched her pull her lips into her mouth and close her eyes like she needed a moment before she could drive. I walked around and got into my car, and sat there and waited for her to pull off first. Didn't look back over at her.

team carter

simone

I'D BEEN HOLDING THE PAPERWORK FOR A COUPLE OF WEEKS. EVERY morning I'd wake up thinking *today*, then find another excuse. The timing wasn't right. Mercury was in retrograde. Next week. But today was different. Today was Raschad's birthday, and Zhaire had been bouncing off the walls since he woke up, already dressed in his favorite Spider-Man shirt, counting down the hours until Raschad picked him up.

A few weeks ago, when Tre had asked what he planned to do for his birthday, he'd said "Just time with my son." When Zhaire heard that, he'd immediately asked if he could spend the whole day with his daddy as his present to him.

"Mommy, you think Daddy will like my card?" Zhaire asked for the third time, holding up the construction paper masterpiece covered in glue and crooked letters spelling out "HAPPY BIRTHDAY DADDY" with a drawing of the two of them holding hands, two identical stick figures with big smiles, one tall, one shorter.

"He's gonna love it."

"Good," he nodded, satisfied, then his face scrunched up. "Are you coming with us?"

"No, this is your time with Daddy. But I'll see you both when he brings you back. And tonight the grown-ups are celebrating his birthday too."

The party. Jesus. My brothers and cousins had insisted on throwing Raschad a proper Lennox Falls celebration at The Obsidian Room, my cousin Khaz's newest spot. He'd opened it a year ago and it was already the place to be in the area.

"Can't let our boy's birthday pass without showing out," Tre had said, booking the VIP section with bottle service like Raschad had always been part of our family.

. . .

After Zhaire left with Raschad, practically vibrating with excitement as he ran to his dad's car, I sat alone in my too-quiet house, staring at that folder again.

Petition for Change of Minor's Legal Name

I'd filled it out three times. The first time, my hand shook so bad the letters came out crooked. The second time, I'd cried and smudged the ink. This third copy was pristine, every letter careful written.

Zhaire Nova Wade → Zhaire Nova Carter

Raschad had shown up. Even when the betrayal should have sent him running. He showed up for his son. He'd earned this. *More* than earned it. And maybe it was my way of saying what I hadn't completely said out loud yet. That I recognized what kind of father he was. That I was sorry for stealing those years of Carter pride from both of them.

My phone buzzed.

> **TARYN**
>
> You ready for tonight? Got my outfit laid out.
> About to shut the club DOWN

> Ready as I'll ever be

> **TARYN:**
>
> You give him the papers yet?

> This afternoon when he brings Zhaire back

> **TARYN**
>
> Good. He's gonna be floored Simi. The best gift.
>
> And that dress you bought? He's gonna DIE

> It's not about that

> **TARYN**
>
> Right. See you at 8

The door burst open, startling me from my thoughts.

"Mommy! Daddy let me get TWO slushies and I played ALL the games and look!" Zhaire ran in, holding a giant stuffed bear nearly as big as him. "I won this for you!"

Raschad followed, lingering in the doorway like he always did now.

"He insisted on the bear. Said you needed something to hug when he's at my place."

"Aww, thank you, sweet potato," I said to Zhaire, hugging the bear. "Why don't you go put your prizes in your room? I need to talk to Daddy for a minute."

"Okay!" Zhaire ran back to Raschad, wrapping his arms around his legs. "Happy birthday, Daddy! This was the best day ever!"

Raschad's face softened completely, and he crouched down to hug him properly. "Thank you, lil man. Best birthday I've ever had."

Zhaire beamed and raced off to his room.

Raschad stepped into the kitchen, hands in his pockets. "He had a good time. Ate his body weight in pancakes. Little man told the waiter it was my birthday, so they came out singing with candles and everything. Had the whole restaurant looking at us." He shook his head, smiling. "He was so proud of himself."

"Sounds about right." I stood, smoothing my hands on my jeans and cleared my throat. "Actually, I have something for you, before you head out."

His eyebrows rose. "Simone, you didn't have to get me a gift."

I retrieved the folder, my hands surprisingly steady and held it out to him. "Happy birthday, Raschad."

Inside was a card and a half-folded letter. The card was simple, "Happy Birthday". I watched as he read the letter that I had placed first:

Raschad,

Happy Birthday. On this day, I thought it only right that I take the time to let you know how grateful I am for the man that you are, and what I see when I watch you with our son.

I see the way Zhaire's whole face lights up when you walk into a room. The way he practices the handshake you taught him over and over until he gets it perfect. How he tries to walk like you and talk like you and be like you in every way a six-year-old can.

I see the patience you have when he asks you the same question five times. The way you get down on his level to really listen to what he's saying. How you never make him feel small or silly or like his thoughts don't matter.

I see you teaching him to tie his shoes with the same hands

that are teaching him to dribble a basketball. I see you reading him bedtime stories in voices that make him laugh until his sides hurt. I see you being everything I knew you could be. Everything I was too scared to let you be from the start.

I watch him at night sometimes, practicing the beats you show him on his little keyboard. The rhythm in his fingers that always came so naturally to him? It's all you. The way he moves to music, the way he hears melodies in everything? That's his father's gift.

Even before you knew him, I could see you in him. His curiosity about how things work. His need to take care of people smaller than him. The way he studies people's faces when they're talking, like he's trying to understand not just their words but their hearts. That gentle strength he has? That's you.

I can't give you back those first five years. I can't undo the choice I made or the pain I caused. But I can tell you this: watching you love our son, watching him love you back, seeing the father you are and the man you are is the most beautiful thing I've ever witnessed.

He talks about you constantly. "My daddy this, my daddy that." He saves his best stories for you. His biggest smiles. His proudest moments. You are already everything to him.

I just want you to know that I see you. I see the father you are, the father you've always been, even when I didn't let you be.

Thank you for loving our son the way you do. Thank you for being patient with me. Thank you for showing up every single day. For choosing him every day.

Happy Birthday, Raschad Nova.

With love and gratitude,

Simone

IT SEEMED LIKE HE READ IT TWICE BEFORE HE FINALLY LOOKED UP. WHEN he did, his eyes were glistening, and I realized mine weren't exactly dry either.

"Thank you," he mouthed to me.

I nodded and smiled back, as he set the letter aside, and a range of emotion settled across his face as he looked at the documents behind it. His whole body went still as he read the header.

Petition for Change of Minor's Legal Name
Zhaire Nova Wade → Zhaire Nova Carter

He stared at the paper for what felt like forever, then looked up at me, voice almost a whisper. "Simone…what is this?"

My tears were a faucet at that point, but I pushed through. "I want to make it right. Zhaire deserves to have your name. You've earned that. You deserve that."

He blinked, like he was trying to focus and a single tear traveled down his cheek. "You're sure?"

I nodded. "Yeah. I'm sure."

He put the folder down, stepped closer, voice rough and eyes glassy. "That… that's not a small thing."

I laughed a watery laugh. "I know."

"I don't know what to say."

"Say you'll sign it," I whispered.

His eyes searched mine, like he was trying to figure out if I was for real, then he pulled me in, hugging me so tight I could barely breathe. "Do you know what this means to me?" he whispered against my hair.

I hugged him back, burying my face in his chest, breathing him in. "I think so."

"No." He shook his head slowly. "This is…" he paused and swallowed hard, then pulled back to look at me. "My name… that's legacy. That's… that's saying he's mine in every way. Not just biology, but *mine*. My son. My family. My blood carrying my name." He turned away, one hand rubbing over his face.

"When I found out about him," he said quietly, "and heard his last name was Wade, it ate at me. I never said anything because what right did I have? I wasn't there. But…I'm the only son. Tamika's married, took her husband's name. Alyssa kept her maiden name but my nephew has her late husband's name. It hit me that the Carter name could stop with me if…" He exhaled shakily. "And here I had a son who didn't carry it. A boy, but he's a Wade, and the Wade name holds weight, so I just swallowed it. I never imagined you'd do this."

The guilt hit me hard, but I stayed silent.

"You're really doing this?"

"Really," I promised. "I already filled everything out. You just have to sign."

He set the folder down carefully on my entry table, pulled out the pen I'd clipped to it, and then paused. "What about you?"

"What about me?"

"Your name. Wade. That's been his identity too. His uncles, his whole maternal side."

"We're still his family," I finished. "But kids usually carry their father's name, Raschad. Especially when they have a father like you. Someone who shows up. Someone who fights for them. Someone who…" I swallowed hard. "Someone who deserved to be there from the beginning, and I'm so sor—."

He cut me off. "Don't do that."

"Do what?"

"The apologies. I know you're sorry, Simone. You don't have to keep saying it."

Before I could respond, he bent over the papers and signed his name. When he straightened, he had to clear his throat twice before speaking. Then he stepped forward and pulled me into another hug, unexpected and overwhelming. His arms wrapped around me completely, and I let myself sink into it.

"Thank you, Peach."

I wanted so badly to turn my head up, to find his mouth, to taste the emotion I could feel radiating from him. My hands gripped his shirt, holding on, holding back. When he pulled away, we stared at each other for a moment too long, electricity crackling between us. His eyes dropped to my mouth for just a second before he licked his lips, then he stepped back, clearing his throat, both of us remembering what we weren't.

"Can we tell him together?" his question was soft and vulnerable.

"Yeah," I managed, my own eyes burning. "Let's do it together."

"Zhaire!" I called. "Come here for a minute, baby?"

We heard the sound of running feet, and then our son appeared, still wiping glitter from his hands.

"What's good?" he looked between us, mimicking the way Raschad often greeted people, trying to sound grown.

Raschad chuckled proudly, then crouched down to his level, and I joined him, the three of us making a little circle.

I took a breath, keeping my voice gentle. "You know how your last name is Wade? Like Mommy?"

"Yeah."

"Well, Daddy and I talked about it, and we decided it's time for you to have your daddy's last name. So you'd be Zhaire Nova Carter. Would you like that?"

Zhaire's eyes darted between us, processing. "Carter like Daddy?"

"Exactly like me," Raschad confirmed, his voice thick.

"Carter," Zhaire repeated, testing it out. "My name is Zhaire Nova Carter?"

"That's right," I said, touching his shoulder.

His eyes went wide, darting between us. "For real?"

"For real for real," Raschad confirmed.

Zhaire was quiet for a moment in that serious way kids do sometimes when they are thinking. Then his face split into the biggest grin.

"That's so cool! Zhaire Carter. Zhaire Nova Carter." He kept repeating it, each time with more excitement. "Wait! Does this mean at school I'll be closer to the front of the line? C comes before W!"

Raschad laughed. "Yeah. You're moving up in the alphabet."

Zhaire launched himself at Raschad, wrapping his small arms around his neck. "This is the best birthday ever, Daddy!"

"I think you got it backwards, little man. This is my present."

Zhaire pulled back, then looked at me with those big curious eyes. "Does that mean your name is Carter too, Mommy?"

I felt Raschad's eyes on me as I answered. "No. Mommy's keeping Wade."

He frowned, curious. "Why?"

I touched his cheek gently. "Because that's my name and it's important to me. But you having your dad's name? That's important too. And I'm proud of both."

His forehead scrunched up. "So we'll have different names?"

"Lots of families have different last names," I explained. "But a name is special. It tells people who you belong to. And this is your father, and he's a great father, so we agree you should have his name." I kissed his forehead. "You're part of both of us. That's what matters most."

He thought about it, then nodded like it made perfect sense. "Okay. Can we go get ice cream? All three of us?" He said simply, already moving on in that way kids do.

Raschad and I exchanged a quiet look over his head, a thousand words between us that neither of us could say out loud yet.

"Get your shoes," Raschad said, and Zhaire took off like a shot.

"Thank you," Raschad said quietly. "I know this couldn't have been an easy decision."

"It *was* an easy decision."

He studied me for a moment, then asked, "The ice cream… you sure you're okay with that? He did have slushies earlier."

"It's your birthday. And we just gave our son your name. I think ice cream is appropriate. Besides," I added, trying to lighten the moment, "you might need sugar energy for tonight. My brothers have plans for you at The Obsidian Room."

He groaned. "Don't remind me. Tre already sent me three texts about bottle service."

"You only turn thirty-one once."

He paused at the door. "You're still coming, right?"

"I'll be there," I said carefully. "Wouldn't miss it."

He nodded. "Good."

"Ready!" Zhaire came running back, shoes on the wrong feet but laced up with determination.

Raschad bent down to fix them, and I watched the two of them—my son and his father, about to share a name, sharing this moment.

Zhaire Nova Carter.

raschad

THE THREE OF US HAD JUST COME FROM GETTING SUNDAES. ZHAIRE HAD gotten chocolate with gummy bears, a combination that made Simone cringe but she let him have it anyway because today was special. The whole time he'd kept saying "Zhaire Carter" under his breath like he was trying it on for size.

We were walking through downtown Lennox Falls, Zhaire between us but not holding our hands, too cool for that now, apparently, when we passed Premier Sports Warehouse.

"Oh, can we look?" Zhaire pressed his face against the window, leaving prints on the glass.

"Actually," I said, "let's go in. Got an idea."

Inside, the store was massive, every team you could think of. NFL, NBA, MLB, everything. Zhaire was naming teams faster than I could track, but I steered us toward the custom jersey section.

"What are we doing?" Zhaire asked, bouncing on his toes.

"You'll see."

The young woman at the counter had a name tag that said Ashley. She smiled at Zhaire's obvious excitement, then looked at me expectantly.

"What can I do for you?"

I took a breath. "Custom youth Knicks jersey, last name Carter, number seventeen."

Zhaire exploded. "That's my new name! Like my Dad's!"

Ashley's eyebrows shot up, clearly charmed. "Really, that's awesome!"

"Yeah," Zhaire beamed, practically vibrating. "I'm Carter now. We just changed it today for Daddy's birthday!" Telling her all our business.

"Well, happy birthday," she said to me, then looked back at her screen. "Just the one?"

"Actually, make it three," Simone stepped forward. "Same name, same number."

My head whipped around. "Really?"

She nodded, her hand finding Zhaire's shoulder. "We're a team, right?"

Zhaire threw his hands up like he'd just won the playoffs. "We're all gonna match!"

Ashley smiled. "Three it is. What sizes?"

"Youth medium," I managed. "Adult XL, and..."

"Women's medium," Simone finished for me.

"Give me about forty minutes," Ashley said.

While we waited, Zhaire dragged us through the entire store.

"Look at these!" He stopped at a sneaker wall, eyes wide. "They have new Jordans! Oh, and those ones that light up!"

"Easy," I said. "Jersey today, that's it."

"But Daddy, look at these Dunks! My friend Liam has the red ones but these are cooler."

Simone shook her head, amused. "Look what you did. You're turning him into a sneakerhead like you."

"Can't help it if the kid has good taste," I said, watching him inspect each shoe like he was appraising art.

Zhaire moved on to the Knicks section, pointing at everything. "That's your old team! Just like our jerseys gonna be!"

"That's right."

When Ashley called us back, she had three crisp blue-and-orange Knicks jerseys spread on the counter, with CARTER 17 gleaming on each one.

I helped Zhaire into his, smoothing out the fabric. "You look official," I told him.

Simone pulled hers over her shirt, she'd worn a white tee, and the jersey transformed her. For a second, seeing my name stretched across her shoulders...*man*. The things it made me think.

"Alright," Simone said, already knowing what needed to happen. She handed her phone to Ashley. "Mind taking one for us?"

"Of course!"

Zhaire jumped between us, throwing up peace signs, cheesing for the camera like he'd just been drafted. I found myself sliding an arm around Simone's waist without thinking, pulling her in close. She stiffened for just a second, then relaxed into it. Familiar heat crackled between us, just under my skin. *My family.* Messy, broken in some places, but still mine. Even if I couldn't claim all of it.

Ashley snapped a couple more shots. "You want one from the back? Show off the names?"

"Yeah!" Zhaire spun around immediately.

We all turned, and Ashley got one of our backs, three Carters in a row.

"Look at y'all," Ashley teased, handing back the phone. "Championship material."

"No doubt," I said, glancing at Simone as she scrolled through the photos, then started texting them to me. "There. Now you have them too."

My phone buzzed with the photos, and I knew what I had to do. I also pulled up the photo I'd taken earlier at her place of the name change certificate, had snapped it thinking I'd want to share with my mom and sisters later.

> 📷 [Carter Fam] 📷 [Carter on our backs] 📷 [Official Name Change Certificate]

> Look at my boy. All the way official!

JORDAN

MY NEPHEW. 😭😭

ALYSSA

Stop. I'm about to cry at work!!!

TAMIKA:

First of all, the jerseys go HARD

JADA

OMG look at lil king!!!

ALYSSA

Wait. Why Simone got one too??

JORDAN

Exactly. miss ma'am you matching now?

It's parental unity. relax.

TAMIKA

Raschad Nova Carter. this is not a text-level update. FACETIME. NOW. Don't play with us.

My phone lit up with the group FaceTime. I looked over at Simone, who was helping Zhaire adjust his jersey.

"You ready?" I asked, half-laughing. "They want to see."

She sighed, rolling her eyes but smiling. "Your sisters don't play, do they?"

"Never have."

"Go ahead."

I answered, and all four of them came on at once, screaming like they'd just won the lottery.

"ZHAIRE NOVA CARTER!!!"

Zhaire grinned and waved. "Aunties! Look!" He turned around proudly so they could see the CARTER on his back.

"Look at his little name y'all, I'm crying" Jada squealed.

"Lord he's gonna break hearts with that name on him, whew!" Alyssa laughed.

"Simone, girl, you looking good too though!" Jordan shouted.

Simone laughed and waved at the screen. "Hey, y'all!"

"So you two are matching now, huh? mmhmm." Jada pursed her lips.

"It's for Zhaire. So he feels supported." Simone tried to explain.

"Girl, you sure that's all? 'Cause the way y'all cheesin…"

I shook my head. "It's a big day, that's all."

"It's a big day, alright. This is a whole soft-launch family rollout." Alyssa laughed.

I covered my laugh with a cough and Zhaire jumped in again, oblivious to the grown folks' games.

"Guess what, Aunties! In school I'll be close to the front of the line now!"

They fell out, all talking over each other.

"I can't take him!"

"He's so proud, look at him!"

"Nova, you did that."

They grinned, warmth filling the whole screen.

"We love you, Zhaire Nova *Carter*!" they yelled one more time in harmony.

After we hung up, Zhaire was still bouncing. "Can I wear my jersey to bed tonight?"

"That's up to your mom," I said.

Simone shook her head, amused. "We'll see."

As we walked toward the exit, Zhaire between us in his new jersey, a guy approached us hesitantly.

"Excuse me, are you Raschad Carter? From the Knicks?"

"Yeah, that's me."

"Man, I'm sorry to interrupt your family time, but could I get a quick picture? My son's not gonna believe I saw you."

"Sure, no problem."

The guy handed his phone to Simone, who took the picture without missing a beat.

"Thanks so much. Your son looks just like you, man. Y'all look good."

After he walked away, Zhaire tugged on my jersey. "Why did he want a picture with you?"

"Because I used to play basketball on TV."

"Oh yeah!" His eyes went wide like he just remembered. "You were famous!"

"Kind of."

"Cool," he said simply.

"Daddy?" Zhaire said suddenly.

"Yeah?"

"Are you gonna wear your jersey to your party tonight?"

"Nah, that's a grown-up party. Different kind of clothes."

"Oh." He thought about it. "But you'll keep it forever, right? All three of us?"

"Yeah," I said. "Forever."

happy birthday to me

This chapter has a soundtrack:

Under The Influence by Chris Brown | *Lemon Lean* by The Dream | *All The Time* by Jeremih | *Could've Been* by

H.E.R ft Bryson Tiller |

simone

THE OBSIDIAN ROOM WASN'T YOUR TYPICAL CLUB. MY COUSIN KHAZ had created something different. Where his other club, The Monarch Lounge was pure sophistication and playlist vibes. Black glass and chrome with purple and gold accents and an atmosphere that promised secrets would be kept. This was high-end, sexy nightlife with choreographed performances that were more art than anything else. Tonight, The Obsidian Room was ours.

My brothers had gone all out for Raschad, booking the entire VIP section that overlooked the main stage. The stage was set up for tonight's signature show, dancers in LED-trimmed costumes that looked like liquid obsidian, ready to perform full choreographed routines. Between sets, the space transformed into pure luxury nightlife.

Our section was already packed. Some of Raschad's boys from his NBA days, my brothers holding court with bottles of D'USSÉ, most of the extended Wade family, and other friends Raschad had made since moving to town, and a few from out of town. The energy was electric.

I wore a burgundy silk dress that had seemed like a good idea at home but now felt like a weapon I wasn't sure I should be carrying. The back was completely open, held together by thin gold chains crisscrossing, and the slit ran high enough that sitting would require strategy.

"You look lethal," Taryn whispered, handing me a drink. "I see my teachings have taken root."

"Taryn." I laughed.

"No, no, I'm proud. This is some master-level work. Give him the most meaningful gift of his life this afternoon, then show up tonight looking like a gift your damn self? Chef's kiss."

"It's not a scheme, T."

"Sure it's not." She grinned wickedly.

Just then, the DJ's voice boomed through the speakers.

"Alright y'all. Tonight we celebrating a real one! Music producer and New York Knicks legend, Raschad Carter. Make some noise!"

The room erupted as Raschad appeared, and my breath caught. All six foot six of him in all black, showing every muscle he'd maintained since retirement, jewelry catching the lights, presence commanding the entire room without trying. Thirty-one years old. He moved through the crowd with an easy confidence, dapping up friends, accepting shots, and his eyes kept scanning until they found me.

The look that crossed his face when he saw me made my stomach flip. He started making his way over, and I gripped my drink glass tighter.

"Birthday boy incoming," Taryn muttered, then disappeared.

His eyes traveled down my body, then back up. "That dress..."

"It's your birthday," I said. "Wanted to look nice."

"Nice?" He shook his head. "Simone, you look..."

Before he could finish, one of the performers took the stage, the beginning of The Fire Glass Show. The lights dimmed, and the dancer emerged in a costume that seemed to glow from within, moving to a mix that had the entire club mesmerized. This wasn't stripping; this was art. Every movement deliberate, athletic, telling a story through motion.

But Raschad wasn't watching the stage. He was watching me.

"You want a drink?" he asked, already knowing I had one.

"I'm good."

Tre appeared with a bottle of Ace of Spades. "Birthday shots!"

The whole section gathered, glasses raised, and Julian made a toast about brotherhood, success, and family. The night progressed in waves. More performances, each one a full production with costume changes, themed music, and choreography that belonged in a Super Bowl half-time show. Between sets, the music switched to trap soul that had everyone moving, bodies pressed close in the VIP section.

For the first hour, Raschad played it cool. He was across the section with his boys, laughing, taking shots, living his night. But every time a man approached me, suddenly Raschad would materialize.

"You good, Simone?" he'd ask, eyes on whoever was talking to me. Or he'd need to get to the bar right behind where I was standing. Or his conversation would mysteriously migrate to my side of the section.

"Your bodyguard's working overtime tonight," Taryn laughed after the fourth time he'd appeared just as a man was offering to buy me a drink.

I was dancing with my cousin Zenobia when I felt his presence at my back, not touching but close enough that everyone else stepped away.

"Dance with me," he said.

"You've been doing fine entertaining yourself," I said, not turning around.

"Stop playing."

Zenobia gave me a look, then melted away into the crowd. Traitor.

I turned to face him. "One dance."

The DJ shifted the vibe as the night got late. The opening notes of Chris Brown's *Under The Influence* floated through the speakers, that melodic beat that made everyone move slower, and get closer.

I let him pull me close, his hands on my hips. Around us, people were coupled up, lost in the music. His fingers spread wide across my back, his hand sliding to the exposed skin of my lower back where the dress chains didn't cover, holding me against him as we swayed.

"Missed this," he murmured against my ear. "Being this close to you."

I didn't answer, because admitting I missed it too would break the fragile control I had left. The song blended into The-Dream's *Lemon Lean* a hypnotic beat that was late-night bad decisions and tomorrow's regrets. Raschad turned me around, my back to him, with one hand splayed across my stomach, the other caressing up and down my arm, and up to my neck, brushing my jaw. We weren't even really dancing anymore, just breathing the same air, teetering on the edge.

Then Jeremih's *All The Time* started, and the VIP section had thinned out completely. People roaming to the lower level, checking out the main floor, getting air on the terrace. It was just us and the shadows and music that sounded like sex.

"You look so good tonight," he rasped, eyes tracing every inch of me. "Good enough to eat."

I let out a breathy laugh, trying to break the tension. "You're drunk, Raschad."

"And?" he shot back, leaning in so close our foreheads nearly touched. "I'm just a little buzzed, but I'm not blind. You knew what you were doing wearing this,"

"I'm not doing anything."

"This dress says different."

"It's not all about you."

His laugh was dark, fingers pressing into my hips. "Everything you do is about me. Just like everything I do is about you."

"That why you keep showing up every time a man talks to me?" I asked.

His hold tightened. "You noticed?"

"You're not subtle when you're jealous."

"I'm not jealous," he said. "I just don't like people trying to touch what's mine."

"Oh, I'm yours again, huh?"

A smile curled his lips. "You'll always be mine, Simone. That doesn't change just because we're not together. Don't play with me."

The possession in his voice should have made me angry. Instead, it made heat pool low in my belly.

"That's not how it works."

"That's how *I* say it works. And don't act like you don't know you *own* me too. Come here."

He took my hand suddenly and led me toward the far back corner, where the velvet booths created shadows the lights couldn't reach. He guided me into the booth, then slid in next to me, pulling me in close, practically in his lap. The music sounded low there, just bass vibrating through the leather seats.

"It's my birthday," he said, voice low and dangerous. "All night, I've been watching you in this dress, remembering things I shouldn't be remembering."

His hand found my thigh where the slit exposed skin, fingers tracing patterns that made me shiver.

"You're drunk," I said again, but my voice came out breathy.

"A little buzzed. Not drunk." His hand slid higher. "Not drunk enough to forget how you sound when I touch you…. How you taste."

"Raschad."

"Tell me you don't think about it," he challenged, leaning closer, peppering kisses on the side of my neck.

I couldn't. Because I did think about it. Often. His fingers found the edge of my panties and I gasped. He pressed his fingers against me through the lace, and my hips lifted involuntarily.

"Feel that?" he growled. "Your body knows what's up."

"Raschad, there are people—" I squirmed.

"They can't see. Just…shhh…let me take care of you right quick." He continued kissing me along my neck and face as he teased my clit. Around us, the party continued, but in our dark corner, it was just us and this thing we couldn't seem to stop.

"Look at me," he commanded, and when I did, his eyes were dark with desire. He slipped two fingers inside me, curling them just right, and I had to grab his wrist to keep from crying out.

My body was on fire, every nerve ending focused on his fingers, his thumb on my clit, the way he was watching me like I was the only thing that mattered. My eyes fluttered shut, head down, heat ripping through my entire body, a moan catching in my throat. He worked me with ruthless precision. I tried to grip his wrist, to slow him down, but he was relentless.

"You gonna come for me, Peach?" his voice was lethal. "That's what I want for my birthday. You gonna come? Hmm?"

I couldn't speak. I couldn't *think*. My body shook, thighs quivering, walls clenching so hard around him I thought I might pass out. He watched every reaction, locked in on me. I bit down on my lip so hard it hurt, trying not to whimper.

"That's it, Peach."

"Raschad, I'm—"

"I know, Peach. Shhh," he coaxed, nibbling my earlobe, "Take what you need, baby." And I did. He placed his mouth on mine, swallowing my cries as I shattered around his fingers, my whole body shaking with the force of it. He worked me through it, drawing out every wave until I was boneless against him.

I pulled on his bottom lip with my teeth as he broke away from our kiss, staring into his eyes with wild fire as I struggled to catch my breath. He slowly withdrew his hand, bringing his fingers to his mouth and licking them clean while maintaining eye contact.

"Happy birthday to me," he mumbled, then kissed me again. I was breathless. Spent. And still wanting him.

I sat there for a moment, and the reality of what just happened washed over me. We were in public, in a dark corner yeah, but still. The thrill of it made me laugh softly.

"What?" he asked, pulling me closer against him.

"We're too old to be doing this in clubs."

"Speak for yourself." He kissed my temple. "And you started it with this dress."

"I need to go clean up. Fix my lipstick." I said, embarrassed, but not moving yet, too comfortable against him.

"Your lipstick's fine."

"It's definitely not." It was smeared all over his lips, so I knew it was smeared over mine. "I like it," he said against my neck. "Evidence."

His possessive tone made me shiver again, but I finally pulled myself together, standing on legs that were steadier now. I escaped to the bathroom, cleaned up and was reapplying my lipstick when Zenobia and Taryn found me.

"That was some grown folks dancing out there," Zenobia teased, coming up beside me.

"The way that man was holding you?" Taryn fanned herself dramatically. "My God today! I thought security was gonna have to intervene."

"We were just dancing," I said, smiling.

"Just dancing," Zenobia repeated. "Girl, you two looked like you were ready to make another baby right there on the dance floor."

"It's his birthday," I said. "We're in a good place. Co-parenting, being friendly."

"*Friendly*," both of them said in unison, then burst out laughing.

"I'm just saying," Zenobia said, "that man is out there happy as hell with his boys, but his eyes find you every five minutes.

I couldn't help but laugh too. Because for the first time in months, things felt possible. The way he'd held me close during the photos, how he kept finding reasons to touch me, my waist, my hand, my shoulder. Like maybe we were finding our way to something new. Maybe we could work out after all.

When I left the bathroom, I saw him by the bar with Julian and Zion. He caught my eye across the room and winked. For the rest of the night, he continued to stay close. His hand on my lower back when I talked. Standing behind me when we watched the last performance. Little touches here and there. It felt natural. Like we were an actual couple.

By two AM, The Obsidian Room was winding down. The performances were over, lights coming up slightly, a universal signal that the party was over.

What was left of our group gathered near the exit, everyone saying their goodbyes. Raschad was definitely drunk now, not sloppy, but his eyes were glassy, his smile looser, leaning against the wall laughing at something someone was saying.

"Where's your car?" Zion asked him.

"Valet has it," Raschad said, patting his pockets. "But Devon drove me here, he was supposed to be DD. Where the fuck is Devon?"

Khairos laughed. "Man left an hour ago with that bartender. Said you'd understand."

"That motherfucker," Raschad shook his head. "He took my keys too. Was holding them for me."

"I got—" Tre started, but his phone buzzed. "Shit, never mind. My situation is waiting for me at the crib."

"I can take you home," I said.

Everyone turned to look at me.

"You know I don't drink like that," I reminded them. "Y'all always joke about how one drink puts me to sleep. Had my champagne at the toast, been on mocktails since."

"You sure?" Zion asked carefully.

"We live ten minutes apart," I said. "It's not a big deal."

Raschad looked at me with soft eyes and drunk affection. "My son's mother y'all. Always taking care of people."

"Come on, birthday boy," I said, grabbing his arm. "Let's go."

We said our goodbyes, and I led him to my car. He folded his long frame into the passenger seat, immediately adjusting the seat all the way back.

"Thank you," he said quietly. "For today. For Zhaire's name. For the jerseys. For being here tonight."

"It's your birthday," I said, starting the car. "And you're his father. Both things worth celebrating."

The drive started quiet, just the low hum of the radio. Then *Could've Been* by H.E.R. filled the car. His hand found mine, and he intertwined our fingers.

"Peach…"

"I know," I said softly.

When I pulled up to his house, he looked at his phone. "Fuck. Devon really did leave with my keys."

He looked at me. "Do you have your copy?"

"I don't keep it on my keyring. It's in a drawer at home. Just stay at my house," I said. "Guest room's always made up. You know where everything is."

When we walked inside my place, the house was still. Zhaire was at Aunt Lorraine's for his sleepover.

"You want water?" I asked, setting my clutch down.

"Yeah."

I went to the kitchen, and when I turned around, he was right there, looking at me with eyes that weren't quite focused but were entirely on me. He took the water but set it down unopened, stepping closer. His hand came up to touch one of the gold chains on the back of my dress.

"This drove me crazy all night," he admitted. "Seeing your back through these chains."

I shivered. "We shouldn't," I whispered, but I was already leaning into his touch.

"I know." But his other hand was on my waist now, pulling me closer.

He kissed me, with his hands in my hair and mine gripping his arms. "Mmmm," I moaned against his mouth.

He picked me up, and my dress bunched up, as he carried me down the hall, kissing my neck, my shoulder, anywhere his mouth could reach.

In my room, he set me down gently, hands already working to get my dress off. He peeled it away, eyes dragging down my body like he'd forgotten what I looked like naked and needed to memorize it all over again. His shirt came next. Then my bra. Then his pants. We moved like thieves, ripping, tugging, taking.

"So damn beautiful," he murmured as the silk fell away.

I reacquainted myself with the planes of his chest, the new "Z" tattoo over his heart, the scar on his ribs from a hard foul his rookie year.

"Simone," he grunted as I kissed that scar, then lower, working at his belt.

"Need you," he said against my skin.

"Need you too," I said.

He lifted me up . "Wrap your legs around me," he commanded.

He hauled me up into his arms with one arm locked under my thighs as he stood tall, the other cradling my back. I wrapped my arms around his neck, clinging to him. My legs wrapped around him, head falling back as his mouth landed on my neck.

"This what you need?" he muttered, rubbing his dick between my lips, teasing me, while coating himself.

"Stop playin' with it," I gasped.

He laughed, but it faded fast. He lifted me higher, then brought me down onto him in one smooth, brutal stroke.

"*Fuck!*" we both gasped.

He held me there, in the middle of my room, my arms and legs wrapped around him tight, then moved. Not a slow grind. He bounced me on him like I was nothing but a damn exercise training drill, *up, down, up, down, up, down,* again and again, his grip locked under my thighs, and my muscles burning to keep pace.

I clung to him, meeting his rhythm, using my own strength to ride with him, chasing the high. His mouth found mine mid-motion, teeth grazing my bottom lip.

"Yeah, Peach…fuck me back…. *shiiii*….like that… damn, girl." He mumbled between bounces.

"Yes…yes…yes," I whined.

"Tell me you missed it," he grunted.

"I did. I missed it. Missed all of it."

"That why you been playin' with me, Peach? Hmm?" he gritted through his teeth as he continued to bounce me relentlessly, "Wearing that dress… smiling in men's faces? Lettin' 'em look at you like they got a shot? Huh, Peach? You forgot who this belongs to?"

"Nuh uh," I gasped in ecstasy, "Not my fault I look goo—"

He slammed me onto him harder, making my back arch as I cried out. "You need to be fucked back to your senses? Hmm?" he choked out.

"Y-Yes…I *doooo*," I sucked and nibbled on his neck.

He carried me to a wall, never slipping out, and pinned me there working me over. My hands gripped the back of his neck, thighs squeezing tight as he drilled into me, one arm under my ass, the other palm spread flat against the wall for balance.

"Mmmph, I love how you feel around me baby. So good."

When my body started to shake, he felt it. "Give it to me, Peach," he gritted. "Give it to me."

I came with a broken cry, nails digging into his skin. He didn't stop. He pressed deeper, harder, chasing his own high. Two, three, four more strokes, and then he lost it too. Eyes shut, jaw clenched, mouth opening on a choked sound that hit somewhere between a growl and my name.

He held me there, still pulsing inside me. Neither of us saying a damn word after that.

At some point I became aware of my ceiling. The dark of my room and his heartbeat steady under my palm. Neither of us moved to say anything. He pressed his mouth to my head once and that was it.

I let myself have it. The way the night had felt like something that was ending and something that was beginning at the same time.

"Raschad," I said.

"I know," he replied. Like we were having the same conversation we always had, just running out of reasons to keep not having it.

I fell asleep thinking… *Maybe.*

birthday regrets

raschad

MY HEAD WAS POUNDING LIKE EVERY OUNCE OF ALCOHOL FROM LAST night was trying to claw its way out through my skull. I dragged myself upright, shoulders aching, and mouth dry. The room was too bright, morning sun streaming through the curtains. I was naked in Simone's bed. Memories from last night replaying in my head. The club. Her in that burgundy dress. My hands on her in the booth. The way she'd felt underneath me, on me, the sounds she made, how perfectly we fit together.

Fuck.

The sex was incredible. It always was with us. No woman had ever made me feel the way Simone did. That connection, that chemistry, since our very first time. Last night had been everything. The way she'd whispered my name, how she knew exactly what I needed without me saying it, that thing she does with her hips that drives me insane.

There's something that happens with her that I've never had a word for. It's not desire. Desire I know. I've had desire with other women. Women who deserved more than the flatness of waking up next to me and realizing I was already somewhere else in my head. That's desire. That's what it looks like when the body wants something the rest of you has no stake in.

This is different.

With Simone the noise stops. The planning, the managing, the constant low-level running of whatever the next thing is. All of it goes quiet. There's just her. Just us. And somehow I feel the most like myself at the exact moment I'm least in control of anything.

I realized this for the first time in San Diego and didn't have language for it. I had language for it by LA and chose not to use it, because using it would have made it real and real things could be taken if you name them too soon.

It *was* taken anyway. And now it's back. Same quiet. A year of careful distance, and before that six years of other women and every flat morning after, and there I was lying there and the noise is gone again. I wanted that every day. Wanted *her* every day. But wanting wasn't enough. The sex, no matter how amazing, didn't rebuild trust that had been shattered.

What the hell are you doing?

Because I'd done this before. Pulled her into my bed then pushed her away. I told myself I wouldn't do that to her again. That the next time I touched her, it would be if and only if I was sure. If I was truly ready.

I still wasn't sure if I was there yet. The guilt of that sat on my chest.

The shower turned off in her bathroom and I sat up, rubbing my face hard, trying to figure out what to say. How to explain that last night was everything I wanted and nothing that I trusted could last. That my body craved her, my heart still loved her, but my mind still couldn't let go of the hurt. We'd made progress. Real progress. But there was still this wall inside me I just couldn't tear down. I needed more time.

The bathroom door opened and Simone emerged in a towel, her skin still damp, looking so beautiful it broke my heart.

"Hey," she said softly, almost shy. "How's your head?"

"Been better."

She moved to her dresser, pulling out clothes. "I can make breakfast. Zhaire won't be back until the afternoon, so we have time to—"

"Simone."

Something in my tone made her freeze. She turned slowly, and I watched understanding dawn in her eyes.

"Don't," she said quietly. "Don't do this again."

I stood, finding my boxers on the floor, pulling them on. "Last night… I shouldn't have taken it there."

Her laugh was hollow. "Which part? The booth? Or here?"

"All of it." I couldn't look at her. "I was buzzed. It was my birthday. The day was emotional. I got carried away."

"Carried away? That's what you're calling it."

"What do you want me to say?"

"The truth maybe?" She clutched her towel tighter. "That it meant something. That we're getting somewhere. That after everything, maybe we're finding our way back."

"I want to, Simone. You think I don't want to? You think I don't want to wake up next to you every morning? That I don't think about you constantly? We've made progress, *real* progress. But I'm not… I'm not all the way there yet."

"So you just keep doing this?" She spat out. "Keep touching me, sleeping with me, making me hope, then crushing me, acting like you didn't want it."

"Of course I wanted it! You're... Simone, you're everything. No one comes close. The way we fit together, it's—" I shook my head. "But that doesn't fix what's broken."

"What's broken is your pride," she said quietly. "I'm not excusing what I did. I've never tried to. I own it. Every day I own it. I made a mistake and—"

"Your mistake cost me years."

"And your inability to forgive is costing us everything else!"

She stared at me for a long moment, devastated, then her expression shifted. "You know what? You're right," she said, voice eerily calm. "You're never going to forgive me. Not really. Not fully. I could give you a hundred years and you'd still be there, wanting me, fucking me, then not wanting to want me, then fucking me again, but not trusting me."

"Simone..."

"I get it now. I've been holding onto this fantasy that one day you'd choose us. Choose *me*. But you won't. You *can't*. And that's... that's okay. It hurts, but it's okay."

She wiped her tears with the back of her hand, straightening her shoulders. "What's not okay though? Is *this*." She gestured between us. "You keeping me on a hook. Making me feel like maybe this time will be different. Maybe this time you'll stay."

"You have no idea how hard it is living on trial with you. Like you're holding a scorecard on me, waiting to decide if I'm worthy enough, if I'm safe enough to love again. Every single day. You think I don't feel that?"

"I'm not trying to—"

"Bullshit!" The calm cracked. "You know exactly what you're doing. You can't have me but you don't want anyone else to either. So you keep me right here, in this fucked up limbo, available when you're weak or drunk or lonely or horny. *Dicking* me along! That's what you're doing."

"That's not what—"

"It is! And I'm done being your maybe. Your sometimes. Your '*I want you but*.' I'm a whole ass woman, Raschad. I deserve someone who chooses me completely. Not someone who sleeps with me like he loves me then leaves before the sheets are cold."

She moved toward me, her towel still clutched tight, and for a second I thought she might slap me. Instead, she just looked at me with eyes that held too much pain and even more fire.

"I understand why you can't forgive me. I do. And I'll carry that forever. But I will *not* carry this disrespect. I'm not your toy. I'm not your backup plan. I'm not here to make you feel good, then disappear on when you remember you hate me."

"I don't hate you, Simone."

"You resent me. Same fucking thing." She laughed bitterly. "And you know what the sick part is? I'd take it. I'd take whatever scraps you threw me if I thought it would lead somewhere. But it won't. We both know it won't."

She stepped back, wrapping her arms around herself. "So here's what's going to happen. You're going to leave. We're going to co-parent like champions because that's what Zhaire deserves. But you don't touch me again. You don't look at me like you want me. You don't whisper lies about me being yours."

"Simone, please, just listen to me. I—"

"NO! I'VE FUCKING HAD IT!" She screamed it, all the pain and rage exploding.

"I'm sorry," I said, because what else was there?

"You're sorry it has to end. But you're not sorry enough to change it." She turned away from me. "Your car keys are on the kitchen counter. Devon dropped them off this morning while you were still asleep."

I wanted to say something, anything, to make this less brutal. But she was right. About all of it. I kept pulling her back in, kept taking what I wanted, kept leaving her destroyed. I'd had over a year to decide and I hadn't. I'd held the door open just enough to keep her hoping and not enough to let her all the way through. It wasn't my intention. But that's what it was.

"I am sorry," I said again quietly. "For all of it."

"So am I," she said without turning around.

I left. Walked out of her bedroom, grabbed my keys, and left her house. As I sat in my car, I could still smell her on my skin, and taste her on my lips.

She was done. Really done. I could see it in her eyes, the final closing of a door I'd always assumed would stay cracked open until I was ready to walk all the way through it. I just needed more time. Thought that eventually I'd wake up and the doubt would be gone, and we could start over. But time just ran out. And I still didn't know how to tear down this wall of pride.

I sat in my car for a long time. Didn't start it. Just sat there.

all in or all out

THIS CHAPTER HAS A SOUNDTRACK

Pink + White by Frank Ocean

raschad

I DIDN'T COME TO ZION'S HOUSE FOR A CONVERSATION. I CAME BECAUSE he'd texted about the game, telling me to come through. I had Zhaire for the evening but he'd fallen asleep and was crashed in their guest room where Taryn had carried him.

Zion and I had been watching the second half, mostly quiet the way we watched games together, commentary when it mattered, nothing when it didn't. Taryn had been in the kitchen, moving around in there. Then she came in during a commercial. Just standing in the doorway with a dish towel in her hand, looking at me.

"Can I say something to you?"

Zion glanced at her and something passed between them, a whole sentence in half a second. He didn't say anything.

"Sure," I said.

She came in and sat on the arm of the chair across from me.

"I heard about your birthday," she said.

I kept my face where it was.

"And before that." She paused. "And the first time, so for the record, I've been sitting on a lot."

"Taryn…" Zion gave her a warning look.

"Look. I'm not here to attack you," she cleared her throat and I could tell she meant it. "But I gotta tell you what I see," she said, "Because I love Simone. She is a beautiful person inside and out, and I've been watching this for a year, and I… just can't hold it in." She looked at me directly. "You keep her on the shelf, Raschad. You go about your life — and you have every right to — but then something tips a certain way, and you reach for her. And then you put her back on the shelf." She shook her head.

"That's not what I'm trying to do." I answered.

"I'm not saying it's intentional. I'm saying that's what it is." Her voice was even. "She made a terrible choice and she has been paying for it every single day since, way before you even knew. And now you've got her in this position where she can't move forward because every time she tries, you give her hope." She paused.

I looked at the game. The commercial was over. I wasn't watching it anymore.

She stood. "If you don't want to be with her, that's a legitimate choice and nobody would tell you that you're wrong for it. But if you do? Then stop making her float in limbo for you to say it." She went back to the kitchen.

The game played. Neither Zion nor I said anything for a minute. Then he reached over and muted the television.

"She's not wrong," he said.

"I know."

"I'm not gonna lecture you, or pile it on." Zion continued. "But I'll tell you what I see, since apparently tonight is that night."

"Keeping Zhaire from you, that was wrong. We've never said otherwise. We were furious with her," he added. "When it came out. Julian, Tre and I, we were all upset with her. She knows that. And there's no excuse for it. Fear, trauma, whatever she was going through, she should've told you. So I'm not here to tell you to get over it," Zion said. "That's not what this is."

"Then what is this?" I asked.

"This is me, as a friend, asking you to be honest with yourself about what you want. I've been where you are, Raschad. Not exactly. What you are going through with Simone and what Taryn and I went through are different situations. But that place you're in? Where you love somebody and you're scared to let them in because they've already shown you what they're capable of? I know that place."

He leaned forward.

"Taryn pushed me away. Countless times. We'd get close, she'd bolt. We did that dance for a while. And there were moments, where I questioned if I was being a fool, where I thought I was done. Where my pride said I'm not chasing someone who keeps leaving."

"What changed that?"

"Therapy." He said it without hesitation or the flinch men usually attached to the word. "I started going years before Taryn and I got together, because the courts made me. Anger management and all that. But it turned into me looking at why I did the things I did. Why I was self-destructive. And the answer was always the same. Losing my mother. Watching her die. That was my original wound. Everything after that was me trying to make sure I never felt that helpless again."

The mention of their mother landed in the room like a stone in still water.

"Sound familiar?" Zion asked.

It did. It sounded like every explanation Simone had given me. The fear of loss, the compulsion to control, the belief that keeping people out was safer than letting them in. It also sounded, in a way I hadn't expected, like me. A man who'd rather live in the in-between than risk getting hurt a third time.

"My therapist said something that has stuck with me," Zion continued. "She said, 'You're not protecting yourself from pain. You're guaranteeing it.' Because the only thing worse than being hurt by someone you love is spending your life without them to avoid the possibility."

"I'm not telling you to forgive her on demand," Zion said. "Forgiveness doesn't work like that. It's not a switch. It's a process. And honestly? There might be things you never fully forgive. Things that scar. But the question isn't whether you can forget what she did. The question is whether you can build a life with her that's *bigger* than the wound."

"And if I can't?"

"Then you can't. And you walk away. Final. Not this…" He gestured vaguely. "Not this purgatory you've both been living in."

"But what I see? When you're not thinking about it, when it's just a normal day and you're here or you're at the house with Zhaire or you're at the studio, you look like a man who has everything he needs."

He paused. "And when there's Simone, standing feet away, you look like a man who's working very hard not to reach for something he desperately wants."

I didn't answer.

"So what's the actual thing?" he asked. "Not the explanation. The real thing underneath it?"

"Pride," I said finally. "Mostly. Part of me, keeps saying I'd be a fool. That a man who goes back after that is a man who doesn't respect himself." I looked down. "Doesn't matter that I understand why she did it. Doesn't matter that I know she's not that person in a malicious way. There's still this voice that says if I walk back through that door, I'm saying that what happened was acceptable."

"That's real. I hear that." Zion's voice was kind but unflinching. "But here's the thing about pride. It doesn't know the difference between protecting you and just hurting you quieter. And pride doesn't raise your son. Pride doesn't keep you warm. Pride is just fear with better posture."

I rubbed my face hard. "I don't want to go all in and get destroyed again. And I don't want to let go and lose her forever. I'm fucking stuck, man."

"The bravest thing I ever did was let Taryn back in when pride told me I'd be a fool to let her in again. I chose her anyway. Not because the fear went away. Because I decided she was worth more than the fear."

"And if I choose wrong? If I let her in and she cuts me."

"Then you'll survive it." Zion looked at me. "But let me ask you this: if you don't choose her, and two years from now she's serious with someone else and Zhaire's calling another man his stepdad and you're wondering what would've happened if you'd been brave enough... will you survive *that*?"

The jealousy that flared wasn't rational. It was primal. Bone-deep. The kind that bypassed every logical argument my pride had ever made and went straight to the part of me that had never stopped believing she was mine.

"No," I said quietly. "I wouldn't survive that."

"Then maybe that's your answer."

"It's not that simple."

"I'm not saying it's simple. It's the hardest thing you'll ever do. Harder than any game, any comeback, any shot at the buzzer. Because this isn't about talent or skill. It's about choosing to be vulnerable with someone who's already proven they can hurt you. That's terrifying. I get it."

He put his hand on my shoulder "But you're not a man who runs from hard things," he said. "That's not who you are. And if you let pride make this decision for you, you might regret it."

"She already said she's done with me."

"She said that because she had to," Taryn shouted from the kitchen. "To protect what's left of herself. That doesn't mean the door is locked. It means you need to use your key."

Zion turned the volume back on and we watched the rest of the game. Didn't talk about it again.

SIMONE ANSWERED THE DOOR BEFORE I KNOCKED. SHE'D HEARD MY CAR, probably.

"He's ready," she said. "His bag's by the door."

"Simone." I stopped on the porch. "Can we—"

"It's all good, Raschad."

"I just want to—"

"Really." Her voice was even. "There's nothing that needs to be said.

We're okay. We're co-parenting. Everything's fine." She looked at me steadily. "You don't have to keep trying to have this conversation."

I didn't know what I was going to say anyway. Behind her, Zhaire appeared in the hallway in his jacket, backpack on. He slipped past Simone to the porch and took my hand without looking up, already moving toward the car.

"Bye, Mommy," he called back.

"Bye, baby. Be good." She looked at me one more time. Not unkind. Just… done. "Have a good weekend."

She closed the door and I stood there for one second. Then I picked up Zhaire's bag and followed my son to the car.

When we got to my house, Zhaire went to play and I sat on the couch. Didn't turn the TV on. Just sat. Zhaire came back from his room with a handful of crackers and arranged himself on the cushion beside me.

"You look like Mommy," he said.

"I look like Mommy?"

"When she's sad." He was matter-of-fact about it, crackers balanced on his knee.

"I'm okay, Z. Daddy's just thinking."

He studied me for another second. Then put his crackers down and turned on his tablet, shoulder against my arm. He started tapping through it, then found what he was looking for. Pressed play.

Frank Ocean, *Pink + White*.

The melody came through the small speaker dreamy and floating. Memories of a bench in the hallway of a hotel in San Diego flashed through my head and I went completely still.

"What is this?" My voice came out careful.

"Mommy's song." He picked his crackers back up and settled back against my arm. "She plays it when she needs to feel better. When she's doing the sad face." He glanced up at me. "You're doing the sad face."

My throat tightened. "You think I'm sad?"

He considered me with great seriousness. "Mhm."

I looked at the tablet. She played it when she needed to feel better. For years she had been pressing play on a song I gave her when she didn't really know me yet. She'd been going back to it, played it so many times that our son knew it by its function. Learned that when someone you love is hurting, you give them things that help. You sit beside them. You play the song. You turn up the volume a little.

"No," I said. "I'm not sad."

Sad wasn't the word. What I was felt bigger than sad, more complicated. What I was felt like a man having been sitting in the dark and finally, finally letting his eyes adjust.

I put my arm around him and he settled in against my side and ate his crackers and neither of us said anything more as the song kept playing.

THE NEXT DAY WE WERE SITTING ON THE SWINGS AT THE PARK, ZHAIRE pumping his legs trying to go higher while I pushed him.

"Higher, Daddy!" he called out.

"You trying to fly away from me, Z?"

He giggled. "I can't fly! I'm not a bird!"

A couple walked by holding hands, the woman laughing at something the man whispered in her ear. Zhaire's swing started to slow as we watched them.

"Daddy?" he said, dragging his feet to stop completely.

"What's up, buddy?"

"Why don't you live with me and Mommy?"

The question caught me off guard. "Because your mama and I aren't together, little man."

"What do you mean?"

I sat down on the swing next to his, trying to figure out how to explain this to a six-year-old.

"You know how Uncle Zion and Auntie Taryn live in the same house?"

"Yeah."

"That's because they love each other, and want to be together all the time, so they got married and live together."

Zhaire nodded like this made sense. "Like boyfriend and girlfriend?"

"Kind of but more than that. Like... when two people love each other so much they want to be a family."

"But we're a family," he said, confusion creeping into his voice. "You, me, and Mommy."

"We are a family. Just a different kind."

"Uncle Tre has lots of girlfriends," Zhaire said matter-of-factly.

I couldn't help but laugh. "Yeah, Uncle Tre is still figuring out what he wants."

"So you and Mommy don't live together like Uncle Zion and Auntie Taryn because you don't love Mommy?"

My heart stopped and I looked at my son. "I do love your mother." I said quietly.

His face lit up. "You do?"

"Yeah, I do."

"You said when you love someone, you want to be with them all the time."

"Sometimes grown-up love is more complicated than that."

"Why?"

I paused trying to find words he could understand. "Sometimes people make mistakes that hurt each other. And sometimes it takes time to figure out how to forgive those mistakes."

"Did Mommy make a mistake?"

"We both made mistakes."

Zhaire was quiet for a moment, swinging slightly back and forth. "How do you know you love Mommy?"

I thought about that beach in San Diego. About the way she'd looked in that blue bikini, laughing at something I'd said. "I loved your mother from the first day I met her," I said.

"Really?"

"The very first day. We were on a beach, and she was the most beautiful woman I'd ever seen. But it wasn't just how she looked, it was how she made me feel."

"How?"

"Like the sun was brighter when she was around."

He started swinging again, then stopped abruptly. "If you love Mommy, why don't you live together like Uncle Zion and Auntie Taryn?" he asked again deciding I still hadn't given him a satisfactory answer to his question.

"Sometimes grown-ups make things more complicated than they need to be." I said again.

"That's dumb."

"Yeah," I said, surprising myself. "It is. Maybe you're right."

"I'm always right. Mommy says I'm too smart for my own good." Zhaire nodded seriously, then suddenly perked up. "Ooh! Can we get ice cream after this?"

I laughed at how quickly his six-year-old brain had moved on to his obsession with ice cream. "Sure."

I'D BEEN STARING AT MY PHONE FOR TEN MINUTES BEFORE FINALLY hitting the FaceTime button. Of all my sisters, Alyssa would give it to me straight while still understanding the complicated parts. Her face appeared on screen, hair wrapped, glasses on, clearly ready for bed.

"It's late," she said. "This better be good."

"I fucked up."

She sighed. "Hold on, let me get comfortable. "

I watched her adjust pillows and settle into her bed.

"Okay," she said. "Talk."

I told her everything. My birthday, Simone's ultimatum, the weeks of awkward exchanges since.

"And now?" she asked when I finished.

"Now I'm sitting here at midnight calling you because I don't know how to fix it."

"Do you want to fix it?"

"Yes."

"Then what's stopping you?"

"I don't know. It's like I'm over what she did, but, then, I'm not over what she did."

"You know what I can't get past? Malik being gone. Three years and I…" she trailed off, and I knew she was thinking about her husband's death, and the betrayal she'd discovered that same day.

"That's different."

"Is it? Loss is loss, Raschad. Whether it's death or deception, you're mourning something that was taken from you. The difference is, you have a chance to reclaim yours."

"It's not that simple."

"Love never is. You think good relationships don't have issues?"

"Not like this."

"The size of the transgression matters less than what you do after it. And from what I can see, your love for Simone is massive. So is hers for you."

"Love isn't enough."

"Bullshit. Love is everything. It's just not *easy*." She adjusted her glasses. "You're headstrong, focused, stubborn, driven, decisive, all the things that make you successful. But love doesn't play by those rules, Nova."

"So what am I supposed to do?"

"You're supposed to decide what matters more to you. Being right or being happy? Feeding your pride or feeding your heart?"

"What if she's already moving on?"

"Is she?"

"I don't know. We don't talk except about Zhaire."

"Then you better figure it out before someone else does. The next man might not fumble."

"I know."

After we hung up, I sat thinking about what she'd said. About what they'd all said. I needed to talk to Simone. Really talk. Put my ego aside and tell her I wanted us. That I want to fight for us.

The next morning I picked up my phone.

> Hey. Can we talk?
>
> Not a co-parent talk.
>
> A you and me talk.

She didn't respond that day. That was okay. I'd said it.

two lines

simone

I THOUGHT BEING DONE WOULD FEEL LIKE GRIEF. LIKE A DOOR CLOSING, the sound of it, the finality. And maybe it was that, somewhere underneath. But mostly it just felt like I'd been holding something very heavy for a very long time and I'd set it down. But my arms were still sore from it, just that the thing wasn't in my hands anymore.

Raschad had tried to talk to me about it a few times since then, but I refused to go there with him. I'd drawn a hard line with him that if it wasn't about Zhaire, it wasn't relevant to discuss. I wasn't putting myself through the hope and the let down cycle again. Not to punish him. I just didn't have anything else to say. We were co-parents. We were doing that well. Everything else was just noise and confusion.

I'd come to terms with the fact that he would never be able to let go of the hurt. I wasn't angry about it. I understood it. If our situations were reversed I don't know that I could have done better. You can understand a thing completely and still have to walk away from it. That's not cruelty. That's just survival. That's where I was at with it.

Then, it happened. I stood in my bathroom, blinking down at the faint pink lines on that cheap plastic stick and exhaled.

Pregnant.

The moment felt like déjà vu and a bad joke. I stood there waiting for the fear that had swallowed me whole the first time. The fear that pregnancy could end the way it did for my mother. It was quieter this time. Not gone. But quieter. Like a scar that ached in certain weather instead of a wound that was open. I'd done this before. I'd carried Zhaire to full term and he'd come out perfect and I'd survived. My body had proven something to me that nothing else could have.

The panic that rose now wasn't about dying. It was about him.

What is he going to think?

Will he assume I did this on purpose? That I was trying to trap him, forcing him deeper into my life? We weren't together. We were coparents who crossed a blurred line, high on jealousy, tension, and tequila.

Was this how my life was supposed to go? Pregnant twice by the same man I never made it with? A tiny part of me felt a spark of excitement. A new baby. Zhaire would have a sibling. We co-parented well. We could do it again, right?

But that spark was crushed by a tidal wave of dread. What if Raschad thinks I'm manipulating him? What if he says we should try again, but only because of this baby? My heart clenched. I didn't want to be anyone's "responsibility." I dropped my face into my hands as tears welled up. *Dammit.*

I pulled out my phone and scrolled to Taryn's name, fingers shaking.

> I need you. Emergency. Come over.

Thirty minutes later, Taryn came barreling through my door, scanning the room like she was ready to fight.

"Okay," she said, hands on hips, "What's going on now?"

I just pointed to the hall bathroom, to the little stick that had decided to ruin my day. Taryn squinted, picked it up carefully, and let out a long, drawn-out, "*Daaaamn.*"

She threw her hands up. "Lord have mercy. Operation Shut Shit Down worked *way* better than I expected!"

I couldn't help it, I laughed through my tears.

Then she gave me a judgmental look. "So I guess condoms are just not in y'alls vocabulary, huh? No birth control or nothin', I swear," she shook her head.

"I don't even have an excuse, T. Don't judge. It's not like we planned to sleep together. It just happened, and we weren't prepared or thinking…"

She squinted at me, dramatic as ever. "Simone, I'm sorry, but that man's sperm's *gotta* have GPS in it, or you are just fertile as fuck. Because *how the hell* you get pregnant twice by the same man you *not* even with? With as little sex as your ass has?"

I shook my head, laughing more and crying all at once. She sat next to me, wrapping an arm around my shoulders.

"What if he thinks I did this on purpose?"

She squeezed me. "You are not about to sit here acting like you tried to trap that man. Stop it."

I bit my lip. "But what if he *thinks* that? What if he thinks I'm trying to reel him back in with a baby?"

Taryn leveled me with an aggravated look. "Girl. Be for real. That man is grown, in his damn thirties. You think he doesn't know how babies get made? He coulda pulled out. Coulda wrapped it up. Coulda said *no* and kept it in his pants. But he didn't. So don't act like is just on you."

I wiped my eyes and nodded.

"And honestly? He wasn't tryna stop it either, was he? Maybe deep down *he* wanted this. Why didn't you think of *that* first? Instead, you're always so busy blaming yourself."

She kept going. "Y'all are two grown, educated, *consenting* adults who know exactly what comes from raw sex. So don't put this all on your shoulders like you ran some diabolical plan. That man was right there with you."

I let out a breath, the weight in my chest easing just a little.

Taryn patted my thigh. "Look. As confused as Raschad's wishy-washy ass has been, there is no denying he loves your emotional behind. He *loves* you. He may not know how to do it right, but he does."

I nodded, sniffling again.

"So tell him. Tell him *soon*," she insisted. "This is not seven years ago, Simi. Y'all are different people now. *You* are different. Stronger. Wiser. It'll be okay."

"I love you," I whispered.

Taryn smiled. "Of course you do. I'm the best."

———

I'D BEEN REHEARSING THIS IN MY HEAD FOR DAYS. IN THE SHOWER, IN the car, in the middle of the night when anxiety woke me up like a slap. Every version felt wrong. But Taryn was right. It had to happen now.

So I texted him:

> Hey, can you come by after you drop Zhaire off at school? I need to talk to you.

RASCHAD NOVA

> Everything okay?

> Yeah. Just come by please.

He showed up maybe an hour later, in a fresh tee and sweats, looking fine. He stepped inside cautiously, keys jangling in his hand.

"What's up?"

I took a breath, trying to slow my heart racing. "Can we sit down?"

He looked apprehensive, but followed me to the couch, dropping onto it.

My throat felt like it might close up. "Okay. Um." I paused and gathered myself. "I'm just gonna come right out and say it."

He stared at me, confused.

"I'm pregnant."

His face went slack. His mouth actually fell open for a solid five seconds. There was just air. No words. No breath. Finally, he found something to say.

"You're...pregnant. With my baby?"

Something in my chest twisted. I winced, defensively "Don't say it like I've been out there spreading it Raschad! YES your baby." I stood up.

He grabbed my hand, pulling me to sit back down next to him. "That's not what I meant. No, no, no, Simone. That's not what I meant. *At all.*" He stood up, then sat back down, then stood again, like he couldn't decide what to do with his body.

"It's just..." he shook his head, and sat down again, almost laughing. "It's a shock. But...a good shock. The *best* shock. My words came out wrong. I-I know it's mine. I would never imply...or think that...I wasn't —." he stopped and took a deep breath in and then a long exhale.

He stood again, ran both hands over his face, and sat back down. "Okay," he said, like he was talking himself into being steady. "Okay."

I'd never seen him so flustered before, I almost had to bite back a laugh. I looked at him. "You're not upset?"

His eyes met mine. "Upset? Simone... I get to do this. I get to be there. That's...God, that's everything to me."

I started crying, overwhelmed as he dropped to his knees in front of me, grabbing my hands. "I know you're scared. I know this is complicated, and not planned. But listen to me." He looked into my eyes. "I'm here. All the way. Whatever you need."

I covered my mouth, sobbing as he got up and sat back next to me, pulling me into his side, kissing the top of my head. "Thank you for this" he whispered.

I laughed through tears. "Raschad, it's literally the size of a blueberry right now."

He cracked a grin, wiping at his own eyes. "Still... thank you. Can I?" he gestured to my stomach.

I nodded and he placed a warm hand over my stomach, like he was holding something priceless. For a minute, we were just quiet. Then I found my voice, moving out from under his arm, enough to look at him straight.

"I need to say something." I said.

He looked at me.

"We are good co-parents. You and me with Zhaire. That part works. And I know it can work again with this baby too." I kept my voice certain, even though nothing inside me was. "You don't have to feel obligated to do anything different than what we're already doing."

He sat up straight. "What are you saying?"

"I'm saying this doesn't have to change anything. We don't have to be together because there's a baby on the way. I mean it, Raschad. I have watched you be a father to Zhaire and it is the most..." I swallowed fresh tears. "It is the most incredible thing I've witnessed. I am not asking you to be anything other than that, for this one too."

"Simone."

"I don't want you to feel trapped."

"Trapped? That's not what I feel. At all."

"You don't have to say that."

He turned on the couch to face me fully. "I'm not saying it because I have to. I'm saying it because it's true. I *want* to try. I *want* our family. I *want* you, Peach. All of it. This is what I want."

I looked at him for a long moment, at what looked like certainty in his face. Everything I had wanted from him since he came back into my life, sitting right there in front of me.

But I didn't believe it. Not because he was lying. I knew this was what he thought he wanted. But I was sure he was confusing being a father again and the excitement of it feeling like a "do over", with actual feelings for me.

I had been in this hopeful space before, where I let myself believe it could be real. I knew what I was like when I let myself want something and then lost it. I knew the way that kind of loss broke me. And I was pregnant and already fatigued. I could not afford to fall toward him and find out later that the baby was the only reason he was there.

"I hear you," I said. "I do. But I need us to stay where we are. Co-parents. Like we've been. And if ...if something changes, when it's not brand new and there's no blueberry involved, then maybe we can talk about it then."

He sat with what I'd said and I watched him decide whether to push back or let it sit. "That's not what this is for me, Simone. I know you don't believe that. But it's not the reason." he said. "But, I don't want to stress you out and I don't want to argue. I'll respect what you want."

"Thank you."

"But I need you to know..." he stopped himself and exhaled. "Never mind. We can talk about it another time."

He stayed another hour. We talked about logistics, doctor's appointments, when to tell Zhaire. The practical things. The things we were
good at.

When he left, he hugged me at the door long enough that I had to
tell myself not to hold on.

that true, peach?

simone

———

IT HAPPENED GRADUALLY, WITHOUT A CONVERSATION, AND WITHOUT AN actual decision I could point to. The first night was when I walked into the living room to find Raschad's groggy face and Zhaire asleep on the couch with his head on Raschad's arm. I told him he could take the guest room. He nodded, and crashed there for the night.

The next time it made sense because it was late and Raschad was just going to have to come right back in the morning to pick me up for a prenatal checkup. Then it started making sense so he could be there to help Zhaire some mornings, to take the load off me. This pregnancy had been particularly draining on my body for some reason. Eventually the reason he'd stay was because I was further along now and he felt better being close, making sure we were good. Honestly, so did I.

I was about six months pregnant and Raschad stayed in the guest room most of the week. Slowly he started handling things around my house that I hadn't asked him to. Then, I realized he had also been handling me. Quietly and consistently. Water in front of me before I realized I was thirsty. Reminding me to eat something. Bringing home odd snacks to fulfill my weird cravings. Getting aggravated if I tried to pick up anything heavier than a book. Reminding me that he was there, and he had it. It was getting harder to pretend I didn't feel it.

Zhaire asked about it at the kitchen table one night, pencil hovering over a math worksheet. "Daddy do you live here now?"

Raschad glanced at me, reading my face, then looked back at our son. "For now. While your baby sister is growing." He looked at Zhaire. "You know what a man does when his family needs him?"

Zhaire looked up. "What?"

"He shows up and makes sure everybody's safe. That's it." He tapped his worksheet. "Finish that last problem."

I went to the sink and my hand went to my lower back feeling tightening. I winced quickly, sure I'd hidden it.

"Simone. Come sit down." Raschad called from the living room, without looking up.

"I'm fine."

"You've been saying that all week. I'll do the dishes. Sit down."

I stood there with my hand pressed to my back, my argument fully assembled. He wasn't performing concern. He'd just noticed the way he'd been noticing everything for weeks without requiring me to acknowledge it.

I put the dish towel down and I sat. The sound that came out of me when I landed on that couch was long, shaky, and embarrassingly honest. He came back with cocoa butter, and sat behind me on the couch, one leg up, one on the floor, and asked me where it hurt. He started with my shoulders and worked his way down. My shoulders dropped, my head tilted forward and everything I'd maintained from the second I woke up started dissolving under his hands. My head drifted back against his shoulder. My hand rested on his knee, and next thing I knew, I'd fallen asleep.

I woke up the next morning with a blanket around me and the couch to myself. The kitchen was clean, the dishes were done, and the counters were wiped down.

The back rubs became a standing thing after that. Not every night, but most nights. He'd find me wherever I was around eight or nine and just start, and I'd stopped pretending I was going to object. I'd sit wherever he directed and feel the day unknot itself under his hands.

I didn't mean to go in there. It was laundry day and I'd folded some of Raschad's things even though he kept telling me he would handle his own laundry. But since I was already doing Zhaire's clothes, it didn't make much sense to me to run additional cycles when their clothes could be washed together. I stacked Raschad's clothes neatly and carried them to the guest suite.

His door was half open, and I nudged it open with my hip.

"Raschad? I've got your——"

The ensuite bathroom door opened, and there he was. Dripping wet. Steam curled out behind him and trails of water ran in slow lines down his body, over his shoulders, between the ridges of his stomach, catching in the grooves of muscle on his legs that had no business being that defined.

He had nothing on. Not a towel. Not boxers. Not a single stitch of anything between his body and the open air and my wide-open eyes.

I froze. He froze.

And then, because this man had been put on this earth specifically to test me, he *smiled*. Not an embarrassed oh-shit-you-caught-me smile. A slow, knowing grin that started at one corner of his mouth and spread like he'd been expecting me. Like it was funny to him.

"I… your clothes. I was just… the laundry…" I held up the stack of folded clothes as evidence. Like proof that I had a legitimate reason for being there that was not to stare at his naked body. Which, I was now staring at because my eyes had completely abandoned my brain and gone rogue.

I tried to look at the ceiling. Looked at the floor instead. Somehow that was worse because the floor led to his feet which led to his legs which led to— *I gulped*.

"I didn't know you were… I should've knocked. I'm sorry, I'll just…"

"You're good, Peach." he walked toward the bed where a towel was draped across the end. Picked it up slowly and started drying himself off with an unbothered energy that told me he was not at all in a hurry to cover up.

"Forgot my towel," he said, like grown men just walked around dripping water everywhere on a regular Wednesday afternoon.

He ran the towel across his chest. Down one arm. Then the other. Watching me watch him. Because I was still watching him. I hadn't moved. My feet had betrayed me just like my eyes.

"Nothing to apologize for," he said. "Nothing you haven't seen before."

He was right. I had seen it before. Every inch of it. But that was before I got pregnant, before he moved into my guest room out of what I'd convinced myself was obligation.

He was bigger now. Thicker through the chest. New ink on his ribs I didn't recognize, something scripted on his left side that I couldn't read from where I was. His arms were ridiculous. His shoulders were ridiculous. Everything was ridiculous. And he was looking at me like he knew exactly what I was thinking.

"Thank you," he said, crossing the room toward me. Still naked and dripping in places the towel hadn't reached. He stopped right in front of me, leaned behind me to reach over and push the door shut, then he took the stack of clothes from my hands, his fingers brushing mine.

He set the clothes on the dresser beside me, never taking his eyes off me. "Thank you, Peach," he said again, his nickname for me landing like a palm on bare skin.

I stood there, six months pregnant in a house dress, no bra, hair in a ponytail, belly round and obvious, and I still did not move. His eyes dropped to my mouth. Then my neck. Then slow, so slow, down my body. Taking his time the way he'd taken his time with the towel. And when his gaze reached my full, stretched belly, his expression shifted. The teasing in his eyes softened into something deeper.

Then it shifted back and there was that grin again. His length had started to respond. Growing, thickening, and he made absolutely no effort to hide it. Didn't angle away. Didn't reach for the towel. He just stood there, letting me see what I apparently did to him.

My eyes widened.

"Miss it?" his voice vibrated through my chest like bass through a speaker.

My face was doing something I couldn't control. Flushed, lips parted, eyes that wouldn't look away no matter how many direct orders my brain was issuing. I licked my lips and swallowed hard.

He tilted his head and smiled wider. "It misses you."

"Raschad…"

"Actually," he said, casually, like we were having a conversation about the weather. "I read something about pregnancy I've been curious about. Maybe you can tell me if it's true."

I swallowed again. "What?"

"I read that when a woman is pregnant…" He was even closer to me now. Close enough that the heat from his body was wrapping around me. "…that she's the most sexual she'll ever be. Wants it more." His voice dropped. "*Needs* it more."

He paused and let the words sit. "That true, Peach?"

My heart was hammering and my skin was on fire. "I-I don't know," I whispered. "Haven't really thought about it." The lie was so obvious it was almost comedy. I'd thought about it every day for months. Every time he walked past me in gray sweats with his chest out. Every time he'd be sitting on the couch, watching a game, with his legs wide and I'd stare at him for too long and have to leave the room before I lost control, and straddled his lap.

He smiled patiently like he knew that my body was telling a different story than my mouth. "Hmph," he said. "Maybe I should do my own research then?"

And then his hands found the hem of my dress. Sliding upward, palms warm against my sides, the fabric moving with them.

"I like this dress on you, Peach."

"It's just a house dress."

"It's sexy." His hands reached my hips, and he paused. His brow lifted. "No panties?"

"They've uh… felt a little tight lately," I managed. "More comfortable this way."

"Hmmm." His hands spread across my bare hips and his fingers slid from my hip and found me already wet, already swollen, already so far gone that the first brush of contact made a sound come out of my mouth that I will deny to my grave.

He didn't react. Just held me there with his hand between my legs, his eyes on mine, and his breath steady while mine fell apart.

"Survey says," he smiled, "that's one hundred percent *true*."

"*Raschaaaad.*" I tried to make it a warning. It came out like begging.

His forehead touched mine and his free hand came up to my face, thumb tracing my cheekbone, cradling my jaw. So gentle it made my eyes sting.

"Tell me to stop," he said, "and I'll stop."

I said nothing. His fingers moved in circles, making my knees buckle. I gripped his forearm and my breath left my body in a shudder.

"Tell me to stop, Peach."

I wasn't going to tell him to stop. We both knew it. I'd been telling myself to stop wanting him for six months and it hadn't worked for a single second of a single day.

"Don't stop," I whispered.

Then he kissed me. Not the way I expected. Not hungry, or urgent. This kiss was slow and intentional. Careful and grateful and testing to see if everything was still where he'd last left it. His hand left the space between my legs and I whimpered at the loss. He kept kissing me and when he pulled back his eyes were different. The teasing was gone.

I pulled his face back to mine and kissed him with everything I'd been swallowing down. The longing, the fear, the gratitude, the desire that had been eating me alive since the day he unofficially moved into my guest room and started making pancakes in the mornings.

He wrapped his arms around me, adjusting for the belly between us, a new geography of my body that he navigated like he'd already mapped it out. He pulled me close without pressing. Held me tight without squeezing, finding a way to fold me into him that kept our baby safe between us.

He slowly walked toward his bed. Kissing me the whole way. His hands in my hair, pulling my ponytail loose. His mouth on my neck sucking the spot that made my knees dissolve. I gasped, clutching his shoulders.

He laid me down like I was the most precious thing in his world, and pulled my dress up and over my head. I had a moment where I wanted to cover myself. My body wasn't what it had been. My stomach was round and stretched, a darker line ran from my navel down. My breasts were heavier, fuller, and starting to become veined in ways I'd avoided looking at in the mirror. My ass had widened. Everything was softer, rounder, bigger…different.

He must've seen the hesitation in my face. My instinct to curl in. "Don't do that," he said quietly. He pulled back enough to look at me. And the way he stared wasn't reassurance for my benefit. It was hunger. Real, unfiltered hunger. The kind that darkens a man's eyes and changes the way a he breathes.

"You know what you look like right now?" he said as his hands traced my sides, up from my hips, over the curve of my belly, along my ribs, caressing my breasts so gently it made me arch into him. "You look like everything I ever wanted and was too stupid to hold on to."

He lowered his mouth to my stomach and pressed his lips just below my navel. Reverently kissing a trail across my belly like he was blessing it. His lips followed the darker line like he already knew it. He did. His hands held my hips, thumbs stroking the stretch marks on my sides. The ones I coated with cocoa butter every night and hated, he was touching like they were beautiful.

"Every part of this," he murmured against my skin. "Every part of you."

He moved lower kissing below my belly, watching my face the whole time, then he pulled back again, and stared at me, naked, pregnant, and stretched wide by the life we'd made together. And the way he looked at me made me feel like the most desired woman who had ever existed.

"Raschad…"

"I got you," he said. "Let me take care of you."

He started at my ankles. Kissed and licked his way up my calves, behind my knees, where I flinched, ticklish, and he smiled against my skin. Then up the inside of my thighs, so slowly I thought I'd lose my mind. My hands fisted the sheets and my breathing went ragged.

He settled between my legs, spreading my legs apart, and I felt his warm breath against me before his mouth was. When he put his mouth on me, my back arched off the bed and I let out a long low moan. He took his time, working his tongue in devastating patterns, remembering what I liked, finding new things that the pregnancy had made more sensitive. My entire body was a live wire. Every nerve ending amplified, every touch landing harder than it should have. He'd been right about the pregnancy thing but I would never admit it.

His hands held my legs open and his thumbs stroked the crease where my legs met my hips. When he found a rhythm, I stopped thinking entirely.

"Raschad — I'm — oh —"

He didn't speed up or change pace. He stayed right there with his mouth on me with devotion. I came apart completely. My whole body seized then released, waves rolling through me so hard I could barely breathe, my hands clutching the back of his head, and my voice breaking. He stayed with me through every pulse and aftershock, gently easing me back down.

When he lifted his head, he looked satisfied but not done. He climbed up beside me, lying on his side, facing me. His hand found my stomach and rested there.

"Hey," he said, softly looking into my eyes.

"Hey," I exhaled, my body still humming at the edges.

He moved over me carefully, bracing his weight on his forearms, keeping pressure off my belly. We shifted to a new position, figuring out the geometry together, laughing a little, and adjusting, my bump between us requiring a negotiation that felt more intimate than the act itself. He finally settled at my side, spooning me close, and when he pushed into me, achingly slow, we both went still. He exhaled against my neck and shuddered.

"Simone," he breathed. "I missed you so much."

I reached back, gripping his hip, pulling him deeper. "I missed you too."

He moved slowly, with one arm wrapped around me, his hand splayed across my belly, holding us in one embrace. His lips kept finding tender spots on my neck, back and shoulders. His breathing was ragged, but his movements were controlled. Every stroke reaching the deepest parts of me without rushing, without anything but love translated into the only language we'd never had trouble speaking.

My hand covered his on my stomach and our fingers laced. And for the first time in a long time, I let myself believe this was real. That he wasn't going to leave. That the man at my back, moving inside me, whispering my name like it was the only word he knew, was exactly where he wanted to be.

Not out of obligation, or because of the baby. Because of *me*.

He pressed deeper and I gasped. He paused. "You okay?"

"Don't you dare stop."

He laughed, the vibration moving through both our bodies and kept going, building slowly. His hand left my belly and found me again, fingers circling where we were connected, matching the rhythm of his hips with precision.

"I love you, Peach," he whispered in my ear. "You hear me? I love you, baby."

I held his arm tighter against my stomach and closed my eyes. I couldn't say it back yet. I wanted to. I felt it so completely. But saying it out loud would have meant trusting it. So I held on instead.

I climaxed again, quieter this time, deeper in a wave that started in my heart and rolled all the way through me, pulling him with me. He came, burying his face in my neck, holding me so tight I could feel his heartbeat against my spine. We stayed like that, connected, breathing hard, with his arm around me.

Neither of us moved. His hand stayed on my belly, massaging in circles. He looked at me for a long time. Then he pulled me in, and tucked my head under his chin.

He didn't go back to the guest room that night. Or the next. Or the one after that. By the end of the week his things had migrated. His toiletries on my bathroom counter, his charger on the nightstand, his pillow denting the other side of my bed. Not with a conversation or a declaration. Just a quiet, steady shifting of his life into mine.

He had his house, still went back now and then, usually to get more things and check on his spot. But he slept behind me every night, arm around my stomach, palm flat where the baby moved. When I got up at 3 AM he'd stir and mumble *you good?* and I'd say *yeah* and he'd be back asleep before I came back but his arm would find me the second I settled in. Like a reflex. Like his body was keeping track of mine even when his brain wasn't.

He was attentive like that.

And yes, we kept sleeping together. Increasingly creative as the weeks went on. He took care of me. I took care of him. It was an arrangement that functioned.

But in the back of my mind, I knew, once the baby came things would settle back into their shape. He had his house, I had mine. We'd figure out the schedule the same way we'd figured out Zhaire's. The comfortable rhythm of two people who co-parented well. This stretch, this in-between time where he was here every night and his pillow was on my side of the bed and Zhaire had started setting a place for him at the table without being asked? That was temporary and practical infrastructure. A good man making sure everyone was taken care of.

That was Raschad. That was just who he was. I intended not to overthink it. It was a good arrangement, and I would just enjoy it for what it was, while it lasted.

probably nothing

simone

———

This pregnancy was harder. More tired. More achy. More of everything. With Zhaire I'd worked forty-plus hour weeks, driven myself to appointments, carried groceries, felt tired only in the way a normal person felt tired, manageably and temporarily. I'd expected this one to go the same way.

But my body had other plans. By the time I hit seven months I was working from home most days. Raschad's insistence, backed by my brothers, all four of them presenting it to me one Sunday dinner, clearly coordinated in advance. I'd looked around the table at all of them and understood that the conversation had already happened somewhere I wasn't invited to and this was just the announcement.

The truth was it helped. My hips ached and my feet were swollen by afternoon, a persistent puffiness that my shoes noticed before I did. I'd had some swelling with Zhaire too, toward the very end. So I filed it under normal, didn't complain, and moved on.

Raschad was... a lot. That was the thing about him being in my home, in my bed, and in the full fabric of the daily routine. He saw all of it. The way I shifted my weight getting out of bed in the morning. The way I pressed my hand to my back without meaning to. The way I ate less than I should have because my stomach had opinions about everything. He tracked it all with the focused, slightly obsessive attention of a man who had missed one pregnancy and was determined not to miss a single detail of this one.

It was sweet. It was genuinely sweet. But it was also a lot.

"You sleep okay?"

"Your ankles look more swollen today than yesterday."

"Did you drink all the water I left?"

"You've been rubbing your back for twenty minutes."

I'd smile and say I was fine and mean it, mostly. Because I *was* fine mostly. Part of me thought the vigilance of his concern, the way he catalogued my symptoms like he was preparing a case, was because he didn't have the reference point of knowing what was normal. I did. Zhaire had been textbook. This pregnancy was harder, yes, but harder didn't mean a problem.

I didn't want him to worry. I wanted to give him a version of my pregnancy that let him relax, and enjoy it. Have the experience he'd missed the first time without it being shadowed by fear.

So when he asked if I was okay I always said yes. When he asked about my ankles I said it was normal. When he asked about my headaches, which had started somewhere in week twenty-four, dull and persistent, I said it was probably screen time, I'd been on my laptop too much, and I'd take a break.

I wasn't lying to him. I was telling him what I told myself, which was that pregnancy was uncomfortable at times. I kept telling myself I was older now and bodies change. What I kept pushing down was the thing I'd carried since I understood what it meant that my mother had been fine right up until she wasn't. I didn't let myself think about that as often as I did when I was pregnant with Zhaire. My body knew how to do this and I was in a good hospital system, being monitored and cared for.

THURSDAY MORNING I HAD ANOTHER HEADACHE. NOTHING MAJOR. JUST a dull throb behind my eyes that made me want to close the blinds and lie down for the rest of the day. Which I couldn't do, because I had ten things on my to-do list that weren't going to do themselves. I took a Tylenol, drank water and went about my day. By Thursday night, my headache was still there. Not worse. But not better. Like a houseguest who wouldn't take a hint.

"You okay?" Raschad asked when I pressed my fingers to my temples at dinner.

"Just a headache." I tried to smile. "Think the baby's sitting on a nerve or something."

He frowned. "How long have you had it?"

"Since this morning. It's not a big deal."

"You take anything?"

"Tylenol."

His frown deepened. "And it's not helping?"

"Not really, but—"

"We should call the doctor."

"Raschad, it's just a headache." I heard the exasperation creeping into my voice. "Pregnant women get headaches. It's on the list of approximately nine hundred things that happen when you're growing a human being."

"I know, but—"

"I'm fine."

That word again. The one I'd been using like a shield because if I admitted something hurt or felt wrong, he'd go into overdrive. And the worst part? I couldn't even be properly annoyed at him. Because I knew *why* he was like this. Knew that my brothers had spent my entire first pregnancy taking turns sleeping on my couch because none of us trusted my body not to do what my mother's did. He'd absorbed that history and turned it into vigilance, the kind that came from love so deep it looked like control if you didn't understand what was underneath it.

He was nervous. And unlike me, who hid behind *I'm fine* and changed the subject, Raschad turned his nervousness into action. Research. Questions. A blood pressure monitor on the bathroom counter.

"Okay." He went back to his food.

But under the table, I saw him pull out his phone. Saw his thumb move across the screen. Adding *headache, persistent, not responsive to Tylenol* to whatever log he thought I didn't know about.

DR. KLINE SMILED AT ME FROM ACROSS THE EXAM ROOM.

"Everything looks good, Simone. Baby's measuring right on track."

"That's great." I smiled back.

"Blood pressure's a little elevated today." She made a note on her tablet. "140 over 93."

My smile faltered. "Is that bad?"

"It's higher than we'd like, but not in the danger zone. Very common in the third trimester."

"Any other concerns?" Dr. Kline asked.

"No, I don't think—"

"She's been having headaches," Raschad cut in.

I closed my eyes. *Here we go.*

Dr. Kline's eyes flicked to him, then back to me. "Headaches?"

"Just one," I said quickly. "Well, one that lasted a couple days. But it's gone now."

"*Mostly* gone," Raschad corrected.

I shot him a look and he ignored it.

"And she had some vision issues earlier last week," he added.

"Vision issues?" Dr. Kline's pen hovered over her tablet.

"It was *nothing*. Just blurry for a moment."

"How long of a moment?"

"I don't know. A minute maybe?" I shifted on the exam table, the paper crinkling under me. "It went away."

"Mm-hmm." Dr. Kline made another note. "Well, like I said, these things are pretty normal. Your body's under a lot of stress right now. Just make sure you're staying hydrated and getting enough rest."

"See?" I looked at Raschad.

He didn't look reassured. "One more thing." His voice was calm. "Her blood pressure last visit was 135 over 88. Today it's 140 over 93. That's an increase, right?"

Dr. Kline's smile tightened. Just slightly. "Technically, but blood pressure fluctuates. This reading is essentially the same."

"*Technically*, it's trending up. Not staying stable."

"Like I said, blood pressure fluctuates, Mr. Carter. White coat syndrome is very common—"

"She doesn't have white coat syndrome." His tone stayed even, but I heard the edge underneath. "And I've been tracking it at home. It's been creeping up for three weeks."

"You've been tracking it at home?" Dr. Kline's eyebrows rose.

"Yeah." He pulled out his phone. "Want to see the numbers?"

Oh God. I wanted to slide off this exam table and melt into the floor. Disappear into the industrial tile like water. He was pulling up a spreadsheet at my OB appointment.

"Mr. Carter, I appreciate your concern—"

"Do you? Because you just dismissed three separate symptoms without running a single test."

The temperature in the room dropped and Dr. Kline's smile was gone now. Replaced by something clinical.

"Raschad," I said quietly.

He looked at me. "Look, I'm not trying to be difficult," he said, turning back to Dr. Kline. "But I read that elevated blood pressure, headaches, and vision changes together can be signs of preeclampsia. Is that true or not?"

The directness of it changed something in the room. Stripped away the pleasantries, the professional niceties. Left just a question that required an honest answer.

Dr. Kline's jaw shifted. "It *can* be, yes. But Simone's symptoms are mild and—"

"So shouldn't we be checking? Running labs?"

"Mr. Carter, if I ran extensive labs on every pregnant woman who had a headache, I'd never leave the office." Her tone had gone crisp. "Simone's labs from last month were perfect. Her BP is slightly elevated but not critically. There's no protein in her urine. She's not presenting with preeclampsia."

He leaned forward slightly. Elbows on knees, hands clasped. "Everything I've read says early detection is key. So what's your threshold? Wait until her blood pressure spikes higher? Until her headaches get worse? Until something goes wrong?"

The silence stretched long enough to hear the clock on the wall and feel the weight of what he was really saying underneath his questions.

Dr. Kline turned to me. "Simone, do you have concerns about your care?"

And there it was. The redirect to put the burden back on me to either validate his concerns or smooth things over and keep the peace. I wanted to smooth it over. Wanted to apologize for him, promise we'd be less trouble, make the tension go away. That was my default. My programming. The part of me that had spent my whole life making things easier for everyone else, even if it cost me.

But then I looked at Raschad, at the tension in his shoulders, and the way he was gripping his phone like a weapon, and I realized something. He wasn't being paranoid or overprotective. He was being *thorough*. He wasn't playing about me or our child. And he wasn't wrong.

"I just want to make sure we're being careful," I replied quietly.

Dr. Kline's expression softened, slightly. "I understand. And I promise you, I am monitoring everything closely. But right now, your symptoms don't warrant intervention. If anything changes, if the headaches come back, if you have any vision problems, if you notice sudden swelling, call me immediately."

"Okay," I agreed.

Raschad said nothing else, and we left.

raschad

I WAITED UNTIL WE WERE IN THE CAR. ENGINE RUNNING, DOORS CLOSED… just us. For a moment, I just sat there. Hands on the wheel, thinking.

Part of me was wondering if I'd just embarrassed myself. Embarrassed Simone. If Dr. Kline was right and I'd just pulled out a spreadsheet in an OB's office like a lunatic because I'd read too many WebMD articles at 3 AM. The look on Simone's face when I'd started listing symptoms, like she wanted to disappear… maybe I was the anxious partner who couldn't let things be okay, projecting my intensity onto every ache and pain.

But then I thought about her numbers. 140 over 93. Up from 135 over 88. Up from 128 over 82. That wasn't being anxious. That was math.

"I'm sorry," Simone said before I could speak. "That was… "

"I don't trust her."

She blinked. "What?"

"Your doctor." I gripped the steering wheel. "I don't trust her. She didn't even want to run basic tests that would take nothing to do."

"She said my labs from last month were good."

"Last month isn't this month, Simone." I turned to face her. "Your blood pressure is going up, Peach. And she didn't seem concerned at all."

"Because it's not that high." She was quiet. Looking at me with those eyes, tired, conflicted and caught between wanting to believe her doctor and wanting to appease me. I hated putting her in that position.

"You really think she's dismissing me?" she asked softly.

I reached for her hand and held it. "I think if you were a white woman in Essex Heights, she'd have already run every test in the book."

The words landed between us heavily.

"Your mother died because of a pregnancy complication, Simone." I said quietly. Not to scare her, but because one of us had to say it out loud instead of letting it sit in the room like furniture you walk around. "And that doctor in there didn't even ask about your family history. Didn't mention it. Didn't factor it in. She looked at your numbers and told you to drink water."

Her fingers tightened around mine. "I hear you," she said finally. "But we can't just….I mean, she's my OB. We have to trust—"

"No, we don't." It came out harder than I meant. But I didn't take it back. "We don't have to trust anyone who isn't taking you seriously. And if she won't listen, we'll find someone who will."

"Raschad."

"I'm not taking any chances with you, Simone. I'm not taking chances with our baby because some doctor decided to stick to the script instead of actually paying attention. So yeah, I'm gonna ask a lot of questions. I'm gonna push. And if that makes me difficult… I don't give a damn."

She stared at me, then leaned over the center console and kissed me. "Okay," she whispered.

"Okay?"

"Okay." She settled back in her seat. "You're right. We should be careful."

The relief hit so hard I had to grip the wheel to keep from sagging against it.

"But you have to promise me something," she said.

"Anything."

"Don't let this pregnancy consume you." She touched my face. "I like you present, Raschad. Not spiraling. Can we do that?"

I wanted to say yes. But the truth was I'd been spiraling for weeks. Since the moment I saw that first elevated reading and the day she told me her vision had blurred.

"I'll try," I said. It was the best I could offer.

---

two weeks later

The frustration of loving Simone was that she was the smartest person in most rooms she walked into, meticulous about everything, the kind of woman who caught details other people missed entirely. But she had a complete blind spot about herself. Her own comfort, her own limits, her own body sending signals she'd decided not to receive. She'd calibrated herself to ignore her own needs so efficiently she didn't even notice she was doing it.

I noticed.

I noticed the swelling in her ankles that was there every morning before she got up, worse than it had been the day before, worse than the week before that. I noticed the headaches she'd mentioned twice and then stopped mentioning, which didn't mean she'd stopped getting them. It meant she'd decided not to tell me about them anymore. I noticed the way she carried herself, more careful, more deliberate, like she was managing something she didn't want me to see.

And now her shoulder.

She hadn't said a word about it. But I'd watched her for two days, pressing her fingers under her right shoulder blade like she was trying to locate a pain she couldn't quite reach. Watched her face in the mornings when she thought I wasn't looking. The tightening around her eyes. The slow careful movements of her collecting herself before she put her game face on for the day.

She was protecting me from information I needed.

That was the thing about her that made me want to yell and hold her at the same time. She'd spent her whole life managing alone and was still doing it. Only now she was doing it in my direction, trying to smooth things for me the way she smoothed things for everyone she loved.

But I wasn't everyone. And I was done being managed.

Sunday evening I watched her standing at the kitchen counter, her right hand pressed to her side, and her fingers tucked under her shoulder blade, breathing carefully. She thought she was being subtle about it. She wasn't.

I crossed the kitchen and put my hand on her lower back. "Peach." I kept my voice level. "What's wrong?"

"Nothing. Just a little uncomfortable."

I moved my hand higher, pressing gently between her shoulder blades until she hissed involuntarily, a sound she couldn't have faked.

"How long?"

"Since yesterday, maybe."

"And you didn't say anything?"

"Because it's probably nothing." She turned to look at me. "The baby's been shifting. Running out of room."

I came around to face her. I didn't know what was wrong, but I could feel something *was* wrong.

"We should call Dr. Kline," I said.

"Raschad, it's Sunday. I'm not calling her for shoulder pain."

"Why not?"

"Because she'll think I'm overreacting."

"I don't care what she thinks."

"I do." The frustration broke through. "Everything aches. My back hurts. My feet hurt. My ribs hurt. That's normal."

I stood there and made myself think about whether I was being rational or not. My eyes moved back to her hand. Still pressed against her side.

"Please," I said. "Just call. Let her tell you it's nothing."

She looked at me for a long moment, then she pulled out her phone. She left a message with after-hours call center rep. And an hour later Dr. Kline called. Pleasant, and professional, trying to feign being gracious about a Sunday interruption.

I listened as Simone explained her shoulder pain and Dr. Kline told her it was probably the baby's position. To take a Tylenol and rest and she would see her Friday for her scheduled appointment.

"Okay, thanks, Dr—"

"Wait." I cut in. "Dr. Kline. This is Raschad. I hear you saying it's probably nothing. But she's been in pain for two days and it's getting worse, not better. We need her to be seen."

"Mr. Carter, back pain in the third trimester is very common."

"It's her *shoulder*. And I understand that. I'm not asking you to diagnose anything. I'm asking if she can come in tomorrow and be checked. That's all."

"That really isn't necessary, she already has her Friday appo—"

"With respect… how do you know it isn't necessary if she hasn't been examined? She's thirty-two weeks pregnant and she's been hurting for two days."

Silence.

"If you won't…" I took a deep breath, "We need you to note this in her chart."

"What?" Dr. Kline asked.

"Put it in her chart. That we called today, at 6:30 PM, reported persistent worsening pain, and requested a visit. And you said no."

The quality of the silence changed.

"Come in tomorrow at eight-thirty," Dr. Kline said.

Then she hung up.

Simone stared at her phone. "She's going to hate us."

"I don't care."

"Raschad."

"I don't *care*, Simone. I don't care if she hates us. If she thinks I'm difficult. If she complains to every doctor in the practice. I care about *you*. And our baby. That's it."

"Okay," she whispered.

"Okay?"

"Okay."

I pulled her into my arms. "It's probably nothing," she whispered against my chest.

I kissed the top of her head. "Yeah," I said. "Probably nothing."

hellp

raschad

DR. KLINE'S OFFICE SMELLED LIKE LAVENDER AND ANTISEPTIC. WE'D been sitting in the exam room for fifteen minutes, Simone on the table and me in the chair by the door, willing myself to sit still.

"You're making me nervous," Simone said.

"Sorry." I forced my knee to stop bouncing. "Just ready for her to get in here."

"She's probably making us wait on purpose. Punishment for last night."

Maybe. Probably. I didn't care.

The door opened and Dr. Kline walked in. Tablet in hand with an expression pulled tight. "Good morning," she said politely.

"Good morning," Simone replied.

I nodded. That was all she was getting from me.

Her eyes flicked to me, then away. "So. Shoulder pain."

"Yes." Simone shifted on the table, wincing. "It's worse today."

"Worse how?"

"Sharper maybe. It feels like a huge heavy ball or knot, and kinda pierces depending on how I move."

Dr. Kline moved closer and pressed her fingers below Simone's shoulder blade. "Here?"

"Ahh!" Simone yelped then pulled it in trying to quiet her reaction. "Yes. *There.*"

I watched Simone's face, trying to hide the pain and failing.

"Any nausea?" Dr. Kline asked.

"No."

"Headache?"

"Not really. A little dull."

"Let's check your blood pressure."

She wrapped the cuff around Simone's arm, then frowned at the reading.

"What is it?" I asked.

"149 over 97." She made a note. "Elevated."

"How elevated?" I was already pulling out my phone. "Last appointment it was 140 over 92."

"I'm aware, Mr. Carter."

"So it's still going up."

"Yes, it's trending upward." She set the cuff aside.

"What number does it have to hit before you're concerned?"

Her mouth thinned. "I *am* concerned, Mr. Carter. That's why I had you come in today."

"Because we forced the issue." I snapped.

"Raschad," Simone said quietly.

I looked at her. She looked washed out. I took a breath and tried to pull it back. "I apologize. I just… we want to understand what we're dealing with here."

Dr. Kline studied me, then her expression shifted. She turned to Simone.

"Given your elevated blood pressure, and the pain you're experiencing, I'm going to run labs. Liver enzymes, kidney function, platelet count. Just a precaution. To rule everything out."

"I don't want to wait on this," she continued, "I'm going to send you over to University Medical Center, the Maternity Unit. They'll run the labs there and monitor you at the same time."

She looked at me. "You can take her straight there from here. I'll call ahead for you."

simone

THE TRIAGE NURSE AT THE HOSPITAL WRAPPED THE BLOOD PRESSURE CUFF around my arm and I watched her face while it tightened. Raschad stood at my shoulder, still, absorbing everything.

"155 over 100," she said, already typing. "Let's get you into a room."

They moved fast after that. Hooked me to monitors, drew blood, collected urine, and threw questions at me one after the other, while Raschad stood at the side of my bed holding my hand, watching the numbers on the screen like he could make them mean something reassuring. They gave me a medication to bring my blood pressure down, and we waited.

The doctor on call came back and checked my vitals. "Let's give it a little more time," he said, and left.

We waited more. He came back again with the same careful expression that wasn't telling us anything. "Let's give it a little more time."

By the third time he said it, Raschad and I looked at each other, beginning to understand that *a little more time* was not reassurance. It was a doctor who was watching something and not ready to tell us what. Three hours in, Raschad texted my family to tell them what was going on and get coverage for Zhaire after school.

Hours passed the way time passes in hospitals. In chunks and gaps, and stretches of silence broken by sudden efficient motion. More blood draws, more panels. The numbers on the monitor not going where they were supposed to go. A new doctor came and went, shift change I supposed, and spoke in the careful language of someone who wasn't ready to say the full thing yet.

"Your blood pressure is not responding to the medication. We're going to keep you overnight and do another round of labs in the morning."

Raschad didn't ask questions. He just nodded, like he'd already been prepared for this answer, and went to text to arrange Zhaire's coverage for the night.

The sofa in the room was too short for his frame by about six inches. He folded himself onto it, legs hanging off the end, and lay there looking across at me and the monitors with an expression he kept adjusting every time our eyes met, smoothing his face into something calmer, that wouldn't scare me. The moment he looked away I could see what was underneath it.

I drifted in and out through the night. Every time I surfaced he was somewhere different in the room. The sofa, the chair pulled close to my bed, standing at the window with his arms crossed watching the parking lot. But he was always there. Every single time I opened my eyes.

At some point I woke up and found his hand covering mine on the bed, his head dropped forward, finally asleep in the chair.

I woke up in the morning to hushed voices. Raschad was there, still in yesterday's clothes, sitting in the chair beside my bed. My brothers were in the room. Julian standing straight, arms crossed by the door. Zion beside him and Tre with his hands in his hoodie pockets, leaning against a wall.

I managed a weak smile. "Hey."

They came to the bed. Julian took my hand first. "How do you feel, Simi?"

"Fine," I said out of habit.

The door opened and Dr. Kline came in with a folder in her hand and a resident behind her. She had a focused look on her face that made the room go still before she said a single word.

Raschad stood up and moved to the side of my bed, his hand finding the rail.

"Good morning, Simone," Dr. Kline said. "We have your full labs back. I need to talk to you about what's going on."

She looked around the room briefly, at my brothers, at Raschad, then back at me.

"You have something called HELLP syndrome." Dr. Kline said. "It affects your liver, your platelets, and your blood pressure. It's serious."

I felt Raschad's hand clamp around mine.

"HELLP," she continued, "stands for, **H**emolysis, the breakdown of red blood cells, **E**levated **L**iver enzymes, which indicate your liver is under significant stress, and **L**ow **P**latelets, which affects your blood's ability to clot properly. It's a severe form of preeclampsia. That's why your pain was getting worse, and why your blood pressure wouldn't respond to medication."

She gave me a moment to let it register.

"The only treatment is delivery. At just past thirty-two weeks your baby is viable with a very strong chance. But the risk to you is too high to wait."

"When?" Raschad's voice was barely controlled.

"Today. Emergency C-section within the next few hours."

"What if we wait," I said. "Just a little longer. Give her more time."

"Simone." Dr. Kline's voice was careful. "If we wait, we risk liver rupture, hemorrhaging, possible stroke or seizures. This condition escalates rapidly. Waiting is not a safe option."

Hemorrhaging.

Mama. I felt cold all over. The word moved through me, and rang in my head. I hadn't let myself go there during this pregnancy. I'd filed it away, told myself this was different. I turned my head toward my brothers. Julian was still and quietly absorbing it. His eyes stayed on Dr. Kline, not blinking. Zion made a low sound like something had hit him. Tre looked at the floor for one second and then looked back up, his eyes bright. He didn't say anything either.

"So you're telling me," Raschad said, and I could hear the control in his voice starting to fracture, "that if we had waited until Friday for her scheduled appointment, she could have died?"

"Mr. Carter—"

"No." His voice boomed through the little hospital room, sending a tremor through the walls. "Answer the question."

Dr. Kline didn't flinch. "Left undetected, HELLP can escalate rapidly. The outcome could have been significantly worse, yes."

"How rapidly?" he demanded.

Dr. Kline held his gaze. "In severe cases, within twenty-four to seventy-two hours. It's…not a slow moving condition."

"Twenty-four to seventy-two hours," he repeated quietly. "And you wanted her to wait five days."

She didn't answer that.

Raschad's face turned to stone. "You will NOT be the one to handle this delivery. We request a different attending."

"Mr. Carter," she said, "I acted on the information available to me at each visit. Your wife's symptoms were consistent with normal third trimester presentations. I cleared my entire schedule and came in this morning because your wife is my patient and I care about her outcome. I am not your enemy."

"That's all well and good. But you are done here," he replied.

She stiffened. "That is your choice. But I must warn you that whatever team you choose, they will need to move quickly. Let my office know what you decide ASAP."

She left.

The second the door closed my brothers turned to each other and the room became something like a command center.

Zion got on his phone, talking low on then corner, Tre in another, and Julian was pacing, firing off texts. "We need to get the best maternal-fetal specialist in the area in here…"

"Already done." Raschad's phone was in his hand. "Dr. Adeyemo. I reached out to her office last night when her pressure wouldn't come down."

Julian looked at him for a second. His eyes moved across Raschad's face, reading and assessing. And then the thing that had been ready to activate in him, the auto pilot of my brother who had spent his entire life being the one who handled it when things went wrong, settled quietly. He took one step back. No words.

"She's too small," I started to cry. "Raschad, she's too small, she's not ready, she's needs to stay in longer."

"Peach. Calm down. It's gonna be ok. Look at me right here." He leaned over me, and took my face in his hands.

My breath was coming wrong. I could feel it happening, the shallow pull, and the edges of the room going soft.

"Eyes on me," he said firmly. "Just my face, Peach."

I found his eyes and held on to them.

"She's small but she's strong," he said. "She's been fighting in there for thirty-two weeks and she's not done fighting. She's a Carter and a Wade. She doesn't know how to quit."

My breath came out in a long, shaky exhale.

"There," he said quietly. "There you go." He kissed my face and took slow long breaths with me, while my brothers stood around us not saying a word.

"Where's Zhaire?" I choked once I had calmed down.

"He's with Taryn. She's dropping him off with Aunt Lorraine, and will be on her way after that." Zion said. "Zhaire's good, okay? You just focus on you."

Less than three hours later, the new team swept in, in crisp blue scrubs, calm but serious. The lead doctor, a Black woman with kind eyes and a no-nonsense voice, stepped forward.

"Hello, Simone. I'm Dr. Adeyemo," she introduced herself. "I specialize in high-risk maternal-fetal medicine. I've reviewed your labs, and I'm going to explain exactly what's happening and how we'll be taking care of you, okay?"

I nodded.

She pulled up a chair and leveled with me, eye to eye. "Your liver enzymes and platelets have continued to worsen, which confirms the HELLP diagnosis you were given. Your baby is doing well right now, but HELLP can shift quickly and become life-threatening for you. The safest plan is delivery."

I swallowed, fighting tears. "Okay." Raschad squeezed my hand.

Dr. Adeyemo continued. "We will do a C-section. We will have a full NICU team on standby ready to take care of your daughter the second she is delivered."

"We will have blood products on standby. With your platelet levels as low as they are, your blood's ability to clot could be compromised. If bleeding becomes difficult to control during delivery, we want to be prepared to transfuse immediately. That is standard protocol for HELLP and we are ready for it. You are in good hands. We do this every day."

I looked at Raschad and watched his chin tremble for a second, before he locked it down. I closed my eyes. My daughter's heartbeat was strong on the second monitor. The sound of a life that was about to begin several weeks too soon.

"I can't." My words came out shattered. "I can't. She's not ready. She needs…"

"She needs you alive." Raschad's voice broke wide open. "We all do."

"But—"

"There is no but." He brought my hand to his lips and kissed my knuckles. I could feel him shaking. "I can't lose you, Simone. I *can't*."

I looked at him. Past his steady voice and strong hands and the man who'd spent months being my advocate and my shield. And underneath all of it, I saw that he was terrified. He was drowning now. Right in front of me. Holding my hand and drowning.

"Okay," I whispered. I turned to Dr. Adeyemo. "When?"

"We're getting an OR prepped now. Probably within the next hour."

I nodded as my brothers gathered at the foot of the bed.

"You trust your team?" Julian asked Dr. Adeyemo.

She met his stare head-on. "I would trust this team with my own family."

Julian nodded.

"And the baby?" Tre asked,

"She will go to our NICU. Which is one of the best in the state." She smiled gently. "Thirty-two-weekers often do very well. Especially girls. I won't lie and say there's no risk. But the outcomes are generally very positive."

Dr. Adeyemo stood. "Try to rest if you can. Nurses will be back shortly to get you ready."

She left and Raschad climbed half his body onto the bed beside me, carefully adjusting around the tangle of wires. He wrapped his arm around my side and nuzzled into me.

"I'm sorry," I said.

"For what?"

"My body. Failing her."

"Stop." His voice piercing enough to cut through the beeping machines. "Your body is not failing her. Your body is trying to protect you *and* her. That's not failing, Simone. That's surviving."

"But the baby..."

"Is going to meet us sooner than planned. That's all." He kissed my cheek.

I turned my face into his chest and let myself break. The kind of tears that come from the deepest part of you. My brothers stepped out as he held me through it, letting me cry.

raschad

They prepped Simone for surgery in the early afternoon. Julian stepped out to call Aunt Lorraine about Zhaire. Taryn sat close to Simone, holding her hand, talking low, I couldn't hear what she was saying but I could see Simone's face, the way it softened and calmed under Taryn's voice.

I sat in a chair and watched our daughter's heartbeat on the monitor. Strong and steady. *That's right,* I thought. *Stay strong. We're coming.*

They started moving Simone. The sounds of the gurney unlocking, wheels finding the floor and the mechanical sound of a bed becoming a transport, set the room alive with activity. I fell into step beside her as they wheeled her out, my hand in hers, our fingers laced.

"You're going to be okay," I said. "You know that."

"I know." Her eyes were on the ceiling tiles moving past overhead.

We moved down the hallway with two nurses flanking us whose names I'd already forgotten. Everything was too bright and too quiet at the same time.

Then we reached double doors. The kind that swing both ways, and a painted line on the floor marking where the sterile zone began. I kept my hand in hers, the other on the bed rail. And then a nurse stepped forward, gently but resolute.

"I'm sorry, but this is as far as you can go," she said to me.

I didn't understand her words at first. They hit my ears but bounced off, like she'd spoken a language I'd never learned.

"What?"

"Her C-section will be under general anesthesia. It's an emergent procedure. We can't allow you into the OR. I'm sorry."

Simone and I looked at each other, both arriving at the same realization at the same moment. The understanding of what it meant that they wouldn't let me through those doors with her. The understanding that this was serious enough that the normal rules of the father in the OR beside the mother, had been set aside. We'd seen C-sections on television. We'd talked about it. We'd both pictured me there if it had to happen, beside her head, mask on, holding her hand, watching our daughter be pulled from her. Neither of us had pictured or prepared for this.

"No." I said fast and automatic. "I'm going in with her."

"Sir, I understand, but protocol—"

"I don't care about protocol." My voice rose. Not shouting, but the kind of volume that makes people in hallways stop walking. "She needs me in there."

"Sir."

"She has panic attacks." I was talking faster now. Desperate. Laying facts on the table. "She has a history of panic attacks. I need to be there."

"I understand your concern, but under general anesthesia, she won't be conscious. She won't know…"

"*I'll know*." I choked out. "I'll know she was alone."

The nurse looked at me with an expression of compassion wrapped in policy. Kindness that couldn't bend the rules.

"Raschad…" Simone's voice was thin and shaky, coming from below me, and when I looked down, she was trembling. Her teeth chattering, her eyes wide and locked on the gray doors like they were the entrance to something she might not come back from.

"I can't," she whispered. "I can't go in there."

My heart *shattered*. Exploded into a thousand pieces inside my chest. But she couldn't see that. She needed me strong. I dropped down and took her face in my hands.

"Look at me, Peach. Just me."

Her eyes found mine terrified and swimming.

"You can do this." My voice was steady. I don't know how. I don't know where I found it. Somewhere in a reserve that only opens when the person you love most in the world is looking at you like you're the last thing standing between them and the dark.

"You hear me? You can do this."

"I'm scared."

"I know. But you're the strongest woman I've ever known." I wiped her tears with my fingers. "You are *going* to be okay. Our daughter is going to be okay. You have been strong every single day of this and we need you to stay strong for just a little while longer. Just a few more minutes and then it's done, and I'll be *right* here when you come out. *Right here*. I'm not leaving."

"But what if—"

"No what-ifs. You're going to go in there and you're going to fight. For our daughter. For Zhaire. For us." I brought her hand to my chest. Pressed it flat against my heart. "And when you wake up, I'm going to be the first face you see. I promise you that."

"Promise?" Her voice was so small. She sounded like a little girl.

"I promise." I kissed her forehead. Her cheeks. Her lips salty with tears. "You're going to be okay. Say it."

"I'm going to be okay."

"Again."

"I'm going to be okay."

"That's my Peach." I pressed my lips to hers and held them there.

"I love you," she whispered.

"I love you more than anything in this world." I kissed her one more time. "Now go meet our daughter. And tell her daddy's right outside waiting to meet her too."

She nodded and tried to smile. I looked up and the nurses were dabbing their eyes. One of them touched my arm apologetically. I stood up straight and forced my face into something that looked like confidence. Forced my body into something that looked like I was calm. For her. The nurses started wheeling her forward, past the line. She turned her head to the side to look back just before the doors and looked at me.

I put my hand over my heart. "Right here. Waiting for you, Peach."

The doors swung open and she crossed the threshold. The gray doors swung shut and then she was gone. I stood at those doors, frozen in place. And something in me that had been held together for the last twenty-four hours gave way.

My fist hit a wall. The sound of it echoing in the hallway. And then my knees went out. But I didn't go all the way down. Julian caught me. Came from out of nowhere, or maybe he had been behind us all along. His hands gripped my shoulders, and he didn't say anything. He just held me up, keeping me from the floor, and walked me down the hallway to the waiting area.

Zion, Tre and Taryn were already in the waiting room. I swear I couldn't breathe when those doors slammed shut. My hands were shaking so bad I had no choice but to pace, back and forth, fists clenched, heart pounding so hard it hurt. She was in there. Alone. And I couldn't do a damn thing. I pulled out my phone, found a seat and started searching.

> *HELLP syndrome prognosis*
> *Emergency C-section complications*
> *32 week preemie survival rates*

Every article made me feel sicker, punching holes straight through me. I clicked another link, then another, spiraling deeper until Julian snatched my phone right out of my hand.

"Yo!" I barked, reaching for it back.

"No," he said, shaking his head. "You will drive yourself crazy with that shit. You have to stay calm, Raschad."

I was about to argue when Taryn stood up.

"Okay, we need to pray," she announced, gesturing for us all to stand. She didn't ask if anyone minded. She just stood and reached for my hand on one side of her, Zion's on the other, Julian and Tre following, and a circle formed, without coordination.

"Lord," she started. "We come to you right now. Boldly, because you said we could. Because you said cast your cares, and Lord, we are casting everything. All of it. Right here, right now, at your feet."

She tightened her grip on my hand. "You know Simone. You knew her before we did. You know her heart. You know the battles she's fought, you know the storms she and this family have survived. You have carried them through every valley, and we are asking you to carry them through this one too."

I closed my eyes.

"We are asking you to cover her. From the crown of her head to the soles of her feet. Guide every hand in that room. Every doctor, every nurse, every instrument, every decision. Let your wisdom move through them, Lord. Let no weapon formed against her prosper. Let your angels be standing guard in that operating room right now."

I felt Julian's hand tighten on my shoulder.

"And that baby girl." Taryn's voice cracked then she steadied. "Protect her, God. Let her lungs be strong. Let her heart be steady. Let every organ do exactly what you designed it to do. Let her come into this world crying and breathing and fighting because she is a Carter and a Wade and she does not know how to quit."

Her words flowed like a river, unstoppable.

"We speak against fear right now. We speak against every dark thing that has tried to attach itself to this moment. And Lord..." she paused and drew a breath that shook. "We remember Niecy Wade. And we are standing here today declaring *this is not that*. Not today. We break that. We break any and all generational curses *right now*. We stand on your promises. We believe you are able, and we will keep believing. We break it right now in Jesus' name."

The room was completely silent.

"We believe you, Lord. We are scared and we believe you anyway. We thank you in advance for Simone's testimony. For that baby's first cry. For our family coming home whole."

Her voice dropped lower and then rose again, stronger. "In Jesus' name. Amen."

The room held it for a moment. I folded over, burying my face in my hands, crying. I couldn't hold it in anymore. All the strength I'd performed, all the fear I'd swallowed, it all broke loose in that moment.

Julian didn't move. His fists were clenched so tight, eyes fixed on the floor like if he blinked, he might fall apart. Tre looked stunned, like the prayer had knocked the wind out of him. He let out a low, broken

"Amen," then turned away. Zion wrapped his arms around Taryn with wet eyes, and mumbled, "Thank you, baby."

She looked up at him and whispered, "It's gonna be okay."

And then, from somewhere in the room:

"Amen."

And another. *"Amen."*

And another. A woman across the room with her hand over her mouth. An older man in the corner, head bowed. A nurse passing in the hallway who stopped walking.

"Amen."

"Amen."

I sat down in a chair, both hands over my face, and let it come. Everything I'd been holding since she was admitted yesterday. I thought about San Diego. The way she'd looked at me, with my headphones in her ears, asking me if I'd called her 'Peach'. I thought about the blanket nest in LA where Zhaire was conceived. I thought about six years of missing her without letting myself admit what it was. I thought about walking out of her bedroom drawing a line and telling myself I was being righteous when really I was just afraid. I thought about every day I'd made it harder than it needed to be. Every door I held open just enough… never wide enough to let her through. Every time pride told me it was self-respect and I believed it.

All that time. All that wasted, stubborn, frightened time.

And then I thought about this morning. Dr. Kline with her folder, looking at me, and saying *your wife* like it was simply true. Like it was just a fact about the world.

I hadn't corrected her.

Not because I was distracted. I hadn't corrected her because the words landed on me and it felt right and I didn't want to take it back. Because standing in that room with Simone's hand in mine and everything stripped down to what actually mattered, *your wife* were the only words that felt true.

I wished they were true.

I pressed my hands harder over my face and breathed through it. She had to be okay. She had to come out of those doors. Because I had things left to say to her that I'd been swallowing, and I was done swallowing them.

Come back to me, I thought. *Come back to me.*

three pounds, two ounces

raschad

———

THE FIVE OF US SAT IN A ROW OF PLASTIC CHAIRS. EVERY TIME THE waiting room doors opened my heart seized. Two hours and fourteen minutes later a neonatal nurse came through the doors in scrubs, with her mask pulled down.

"Mr. Carter?"

We all stood at once as she gestured for us to step into the hall.

"Your daughter is here. Three pounds, two ounces. She's breathing with some support and we're taking her to the NICU now. She's doing well."

I let out a long exhale. Next to me Taryn hugged Zion, "Thank God." Tre nodded over and over, and Julian closed his eyes.

Before I could move, another nurse appeared from the corridor pushing an isolette, clear and enclosed with warm light glowing from inside it. She slowed as she approached us.

Inside, wrapped in a blanket no bigger than a hand towel, with a white knit cap pulled low on her forehead, was the tiniest person I had ever seen.

"Oh God," Zion breathed.

Tre stepped forward. "She's so tiny."

I couldn't speak or move. I just looked at her. Dark curls were peeking from under the cap. She had Simone's mouth, and one impossibly small hand was visible, fingers loosely curled.

"She's beautiful," Julian said quietly.

The nurse smiled. "Say hi to your family, baby girl." She paused long enough for us to have her. Then said, "We need to get her settled. You can walk with us to the NICU."

I took one step. Then stopped.

"Simone?"

The nurse's expression shifted. "She's still in surgery. Someone will be out shortly with an update."

Still? She was still open. Still on that table. My feet wouldn't move. I was torn in two directions. My daughter going to the NICU. And my woman still in surgery.

"Stay," Zion said, already moving toward the isolette. "We've got the baby. Go wait for Simone."

I looked at my daughter one more moment. "Hi, Zaria," I managed. "Hi, baby girl. I'm your daddy. I'll be back with you soon."

They started wheeling her away and I watched her disappear down the hallway, with Zion and Tre following behind. I turned back to the waiting room.

Thirty minutes later Dr. Adeyemo came through the doors. Her face was composed but not relaxed. "She delivered successfully," she told me, Julian and Taryn. "But she experienced more bleeding than we anticipated. Her platelet levels were critically low going into surgery. Because we had blood products on standby we were able to manage the hemorrhaging as it developed."

"Is she stable?" Julian asked.

"Right now, yes. Her vitals are holding. The bleeding was significant but controlled. She's receiving blood and platelets now. Another thirty to forty-five minutes and she'll move to the ICU for close monitoring."

"ICU?" I said. "She's not out of danger?"

"It's the most controlled environment we have. Precautionary, given what her body has been through today. The preparation, having blood ready, that put her in the strongest position possible. We'll update you as soon as she's settled." She disappeared back through the doors.

Julian's hand moved from my shoulder to the back of my neck. "You did good," he said. His voice carrying a roughness I'd never heard from him. "The labs. The specialist. Making them take her seriously. You did that."

"I just did what—"

"What anybody would do?" Taryn shook her head. "No. Everybody doesn't. Black women die because everybody doesn't. Because the doctor says it's nothing and she goes home. You pushed, Raschad. You *literally* fought for her. Don't downplay it."

I didn't have a response. The words hit me in a place I couldn't argue from, not because they were flattering, but because the truth of them was terrifying. Because the thing they were praising me for was the thing that almost didn't happen. The appointment I almost didn't demand. The lab order I almost accepted as unnecessary. The moment I almost said okay, I'm sure it's fine because that's what the expert was telling us and who was I to push back?

If I hadn't?

The thought tried to form and I wouldn't follow it to its conclusion. Because behind those doors, Simone was alive. And our baby girl was alive.

simone

THE FIRST THING I FELT WAS PAIN. A DEEP, SETTLED WRONGNESS IN MY body. I tried to shift and everything said no at once. My abdomen, my back, my arm where something was taped. The ceiling was wrong. Too white. The sounds were wrong. Then I thought I heard Frank Ocean. Not fully. More like the way you hear rain while you're sleeping and the sound arrives before you know whether you're dreaming or awake. A melody floating. *Pink + White.*

It was playing somewhere close. The volume of a phone speaker, the way Raschad played music all the time, because silence made him restless. My body knew he was there before I fully opened my eyes.

"Raschad..." My voice came out ruined. My throat burned and was dry and raw.

A chair scraped against the floor. And then he was right there. Leaning over the bed rail, his face filling my vision. His eyes, red-rimmed and bloodshot, the whites carrying the evidence of days without sleep. His beard was fuller and rougher than I'd ever seen it, past the point of deliberate and into the territory of a man who had forgotten grooming existed. The same clothes I'd been seeing him in for… how long? His hands found my face, shaking slightly.

"Hey," his voice was low and fractured. "Hi, Peach. I'm here."

I tried to orient myself. Machines to my left, an IV pole with two bags. Something tight around my finger. A cuff on my arm, squeezing at intervals. The smell of antiseptic and cold air.

Then it hit me. *The baby.*

I grabbed for him. My arms were weak, the muscles responding at half speed, my fingers closing around his forearm with a grip that would've embarrassed me if I had the bandwidth for embarrassment. My body didn't feel like mine. It felt borrowed. Evacuated. Like someone had taken everything out and put it back wrong.

"Did she—" My heart constricted.

"She's here. She's in the NICU. She's breathing." His voice roughened on the last word. "Three pounds two ounces. She came out fighting." He shook his head slightly. "She came out crying, they said, Simone. The second they got her out. Three pounds and she came out crying."

A sob came wrenching out of me as my whole body shook with it. The monitors beeped faster.

"She's alive?" I asked again, even though he'd just told me.

"She's alive."

He pressed his forehead to mine "And you are too," he whispered.

Those four words stopped me. *And you are too.* Like my survival wasn't assumed. Like there had been a period when the outcome was undecided.

"How long have I..." My voice scraped.

"Almost three days." He said it softly. "You've been in and out. Mostly out."

Three days. I'd been out for three days. My daughter had been alive for three days and I hadn't held her. Hadn't seen her. Hadn't been conscious enough to know she existed outside my body.

"I want to see her."

I pushed myself up. My arms took my weight for half a second before the pain detonated. A deeper, full-body protest from my stomach that had been cut open and sewn shut and was nowhere near ready for what I was asking those muscles to do. My arms buckled.

Raschad caught me, lowering me back down. "Simone." His voice was tight. "Don't do that."

"I can't even sit up. Why am I so weak?"

"Because your body just went through hell," he held my hand. "You lost blood. A lot of it. You had surgery. You're on magnesium to keep your blood pressure down. You're expected to feel like this."

"I need to see her, Raschad. She needs me."

His jaw flexed. "I asked. The doctor said your blood pressure is still unstable. They don't want to move you yet. Maybe tomorrow."

"My baby is here," I whispered, "and I can't even hold her?"

He pulled out his phone and paused the song.

"I got something." He turned the screen toward me. And there she was. So small she barely filled the frame. A knit cap on a head the size of an orange. Clear plastic walls around her keeping her warm in the way I should have been keeping her warm. Her fingers were curled into tiny fists and there was a tube running through her nose and an IV in her arm.

"Zaria," I whimpered.

"That's our girl."

He swiped and a video played. Her chest was rising and falling. She made a tiny stretch, one arm extending, her fingers splaying. And then a sound. A faint, squeaky cry. Not distressed, just the announcement of a tiny person who was here and wanted it noted.

That sound broke me, and I sobbed again deep from the floor.

"I'm sorry." I cried.

"Simone." He wiped my tears with tissue and kissed me. "Your body kept her alive for thirty-two weeks. You grew her and fed her and kept her safe while your own body was turning against you. Sorry for what? You saved her. And the second you walk into that NICU and she hears your voice, she will know exactly who you are."

He pulled me in as carefully as he could, one arm around my shoulders, my face against his neck. I felt the roughness of his beard against me.

"I didn't leave, Peach. Not for one hour." He wanted me to know.

I knew it. I could see it in the wrinkles of his clothes and the exhaustion in his eyes that had nothing to do with sleep.

"Who do you think she looks like?" I whispered.

I felt him smile against my hair. "Like us," he said. "Like the best parts of both of us."

THE NEXT AFTERNOON THEY PUT ME IN A WHEELCHAIR AND TOOK ME TO her in the NICU. I knew she would be small. Three pounds two ounces, Raschad told me, but numbers don't prepare you for the actual sight of your child fitting in a space the size of a shoebox. Her skin was so thin it was nearly translucent, her chest was rising and falling with the CPAP machine.

She had Raschad's long fingers. Even that small, the length of them proportionate to her body was unmistakably his. I reached through one of the ports before the nurse finished explaining that I could. Zaria flinched one small, full-body startle. Then she settled.

"Hi," I managed through quiet tears. "Hi, baby. Mommy's here."

"Zaria," I whispered, testing the name against this small face. "Zaria Denise Carter."

Raschad crouched beside my wheelchair. His hand went through the other port, enormous against her tiny frame. We stayed like that for a long time, neither of us speaking, with our daughter breathing under our hands.

. . .

I was released to go home one week later, but Zaria spent another twelve weeks in the NICU. Eighty-four days of driving back and forth to that hospital, pumping milk every three hours whether she could take it or not. Raschad covered most mornings, going there after dropping Zhaire off at school. I stayed from the afternoons into the evenings, and he came back at night. Children were not allowed, so Zhaire had yet to meet his little sister other than through the photos and videos we'd share with him. The NICU nurses knew us by name by the second week. By the third, one of them had started saving the better rocking chair for me. We built a life inside that building the same way we'd built everything else, just showing up, until the shape of it was undeniable.

We finally brought her home on a Tuesday. A little over two months after she was born, five pounds twelve ounces, and off the CPAP, taking full feeds, and according to her primary nurse already a legend on the night shift. Her day nurse hugged me at the door and Raschad buckled Zaria into the car seat and checked it five times as the nurse watched with patient amusement.

I sat in the back beside her for the drive home. She slept through all of it like she had absolutely no idea what the last two months had cost us.

That's our daughter, I thought. *Unbothered.*

Valencia had the door open before we made it up my porch steps. She didn't say anything, just stepped back and let us in, with her hand going to her mouth. Aunt Lorraine was right behind her. These two women had been running my house for over a month and had become fast friends. When I came home from the hospital, still slow and sore, they had everything handled. Zaria's nursery finished. The refrigerator full. House clean. I don't know what I would have done without them around.

Raschad lifted Zaria out of the carrier and held her out to his mother.

"Oh," Valencia said with wet eyes. "Oh, Nova."

She took her granddaughter and her whole face changed. "Hi, sweet girl," she whispered. "Grandma's been waiting so long for you."

Zhaire came downstairs mid-sentence about still wanting a dog. He stopped. He looked at me, then at Raschad, then at Valencia, holding Zaria in the armchair.

"She's here?"

"She's here."

He crossed the room slowly and stopped, looking at the tiny face he'd only seen in photos. Zaria was awake, eyes open taking the world in. She looked up at Zhaire and he stared at her.

"Hi Zaria," he said softly. "I'm Zhaire. I'm your big brother." He leaned in, studying her face. "You're too little right now. But when you get bigger I'm gonna show you everything. I've been saving my best Beyblades." He paused. "I'm gonna protect you. Okay?"

Zaria made a squeaky sound and his whole face split open. "She heard me!"

Nobody moved. Raschad turned away and let out a deep exhale. I didn't try to hide it. I just let my happy tears fall. I looked at my son, who had channeled every man who loved him without knowing it and thought: *we're going to be okay. All four of us. We really are.*

comfortable

THIS CHAPTER HAS A SOUNDTRACK

Comfortable by H.E.R.

simone

ZARIA WAS FIVE MONTHS OLD, FINALLY SLEEPING IN HER CRIB FOR THREE-hour stretches at a time, and I felt like a human again. Mostly. My incision had closed up and my scar was neat. A reminder of how we'd survived. I was starting to feel…*normal.*

Raschad and I were good. Better than good. He'd been gentle, affectionate, touching me with nothing but tenderness, hugging me from behind, massaging my shoulders after a long day, holding my face and peppering me with kisses. But beyond that? Nothing. There was still this awkward, weird distance when it came to sex. He hadn't pushed. Hadn't even hinted.

So naturally, of course I told Taryn. "Girl, what? FIVE months? Simone. You have a man built like a superhero living in your house, who worships you, practically saved your life, and you haven't ridden the daylights out of him yet?"

"Taryn, it's not that simple. I had a whole baby cut out of me. Been taking care of a preemie."

Taryn nodded, serious for a second. "You're… healed, though. Right? I mean you're cleared? You feel good?"

"Yeah. But what if he doesn't even want me like that anymore? My body has changed. I have scars. Or, maybe he thinks I'm off-limits now or something."

Taryn slapped her thigh, laughing so loud Zaria stirred.

"Off-limits?! He looks at you like you are his whole meal, plus dessert, plus seconds. Trust me, I've clocked it."

I shook my head, embarrassed. "I don't know. It feels weird. And things are great otherwise. I don't want to mess up the peace."

"Ain't no peace if y'all keep tiptoeing around each other. At some point somebody gotta bust a move, and bust a —"

"Don't say it!"

We cackled.

THAT NIGHT, THE TENSION PRACTICALLY PULSED OFF ME. RASCHAD WAS helping fold a load of laundry, his big hands carefully pairing up tiny pink socks. *Those hands.* I swallowed. Hard.

He caught me watching him, eyes crinkling. "What?"

I looked away. "Nothing."

He walked over to me, leaning against the dresser, so close I could smell the soap on his skin.

"You sure?" his voice sent a spark straight through me.

I laughed nervously. "You've been really good. You know. About… everything."

He tilted his head, searching my face. "About what?"

I hesitated. *Say it, Simone.* "You've been… really gentle with me. Since everything."

He nodded slightly. "Yeah."

"I mean… with all of it. Being affectionate but not—" I stopped.

"Not what?"

I made myself say it. "I don't know if you still… see me the same way. My body is different. The scar, my weight…" I looked at him. "I can't tell if you're being careful because you want to be careful. Or because…"

"Because what?"

I shrugged. He looked at me for a second, then stepped closer and ran the back of his finger down my face.

"You think I don't want you?"

I looked away. "Do you?"

He turned my face back to his. "Peach," he smiled. "I've wanted you every day since you came home from that hospital. I *always* want you."

I let out a shaky exhale.

"I haven't gone there because I don't want to pressure you. You almost died Simone. Your body went through hell. What I look like trying to push sex on you after that. And seeing you that way…" he choked back emotion. "I don't know… it did something to me, Peach. You're precious to me. I don't wanna mishandle you. I don't want to hurt you. So… I'm fine with taking your lead."

A tear slipped down my cheek and he wiped it away

"Whenever you're ready, you just let me know."

My body was screaming *yes, now.*

"Okay." I nodded. "I needed to hear that."

raschad

The next day

<hr>

WHEN I GOT HOME, THE FIRST THING I HEARD WAS SIMONE'S VOICE floating, softly singing along to H.E.R's *Comfortable*. I stood there in the doorway of our room, just watching her. She was putting clothes away, hips swaying and her robe slipping off one shoulder, completely unguarded. God, she was beautiful.

I'd been holding myself back for months. Telling myself she wasn't ready. Standing in that doorway, watching her hum, hips swaying... I was done holding back. She had all but given me the all clear signal the day before. She didn't have to tell me twice.

"Hey."

She jumped and turned around "Hey," she smiled. "You're home."

"Long day," I said. "Kids sleep?"

"Yeah. I just fed Zaria and put her down half an hour ago. Practically dragged Zhaire to bed. He's finally knocked out."

I went to her and pressed my lips to the curve of her neck where her robe had exposed her shoulder. She melted against me, breathing me in.

"Come take a shower with me." I leaned down and kissed her deeply, tangling my tongue with hers, while squeezing her ass, then pulled back and looked at her. "Five minutes."

She nodded, speechless, "Mmhm."

I WAS ALREADY IN THE SHOWER WHEN I HEARD THE DOOR OPEN. SIMONE stepped into the steamy room and I turned, my eyes tracking her like a hawk. Her robe fell open, sliding off her shoulders. And she stood there naked and vulnerable. I slid the shower door open, water splashing off me, a slight grin playing at my mouth.

I didn't say a word, just reached a hand out and gestured for her to come in. She came to me with no hesitation, as I pulled her into the shower and kissed her, tasting every damn reason I'd rushed to come home to this.

She moaned into our kiss, grabbing at my shoulders as I spun her gently under the spray, water sluicing across her breasts, stomach, and sliding down her body. I stepped back to look at her and she tried to turn to hide herself. I caught her hands.

"Don't do that. Let me look at you, Peach."

Five months of quick glances and tonight I was looking at all of her. Her fuller hips, the breasts she'd been hiding in robes for weeks. The dark line still running down her belly. Her c-section scar.

She was different. She was also *more*. I moved her from under the water and lathered soap in my hands and started at her shoulders. Slowly, I worked it down her arms, the sides of her hips, then around her thighs making her tremble. I moved back up to her collarbone, down to her breasts, palming them, watching her bite her lip when I rolled my thumbs across her nipples.

"Look at you."

Her eyes went glassy and a small sound escaped her as I worked my way down her stomach, down the line, to the scar. I dropped to one knee and pressed my mouth to it.

"This is where my whole life came from." I whispered as she moaned and gripped my shoulders.

I stood up and kissed her again. She pulled back, eyes wide, and smiled at me. She took the soap, and started working it across the lines of my chest, down my abs, tracing the faint trail of hair below. I hissed out a breath, muscles flexing as her fingers teased my dick, already fully erect and heavy.

"Peach…" I warned.

She bit her lip, then sank to her knees on the steamy tile and I nearly lost my mind. Her mouth was on me a second later, looking up with her eyes locked on mine. I groaned, hand braced on the tile, trying to stay upright while she pulled me deeper and sucked me slow. For a moment, I let myself feel her. The heat, her tongue, her hand at my base, the sounds she made that reverberated through me. My hips bucked and my head dropped forward.

"*Peach…*" I choked out again.

She took me deeper and somewhere in my haze of pleasure, my head cleared. *Not like this.* Not the first time. Not her on her knees on tile after five months of being scared of her own body. Not me standing over her finishing in two minutes because I'd been holding it back for months.

I wanted to lay her out. I wanted to be inside her. To take my time with the body that almost didn't make it back to me. I tangled my fingers in her hair and tugged back gently.

"Come here, baby."

She didn't stop, taking me deeper, letting me hit the back of her throat, tears mixing with water on her face.

"Peach…please." I warned. "Come here."

She pulled back slowly, lips swollen, water and tears on her face, breathing ragged. Then she shook her head.

"Let me." Her hands were gripping my thighs. "Raschad, let me. Please."

"Baby—"

"Let me give you this." She pulled back just enough to swirl her tongue around my tip, then sank down again, hollowing her cheeks, moving faster.

Damn. My hips jerked but I gathered the strength to pull out, bent down to her level, then pulled her up and against me.

"Listen to me." I held her face. "Right now? I need to be inside you. I need to feel you."

She let out a shaky breath.

"Let me have you first." I kissed her and shut the water off and lifted her in one easy motion, her arms around my neck, legs wrapped around my waist, water still dripping from both of us, and kissed her as I carried us carefully out of the bathroom and straight to the bed, not caring about the wet mess. I lay her down on the cool sheets while I hovered above her.

"We're here, Peach," I kissed down her neck, then down to her belly, pausing again to run my lips and tongue over her scar, tracing it.

She let out a sob, hands gripping the back of my head, and I crawled up to kiss, swallowing her cries. I wanted to see her on top, strong and powerful, so I guided her to straddle me, her hands on my chest, her wet, curly hair clinging around her face and shoulders.

She sank down on me, eyes locked on mine, and I could have come right then. I mustered up all the restraint I had, holding back as she moved her hips in circles, rolling, riding, and gasping out my name. I gripped her hips. Held still. Let her feel me. Let her set the pace.

"Take your time, Peach."

Watching her ride me I was wrecked. This was my woman. My *whole life*. She leaned down and kissed me. Then tried to flip us.

I grinned against her mouth. "Nuh-uh." I held her in place. "Stay up there. Let me look at you."

She bit her lip and kept moving as I thrust my hips up meeting her grinds. I pulled her down to my chest, wrapped her in my arms, sucking her neck, whispering how perfect she was, while she continued grinding on me.

Then I rolled us over, until she was under me again. "I love you." I said, staring into her eyes as I rocked into her. "I love you. I love you, Peach."

"I love you, too." she gasped. "I love you… I love you…"

I kept moving. Watching her come apart, both of us saying it over and over like we were making up for every day we didn't. Her body gripped around me, and I felt her breaking first. Her climax came like a wave, as her body locked up around me, walls fluttering. I rolled my hips into hers one last time, my own orgasm tearing through me so hard I saw white.

We stilled, trembling, wet and tangled together. I pulled her close, and wrapped us up in a blanket, skin to skin, nothing between us. Her face was pressed into my neck, still trembling.

"You okay?"

She nodded against me. "I'm better than okay."

A minute passed, and our breathing slowed. "We made it," I told her.

She was quiet for a moment, her fingers tracing across my chest. "I didn't know if we would."

"Me neither."

She tilted her head up to look at me. "But I wasn't gonna stop hoping." I said.

She tucked her head back under my chin, and took a long breath.

"You're stuck with me, Peach," I held her tighter.

She smiled against my chest. "Promise?"

"Forever."

you were always mine

THIS CHAPTER HAS A SOUNDTRACK

I Do by Leon Thomas

simone

I HADN'T WASHED MY HAIR IN FOREVER. THAT'S WHERE I WAS AT. A SILK scarf and head wraps had become my go-to and my robe had become my uniform. Zaria was thriving and Zhaire had adjusted to our new normal. He wants to hold her constantly and had taken to calling himself "Big Z" and referring to Zaria as "Little Z," which was the cutest thing I'd ever heard and also made me cry. Everything made me cry.

Raschad had been everything. He'd moved in officially, however he still had the home he'd purchased in Lennox Falls, so we'd been back and forth on which home should become our official home base. Or, if we wanted to start fresh and build something new from ground up. We'd stopped pretending we were just co-parents. We were a family. A real one. The kind I used to think I didn't deserve.

But I was also a mess. Physically. So when Taryn showed up on a random Friday evening with garment bags and a makeup case, I should've known something was up.

"Go take a shower." She breezed through the front door. "We're going out."

I looked up from the couch where I was holding Zaria, burp cloth draped over my shoulder, hair wrapped in the scarf I'd been wearing for four days straight. "Excuse me?"

"You heard me." She dropped the garment bags on the armchair. "You've been cooped up in this house for weeks. You look like you've given up on life."

"I have a newborn."

"You have a six-month-old who sleeps hours at a stretch now. You also have a man, an Auntie, three brothers, and a mother-in-law who can watch her for one night. Get. Up."

"She's not my mother-in-law." Raschad's mother had come back in town two days ago, to stay for two weeks.

"Mmhmm. Let's go."

"Taryn."

"I already talked to Raschad. He said go enjoy yourself. Valencia will watch the kids. She already knows too."

I looked down at Zaria, who was staring up at me. I swear she blinked at me like *go ahead, Mama.*

"Where are we even going?" I asked, already standing.

"Somewhere that requires you to not have spit-up on your chest." Taryn reached for the baby. "Give me my goddaughter and go wash your ass. We're going to a spa and then I booked a glam team. I got you a dress, but I need to raid your closet for the right shoes to match it. We're leaving in forty-five minutes."

"A glam team?"

"Did I stutter?"

"What are you up to?" I asked slowly.

"Nothing. Can't a girl take her best friend out? You almost *died,* Simone. I think that earns you a night where you look stunning and drink something that isn't lukewarm chamomile tea."

She had a point. "Fine," I said. "But I need to pump first."

"Obviously. Now *go.*"

I took and shower, got dressed and I kissed Zhaire goodbye he was on the couch with Valencia, eating popcorn and watching a movie, unbothered by my leaving, I leaned over Zaria's bassinet by the sofa. She was sleeping.

"I'll be back," I whispered. "Mama's just going out for a little bit."

Valencia caught my eye. "Go have fun, sweetheart. We've got everything handled."

Taryn and I spent three hours at a spa and it was glorious. We left there and Taryn drove playing Snoh Aalegra and Jhené Aiko, making small talk about absolutely nothing. I watched the city blur past the window, feeling lighter than I had in months. We ended up back at Taryn's house where her glam team was waiting.

"We're going out tonight, babe. But you're getting dolled up first."

The glam team was two women who worked on me like I was a canvas. Washed and deep conditioned my hair, blew it out in big loose waves that fell past my shoulders. Beat my face so good I almost didn't recognize myself. Soft glam, dewy skin, a nude lip with just enough shimmer, lashes that made my eyes look enormous.

The dress Taryn brought fit like it was made for me, hugging my postpartum body in a way that made me feel powerful instead of self-conscious. Raschad always told me he loved my every version of my body, but standing in front of that mirror, I believed it for the first time in months.

Taryn watched me from the doorway, with a smile too wide.

"What?" I said, adjusting an earring.

"Nothing." She blinked fast. "You just look really beautiful."

"Are you about to cry?"

"No. Shut up. Let's go."

We pulled up to a venue I didn't recognize, a garden estate tucked behind wrought iron gates with jasmine hedges. A valet stepped forward before we'd even fully stopped.

"This is where we're going?" I looked at Taryn. "What is this place?"

"Just come on." She was out of the car before I could press.

I stepped out and followed her up a stone pathway lined with lanterns. The air smelled sweet, like roses. Then I noticed layers and layers of roses lining our path, the scent getting stronger with every step.

"Taryn."

"Hmm?"

"What is this?"

She didn't answer. Just looped her arm through mine and walked me toward a set of tall wooden double doors at the end of the pathway. My heart started beating faster as she stopped in front of the doors. She turned to face me and her eyes were glistening.

"What's happening?" My voice came out shaky.

She squeezed both my hands. "Go." She dropped my hands and reached for the door handles. "Go on, girl." Then she pulled the doors open.

The first thing I registered was the light. Hundreds of candles were everywhere, lining the pathway, clustered on stone ledges and floating in shallow pools of water. The entire courtyard glowed golden, like someone had trapped the sunset. Then more roses. Walls of them climbing the stone arches, cascading from overhead pergolas, gathered in lush clusters of deep reds and soft blush pinks and creamy whites. Petals were scattered across the ground.

And people. *My* people.

Julian stood to the left, as I walked in, his hands clasped in front of him, wearing a suit. Tre was beside him, suited with a smile fighting through what I could already tell was emotion he was trying to hold back. Zion was next to him with one arm around Taryn who was wiping her eyes. When had she gotten beside him?

Next to them was Aunt Lorraine with her hand pressed over her heart, and Uncle Reggie, Zenobia, Marlow, Kendra. Khaz and Khairos all there smiling.

Then I noticed Raschad's sisters. Tamika, Jordan, Alyssa and Jada all of them dressed up and smiling, Jordan surprisingly already crying openly.

Valencia was standing with her daughters, smiling wide and holding... Zaria. My baby girl was in a cream lace dress I'd never seen before, with a tiny bow in her hair, sleeping soundly in her grandmother's arms.

And Zhaire, my baby, in a little navy suit with a tie, standing at the end of the aisle like a tiny groomsman. He saw me and his whole face split open.

"Mama!" he whispered loudly the way seven-year-olds whisper, which is not a whisper at all. "You look like a princess!"

I couldn't breathe. Because there, at the center of it all, standing beneath an arch dripping with roses and greenery, with his hands at his sides, in a tailored tux that made him look like he'd stepped out of a painting, was Raschad.

The father of my children. The man who'd held me through the worst of my life. Who'd fought doctors for me, slept in hospital chairs next to me, learned to change preemie diapers and check oxygen levels and never made me feel like I was too much. He was looking at me like I was the only person in that courtyard.

I was already crying before I reached him as Leon Thomas' *I Do* started playing.

He caught both my hands when I got close and held them. "You're stunning," he said low. "I just... I needed you to know that first."

I laughed through the tears. "Raschad..."

"You know what this is," he squeezed my hands.

I did. The whole garden told me. Every candle, every rose, everyone I loved assembled in the same place... I knew.

"Before I get to it," he said, "I made you something." He glanced past my shoulder and I turned.

There was a platform to the side of the arch with a keyboard, and a microphone stand. Tre started walking toward it, adjusting the mic height, rolling his neck the way he did before he was about to perform.

My breath left my body. Tre had not stood at a microphone to perform in almost a decade. He had made himself the man behind the music, the producer, the architect, the one who built what other people stood up to sing. He had stepped away from this years ago and nobody outside our family knew exactly why and nobody had pushed him on it.

But there he was standing at a microphone.

"Took some convincing," Raschad said quietly beside me. "But he's the only one with the voice to do it right." He paused. "I wrote this for you. He's singing it for you."

Taryn appeared at my side and pressed a folded handkerchief into my hand, as Raschad walked to the keyboard. Took his place and set his hands on the keys.

He played one chord, and Tre began.

YOU WERE ALWAYS MINE
written by: R. Carter
produced R. Carter & Tre Wade
performed by Tre Wade
(c) WadeHouse Records

VERSE 1
Thought it was a weekend
Turned into a lifetime
Tried to moved on
Carried you the whole time
Left me once
Hurt me twice
Almost died carrying our life
I'd walk it all again
Every wrong turn
Every dead end
To end up right back with you

CHORUS
Took the long road
Every wrong sign
Every road led back to your line
'Cause you were always mine
You were always mine
Written in fate,
Inevitable by design
Baby you were always, always mine

I pressed the handkerchief to my face. Raschad was watching me from behind the keys, with tears threatening in his eyes.

VERSE 2

Wore my name before I gave it
On our son before I knew him
Tough outside, sweeter when you let me in
You a peach for a reason
Been my favorite ever since
Now I know what love looks like on skin
The proof of us written where only I've been

I pressed both hands over my mouth and stopped fighting it entirely.

CHORUS
Took the long road
Every wrong sign
Every road led back to your line
'Cause you were always mine
You were always mine
Written in fate,
Inevitable by design
Baby you were always, always mine

OUTRO
The reason I stayed
The reason I'm here
Don't need heaven to find me
You brought it here
You were always mine
Just had to turn around
Always mine
Always
Mine

Tre held the last note and let it go. The courtyard was so quiet I could hear the candles. Tre stepped back from the microphone. He nodded at me once and stepped down.

Raschad lifted his hands from the keys and walked back to me. He stood in front of me, reached up and wiped both my cheeks.

"Hi," he said.

"Hi," I managed.

raschad

SHE WAS STUNNING. I'D SEEN THIS WOMAN IN A HOSPITAL GOWN WITH tubes in her arm and thought she was the most beautiful person alive. I'd seen her at 3 AM with breast milk on her shirt and bags under her eyes and still wanted to devour her. But tonight she was glowing. The dress, the hair, the way she looked at me like she couldn't believe this was real.

I couldn't believe *she* was real. That we were here. That after everything we were standing in this garden with our families and our children and a future I'd once stopped believing was possible. I held her hands. The music softened to a hum behind us and everyone went quiet.

"Simone. I had a whole speech planned. Wrote it down. Practiced it countless times." I let out a shaky laugh. "But I'm standing here looking at you and I can't remember a single word."

She laughed through a sob.

"So I'm just gonna talk," I said. "The way we always have. Late at night. No filters. Easy. Just us."

I squeezed her hands.

"Eight years ago, I met a woman at a pool in San Diego who ruined me for everybody else. She didn't know it yet. Neither did I. But that weekend changed my whole life. Everything that came after that I measured against the time that I spent knowing you. And nothing ever came close."

"When you came back into my life, you brought my son with you. And yeah, I was hurt in a way I didn't know a person could be. But even in the middle of all that, even when I wanted to stay mad, I couldn't. Because loving you isn't something I choose, Simone. It's just something I *am*."

The tears were rolling down her face, carving clean lines through her makeup.

"You gave me Zhaire. You gave me Zaria. You gave me a family I didn't even know I was allowed to want. You gave me your whole heart, messy, scared, imperfect, *brave*, and those are the greatest gifts anybody has ever given me."

"You almost died bringing our daughter into this world." My voice cracked. "And sitting in that hospital waiting room, not knowing if you were going to make it, that was the moment I knew. Not that I loved you. I already knew that. But that there was no version of my life that works without you in it. Not one."

"So…" I let go of her hands and reached into my jacket pocket. "I'm not asking you to be mine, Simone. You've always been mine. Since our first conversation where hours felt like minutes."

I got down on one knee and she gasped, her hand flew to her mouth. I opened the box and the ring caught every candle, every string light, every bit of glow in that garden and threw it back like a small sun.

"I'm asking you to let me be yours. Officially. Permanently. In front of God, our families, and our babies." I looked up at her. "Marry me, Simone Denise Wade. Let me give you my last name. Let me give you the promise that I'm never going anywhere."

For a second, the world stopped. The music. The stifled crying of our family. All of it. Then Zhaire's voice cut through the silence like a bell.

"Say *yes*, Mommy!"

simone

I LAUGHED. OF COURSE OUR SON WOULD BE THE ONE TO BREAK THE spell of my tears. To crack the moment wide open and make it real. I looked down at Raschad on one knee holding a ring that caught light like it was arguing with the moon. Shaking. This six-foot-six, broad-shouldered, stubborn, beautiful man, was *shaking*.

"Yes," I whispered. Then louder, because he deserved to hear it ring. "Yes. *Yes!*"

He slid the ring on my finger and I didn't even really look at it. I was too busy looking at *him* the way his face crumbled with relief, like he'd actually been afraid I might say no. Like there was any universe, any reality, any version of my life where I would say anything other than yes to this man.

He stood and pulled me into him so fast my feet left the ground. Lifted me clean off the ground, arms wrapped around my waist, my hands gripping his shoulders, and the sounds that came out of the court-yard, the cheering, the crying, the clapping, felt like a wave crashing over us.

He lifted me off my feet again and kissed me. Not a polite kiss either. The kind that made my cousins hoot and my brothers groan and someone whistle loud enough to scare a bird out of a nearby tree.

When he set me down, I was dizzy. From the height, from our kiss, from all of it.

"Look at the ring," he murmured against my lips.

I looked. And then I almost needed to sit down. A deep emerald-cut diamond. Massive, elegant, and catching every light source, set in a band that was delicate and intricate at the same time. It was the kind of ring that made people stop talking mid-sentence.

Zhaire crashed into us wrapping his arms around our legs, face buried somewhere between my hip and Raschad's thigh.

"Do I get to be in the wedding?"

"You're gonna be the best man." Raschad said.

Zhaire's eyes went wide. "Deadbutt?"

"Deadass." Raschad laughed

I couldn't do anything but shake my head.

He pumped his fist and took off running toward his uncles. "UNCLE JULIAN! I'M THE BEST MAN!"

Julian caught him mid-sprint, lifting him up. "I heard, Z. I heard." His eyes found mine across the courtyard and held them. Everything he didn't say lived in that look.

Champagne appeared, someone popped a bottle and the sound made Zaria fuss in Valencia's arms. Valencia bounced her gently, whispered something I couldn't hear, and Zaria settled immediately. That woman had magic hands.

Valencia handed Zaria to Aunt Lorraine and made her way over.

"Come here," She pulled me in for a hug, and I fell into it. Into the solid, certain warmth of a mother's embrace that I hadn't felt in almost twenty years.

"I have watched you with Zhaire," she said. "That boy… the way he moves through the world, the way he loves people, the way he looks out for his little sister already, that is you. You did that."

"And Zaria. The way you fought for her. That's a rare thing, baby."

"And my son." Her voice softened on it. "I know my son. I know how he loves and I know how long he waited to find somebody worth loving like that." She looked at me steadily. "The way he looks at you, I haven't seen him look at anything that way, ever. You gave him that. You and those babies."

She smoothed a hair back from my face.

"You are beautiful, Simone. Inside and out. And your mama, I know she is so proud of you. I know it." Her voice broke, just slightly, just enough. "I'm not her. I would never try to be. But I want you to know, from this day forward, I am here. Same as my own daughters. Any time. For anything." She held her eyes. "I love you. And I am so grateful you are ours."

I broke. Full, body-shaking, ugly-cry broke. Right there in the garden, in my emerald dress, with a diamond on my finger and a woman I hadn't known two years ago mothering me like she'd been doing it my whole life.

Raschad appeared beside us and wrapped his arms around both of us.

JULIAN FOUND ME LATER, AFTER THE CHAMPAGNE HAD BEEN POURED AND Zhaire had eaten his weight in hors d'oeuvres. He stood beside me near one of the stone arches, both of us watching our family. He didn't say anything for a long time. Just stood there, shoulder to shoulder with me, the way he'd been standing with me since I was twelve years old and our world fell apart.

"You good?" he finally asked.

I looked down at the ring on my finger. At the courtyard full of people who loved us. At the man across the garden who had my heart.

"Yeah," I said. "I'm really good."

Julian nodded. "Good." He kissed the top of my head. "You deserve this."

And for the first time in my life, I believed that. Not because someone told me. Not because I'd survived enough to earn it. But because somewhere along the way I had stopped letting fear make my decisions. Stopped shrinking myself to protect everyone else from the weight of my wanting. Stopped deciding in advance that I wasn't worth the risk of being chosen.

I had been so certain, for so long, that loving someone that completely was a liability. That need was dangerous. That asking for what you wanted was just another way of handing someone the thing that could hurt you.

But here was Raschad, who had chosen me in our twenties and chosen me again in out thirties, through every hard thing, through everything I had done and everything my body had put us through. Who was standing across the garden looking at me the way he had always looked at me. Like the noise had gone quiet.

He had always been worth it. And so had I.

It found me. It chose me. And I let it.

mr. suit & tie

julian

SIMONE AND RASCHAD'S WEDDING RECEPTION WAS STILL GOING STRONG when I found the edge of it, just watching. That's always where I ended up at these things, present but at the perimeter, watching what people do when they let themselves be happy in public. I didn't begrudge anyone that. I just preferred to observe it from a comfortable distance.

That's when I spotted her again.

Alyssa Carter. Raschad's sister. Head thrown back, laughing at something with her sisters, completely unselfconscious about the sound of it. She'd changed her hair, longer tonight in a sleek bob with highlights. I looked away, but found myself looking back again. And of course, my brothers noticed.

"You're doing it again," Zion said, appearing beside me.

"I'm not doing anything."

Tre materialized on my other side. "You've looked over there three times in the last ten minutes."

"Drop it."

They didn't drop it. The two of them, plus Taryn who joined their peanut gallery out of nowhere, and suddenly I had three people beside me who had decided that their evening's entertainment was standing next to me, watching me pretend I wasn't watching Alyssa Carter. All three of them useless and laughing and delighted about it.

Zion leaned into me, grinning. "So what'd she call you again? '*Mr. Corporate*'?"

"Don't start," I warned.

"Oh, I'm starting," he replied. "'*Forbes List*', that what she called you."

Tre corrected him, "Nah, it was '*Mr. Suit and Tie*' that's what she said. Man wasn't even wearing suit." he cackled.

Taryn nearly choked on her champagne. "Wait, y'all talking about when Alyssa cussed Julian out? Read his ass for filth on the foot—?"

I shot her a look. "Finish your drink, Taryn."

Zion pointed at me, still grinning, "She got under your skin, huh? You've been off your game ever since."

I shook my head, keeping my face neutral, eyes forward.. "I'm never off. Don't you three have anything better to talk about?"

"Nope," the three of them said in unison, then commenced to laughing like they were front row at a comedy show.

I didn't flinch. Just took another sip of my drink, staring straight ahead like their noise didn't matter. But my eyes slid back to Alyssa anyway. She was talking to someone else now, radiant and bright smile, one hand moving through the air to make a point, Jersey-girl confidence worn like a second skin.

For the rest of the evening, I kept finding where she was. Kept looking away, then finding her again like some malfunction in an otherwise reliable system. Wasn't even trying to. Couldn't help it.

It bothered me that I couldn't help it.

Up Next: Always Yours (Wade Legacy Series, Book 3)

If you enjoyed this story, please consider leaving a rating or review on Amazon or Goodreads. Even a sentence or two helps more than you know. Indie romance lives and dies by word of mouth, and your review is what helps our books reach readers.

See you in Book 3.

between us

raschad

You watched me carry something that almost cost me everything.

Not my anger. The anger was deserved. What Simone did was wrong. I don't need to dress that up. She kept my son from me for five years. Five years I don't get back. First words I didn't hear. First steps I didn't see. Milestones I wasn't at. That's not small and it's not something you minimize because the love story ends well.

Hold that. Before I say anything else.

Because what I'm about to tell you doesn't make the wound go away. It just means I chose not to let that wound be our whole story.

I want to talk about pride.

Pride kept me alive when I was young. Watching my father come and go, watching my mother hold everything together by sheer will, I made myself a promise. I would never be the one left behind. Never let somebody make me feel small and just take it. And I would never do that to the people I love. I built myself around that promise. My discipline, my work ethic, my career. All of it had pride underneath it. A man's gotta have a code to stand on.

But pride is a bad long-term strategy for love.

Because love asks you to be wrong sometimes. Asks you to be soft sometimes. Might ask you to choose the person over the principle. And pride doesn't know how to do that. It just knows how to protect itself.

I stayed angry longer than the anger was useful. I told myself it was about trust. And it was, in part. Trust was real, and broken, and I had every right to take my time with it. But somewhere in there, my anger stopped being about what she did and started being about my pride not knowing how to put down its sword. I was scared that forgiving her meant I was a fool. That choosing her again meant I didn't respect myself. That going back was weakness.

Like Zion told me once; that's fear with better posture.

If you're reading this and you've been hurt, the kind of hurt that changes how you move through the world, I'm not going to tell you to let it go. Make sure you're choosing to heal, not just choosing to go back because the alternative is loneliness.

But I'll ask you this: is the pride keeping you safe, or is it keeping you stuck?

There's a version of strength that looks like holding the line forever. Never backing down. Never giving an inch. And sometimes that's the absolute right call.

Sometimes the person who hurt you isn't sorry, hasn't done the work, isn't respectful, or safe. Walk away. Don't look back.

But sometimes the strongest thing you can do is decide that what you have with someone is worth the risk. That the love is real enough, the growth is real enough, and you are solid enough in yourself to choose to trust again without losing yourself in the choosing.

Simone had been alone for six years. Six years of raising my son, carrying a secret that was eating her alive, playing the same Frank Ocean song when her panic came because that was the only way she knew how to get back to a moment she'd felt safe. She hadn't moved on. She hadn't replaced me. She'd been in a prison of her own making, punishing herself every single day. And I was so busy protecting my pride I couldn't see it.

It didn't make what she did right. It made her human. And it made me realize I was holding out for a kind of perfect I was never going to get. Because perfect people don't need forgiveness. And I didn't want a perfect woman. I wanted her.

I almost let pride take my family from me. My son. My daughter. My Peach. The life we were supposed to have.

I got there eventually. Took a while, but I got there.

Putting the sword down didn't make me weak. It made me free.

If you're carrying anger at someone who hurt you, only you can decide what to do with it. But don't let pride write the ending to a story that love was supposed to finish.

Take your time. Protect yourself. Heal.

But ask yourself honestly: what you're protecting. And is it worth what it may be costing you.

—Raschad

simone

I was hiding for years.

Not from him. From myself. From my own life. From the version of me who got to want things and actually have them.

What I did was wrong. I kept a man from his son for five years because of my own trauma. Because I didn't know how to undo what my fear had built. Because every day that passed made it worse.

I had reasons. Some of them were real. Grief; fear; my mother's death living in my body; panic with nowhere to go. But reasons aren't the same as right. And I spent a long time hiding behind mine.

Here's what I want to talk to you about, though. Not my mistake, but what came after.

I punished myself for years, quietly. Hollowing myself out so slowly. I didn't notice how empty I'd gotten. I stopped dating, stopped letting myself want things beyond Zhaire and work and the careful, controlled life I'd built. It was a silent form of purgatory. A sentence I'd handed myself because I couldn't figure out how to forgive what I'd done, so I just decided not to try.

What I know now is that self-punishment is not the same as accountability. Accountability says I was wrong, and I'm going to do the work to be better and to show up differently. It faces the thing and grows from the thing. Self-punishment says I did something wrong, and I don't deserve good things anymore. It collapses into you, until you've disappeared.

I disappeared for seven years, longer if I am being honest, since I was twelve years old. Like if I suffered enough, for long enough, eventually the ledger would balance and I could exhale.

Life doesn't work like that. There's no amount of shrinking that makes you worthy of love. You don't earn your way there. You choose your way there.

And that choice was the hardest thing I have ever done. Because at least when you're suffering, you feel like you're doing something. The pain feels like proof. Choosing to live again felt dangerous.

If you're reading this and you see yourself in me, not the thing I did, but the pattern, the way guilt can become a lifestyle. How one bad choice or bad season can turn into a whole identity you can't find your way out of. I want you to know something.

You are allowed to be flawed, while doing the work and still want good things.

You are allowed to take responsibility and still deserve love.

You are allowed to be a person who made a mistake and also the person who heals from it.

Staying small forever doesn't undo it. It just adds more loss to the pile.

Raschad forgave me. Not fast or easy. But he chose me on the other side of everything, with his eyes open and his history intact. And I had to learn how to receive that without waiting for him to realize he'd made a mistake, and without shrinking back into myself the moment something got hard.

That's still work. Every day. Learning to stand in good things without apologizing for being in them.

You don't have to earn your way to being worthy. You were already worthy. You just have to stop arguing with that long enough to let it be true.

I almost missed my whole life waiting to deserve it.

Don't do that.

—Simone

don't shrink yourself

Message from N.W. Brown

This book was personal to me.

Before my youngest child was born, I lost a pregnancy at the start of my second trimester. I had felt something was off, and I told my doctor. I was dismissed. Belittled, actually. So, I convinced myself I was being paranoid, and kept my worrying quiet. Three weeks later, at a routine ultrasound, they found that my baby had died. Had stopped growing right around the time I'd first raised my concerns to my doctor.

I have thought about those three weeks many times since.

When I became pregnant again with my fourth child, three kids already at home, I had a better doctor. But I did what so many Black women do. I downplayed pain. I pushed through. I told myself I was strong, that other people had it worse and I shouldn't make a fuss. The pain got bad and I pushed through it. Until finally it got bad enough that I called my doctor and asked if there was anything I could take.

Her response stopped me cold: Go to the emergency room. Right now.

Twelve hours and multiple tests later, I was diagnosed with HELLP syndrome. I was put in an ambulance and transferred to a hospital with better neonatal care. My daughter was born at 29 weeks, weighing less than two pounds. She spent four months in the NICU.

She is here. She is fine. And I am one of the lucky ones.

Black women in the United States are three times more likely to die from pregnancy-related complications than other races of women. That statistic holds *regardless* of income, education, or access to care. We are at times dismissed in examination rooms. We are sent home when we should be admitted. We are told our pain is manageable. And we some-times participate in our own dismissal, because we have been taught to be strong, to not be a burden, to put ourselves last.

This is true not just in pregnancy. It's true in our daily health, our bodies, our lives. We often minimize ourselves until there is a crisis, and then sometimes the crisis is too far along to stop.

We are at times dismissed in examination rooms across every specialty, every stage of life, every kind of complaint. We present with symptoms and are sent home. We describe pain and are told it's stress. We say something feels wrong and are handed a pamphlet. The dismissal is often so normalized, that too many of us have stopped expecting to be believed, or worse, edit ourselves before we even open our mouths. We walk into appointments already rehearsing a version of our symptoms that sounds reasonable enough not to be brushed off.

And when the doctor confirms our thoughts that we're overreacting, we leave relieved. We go home and keep moving. We push through. Because calling again feels like being difficult, like being the patient who cries wolf, taking up space we weren't sure we were allowed to take.

I did this. I have done this more than once. And I know I am not alone.

This is also about self-care. Not the candles-and-bubble-bath version, but the annual appointments we keep putting off. The way we run ourselves into the ground taking care of everyone else and call it strength. We are the ones who show up for everyone. We are often the last ones anyone shows up for… including ourselves.

Raschad's advocacy in this story was not a dramatic plot device. It is the minimum of what saved Simone. It is what too many women never get.

You are allowed to take up space in your own care.

You are allowed to go back when something still doesn't feel right.

You are allowed to ask for a second opinion, to change providers, to say I *know my body and something is wrong* and **keep** saying it until someone listens.

You are not being dramatic.

You are not being difficult.

You are doing the minimum that you deserve.

If you have been dismissed, by a doctor, by a system, or by the voice in your own head that told you to stop complaining, I want you to know that your instincts are **worth** something. That what you feel in your body is **data**. That being taken seriously is not a privilege. It is a **right**.

If something doesn't feel right: say it. Shout it. Then say it again. And again. And again. Don't leave the office until someone has written it down. Ask for documentation.

To the advocates, researchers, doulas, and organizations fighting for Black maternal health, and the many people doing this work quietly and without enough recognition, this story is my small contribution to that conversation.

To the readers who found this book before you had proof it was worth your time: **Thank You.**

Being a new author means asking strangers to spend hours with characters who only live because you invested in them enough to finish. That is not a small ask. To every early reader who posts, shares, recommends, or simply tells one person, you give this book a chance to find its people. You took the risk before there was any reason to, and I will be forever grateful for your support.

To be honest, I am so much better at writing these books than I am at promoting them. My head stays buried in the next chapter, the next character, the next corner of this world I'm still building. Which means your reviews, posts, and word-of-mouth carry weight I cannot carry on my own. You are the reason this book reaches the next reader. Thank you again.

If this story moved you, please consider leaving a review, posting about it, or sharing it with a friend.

Thank you for reading.
With love,
N.W. Brown

TikTok: @nwbrownwrites

Instagram/Threads: @nicolewbrown

Goodreads: goodreads.com/nwbrownwrites

Amazon: amazon.com/author/nwbrown

BookBub: @nwbrownwrites

Website + Mailing List: www.chapterandsoul.com

Simone's story asked more of me than Taryn's did. While her story is book two, it was actually meant to be book one. Before Taryn and Zion, before *Always Running* had a title, I was writing Simone's book *Always Mine.* Her wound was the one I found first and the story I kept returning to.

I write in the order my mind moves me, not at all linearly. I tend to move back and forth between characters, focusing on whoever is pulling at me on a given day or week. So, Simone, Taryn, Zion, Julian and Tre, were all being written at the same time, each one informing the other. And as their stories took shape alongside each other, I realized that Simone's story was too delicate, and maybe too much to hand you before you got to know the Lennox Falls world, or trust me as the person telling it.

So, Taryn and Zion's story supplanted Simone and Raschad's to become book one. Not because Taryn's story was smaller, but because she and Zion became the on-ramp.

Taryn's version of running is easier to recognize. It's loud, combustible, impossible to miss. Simone's is quieter. She runs so carefully, and so completely convinced she's doing the right thing, that she almost convinces you too. So I held her back. And I kept writing.

This book was also originally planned as two books split across separate releases. But Simone's story refused to be cut in half. What she and Raschad go through doesn't have a clean break in the middle. It has a wound that has to be carried all the way through before it can begin to heal. So you're holding one complete story. All of it. The way it was meant to be told.

Writing a woman who does a deeply wrong thing out of a deeply human fear required the belief that both of those things could be true at once. That love and harm can live in the same choice. That a wound you carry for years can rewrite decisions you *think* you're making freely. That some of us spend years trying to protect people from pain they never asked to be protected from, when really we're just protecting ourselves.

If you're here because Taryn and Zion brought you, thank you for sticking with me. Simone and Raschad's story feels different. It was meant to. The Wade family goes deeper with every book, and deeper isn't always comfortable. But I hope you find it worth it.

If this book is where you started, welcome to Lennox Falls! You didn't need book one to find your way into this one. But I hope Simone and Raschad made you curious about what came before, and what's coming after.

Either way, I'm glad you're here.

This series is about Black women who feel deeply and deserve to be loved well, even in their imperfections. Even if they get in their own way. Even when the love they need most is the one they're most afraid to reach for.

Simone finally reached. This was her story. I hope it stays with you.

With love and gratitude,

N.W. Brown

- **Goodreads:** goodreads.com/nwbrownwrites
- **Amazon:** amazon.com/author/nwbrown
- **Instagram:** @nicolewbrown
- **TikTok + Threads:** @nwbrownwrites
- **BookBub:** @nwbrownwrites
- **Website + Mailing List:** www.chapterandsoul.com

before you go

If Simone and Raschad's story moved you, I'd love it if you to left a rating or review on Amazon and Goodreads. Reviews are how indie authors like me reach new readers. They help other people find this book. Even one or two sentences makes a real difference.

No pressure if it's not your thing. Just know that if you do, I'll see it. I read every single one.

Thank you for reading!

— N.W. Brown

- **Goodreads:** goodreads.com/nwbrownwrites
- **Amazon:** amazon.com/author/nwbrown

***Don't miss Book 3: Always Yours**

book club questions

LOVE, TRUST & SECOND CHANCES

1. Simone and Raschad's relationship isn't linear. Did that make their love feel more real, or more frustrating for you as a reader?
2. How did your feelings about Simone keeping her pregnancy a secret change as the story unfolded?
3. At what point did you personally feel like they might actually make it?
4. Do you believe love alone is enough to rebuild trust?
5. At what point did you understand Simone's choice, even if you didn't agree with it?
6. Raschad's internal anchor is that the noise stops when he's with Simone. What does that say about what he's been looking for his whole life?
7. Zion calls Raschad's pride *"fear with better posture."* Do you agree? Can pride ever be legitimate self-protection?
8. Raschad says *"That's my—"* and stops himself. What word do you think he almost said?
9. Simone's journey includes learning how to receive love, not just survive it. Where did you see that shift happen?
10. What does this book say about what it means to truly "show up" for someone?
11. Raschad and Simone "slip-up" intimately three times in the book before official reconciliation. Each moment had a different emotional register. Did you feel the distinction between these spicy moments?
12. *"Loving you isn't something I choose, Simone. It's just something I am."* Do you believe love can be a state of being rather than a choice, especially after hurt?

FAMILY, LEGACY & IDENTITY

1. Zhaire's introduction to Raschad is one of the most emotional threads in the book. What moment between them impacted you the most?
2. How did the presence of family, both the Wade family and Carter sisters shape the story?
3. Children are often peripheral in romance. What did giving Zhaire such a central role add to this story?
4. Zhaire tells the locker room *"That's my mommy and that's my daddy"* in six words. What does that say about what children see that adults can't?
5. Zhaire plays *Pink + White* for Raschad because his mother plays it when she needs to feel better. He learned the function of the song without knowing its origin. What did you think about that moment?

TRAUMA, FEAR & SELF-PROTECTION

- Simone often holds back emotionally. Did you understand her hesitation? Why or why not?
- How did Simone's past (especially her mother's death) influence her decisions in the present?
- Raschad struggles with control, pride, and fear of being hurt again. Which of his emotional barriers felt the most real to you?
- Have you ever found yourself protecting your peace in a way that also kept love at a distance?
- Simone's final line is *"It found me. It chose me. And I let it."* Is that about Raschad, about love, or about herself?
- If you could go back and tell Simone something the moment she found out she was pregnant what would you say? Do you think she would have listened?

On Black Women's Health

1. Simone minimizes her symptoms throughout the pregnancy, to Raschad and to herself. Do you see this pattern in your own life or in women around you?
2. Dr. Kline genuinely believes she's doing her job. Did that make the dismissal more or less frightening?
3. *"Note it in her chart"* is one of the book's signature acts of love. Why does that specific gesture land hard?
4. Taryn's prayer names the generational pattern out loud *"We remember Niecy Wade. And we are standing here today declaring that is not this."* Do you believe naming a pattern is part of breaking it?
5. How did the HELLP syndrome storyline impact your reading experience? Were you expecting it?
6. Raschad advocated for Simone when her concerns were being dismissed. What did that moment say about his growth?
7. Did the medical scenes feel realistic and emotionally grounded, or overwhelming?

FUN & LIGHTHEARTED

- Music plays a role throughout the story. How did it enhance your reading experience?
- If you had to pick one song that represents Simone and Raschad's relationship, what would it be?
- What scene had you laughing or smiling the most?
- Your Favorite Moment: Which scene stuck with you the most and why?
- Cast the movie. Go.
- Three words to describe Simone. Three words to describe Raschad.

CRAFT & STORY STRUCTURE

1. Did the dual POV add to your understanding of the relationship, or did one POV resonate more with you?
2. Which chapter or moment felt like the book's turning point?
3. Which scene felt like the emotional center of the book?
4. What was the hardest moment in the book for you to read?
5. What did this story make you think about in your own life or relationships?
6. After finishing this book, whose story are you most excited to read next, and why?